I WILL FEAR NO EVIL

JOHN E. JACOB

Contents

Dedications

Dedicated to my wife, Barbara Singleton Jacob, my daughter, Sheryl Jacob Desbordes and especially my granddaughter, Nichelle Renee Desbordes.

Acknowledgment

While this is my life's story, it only became a book when I teamed up with the very capable Lee A. Daniels. Lee, a noted journalist, having served for 20 years as a reporter for the Washington Post and the New York Times, brought to my endeavor his knowledge of writing skills, research, and an in-depth understanding of the civil rights movement and the struggles of Black people in our America. A graduate of Harvard College, he had served as the Director of Communications for the NAACP Legal Defense and Education Fund as well as the Editor of the National Urban League's public policy journal, The State of Black America. In addition, he collaborated with my predecessor, Vernon Jordan, on his book Make It Plain: Standing Up and Speaking Out. With those credentials, he proved to be the perfect partner for the writing of my memoir. His technical assistance was invaluable in the production of every page of my book, and he helped me bring this book into existence. Lee, I thank you.

Foreword

This is an American story. John Jacob grew up in Houston, Texas, a booming city which attracted thousands of people from smaller rural locations. John's parents left a small town in Louisiana with a population of about 1200. They came to Houston, whose population of 99,000 white and 34,000 black citizens who lived in strictly segregated areas. Rigid segregation was enforced; busses were segregated, and public schools were segregated by race. John refused to ride the busses and walked to reach the school he attended for black children.

His family lived in a three-room shack with one bedroom for the parents, one room for the children, and a kitchen. There was no electricity or gas. His mother cooked on a wood stove; they read by kerosene lamps, and the outhouse was located on the front side of the house. In spite of his parents' lack of money, they instituted and required their children to live by a set of four rules: the first was children must be in school. The second, when not in school, you must have a job. Third, if you get a girl pregnant, you're going to marry her, and fourth, if you go to jail, you are going stay; and, his father added for emphasis that he may not have gone to college, but he knew the difference between an "A" and a "C"; don't bring home any "C."

John, small in statue, became a top student, member of and President of the Honor Society, and president of his graduating class. He planned to attend college after graduation, even though he had no idea as to how he was going to pay for it. He had had part-time jobs on week-ends and during the summers, but he understood that would not be sufficient to cover the cost at most institutions. And, like most Black children growing up in the segregated south, he knew all of the white institutions in Texas were off limits to him, and those outside the state were out of reach because he didn't have the funds to attend them in spite of his grades. However, much to his surprise, the summer before his graduation, Mr. Evan E. Worthing, a successful real estate entrepreneur, passed, but he left a $500,000 trust fund to provide scholarships for poor but bright Black students. John was one of four students in his graduation class to receive one of those scholarships. John chose to apply to Northwestern University because it was the one school he had heard one teacher in his school speak fondly of it because he had worked on his graduate degree at that institution. John was accepted for admission at Northwestern, but learned during that summer that his Worthing Scholarship funding would only cover two years of cost at that University, and knowing that his parents couldn't provide the additional funding needed, a sense of panic engulfed him. It was during that sense of panic that a young Black woman who served as the teen counselor at the YWCA stepped in and sent a telegram to Howard University about him, and that school changed the trajectory of his life forever. Howard sent him a telegram inviting him to join the Class of 1957,

John entered Howard in September 1953 and earned his undergraduate degree in Economics, minored in political science, finished four years of ROTC, and was commissioned a 2nd Lieutenant in the US Army Infantry Branch. After 17 weeks in the Basic Infantry Officers' training, John applied for and was accepted into the Airborne Training program, which he completed, earning his wings as a qualified military parachutist. At this point, he considered making the military a career, but as faith would have it, the country was in a recession, and John left active duty and spent 12 years in the active Army reserves. He pursued a variety of jobs; Post Office, Baltimore City Welfare Department, and Washington D.C. Urban League. He also earned his Master's Degree in Social Work. And, later he was recruited and convinced to become head of the San Diego, California Urban League. This continued a career in the Urban League.

Several things became clear during these years; John always knew precisely what his responsibilities were in any position. He knew how his performance would be judged and when it was time to leave the position and move on. Although he had not pursued or sought positions at the National office of the NUL, he was recruited to a position when Vernon Jordan became CEO after the unfortunate death of Whitney Young. And, when Vernon decided to leave the League and take a partnership in a D.C. Law firm, he felt strongly that John Jacob should succeed him. Vernon Jordan shared his position with me, and having known and observed John for many years, I agreed with Vernon's position. However, as the Senior Vice Chairman of the National Urban League's Board of Trustees, a careful and diligent national search was conducted before the Board decided on its selection of John. After discussion and agreement on the position, John accepted the position. When asked what was the difference between Vernon and John, John answered other than the fact that Vernon is 6'5" and he was 5'6", Vernon was a lawyer and advocate engaged in social work activities; John was a social worker who would engage in advocacy activities.

John became President and CEO of the National Urban League in 1982 following an attempted assassination of Vernon Jordan in 1980. Vernon's decision to leave the National Urban League surprised both his Board and his Executive Vice President, John Jacob, but to his credit and the credit of the NUL Board of Trustees, it had had the opportunity to work with John and develop the confidence that the League would be in good hands with him as its head. John informed his board in the eighth year of his term that he would like to depart at the end of his tenth year. And, while his Board took its own time in selecting his successor, he spent an additional two years as the League's leader for a total of 12 years. But, again, he knew when it was time to leave. He retired and continued his life's work of helping through his participation as a member of several corporate boards and joining the management team of one of America's Premier Fortune 200 companies. This is a life that has made every place he stopped better; the Urban League movement is better; the nation is better, and the world is a better place because John Jacob has shared this space with us.

BERNARD C. WATSON, PH.D.

PRESIDENT & CEO, William Penn Foundation, Retired

Sr. Vice Chairman, National Urban Board of Trustees, Retired

Chapter 1 — "Vernon's Been Shot!"

In the six-decade-long history of the National Urban League, I was the first Executive Vice President to the organization's top officer, Vernon Jordan. Vernon's choosing me for the new post in 1978 wasn't just a reflection of my fifteen-year record at the League, including leading two of its major affiliates. The bitter economic troubles of the 1970s had produced a severe recession, throwing millions out of work. It had also immediately pushed the official Black unemployment rate above ten percent.

That rise in those years, when certain occupations at the bottom of the labor market—where Black men were concentrated—began to shrink rapidly—set off alarms at the Urban League. It meant that to meet the needs of Black Americans and other disadvantaged people in what was going to be tougher times, we would have to "bulk up," both in terms of expanding present programs and devising new ones and in raising more money to help us do that. So, the League needed to revise its structure to., among other things, free the top officer from the routine tasks of supervising the League's ever more complex work on a daily basis in favor of prioritizing the position's fund-raising and "national spokesman" duties. I was to be the Urban League's "Mr. Inside" to Vernon's "Mr. Outside."

One of the first things Vernon and I did when I got to New York was to have our home telephones connected via the extensions of our headquarters offices. We thought of it, of course, as merely a convenience, and that's how it functioned—until the terrifying moment in the early morning of May 30, 1980. That shortcut is how the call came to me at 3:30 am from a man whose voice I didn't recognize, jolting me fully awake: *Mr. Jacob. Vernon Jordan asked me to call you. He's been shot. He's here in the hospital in Fort Wayne.*

Vernon had been shot in the back in Fort Wayne, Indiana, the man said calmly. He told me he was calling from Parkview Memorial Hospital there. Doctors at the hospital were operating on Vernon at that moment, but it wasn't clear what level of danger he was in.

The stranger was, Vernon told me later, one of the emergency room attendants whose job it was to safeguard his belongings. Vernon had asked him to say I should call Shirley—that it would be better for her to hear the news from me.

Vernon had flown to Fort Wayne to deliver the keynote address at the Fort Wayne Urban League's annual dinner. His message, as he put it in recounting his assault and recovery in *Vernon Can Read!: A Memoir* was that "blacks were terrified at the prospect of the Republican candidate, Ronald Reagan, defeating Jimmy Carter and rolling back many of the gains we had made in the previous two decades. That was pretty much Reagan's stated goal, wrapped in language about 'state's rights' and traditional values. He signaled this by beginning his campaign in Philadelphia, Mississippi, the site of the 1964 killings of three young civil rights workers, Andrew Goodman, Michael Schwerner, and James Chaney."

Vernon's speech, before an audience he estimated at about a thousand, drew an enthusiastic response, and then, as he was dropped off at his hotel by one of the affiliate's board members, catastrophe struck. Vernon described it in *Vernon Can Read!*:

As I was getting out of the car, a bullet fired from a 30-06 hunting *rifle tore i*nto my back. *I didn't hear the gunshot, but the impact lifted me into the air, and I had a sensation of floating—unreal, as if I were in a dream. And then I was on the ground.*

One of my first thoughts was that I had to get back to my room and go to bed so I could make my flight to Houston [[where he was scheduled to speak the next evening]] *... But when I began to feel blood soaking my shirt, I knew I would not be catching that plane to Texas.*

The pain was indescribable, brutal beyond all measure. I have often heard that human beings shut down in the face of overwhelming pain. I did not. I remained wide awake, and I could feel the blood running out of my body. 'This is it for me, 'I thought. 'My life is over.' ...

Then, there was a wonderful sound—a siren. I heard it in the distance and tracked its progress as the ambulance eventually rolled up near me with its lights flashing. To this day, I always have a buoyant reaction to hearing a siren. Others may take it as a negative sign that someone is hurting. But to me, a siren means that someone is going to get help. The paramedics put me on the stretcher, and I talked to them all the way to the hospital. In all of the uncertainty, with all the mixed-up thoughts, I was sure of one thing: I knew I could not go to sleep. Doing that would surely be the end of me. [i] **(F. 1)**

My shock at the news quickly disappeared, submerged beneath the imperative for action. I've got to let the Board know what's going on, I thought, and I've got to get to Fort

Wayne fast so I can make sure Vernon gets the best kind of medical care that will help him recover fully and come back to the League.

I made my call to a Board member, waiting until nearly 6 o'clock to call David Mahoney, the chairman and chief executive officer of Norton Simon, Inc. David and his wife, Hilary, lived on Manhattan's Upper East Side, as did Vernon and Shirley. He and Vernon were close friends. I played tennis with the two of them from time to time. But that morning, my call had a double purpose: I knew David had a company plane at his disposal.

At that time of the morning, my call to David went through their cooperative's switchboard. But the operator told me I'd have to call back at 8 o'clock; it was too early for the Mahoneys to be disturbed. "I can't wait until 8 o'clock," I said with more than a little sharpness in my voice. The operator was in the middle of repeating his refusal to put me through when David's wife, Hilary, picked up the line. Much later, when I had time to reflect on that morning, I felt that she, whose husband was one of the most prominent businessmen in the country, had probably developed a sixth sense about early morning calls: No one would likely be calling at that hour unless it was a matter of critical importance. She and I had never met, but now I explained who I was and why I was calling. She roused David, but he quickly interrupted my torrent of words and put me on hold for what seemed like an eternity.

When he returned, he explained that he had just flown in from California that evening and had taken a sleeping pill to help him sleep soundly. "Now," he said urgently, 'tell me again what you've just said."

4

Once I did that, he immediately said, "Give me time to find my pilots. I'll meet you at your office at 7 o'clock. We'll be wheels up by 8 o'clock."

So I made a mad dash to get to the office. When I got there, David was already pacing in front of the building, with the car that had brought him idling at the curb.

As soon as I had exited my car, he said, "Get in," and we drove to Teterboro Airport in suburban New Jersey, where the Norton Simon company plane was parked.

As soon as we took off, I called Jim Compton, the CEO of the Chicago Urban League affiliate, and told him to meet us in Fort Wayne with an attorney and a PR person. I didn't know what the situation on the ground there was, and I wanted to make sure we were in a position to manage our way through the first day of the crisis.

One of the things that made me appreciate David even more that day was that, while we were en route, he said, "Give me some of your business cards because from now on, I work for you." In that quiet moment on our way into what was sure to be a whirlwind of action, it provoked a fascinating feeling: to have the CEO of a global corporation tell me that he now worked for me. But, of course, he was absolutely right to say that because Vernon, my boss, was incapacitated. I was the guy in charge now, and his role was to support me.

The media coverage, involving national networks and local and national newspapers and magazines, was already intense when we landed mid-morning in Fort Wayne and was to remain so for days. When CNN, the new Ted Turner venture that was to revolutionize the news media, began broadcasting two days later, on June 1, Vernon's attempted assassination was the very first story it discussed.

The *New York Times* story of the attack appeared in the top right column of the front page—signaling that its editors considered it the day's most important story. Under the headline, 'Vernon Jordan Shot at Motel in Indiana; Wounds Are Severe,' it reported that surgeons had undertaken a four-and-a-half hour operation to remove bullet fragments from Vernon's body and close the wound and that after the operation, Vernon was sequestered in its intensive care ward.

The article went on to say that in Washington, FBI Director William H. Webster said he had ordered the agency to undertake a full-scale investigation. He said evidence collected at the scene suggested 'an element of premeditation'—without describing what that evidence was—and 'was in furtherance of an apparent conspiracy to deprive Vernon Jordan of his civil rights.'

As numerous civil rights figures, including Jesse Jackson, Joe Lowery, and Ben Hooks, quickly converged on Fort Wayne, I told the crowd of journalists gathered outside the hospital in the early evening that I had spoken with Vernon, and he was resting comfortably in his room. President Carter would visit him the following day, June 1.

Unlike Vernon's attitude about the shooting, which was soon to become evident, the local and federal authorities' seeming lack of progress that summer in identifying suspects in the shooting provoked intense frustration and sharp criticism throughout the civil rights community and among many Black Americans. And, of course, given the unforgettable trail of assassinations in America in the 1960s and 1970s, suspicions that a white-racist conspiracy had targeted Vernon immediately began to be voiced. But throughout the summer and early fall, Fort Wayne police and the FBI hadn't publicly announced any credible leads until October 28, when the federal agency said it had arrested a man in Lakeland, Florida, in connection with the attack.

That man's name was Joseph Paul Franklin. Franklin would soon become notorious as an avowed white racist murderer who had been roaming the country since the late 1970s—with a 30.06 hunting rifle—targeting Black men and Black-White interracial couples.

In one instance, he was suspected of shooting a Black fast-food restaurant manager who had just spoken in the restaurant to a white female co-worker. In another, he later confessed to shooting to death two Black boys who were cousins, aged 13 and 14, simply because he had grown impatient waiting to spot an interracial couple. Franklin would also later confess to the 1977 firebombing of a synagogue in Chattanooga, Tennessee, and the 1978 ambush of Hustler Magazine publisher Larry Flynt and his attorney in retaliation for an edition of the pornographic magazine displaying an interracial sexual encounter.

Untangling the full extent of Franklin's murderous crimes took much of the next three decades because he was only ever charged in some of the killings and only confessed to others years later. At the time of his arrest in Florida, he was wanted by Salt Lake City police for the murder of two Black men who had been jogging with two White women in a city park that August. That and his ownership of a 30-06 rifle drew the FBI's interest.

Franklin, who denied then that he had shot Vernon, was quickly indicted for the attack—but only on the charge of not attempted murder, but of violating Vernon's civil rights: that is, attempting to prevent Vernon from going into his hotel because he was Black.

Because no one had actually seen Franklin at the site— even though other evidence placed him in Fort Wayne on the day of the shooting—the case against him was widely considered weak. On 17 August 1982, after a trial that took seven days, a Fort Wayne jury deliberated for eight hours before finding Franklin not guilty of the civil rights charge. "Mr. Franklin raised his fingers in a victory sign and smiled broadly at the jury." the *New York Times* reported. [ii]**(F. 2)**

Years later, in 1996, Franklin would claim that he had indeed stalked and shot Vernon. He had gone to Chicago in May 1980, intending to kill Jesse Jackson. When he discovered Jesse was out of town, he left. "While driving through Indiana," Vernon wrote in his memoir, "he heard that I was going to be speaking in Fort Wayne. He went there, found out where I was staying, and lay in wait for me in a grassy area just beyond the parking lot outside of my room." [iii] **(F. 3)**

The acquittal in Vernon's shooting did not change Franklin's own circumstances, however. By then, he had already been sentenced to four life sentences on dual state and federal charges for the Salt Lake City murders. Further, he would be later sentenced to serve two more life sentences for two more racial murders. In still another case, Franklin was sentenced to death in Missouri in 1997 for the murder of a man as he stepped from his synagogue. For that murder, at age 63 in November 2013, he would be executed in the Missouri state prison at Bonne Terre.

In an interview shortly before being put to death, Franklin said he had given up his racist views, having learned from interacting with Blacks in prison that, 'I saw they were people just like us.'

In his memoir, Vernon wrote that, beyond testifying at Franklin's trial in his case, he paid scant attention to that trial, its outcome, or subsequent stories about Franklin.

"That was for law enforcement to deal with," he said. "It was enough for me to tackle my health problems and get back in shape for the Urban League without playing sleuth or following the trial on a daily basis ... Franklin's acquittal or conviction was not my issue. [Long before the trial began] I was well, back home, back at work, playing tennis, living my life. ... it was useless for me to be embroiled in Franklin's fate. ... The one thing I am certain of is that having lived the experience [of getting shot and surviving], I preferred to close that chapter and concentrate instead on Reverend [Gardner] Taylor's [iv] **(F. 4)** belief that I had been spared for a reason. It was for me to discover in the quiet of my own mind just exactly what that reason was. [v] **(F. 5)**

During those first hectic days of early June in Fort Wayne and throughout the summer, I, too, paid attention to the search for Vernon's assailant only as much as necessary to safeguard Vernon's and the Urban League's interests. There was too much else to do. My two overarching concerns were to do all I could to help Vernon get back on his feet as quickly as possible and to keep the organization's staff operating at maximum efficiency. Although Whitney Young's death while swimming at a beach in Lagos, Nigeria, had occurred a decade earlier, it was still deeply felt within the League. I couldn't let the staff—many of whom, like I, had worked under Whitney—be overwhelmed by this new calamity.

To me, that meant I had to get Vernon back to New York as soon as possible; the fine surgeons and staff at Parkland Memorial Hospital had undoubtedly saved Vernon's life. However, I felt that now, for the recovery phase, I had to bring him back to the environment he knew best and surround him with as many people he knew in that environment as medically allowable. But Vernon was to spend the next twelve days at Parkland as the doctors there sought to determine the cause of a persistent and worrisome low-grade fever.

One of my first actions after Vernon's hospitalization was to assign two staffers based in Ft. Wayne to keep me updated on his condition. After several visits to Ft. Wayne to check on Vernon myself, I became more concerned about his recovery. I received frequent calls daily from the on-site staff about his treatments. I finally concluded I had to do more to ensure Vernon recovered and returned to his post at the National Urban League. So, I made a call to Dr. LaSalle D. Leffall, Jr. of Howard University Medical School. In addition to being a brilliant surgeon who was then serving as the first Black president of the American Cancer Society and the first Black president of the American College of Surgeons, LaSalle was a very good friend of Vernon's—and he was a man who had enormous influence and access to tremendous resources.

We had never met in person, but I served as Vice Chairman of Howard University's Board of Trustees at the time, so I felt he would at least know my name. So when I called him, I began by saying, "Dr. Leffall, I know you're a

10

good friend of Vernon's,"—and he quickly interrupted me. 'I'm a good friend of yours; what can I do for you?'"

I told him I would like for him to go to Fort Wayne and examine Vernon himself and tell me what I needed to do to get Vernon healthy again. He said that he could do that on Sunday, two days later. I agreed that would be fine.

But the moment we hung up, I got a call from the staff members stationed in Fort Wayne: they informed me the doctors there had scheduled Vernon for another exploratory surgery, and I was immediately worried. *What's going on? What are they looking for? What are they trying to fix?*

I called LaSalle back, told him the latest news, and said I couldn't wait until Sunday. He immediately replied, "Give me thirty minutes to rearrange my schedule. I'll get a plane from J & J (Johnson & Johnson, the pharmaceutical giant) and go this afternoon."

Later that day, he called me from Fort Wayne. He said that while the hospital was a fine facility overall, we should move Vernon to a facility in New York that LaSalle knew had the most sophisticated equipment, New York Hospital—Cornell Medical Center Presbyterian. [vi]

I hung up and immediately called the staff on-site in Ft. Wayne, asked them to call the White House, and asked them to provide a Medi-Vac plane to transport Vernon back to New York.

Then, I flew back to Fort Wayne to check on Vernon directly.

When I arrived, I met with staff to inquire as to our progress on getting a Medi-Vac plane for Vernon's return to New York. They informed me they hadn't been able yet to reach the President or Hamilton Jordan, Carter's Chief of

Staff. I exploded. "Why are you trying to reach the president and Ham Jordan." "This is a job for Louie Martin!" I said, "Give me the phone." [vii]

I called Louie myself. When I explained why I was calling, he responded by saying, 'John, the criteria for a Medi-Vac plane is ...' and I quickly interrupted: "Louie, if I could meet the criteria, I wouldn't be calling you. I need a plane!"

He said, "Oh, I'll call you back," and hung up.

He did call back soon—with the name of the captain piloting the plane and the time the plane would be in Fort Wayne ready to transport Vernon to New York. I then called Dr. LeFall to give him the plane information as a courtesy since he had put this action in motion. What happened next came as a big surprise. On the day the plane was scheduled to transport Vernon back to New York, Dr. LaFall got on a plane, flew back to Fort Wayne, met the Medi-Vac plane and accompanied Vernon on it back to New York.

Winging the way back to Gotham, I was told Vernon radiated confidence, even as on arrival, he was carried out of the plane on a stretcher (and some fifty-five pounds lighter from the ordeal), then driven to the hospital in a private ambulance amid a seven-car motorcade accompanied by LaSalle and another of his personal physicians, Dr. Adrian Edwards, also of Howard University Medical School.

In a statement released after he arrived at the hospital, Vernon said: "I am well on the way to a complete recovery, to the full resumption of my duties as president of the National Urban League and the continued advocacy on behalf of America's dispossessed. In my personal struggle for recovery health, as in the struggle for social justice, I continue to believe 'we shall overcome.'

Having Vernon back in New York was not only great for him and all his friends in the city and along the East Coast but also great for me, and especially the staff. Although his visitors were, of course, sharply limited to just a handful, knowing that he was just blocks away from our East 62d Street offices in midtown Manhattan was a great morale boost. [viii]

Vernon, like me, was a workaholic and had planned on being back to work in time to lead the League's seventieth annual conference in early August, especially because it was being held that year in New York City itself. He loved the bustle and excitement of the annual conference, especially delivering the keynote address. That year's had promised to be suffused with a special intensity, given the upcoming presidential election: All of the major candidates— President Carter, Senator Edward M. Kennedy, who was then challenging Carter for the Democratic Party nomination, Senator John Anderson, of Illinois, who was running as an Independent, and Ronald Reagan—had accepted invitations to speak. Now, the attempt on Vernon's life and his promise to once again lead the Conference had pushed demand for attendance to record levels; more than 16,000 people were coming to our workshops, candidates' speeches, and other venues.

Vernon's presence at the Conference was not to be, however. The routine of his treatment, his doctors's insistence that he stay put in the hospital, and his own common sense quickly led him to realize his confidence in his own strength was overmatched. He was to spend the entire summer in the hospital, receiving visitors from time to time but otherwise giving himself over completely to the task of getting fully well.

But that didn't mean he was detached from the League's work, particularly in preparing for the Conference, set to run from August 4 to August 7 at the New York Hilton Hotel. Once it was clear that he couldn't attend, Vernon informed me, that his second in command, I would have to step in and give the Conference's Keynote address. I immediately got with Dan Davis, [ix] Vernon's estimable speech writing assistant, and we began meeting to discuss what the conference opener, the keynote address I was now to deliver, should focus on.

Most of all, the tone I wanted to strike was that *I was not trying to be Vernon, nor was I campaigning for Vernon's job. I was his Executive Vice President, representing him.* Vernon Jordan was still the President and CEO of the National Urban League, and the responsibility of League staffers and supporters was to keep the organization moving forward while he was recovering. Our staying on course in the tasks we had to do to serve our constituents and represent their interests to the rest of American society was now more important than ever.

Officially, the general election campaign had only just begun. But few could have doubted that Jimmy Carter and the Democratic Party faced a gloomy prospect. My delivery of the keynote speech was, of course, rigorously nonpartisan as I urgently demanded that vigorous measures be undertaken by the public and private sectors, the Black civic society, and individuals, too, if the catastrophe looming over poor people—especially black poor people were to be averted.

I said that the Black electorate needed to turn out at the polls in huge numbers that November to send a message that black voters do more than "just talk black political strength. Let's show it. Let's demonstrate it. Let's prove it ... so that, come election day, black political power will be the decisive factor in the political leadership of this country for the next four years." [x]

The Urban League would do its part, I told the gathering, by having its 118 affiliates across the country participate in voter registration campaigns as part of the "Operation Big Vote" effort being staged by 70 national, nonpartisan organizations. "We want the candidates to understand," I declared in the speech, "that black people want jobs, not reasons why we can't get those jobs. And we want candidates to understand that the black vote is up for grabs this year." [xi]

But, of course, I knew that Black Americans' vote was not "up for grabs"—because the Republican Party didn't want it. Instead, since the presidential campaign of Arizona Senator Barry Goldwater in 1964, the GOP had wanted only a very small percentage of it—just enough to be able to pretend to White voters that they were pursuing it. Goldwater had opposed both the 1964 Civil Rights Act and the 1965 Voting Rights Act. So had a Republican activist with a growing reputation: the former actor Ronald Reagan. [xii]

Blacks in 1980 were well aware of Reagan's long-standing hostility to racial equality measures—and that reputation was reinforced by the political jujitsu act he pulled right before his August 5th appearance at our Conference.

I'm referring to the you-know-where-I-stand message on race he had sent to White conservatives and racists throughout the country by making a quick trip to the Neshoba County Fair in Philadelphia, Mississippi—the *Times* news report characterized it as "his first real political foray since his nomination in Detroit last month."

This, of course, was the county where the notorious 1964 murders of the three civil rights workers occurred. The *Times* article noted that Reagan was "the first presidential candidate of a major party to speak here since the event was organized in 1889" and drew "thunderous applause" from the 10,000 fairgoers.

It then reported that "in a speech before a crowd almost entirely made up of whites, Mr. Reagan said, 'I believe in states' rights; I believe in people doing as much as they can at the private level." He added that if elected, he would "restore to states and local governments the power that properly belongs to them."

Reagan then immediately flew to New York, where he visited briefly with Vernon at the hospital, a visit which, of course, was covered by the media, and then the next day delivered a thirty-minute address to the Conference.

He drew a polite but chilly reception from our audience, which was undoubtedly aware of the true meaning of his advocating the infamous notion of *states 'rights*. They were also aware that Reagan had declined an invitation to speak before the NAACP conference in July. [xiii]

The *Times* article further noted that during his speech, Reagan likened his appearance at our conference to John F.

Kennedy's 1960 appearance before a group of conservative Protestant ministers in Houston to allay fears that, as President, he would be under the sway of the Roman Catholic Church. Reagan acknowledged that he was facing "a skeptical audience that was filled with doubts as to whether he should be elected leader of all the American people." And that "for too many people, *conservative* has come to mean anti-poor, anti-black, and anti-disadvantaged.

"Perhaps some of you question," he asked rhetorically, "whether a conservative really feels sympathy and compassion for the victims of social and economic misfortune and of racial discrimination. ... If you think of me as a caricatured conservative, then I ask you to listen carefully, and maybe you'll be surprised by our broad areas of agreement." ... [The] "perceived barriers between my political beliefs and the aspirations of black Americans ... are false. What I want for America is, I think, pretty much what the overwhelming majority of black Americans want."

According to The *Times,* the claim "drew no response from his listeners. Nor," it went on, "did his declaration that 'I am committed to the protection and enforcement of the civil rights of black Americans. This commitment is interwoven into every phase of the programs I will propose.'"

The *Times* noted that Reagan had said "he would like to see many programs, such as welfare and education, transferred from the federal government back to states and localities. But he did not use that phrase 'states' rights,' which in the South has come to stand for resistance to desegregation." [xiv]

17

About a month after our conference and 98 days after being shot, Vernon left New York Presbyterian on September 4th for his home in Manhattan. He was, as he noted in *Vernon Can Read!*, down 55 pounds, and so he, who always dressed immaculately, immediately called for his tailors.

When he returned five days later to the League headquarters and an adoring welcome from the staff, instead of his usual business suit, he wore a natty navy blue double-breasted blazer, white shirt with a patterned tie and gray slacks that, with his broad smile and usual take-charge air, presented the very image of a forward-looking executive: the man in charge. As the *Times* report of the following day noted, although he moved a bit more slowly than normal, "Mr. Jordan smiled broadly and exuded the confidence that has been characteristic of his style as the League leader."

And Vernon had a great deal to say to the press corps that awaited him there and to the society beyond. First, responding to a question about the fact that his assailant at that time had yet to be publicly identified, much less caught—and thus, might still be a threat to him—he declared he would "refuse to let the possibility of renewed violence stand in the way of my beliefs and my duties."

But making clear he had no intention of dwelling on the attack, he quickly moved on to call for a meeting of national black leaders to, as he said, "reassess the black political agenda, maximize the black vote, and clarify questions of black leadership." [xv]

To underscore the point, four days later, Vernon sat down with Thomas A. Johnson, a black *Times* reporter, for a lengthy, wide-ranging conversation. Among other things, he declared that he intended to sharply expand the number of Urban League affiliates, then numbering 118, in order to press forward with the Urban League's agenda and combat the "conservative trend in this country, a drift to the right," and again pledged to "continue to speak my mind [whatever] the issue ... even when I am at variance with my colleagues [among the civil rights leadership."

It was vintage Vernon Jordan, as Tom Johnson made reference to when he wrote of Vernon, "In shirt sleeves, gesturing on occasion, Mr. Jordan often smiled in the forty-five-minute talk, moving deliberately in and out of standard English and deep South colloquialisms. 'It is good to be back, really good,' he declared."

Vernon soon demonstrated the truth of his declaration that he had put the assassination attempt behind him when, in October, he journeyed to the famed Tuskegee Institute in Alabama to give a speech. The FBI, which by then had identified Joseph Paul Franklin as his assailant but had not yet captured him, urged him not to go. Vernon was undeterred.

There, amid a resounding welcome, he expressed concern about White evangelical Christians' support of political conservatism—describing it as a "heady mixture of fundamentalist gospel with extreme right-wing political ideology" that must be countered by a massive turnout of Black voters. "Black citizens don't have the wealth or power to enforce our just demands for equality," he declared, "but we do have the latent political power of our numbers. The black vote is concentrated in key states. The black vote can punish enemies and reward friends." [xvi]

19

The 1980 Election proved right the gloomy expectations of both the Black leadership and the Black masses: It was a disaster for the Democrats. In the three-way contest, Reagan won 50.7 percent of the popular vote and 489 electoral votes, the highest number ever won by a non-incumbent presidential candidate. Carter got 41 percent of the popular vote but carried only six states and the District of Columbia. (Anderson won 6.6 percent of the popular vote.) Reagan won 43.9 million votes to Carter's 35.4 million. Reagan gained 56 percent of the white vote, Carter 36%. Carter got 83 percent of the Black vote to Reagan's 14 percent. Reagan massively won White middle-, upper-middle-class, and wealthy households. Further adding to the gloom among Blacks and Democrats, Republicans also won enough Senate seats to gain majority status there—which meant that staunch conservatives such as Orrin Hatch and erstwhile Jim Crow segregationists Strom Thurmond of South Carolina and Jesse Helms of North Carolina gained key committee chairmanships.

M. Carl Holman, president of the National Urban Coalition, spoke for much of the established civil rights leadership—and Black America—when he told a *New York Times* reporter, "It's like after an earthquake when you try to see how many buildings are left standing. When I hear (that Reagan) is going to up the defense budget sharply, cut taxes and thus revenues sharply, and, at the same time, cut government spending but maintain the really important programs, I think I know where the ax is likeliest to fall. It's likeliest to fall on the areas of most concern to us. We are now trying to focus on what can be saved from the wreckage."

Vernon was far more circumspect. He told the *Times* Reagan's expressed interest in using Federal and local incentives to establish so-called enterprise zones in poor central city areas in order to spur job creation for minorities and the poor was a hopeful sign.

Vernon was undoubtedly trying to offer the incoming administration a way they could hew to its conservative ideology and still positively respond to the needs of Black Americans and the society's disadvantaged citizens. [xvii]

It would quickly become apparent the offer was not going to be taken up. Once past the January 20, 1981 Inauguration, the Reagan Administration would quickly show that the words the new President had spoken at our Conference the previous August were a smokescreen for his actual intentions.

Vernon and I both loved to work; in fact, we were compulsive about it. It was not at all unusual that, once the Annual Conference ended, while the League's staff would take the rest of the week off, Vernon and I would return the next day to our offices at the opposite ends of the building's sixteenth floor. That's why I was at my desk that Thursday when Vernon called at midday and asked me what I was doing for breakfast Friday. I told him I had no appointments; I just planned to get some work done in the office.

"Well, meet me at the University Club," he said, "I want to have a talk with you."

So, the next morning, shortly before 8:00, our appointed meeting time, I was waiting for him in the lobby of that august private institution on Fifth Avenue near Rockefeller Center in midtown when one of the Black staffers at the Club, recognizing that I wasn't one of their Black members, came over and asked me who I was there to see. I said, "Vernon Jordan." He replied, "Oh, Mr. Jordan's already upstairs in the dining room. He's waiting for you," then escorted me to the elevator and directed me to the Club's dining room on the seventh floor. On the way up, I had a premonition that something significant was about to occur because Vernon had gotten there before I did. I'm so compulsive that throughout my career, I've always made sure I was quite early for my appointments.

Soon after I sat down and ordered from the menu, Vernon told me that he was resigning from the League.

I was shocked. I had not seen this coming. Vernon resigning? Since recovering from his being shot fifteen months earlier, he had shown no diminution in zest for leading the Urban League. No one loved standing up before an audience and giving a speech more than Vernon Jordan. No one loved operating in all of the arenas an Urban League chieftain had to operate in than Vernon Jordan. My immediate thought was that, understandably, he had been more affected by the assassination attempt than he had let on and was trying to figure out what to do with the rest of his life.

I began to ask what was bothering him, with the idea of helping him work through it, but he cut me short.

"Oh, no, no. I don't think you understand," he said, "I have already accepted an offer from a D. C. law firm, Akin Gump Strauss Hauer & Feld. I've already seen my office. I've already ordered my furniture, and I begin work there on January 2nd."

He was that matter-of-fact, that definitive. ^{xviii}

And then he said to me, "And you ought to want this job."

It was not until Vernon had said those words that I had even thought about wanting the League's top job because, thinking Vernon would be heading the League for years to come, I had come to New York to get discovered by Corporate America, not to become the CEO of the National Urban League.

But Vernon's insistence that I should want to succeed him forced an immediate re-calibration. I realized that I had spent every second of every minute of every hour of every day of every week of every month of every year for the past seventeen years doing exactly that—preparing myself to lead the National Urban League. My career proved that. No one in the country was better prepared than I was. So, yes, I thought to myself: I ought to want the job.

I never had any doubts about my ability to lead the National Urban League. In fact, while leading the Washington Urban League, I was once interviewed by legendary journalist Chuck Stone for Washingtonian Magazine, after which he asked, "When are you going to run for Mayor?" I told him I'd rather be chairman of the Chrysler Corporation, the Big Three automobile company, and I meant it. In other words, I always believed I had the ability, knowledge, and intellect to perform in that capacity. It simply wasn't what I had set my sights on. All the things you are called to do at the level of national president of the Urban League were just an amplification of the many tasks one has to perform as a local executive.

I'm reminded of something Dan Collins said to me soon after I became president. Dan was a long-time national trustee, and I was in San Francisco, his hometown, to speak at the local affiliate's annual dinner. After dinner, he came to me and said, "Jake, I always knew you could manage the League. What I needed to see was, could you move the troops, and tonight, you proved to me that you could."

So, the issue for me has never been could I do the job, but rather, would I get the opportunity to do the job.

In fact, Vernon and I had, separately, been thinking along the same lines all along in terms of the ambitions each of us had and the skills we had acquired working at the top of the unique organization that was the National Urban League. We both understood that those skills were valuable assets in trying to navigate the pathways into the private sector that *could now be open for Blacks like us.*

And in its broadest meaning, the term *Blacks like us* actually encapsulated those Black men and women of the generation born in the 1930s and early 1940s as well as the Black Boomers of the postwar years who constituted a new Black American cohort. I call them the *Fortunate Few.* Yes, in earlier decades this cohort was named the *Talented Tenth* because then their numbers were truly small. Now, however, thanks to the explosion of Black college-going in the 1960s, at the dawn of the 1980s, this cohort was sizable and growing. It included the seasoned veterans of the civil rights and social justice wars, like Vernon and me, of the 1930s and early 1940s generation, and as importantly, well-educated Black Boomers who had been inspired in one way or another by the civil rights victories—and trained by their pursuit of higher education credentials—to not let their thinking about and pursuit of their own ambitions be limited by the old barriers.

As he wrote in *Vernon Can Read!*, he had since 1979 been quietly discussing moving into the corporate world with a few corporate chieftains and high-powered attorneys:

The work of lawyers and corporate executives who were volunteering with the College Fund and the Urban League had always interested me. I heard them talk about their deals, transactions, and cases. My membership on corporate boards was an even more direct window into this world. Put simply, I wanted to be a part of it—a real part of it. ... I wanted to practice law in a private law firm with corporate clients. ... I asked myself, 'What has all this been for if someone in my position could not if he wanted, make the transition from the not-for-profit world into the corporate world? 'White people did this kind of thing all the time, and no one thought anything about it. It was the accepted prerogative of white people, particularly white men, to establish themselves in one field and then go into another. Success was their calling card. Once they had that identity, they could go almost anywhere they wanted. My whole life had been geared toward saying that the horizons of black Americans should be as unlimited as those of whites ... Why shouldn't I try this? ... That civil rights leaders tended to stay in their positions forever was, in part, a function of the limited opportunities open to them ... Certainly, some of them would have continued on their paths no matter what. But by the 1970s and 1980s, the world has changed enough so that the leader of a black organization could get a job in corporate America ... [xix]

These kinds of ambitions among the most fortunate of Black Americans were also being propelled by the relentless demand of a *global* consumer society and the fierce

25

competition between consumer companies at all levels of the business structure to reach and develop new markets for their products. Businesses needed as much talent for the greater competition they faced as they could muster.

But, for Vernon and also Ron Brown, and, later, myself, there was an additional dynamic at work—something rooted in the very founding, mission, and practice of the Urban League itself. That *something* was the by-product of the long-ago deliberate integration of not only the League's staff but its trustees, too. That is to say, the League's national unit and local affiliates had always deliberately included a substantial number of White business leaders as trustees— and their board chairmen (and yes, until the end of the 20th century, the head of the board was, overwhelmingly, a man) was almost always White.

That practice was both idealistic and pragmatic. Given that the League was founded in 1910 to provide social services to and develop job opportunities for the flood-tide of migrating Black Southerners gathering in America's cities and towns outside the South, it was clear that couldn't be accomplished just by stimulating the development of black-owned businesses within the rapidly growing Black urban ghettos. Training Blacks for jobs in the factories and private businesses, as well as the White-dominated niches of the civil service, was crucial.

In that, White businessmen were potentially invaluable allies. They could hire Black workers for their places of business. They could influence other businessmen and government officials to do so. They could contribute money to support League initiatives, and help convince public officials and the citizenry at large to do likewise.

In other words, White business leaders could 'translate ' and vouch to their fellow Whites for at least some of Black Americans 'determination to forge their way into the American mainstream—and the larger society's need to help them do so.

That this process of building Black America's occupational and economic resources was unquestionably a very slow one over the first six decades of the twentieth century doesn't mean it wasn't a worthwhile pursuit. Nor does it mean that the League's work wasn't part of the overall thrust of civil rights activism during this period. In fact, one could well say that the League combined to great effect the two major streams of the centuries of black political thought: the emphasis Booker T. Washington placed on self-development and self-reliance, on the one hand, and, on the other, the emphasis W.E.B. Du Bois and the fledgling coalition of Blacks and Whites who were to found the NAACP placed on Black Americans being able to enjoy without delay the full range of civil rights that was theirs by birth.

There was another consequence of the League's internal integrationist requirement, which was persuading White business leaders to become allies of the Black freedom struggle. That was, inexorably, its arming by experience of its senior officials with the diplomatic skills necessary to navigate and narrow the chasms between the "two nations" of Black America and White America.

As the century deepened and Blacks 'pursuit of racial equality outside the South became more assertive, it took a particular kind of *leader t*o knit together the needs and interests of the League's different constituencies—poor, poorly-educated Blacks; striving, well-educated Blacks; local, state and national elected officials and government bureaucrats; and top-shelf corporate leaders and philanthropically-minded White foundations and individuals.

Of course, many Black individuals had always possessed such skills. But no other organization had *institutionalized* its practice—had made that ability a requirement for rising to any significant level of leadership within it. To lead the National Urban League or one of its scores of local affiliates, one had to be able to practice the arts of not servility to the White Establishment but racially progressive advocacy, bridge-building, negotiation, and meaningful compromise that produced results.

That we could think it was now possible to realize such ambitions was furthered by the remarkable successes of such new Black entrepreneurs as Earl Graves, publisher of Black Enterprise Magazine; Edward Lewis, publisher of the Essence Magazine conglomerate; Reginald Lewis (no relation), the first African-American to build a billion-dollar company and others.

So, in hindsight, it wasn't surprising that in the 1980s, when a number of African Americans forged remarkable achievements in the business world, the ties between the Urban League and the business community would expand to a new dimension. In hindsight, it was not surprising that Vernon, my boss, would leave the League in the early 1980s and forge an unprecedented second career as a "private sector public figure" and later as "First Friend" to a President of the United States; nor that, a decade later I would be recruited into the highest reaches of corporate America by the chairman of one of its iconic companies on whose board I served—and who became a close friend.

Word that Vernon would be resigning from the League hit the front page of the *New York Times* on September 9, the ninth month of the Reagan Administration's first year in office. There, it vied for attention with the announcement of the death from illness of the 80-year-old Roy Wilkins, the venerated leader of the NAACP. Predictably, the coincidence of the two events quickly brought musings in the media about the supposed decline in energy and talent of Blacks 'drive for racial equality. [xx]

But Roger Wilkins, Roy's nephew whose own glittering career had included governmental service and stints on the editorial boards of both *The Washington Post* and the *New York Times*, offered a trenchant observation.

"My uncle's death brought out a lot of nostalgia about struggles sustained, victories won, and leaders gone. Vernon Jordan's resignation is apt to resurrect that old dumb question that the press always raises at times like these: Who is the new black leader? … But though Jordan was the most prominent of the black leadership cadre, he is not *the* leader, just as there was no single leader in the 1950s and 1960s. … the question, Who will be the new leader? Is exactly the wrong one. The better questions are: What are the current needs of the black community? How can we blacks augment the competent leadership we now have in order to best meet those needs? … Times are hard and changing. We blacks need to be innovative and sacrificing to meet the old challenges in new forms as well as the truly new challenges … " [xxi]

That is what I intended to do in the job. I quickly agreed with Vernon that I "ought to want," and I did want.

But I also immediately decided as we sat there in the University Club dining room that I wasn't going to campaign for the job. My record in the Urban League was clear, and the national board of trustees and the members of the selection committee had gotten a clear look at my management skills during the three years I had served as Executive Vice President, Vernon's No. 2. I knew there was a top-quality list of names mentioned as being interested in the job. Among them were Maynard Jackson, Ron Brown, and H. Carl McCall—all of whom had much greater public visibility than I, so it seemed not at all certain at the outset that I would be the choice.

But Vernon worked exceedingly hard lobbying the selection committee and the full board on my behalf. And it worked out for the best.

I was home in Hartsdale on Sunday morning, December 6, when I got the call telling me that the Board had met that morning and made its decision and that I should come in immediately and meet with them. I had known they were close to a decision but I was not sitting at home waiting for a call. In fact, I was home watching a football game. So it took me a little while to get to the hotel where the meeting was being held.

The next day, Monday, December 7, America learned the National Urban League had a new leader.

Chapter 2 — Family Beginnings: Houston

I was blessed with having had two wonderful parents. Emory Jacob (EMORYJacob) and Claudia (CLAUDIA) Sadler Jacob. I'm spelling out their first names because years later when I saw the birth certificates of both, my father's first name had been spelled not EMORY, but rather EMERICK. And when she was born, my mother's first name was listed as CLAIDIS. Both my parents were born in Marksville, Louisiana: Dad, on July 9, 1905; Mom, on May 8, 1908. They were married on November 9, 1926, in Marksville by Reverend S. H. Lockwood.

Marksville was a very small community almost at the state's eastern border with Mississippi, near the "crook" of its L shape. It's a little more than 70 miles northwest of Baton Rouge and about 164 miles northwest of New Orleans. **(F. 1)**

Marksville remained a small community well into the 1920s. Because its 1,185 residents were heavily dependent for work on the agricultural character of the surrounding area, it, too, was devastated by the catastrophic Great Mississippi Flood of 1927. That inundated the river's alluvial plain from the Gulf of Mexico to as far north as Arkansas, killed more than 500 people (the official government toll; many believe the actual number of dead was far higher), and left at least half a million homeless. It also ensnared the African American population (in the Mississippi's Delta lowlands, Blacks comprised 75 percent of the population and supplied 95 percent of the agricultural labor) in a particularly cruel oppression. Many were forced into work gangs for the recovery effort under conditions that approximated slavery. That worsening of the predicament of Blacks in Mississippi and Louisiana, many of whom had been independent farmers and sharecroppers, fueled a substantial migration northward and westward. **(F.2)**

Amid the devastating loss of life and appalling suffering that affected nearly a million people, Emory and Claudia Jacob were luckier than most. Dad found work in a sawmill in Trout, Lousiana, 40 miles northwest of Marksville, and, bearing their meager belongings, they moved there in 1928. **(F.3)** Here, my oldest sibling, Robert Cleveland, was born. Actually, my mother and father gave their firstborn only the initials "R.C." at birth, but later in life, he gave himself the first and middle names of Robert Cleveland.

Three more children were born to the Jacob family in Trout. Gladys, Emory, Jr., and me, John. Gladys, born in 1929, lived only to the age of 12, dying in 1942 from an illness that we never were clear about. In 1932, my parents' second son, Emory Jacob Junior, was born. But he and the Jacob family as a whole were again subjected to one of those numerous minor occurrences that showed how the South's system of racial oppression intruded upon Black Americans' lives in small ways, too.

While my parents named him *Emory* when he received his birth certificate years later, he discovered someone in the state's bureaucracy had put his first name as *Emerick (as Dad's name had been misspelled when he was born)*—and they had added an "*s*" to the last name. Robert would later discover the same had been done to the Jacob name on his birth certificate. Both of my older brothers accepted the bureaucracy's carelessness, and so the Jacobs family was ultimately to have two brothers with the last name of *Jacobs*, and three brothers with the last name of *Jacob*.

I was the last of the Jacob children born in Trout. Two years after my birth in 1934, we moved to Houston, where my two younger brothers were born—Norman Louis in 1939 and Billy Joe in 1943.

The Houston, Texas, I grew up in from the 1930s to the early 1950s was a vibrant, multiracial city, bustling with money from two spectacular natural events that occurred within hailing distance from the city and months of each other at the turn of the twentieth century.

The first, chronologically speaking, was the catastrophic hurricane that, on September 8, 1900, nearly obliterated Galveston, Texas, the city on a sandbar in the Gulf of Mexico just off the Texas coast. Little more than 50 miles due south of Houston, Galveston had served as the former's port for decades; its destruction convinced Houston officials they needed their own port. The second event was the Spindletop oil strike in early January 1901 in the oilfields near Beaumont, Texas. The volume of oil it immediately began producing made Texas the center of the oil industry in the entire world and instantly vaulted Houston into the top ranks of the nation's port cities. **(F.4)**

The population figures tell the tale succinctly and dramatically. The city's total population in 1900 of 44,663 included 30,025 Whites (including residents of Mexican descent, who were always classified as *White* under Texas law) and 14,608 Black Americans. By 1920, the figure for Whites (and residents of Mexican descent) had tripled to more than 99,000, and that of Blacks more than doubled to nearly 34,000. The population boom would continue on into the mid-century and beyond: to more than 226,000 and 66,000, respectively, by 1930; to more than 298,000 and 86,000, respectively, by 1940; to more than 471,000 and nearly 125,000, respectively, by 1950.

That massing of people pushed Houston up the ladder of the nation's largest cities with astonishing speed. In 1930, it ranked 26th; in 1950, it ranked 14th.

Further, the city's growing prosperity attracted a deeply diverse population: Anglos, some of whom traced their lineage back to before the Alamo; White ethnic immigrants and immigrants from Mexico; *Tejanos*—Texans of Mexican descent whose families had settled in Texas when it was an unchallenged part of Mexico, **(F. 5)** and African Americans.

The post-1900 wave of Black migrants to Houston settled just where those that had preceded them in the previous decades had — overwhelmingly in the neighborhoods of the Third, Fourth, and Fifth wards abutting on three sides of some part of the city's downtown.

The pervasive racist dynamics of the early and mid-twentieth century America left Black Americans profoundly isolated from the mainstream currents and opportunities of the larger society. But it also compelled them to create, behind the barriers that hemmed them in, neighborhoods that could provide its residents a large sense of urban self-sufficiency and relief from the "war-footing alertness" required when one went into the greater White world.

So, it was in Houston, facilitated by the city's ward system established with the city's formal founding in the 1830s. **(New F. 5)**

There, despite the harsh limitations of discrimination and segregation, the overall Black community's location at the

34

center of the city, next to downtown and essentially next to each other, brought into being both a geographical sense of unity along with a strong sense of each ward's uniqueness that enabled multiple individuals and groups to significantly exercise their ambitions in, so to speak, their own space. Businesses, churches, civic groups, nightclubs, and individuals thrived in each ward—although the Third Ward, southeast of downtown and bisected by the Gulf Freeway super highway that went from downtown to the Gulf of Mexico, was clearly the most prominent in the minds of Black Houstonians and those elsewhere. **(F. 7)**

None of the wards's populations was completely Black. Indeed, the Third Ward had a considerable White population—in part because it also contained the expansive campus of the segregated University of Houston. But the Third Ward's prominence also stemmed from its place in the national history of Black Americans. It was where Houston's first Black institution of higher learning, the Houston Junior College for Negroes, was established in the 1920s. **(F. 8)** Twenty years later, trying to ward off increasing pressure from Black Houstonians and the National Association for the Advancement of Colored People (NAACP) for access to the University of Texas, Texas state officials hurriedly elevated the school to four-year college status and added a law school to it, renaming it Texas Southern University. The attempt to stymie that effort didn't work.

In June 1950, the Supreme Court ordered in that case, *Sweatt vs. Painter*, that the university admit Black students to its law school, thereby ending discrimination in graduate and professional school education in the U.S. **(F. 9)** The family of the named plaintiff in the case— Hemann Marion

35

Sweatt—had lived in the Third Ward for decades and in the 1920s he had attended the elementary school I was to briefly attend a decade later. (**F. 10)**

As the city's commercial development after 1900 sparked an immense ongoing influx of Whites, creating new segregated neighborhoods further and further from the city center, city officials formally eliminated the ward system. But those areas, especially in reference to Black Houston, would remain in continual popular use throughout the twentieth century.

As a group, Houston's Black population was significantly more diverse than in any other city in the country but for New Orleans. Some could trace their ancestors (some enslaved; some free) in Texas back before the Civil War. Others had arrived immediately after the Civil War had ended, bringing to the small Black population of that now-defeated Confederate state the news that Negro Slavery had been abolished—news that led to the tradition of Juneteenth. In fact, the high school I would attend, Jack Yates High School, was named for the minister who, with his wife, had arrived in the city in 1868 and would become the most prominent of the leading Black figures of that era who could be said to have *founded* the Black Houston community. (**F. 11)**

Finally, the explosive need for workers of all kinds was generated by the oil strike and the dredging of the Houston Ship Channel to the Gulf of Mexico. Those two developments produced a need that drew Blacks from all over the South—my parents included. In that regard, Houston offered the most striking proof that some of the Black migrants escaping the rural South during the early and middle decades of the twentieth century headed for Southern cities, too. The mixture of Black customs, speech patterns, and musical styles produced a Black Houston "culture" of great vitality—one that was also influenced, especially in the musical style of jazz, by the music of Cajuns from southern Louisiana and Mexicans and Tejanos.

Although these groups *as groups* largely remained separate, their musicians "borrowed" extensively from the musical patterns and innovations of the different styles. For Black Houstonians, the development of a Houston style of jazz was significantly rooted in the integral role the city's high schools for Blacks played in Black civic life from the 1920s to the late 1950s. That influence was particularly grounded in the rivalry between Phillis Wheatley High **(F. 12)** of the Fifth Ward and the Third Ward's Jack Yates High, which would become my high school. This development was a direct result of the heavy Black migrations from the World War I years onward. Before that, city officials had deemed Booker T. Washington High School, in the Fourth Ward, sufficient to pack in Black adolescents. Now, the exploding population growth in the Third and Fifth wards required each to have its own facility for the upper grades; both schools were built simultaneously. Though officially supervised by the all-White school department, the schools were staffed by Black principals, teachers, and other administrative personnel, and the principals had, within the boundaries of the over-arching rules of Jim Crow, significant leeway in supervising their schools.

The quickly-developed rivalry between Wheatley and Yates, which had both serious and a great heaping of humorous elements, epitomized the classic American high

37

school rivalries of those decades that were centered on their athletic teams' prowess in general and that of their football squads most of all. It was widely acknowledged that both schools' teams were annually among the best teams, Black and White, in the entire country, added to the electricity surrounding the annual Thanksgiving Day game, the *Turkey Day Classic*. This was not just a football game but a civic festival, usually drawing tens of thousands of alumni from near and far to join students, neighborhood residents, and partisan bystanders to cheer on their respective teams to deliver them bragging rights for the next twelve months.

But what distinguished the Turkey Day Classic from myriad similar high school Thanksgiving Day contests was the superior quality of each school's band. Their parade to the stadium before the game, amid the automobile convertibles carrying each school "Queen" of the game and her court, various prominent alumni, and even owners of businesses taking advantage of the priceless advertising opportunity, as well as their play during the game's halftime was considered as important for bragging rights as the footballers' on-the-field exploits.

One reason sprang from the fact that after the 1920s, big band swing music became the most popular form of jazz for the next two decades, and Yates' and Wheatley's leaders organized superbly led music programs to take advantage of it. This, of course, was just the moment when, on the one hand, Houston's migratory stream had brought to the city substantial numbers of adults with a deep attachment to particular race- or ethnic-based musical traditions. And on the other, it had also brought a substantial number of children of those different groups to the schools who would take full advantage of the programs' offerings.

Those programs enabled students to learn how to write music, which was one way to help spark not only their technical knowledge of how music is made but also their own creativity. And, since many students came from families too poor to buy an instrument, the schools' programs gave them access to instruments they both did and did not have experience with. In addition, because big bands included many more instruments than the small-combo jazz unit of prior decades, that meant that students could indulge in learning to play more than one.

The Yates and Wheatley bands of these decades were a unique phenomenon. Not only did they include such students who went on to prominent national careers as Arnett Cobb, Illinois Jacquet, and Eddie "Cleanhead" Vincent. They also contributed substantially to the development of the saxophone, replacing the clarinet as a central element of jazz music. Writ large, that instrument's aggressive sound—be it brassy or piercing—was a response to the broader *urbanized* society's increasing complexity. But, more immediately for the Yates and Wheatley bands, it answered their need for an instrument that could make them *be heard* above the exuberant, raucous din of the Third and Fifth wards parade watchers and football game spectators.

Each of the schools' bands was so good as a unit that the trumpeter and singer Milt Larkin were the most active of several bandleaders in Houston who either included student musicians in professional bands for gigs or, on several occasions, led bands composed entirely of current and recent students from the schools in Black Houston's nightclubs and ballrooms. That meant, in some instances, those high school musicians were earning as much per week as adult workers on the docks. In fact, the bands' excellence contributed in numerous ways to Black Houston's considerable sense of itself, despite the heavy burdens imposed by Jim Crow, as a community of importance.

That vitality was often boasted of by Black Houstonians and praised by visitors alike. Many compared it favorably to Atlanta for its cosmopolitanism, scope of Black business development, and — compared to the rest of the South — relative lack of constant anti-Black violence. All well understood, however, that situation was completely dependent on limited contact between Blacks and Whites — and the former remaining in their designated 'place.' While Houston's Jim Crow culture was significantly less virulent than that of rural East Texas and the Deep South's countryside and cities–didn't mean it was fundamentally benign. It followed all the major and petty laws and customs of the White South's rule of apartheid: segregated public schools; exclusion from the public University of Houston and the private Rice University; segregated residential neighborhoods; inferior government servicing of their neighborhoods; exclusion from all but the lowest rung of jobs in private companies and government agencies; and a police force that was routinely brutal toward Blacks, even if they had committed no crime.

But, quite possibly, the most hated Jim Crow practice of all was the mandatory segregation on the city's buses. It was a constant topic of discussion in the city's Black newspapers, Black churches, and Black Houston's civic clubs. Adding to the humiliation was the fact that the "colored section" on the buses shrank whenever any white rider wanted a seat occupied by a black person. Blacks sitting in the single seat or a two-seat row past the halfway point of the bus had to move further back—which, of course, actually meant they had to stand up since all the seats "further back" were already taken. And the "order" to get up by a White passenger or the bus driver himself was often accompanied by, at best, a preemptory tone or, at worst, a grab, a shove, and a racial epithet.

The practice infuriated Blacks of all ages and classes because it struck in the most public of spaces at the foundation of one's individualism and dignity. It declared that you, being Black, were worthless and helpless before the power of not just the *White* state but any *White person* in it. There's plenty of evidence in the chronicle of Black Houston life during the Jim Crow decades that Black women also expressed their fury about the segregation on the buses and their being subjected to the petty cruelties of apartheid whenever they went downtown. But, given the distinct "gender politics" of American society of that era—that men were supposed to protect women and children—the "mobile" nature of where the *line of separation* was to exist on the buses was even more galling to many Black males— for that line could, and most often, did change on every bus and every bus ride and at every stop.

Resistance by any Black person, old or young, male or female, to being told to move sharply ratcheted up the tension inherent in the situation: At that point, violence from either the bus driver (some of whom carried pistols) or white male passengers, or an ad hoc mob on the street, or the police became not just a possibility but a probability. But, even if

41

an individual Black passenger was, out of frustration, willing to face that probability for himself or herself, they also had to consider that they were endangering other Black riders on that bus as well. That predicament embodied the fundamental message of Southern apartheid: *Suffer the humiliation—or else.*

Words spoken by Dr. Benjamin J. Covington, whom Lorenzo J. Greene interviewed on his visit to Houston, indicate how deeply Blacks of all stations resented the bus rule—and how much it represented for them the injustice of the whole of apartheid. Covington was the most prominent of Houston's Black doctors and, with his wife, was a leading pillar of Black Houston society. Their daughter, Jesse, was a well-known classically trained pianist who subsequently married Albert Dent, the educator who became the longtime president of New Orleans' Dillard University.

Speaking to Greene, obviously, with some heat in his voice, he said that he never rode the buses because "he could not 'be a man' and protect women from an insult hurled at them by white people." * For any Black man to object to the woman he was with being insulted by a White man or woman, Covington said, "whether he be husband, father, brother, or sweetheart, would be tantamount to suicide. … it is such things as this … which make the Negro's situation in the South so insecure that it is equivalent to sitting on a volcano. One never knows when an eruption will occur." **(F. 13)**

Greene wrote in his memo that "I left Dr. Covington, but his words made me realize as never before the racial dilemma faced daily by Southern Negro men who love their women yet who feared to protect them against the insulting advances of the most ignorant white man." **(F. 14)**

It's not likely that I, as a young boy growing up in mid-twentieth century Houston, could have, like Dr. Covington, fashioned such powerful words. But I was not so young as to not know that I, and all the people who looked like me, were surrounded by a special, *racial* danger. The anger among Blacks about the segregated rules of public transit told you your *place*. The overcrowded schools and often decrepit textbooks for Black children told you your *place*. The poor housing and lesser services the city devoted to Black neighborhoods told you who you were and what White America thought of people like you. Like Dr. Covington, I, too, never rode Houston's buses. I walked everywhere—to elementary school and high school, to run errands for my parents, to my part-time jobs after school and on Saturdays, to visit friends. My living in the Third Ward and the substantial degree of *Jim Crow-driven self-sufficiency* in social and commercial activity made that an easy choice. The only reason I moved beyond the boundaries of the Third, Fourth, and Fifth wards was to go to the after-school job I had downtown. And when I went downtown, I kept my eyes downcast—so as to not get accused of looking any White man or woman in the face.

When I was head of the Urban League, I kept in my office a framed picture of the second of the two family homes—actually, they were shacks—I grew up in. One day, when a friend came for a meeting, he caught sight of it. His eyes widening, he said with astonishment, "Jake, I knew you had grown up in poverty. I didn't realize your family was that poor."

I laughed. "Man, that was our second home—the one we *moved up to* because my parents had more money. You should have seen our first house!

A few years ago, I purchased a sculpture by Woodrow Nash of a young black boy, about the age of six, seven, or eight, dressed in a pair of blue-bibbed overalls and wearing a floppy hat. He is sitting on a box, looking sad. I was attracted to the piece because it reminded me of when I was about that age—looking sad because I was sad. In fact, I named the piece Johnny B because that's what my mother called me. And my sadness was because I was poor. Not that I imagined I was poor. I knew I was poor even at that early age, and I hated it.

I'm not so sure my deep feelings were shared by all the people on my block and the nearby streets because one of the by-products of the "old" segregation—the Jim Crow segregation that governed life in the South before the 1960s—is that it camouflaged the full impact of one's poverty because segregation threw Black people of all economic levels into the same neighborhood and often on the same block. For some, that might have indicated all black folks were equal because we were all facing the same problem: white racism. But for me, even at an early age, I could see the differences among us.

For example, Nurse Johnson's big house on the corner had gas for cooking and heating and electric lights. The postman next door to her had the same utilities. But my house was a three-room shack. Not three bedrooms, *three* rooms: the front room where my parents slept; the middle room where all of us six children slept; and a kitchen. The shack had no gas, no electricity, and an outhouse in the front yard. We weren't living on the street poor or living in a car poor. And while my mother and father had little money, they were a loving couple, childhood sweethearts who had married young— Dad had been 21; Mom, 18—and built a close, stable family. As small as our homes were, I never heard them argue. They always felt that God would make a way somehow and they lived that every day. But we were poor. I knew it, and I felt it every hour of every day.

However, despite their economic poverty, my mother and father didn't think of themselves as *poor*. Oh, they were well aware they didn't have much money at all. *But they did not consider themselves poor.* This belief held even as they, like everyone else, were trying to make do in the midst of the greatest economic crisis America had ever faced—the Great Depression.

Perhaps that was because they had come of age in an era when many Americans believed that there was a clear distinction between not having much money, on the one hand, and, on the other, *being poor*. The former was merely a matter of economics. Most Americans—especially most of the people that most Americans interacted with on a daily basis in the places they lived—didn't have much money, a situation common even in the late 1940s. The rich and even the upper middle class were few and far between in the places most Americans lived, whether urban or rural. Before the 1960s, the media—that is, newspapers, radio, and television in its early form—largely hewed to the portrait of an American society where most everybody (meaning most everybody who was *White*) was more or less in the same economic strata. Those who were wealthy, or even upper-middle-class, were the exceptions.

Even more to the point, the *moral stigma* attached to being poor—the suspicion that *being poor* was one's own fault—led many people, including those who were poor and those who were not but knew people who were poor, to *not* consider many people who had very little money as poor in that sense. In this, upstanding personal behavior counted for more than the hard economic facts. If one were God-fearing, as the saying went, personally honest, and conducted oneself with integrity in your relationships with your neighbors and other people, one would not be *poor* in negative terms.

Among Black Americans, there was a racial element to holding this belief as well. White America's claim, asserted again and again—that Black men and women, too, cavalierly abandoned their family responsibilities—put heavy pressure on both Black husbands and wives to make having a family work. And it puts especially heavy pressure on those whose incomes put them at or below the poverty line to *make being poor work.* From what I saw growing up in Houston, it was vitally important to men's and women's sense of self and their sense of place in the community that—even if the wife of the family worked—*they* were seen as financially taking care of their families.

Of course, as a group, Black Americans were disproportionately deeply poor. That's because in Houston and throughout America, racial discrimination was a system of economic as well as social and political warfare against them. The way it operated in the South made that unmistakably clear. In these decades, their lack of formal schooling or training didn't prevent most Native-born Whites and White-ethnic immigrants alike from finding an economically comfortable niche on the ladder of opportunity and, for many, rising beyond the working class. But that route up the economic ladder was closed to all but a minuscule number of Black Americans, no matter how— with or without formal credentials— talented and hard-working they were.

My father was able to support his wife and six children, working five days a week on his regular job, first as one of the legions of Black itinerant laborers who found regular employment in a region characterized over the decades by constant expansion. The building-out of Houston's Ship Canal and the area's road network, not to mention the new office buildings and homes being built in the white-only subdivisions, required tens of thousands of men whose physical strength and willingness to work hard for little pay was so undervalued but so necessary. As he got older, he found a steady job building caskets for the Houston Casket Company.

But Dad also had a second job—really, a labor of love and commitment to his people and God. My parents were very religious, and as a result, we spent our Sundays and many of our evenings during the week in church. Because we never owned a car, church for us was not only a place for religious nourishment but also our principal family extracurricular activity. At church was where I first developed my public speaking skills, giving my Easter and Christmas speeches every year and competing against other children reading and interpreting various passages of scripture and books of the Bible. But Dad was never with us on those Sundays. That's because in migrating to Houston for better work opportunities, he had not given up his commitment to spreading the word of God.

Black Houston (and the White and Hispanic Houston communities) was chockablock with churches and formally credentialed ministers. The Jacob family attended Jordan Grove Missionary Baptist Church at 2017 Dowling Street, a couple of blocks from our home, next to the HT Taxi Company, and across the street from a pool hall. But, as it was throughout the South, many Black churches in the hamlets and rural areas of East Texas were too small and their congregants too poor to afford a full-time minister. They depended on men (although, of course, women knew their Bible at least as well as men; the ministers in that era were almost always men) like Dad— men who had little formal schooling but who were, in fact, *ordained* ministers, men who knew their Bible and had a fervent commitment to deliver the Word of God to a sorely tried people. These men would be hired on an informal basis, usually with no fixed duties beyond preaching at the Sunday morning and Sunday afternoon service—and no fixed salary.

So, on every Saturday morning, Dad, having packed his suitcase with one of his two suits and wearing the other, left home to catch the segregated bus for downtown Houston. There, he took a segregated Greyhound or Trailways bus to head for one of the two churches he pastored and preached to on alternate Sundays. One of the churches was forty-six miles southwest of Houston in Wallis, Texas; the other, about seventy-four miles away in Brenham, northwest of the city.

It was years before I realized I'd actually never heard my father preach. Perhaps it was because we didn't have a car and couldn't afford the bus fare for the whole family to traverse the rural areas of Texas that seemed so far away.

The family only journeyed to those churches, via getting a ride from friends, to celebrate his anniversaries. And on those occasions, there was always a guest minister preaching the sermon in his honor. I did hear, however, that he was a great preacher. I remember him returning home late Sunday nights, tired and worn, with his compensation being only what was left from the collections (after what was needed for the church's operational expenses had been taken out). He'd have what was left tied up in his handkerchief: nickels, dimes, quarters, and a few dollar bills. And I would hear him softly tell my mother: *Do what you can with this.*

It was that commitment to being responsible and behaving properly in one's dealings with the outer world that my parents insisted on. Dad put the rules succinctly.

Rule Number One was that if you were going to live in his house, you must be in school. He added that he may never have gone to college, but he knew the difference between an "A" and a "C." "Don't bring me any "Cs," he would say.

Rule Number Two was if you're not in school, you must have a job.

Rule Number Three was if you get a girl pregnant, you're going to marry her.

And Rule Number Four was if you go to jail, you're going to stay there.

It was always clear he meant every word and would hold us to them.

So, when my brother Emerick, their second son, two years older than me, came home one day in his senior year of high school in early 1950 and told Dad his girlfriend was pregnant, I don't believe my father even bothered to look up from his chair; he simply asked Emerick when was the wedding to be.

Emerick graduated from high school in January of the new year, celebrated his 19th birthday that February 12th—and he and his girlfriend were married on February 13th.

Because my sister Gladys died at twelve years of age in 1942, only Robert, the oldest, who was one year older than she, had the best chance of having more than hazy memories of her. That included me, who was only seven at her death. What I do recall is that she was very smart in school and very well-liked by the adults and children in the neighborhood. We brothers never could say that we knew her well; we were just children ourselves. But we never forgot her place in our family.

All the Jacob brothers were to go to college except for Emerick. He, in early 1951 a husband and father-to-be, was in need of a job. Fortunately for him, a member of our church at Jordan Grove was a longtime employee of the Houston Water Maintenance Department. Uncle Doc, as we called him, Uncle Doc Faultry. Despite the fact that Uncle Doc could neither read nor write, he had his own crew of men working for him and was in charge of a water department truck. Respected on the job and in the community, his word was good enough to get a man an entry-level job with the agency, and he got Emerick his first job on his truck digging ditches. That chance was all Emerick needed. He retired from the water department 35 years later as a division manager.

Emerick's first marriage produced two girls before ending in divorce in the mid-1950s. He married again in early 1961 and he and his second wife had three girls, and

Emerick adopted his wife's son from a prior relationship. My brother Emerick passed in May 2003, exactly nine months after the death of our mother.

Robert, the oldest of us, left high school after the 11th grade and joined the Navy. When his tour was up, he returned to Houston and used his G.I.Bill benefits to enroll in the Jackson School of Horology to learn watch repairing. He soon moved to San Francisco, where our Mother's oldest Brother, Burt Sadler, was living. But his business prospects must have collapsed because soon after, he had joined the Air Force and was assigned to the branch's Perrin Air Force Base in Denison, Texas, five hours by car from Houston. Marriage followed in 1949, and over the next sixteen years, so did five girls and one boy. In the early 1950s, after completing his tour of duty, he and his wife moved to San Francisco, where Robert took jobs as a porter in hospitals and the airport to support his growing family.

I don't know if my going off to college in 1953 was his motivation, but by the mid-1950s, Robert had fallen in love with education. While working his two jobs as a porter, he enrolled in Cal State University. And he went to school continuously for 10 years. Just to show you how enthralled he was with education when our younger brother Norman graduated from high school and joined him in San Francisco to enroll in an engineering program, Robert started taking some engineering courses, too—and he kept on taking engineering courses for the ten years of going to college part-time to gain a degree in psychology. With that degree in hand, Robert began working in the San Francisco city poverty program.

It was while working in that capacity that he was approached by a civil engineering company that had been awarded a contract to construct a highway in the black community of San Francisco. They wanted his knowledge of the community and contacts with community leaders to help promote acceptance of the project. Robert accepted their offer on condition they let him spend a week reading books on civil engineering in their library to acquaint himself with some of the technical details of the road-building project. The firm readily agreed; after all, such knowledge would be valuable in showing community leaders the firm's concern.

What Robert was actually doing was brushing up on the knowledge about engineering he had acquired from taking engineering courses during his 10 years of college study. Once he completed his review in its library, he went straightaway to the city's engineering department and registered to take the qualifying civil engineering examination to become a certified civil engineer. He passed the test, joined the city engineering department, and was assigned to monitor the project work of the company that had originally hired him to sell the community on the project. Robert retired from the engineering department of the county after some twenty-five years of service. By then, he and his first wife had divorced, and he had remarried and adopted the daughter of his second wife. Robert died on June 26, 1997, at 69 years of age.

Norman Louis, my parents' fifth child and fourth son, five years behind me, was always a happy child. He loved to joke, and he loved having fun. I don't remember us doing a lot of things together because when you're five years older than your younger brother, you don't have a lot in common.

But he was very smart and talented in many ways. But, as he once told me later in life, he had two huge disappointments as a teenager—one of which shadowed our relationship all his life.

The first was that from elementary school through high school, Norman had wanted to go to West Point. But he was Black, and in Texas in the mid-1950s, no member of the Texas delegation to Congress stepped forward to give that a chance of happening. The second was even more bitter to him and dismaying to me. School officials said he was ineligible to receive the particular lucrative scholarship I had gotten because it wouldn't be fair to other students. I believe Norman went through life feeling that I had denied him the scholarship opportunity because I had gotten one before him.

After he graduated from high school, he moved to San Francisco and moved in with my brother Robert and enrolled in an engineering program at Cal State. While matriculating at that institution, he met and later married a Chinese-American named Janet Chan on January 18, 1962. From that union they had one child; a daughter, Askia, who has been for many years the wardrobe manager for Samuel L. Jackson, the movie star. And, if you watch the credits for any movie he's in, you'll see her name.

It was during Norman's college years (during which he had married) that he connected with a group of talented actors, writers, singers, and dancers through which his passion for theater blossomed. They called themselves the Afro-American Folkloric Troupe of San Francisco and came to New York to seek their fame and fortune. My first trip to New York City was to see them perform. I was blown away by how talented they were particularly how talented Norman was. Norman quickly abandoned his engineering goals and concentrated his efforts on the theater. It clearly paid off. Six years later, in April of 1969, when the troupe, clearly well known among dance aficionados, performed again in New York, a *Times* theater critic praised "Norman Jacob" in an article, "Afro Folkloric Troupe Opens Talent Fete" for being "a limber-legged fellow with flashing teeth and a natural sense of comedy."

Norman would continue with the troupe until being incapacitated by a stroke in the mid-1980s. It left him temporarily unable to speak and with a permanent limp, ending his career on the stage. However, resilient as ever, he went back to college, earned degrees in early childhood education, and taught for a time in several New York private schools. But, just as things seemed to be going well again, he contracted a case of hepatitis from a student that ultimately forced him to give up teaching, broke apart his second marriage, and sent him on a downward spiral physically and in spirit.

Mom had made me vow that I would look after Norman; after all, I was in New York, too. But his troubles were not over. Ultimately, over more than a decade, they took him all the way back to Houston, which he had left a half-century earlier, and to a bout with drugs and near-homelessness until one of his nieces, a daughter of Emerick's, who lived in Houston undertook the daily supervision he needed. Now, my checks for his support were sent to her. I flew to Houston to see him, and we reconciled; in fact, the three of us went off to lunch that day, and we had a great time. Things were looking up again, and the surgery he had to repair a hernia he looked upon as part of his getting back in good physical shape.

But, days later, in mid-December of 2015, as he lay in his bed in his nursing home in Houston, he went into cardiac arrest. He never regained consciousness. We buried my brother Norman Louis on the 19th of December, after a beautiful funeral service, near the gravesite of our father and mother and our brothers Emerick and Billy.

Billy Joe, my baby brother, was born in May 1943 in Houston, the second and last of the boys born outside of the state of Louisiana. Because we were nine years apart, I really never got to know Billy as a child. I went off to college when he was only 10 and I never lived in the same home or in the same town during his lifetime. What I do know, however, is that Billy had a brilliant mind. He did exceptionally well in school and he, too, received a scholarship to college.

It wasn't the Worthing scholarship, but it was substantial. He attended Texas Southern University, the successor four-year college and law school for Blacks right in the Third Ward, the original Houston Junior College for Negroes. He graduated with honors with a degree in English, then scored the highest grade of anyone taking the teacher's examination that same year. Later in his career, when the Houston School System instituted a requirement that all teachers and administrators had to take and pass a re-certification exam, he did so well on the test that he was recruited to tutor others for the exam. He loved his job, and he loved teaching children.

What I didn't know about Billy for a long time was that he was gay. I became aware of that as I visited my parents and began to meet Billy's friends and associates. They were all teachers; they hung out together, and they loved being around my parents. Billy was a great son; he even bought a house across the street and down the block from where my parents lived so that he could check on them every day and do whatever he needed to make their lives comfortable.

Billy was the go-to brother, and he made it easy for those of us living outside of Houston. What I found fascinating was that my father and mother, being Southern Baptist people, had no difficulty accepting Billy and his homosexual friends. And I should have said Billy had a great sense of humor. He was smart, he was interesting, he was sophisticated, he was intellectual and he was adventurous. He was successful as an educator, moving up to the position of assistant principal.

But his career came crashing down when he was arrested for purchasing drugs from someone on the street. He explained later that his partner needed some drugs, and he went out to get them and was arrested for purchasing drugs. It was front-page news that a high-ranking official from the Houston Independent School District had been busted buying drugs. It was embarrassing, and he was looking at a criminal record.

But in stepped my good friend from my high school days, Andrew Leon Thomas Jefferson, Jr., who had been Houston's first Black State judge. Jeff was able to negotiate a deal for Billy that if he did not commit any crimes for a period of time his record would be expunged. While that took care of the legal side of the issue, he still was faced with the public relations side of the problem. Because of his value to the school system, they found a way to keep him employed in a useful way. But they did not want him in the classroom with children again.

Billy was a loyal attendee at every National Urban League National conference during my tenure. For him, the conference was a brothers' family reunion because Emerick and his wife would come with my mother from Houston, and Robert and his wife would come from California, too.

Billy became very ill in 1995 and was hospitalized and diagnosed with the AIDS virus. I sent him a tape of a sermon Rev. Dr. W. Franklin Richardson had preached regarding the subject of AIDS because he had a brother who had the same condition, and I wanted him to know he was not alone, and then I called him to see if he had received it.

When I talked with him, he said he was so glad to hear from me because he thought that I didn't love him because he was gay. And, I said to Billy that I had never stopped loving him, that I didn't have a problem with his being gay, and that it pained me to know that he thought I did. I told him that he was and would always be my baby brother, and I loved him very much. I told him the message of the sermon was that AIDS didn't just affect the person with the disease. All the family who loved that person felt his pain. I don't think he ever got to listen to the sermon because Billy passed on April 13, 1995.

Despite the power of my parents in shielding us from the desperateness of rock-bottom poverty and despite the camaraderie we brothers forged all while living in what was a shack, I found my childhood painful because we were so poor. For me, the two most painful days in the year were my birthday and Christmas—because we never had the money to celebrate with the exchanging of gifts. Decades later, I could crack a joke about the houses we lived in. But it was very far from a laughing matter to me then.

Of course, it was easy to see that our housing situation was not unique in Houston. A large swath of Black Houstonians (and some White Houstonians) lived in deep poverty. So-called shotgun houses were common in most of the Third Ward's Black neighborhoods (as they were in many Black communities throughout the Deep South) because that was where the Black community first took shape in the years immediately after the Civil War. *

These structures were one room wide and one story tall, with the rooms arranged in a row without hallways and doors at the opposite ends of the structure. The name came from the fact that if one aimed a shotgun through the door and pulled the trigger, the shell would pass through both doors without obstruction.

Shotgun houses became less common as Houston's zoning code and building regulations brought a uniform modernity to residential housing within the city limits; the city began to build housing projects for families in the deepest poverty; and the city's Black middle class and the lower middle class began to grow and use their resources to build modest to grand homes in the ward.

From a more distanced perspective, one could see in these rudimentary homes the determination of people without resources to take some measure of control over their own lives. My own parents exemplified that human response, and as I've said, I celebrated that about them.

But then, awareness of the depth of my family's poverty never left me as I progressed through school and, particularly in high school. I thought that my friends were as aware of it as I was. It was only years later that one of my classmates told me it wasn't a factor at all in the friendships I had with others, either with other students who came from poor families or those who came from well-to-do ones. She said it didn't seem to bother me—I was a student who compiled top grades and was involved in significant extracurricular activities, so no one else thought anything of it.

My childhood centered around basically two institutions, the public school and the church. Later the YWCA became one of those institutions where I spent time. In Houston in those days, there was only one public recreation center in the ward in which I lived; the Emancipation Park. * And, because my mother was very protective of us, the time we spent at the park was limited.

Because I turned six years old in December 1940, I wasn't allowed to enroll in school until the following September. My first school was the nearby Frederick Douglass Elementary, * where Robert, Gladys, and Emerick had preceded me. **(F. 16)** But I never made it to the fifth grade at Douglass because, in 1945, the city began building the I-45 superhighway, the Gulf Freeway that began downtown and ran the fifty miles to Galveston and the Gulf. The Freeway split the Third Ward significantly, and Pierce Street was right up against it. It had, in effect, become an access road to the Freeway.

Those changes led the city's all-white school board to order that the children living on our side of the highway would be transferred from Douglass Elementary to Dodson Elementary, several blocks further from my home than Douglass and in an all-White neighborhood. Dodson had previously been a Whites-only school, but the city had built a new school for that neighborhood's children. So, they got a new school, and we Black children got their hand-me-down school building.

As one might have guessed, Dodson was located in one of the ward's lower-middle-class white neighborhoods, and it was there I was called a *nigger* for the first time. That happened when I was serving as a school crossing guard, which essentially was providing safety for children crossing the street. On my crossing guard duties one day, I, clad in a white X-shaped belt, wanted to find out the time, so I simply stuck my head—not my body, just my head; in the white barber shop's doorway; I had no intention of entering the shop— in the doorway of the barbershop not far from the corner I was patrolling to see the time. The owner, an old white man, yelled at me, saying *nigger don't you set foot in my shop.*

And it didn't end there. He proceeded to walk down the street to the school, demand to see the principal, tell him of my transgression, and say he should see to it that *it never happens again.*

Dodson was a smaller school with fewer students than Douglass, and even the principal, who also owned a funeral home, taught classes. After two years at Dodson Elementary, I graduated in June 1947 and enrolled in Jack Yates High, which in those years included grades seven through twelve. And when you went to Yates, you were in *high school*, not junior high school. All the students there were in the same school. **(F.17)**

As a child, I really didn't have a lot of interaction with kids in elementary school or in my neighborhood. We may have had nine houses on my block of Pierce Avenue, with children of my age living in only four of them. On the corner of Pierce and Live Oak was the house of Nurse Johnson and her son, Henry, whom we called Snappy. And then there was Sonny and his younger brother Donald Larue, and the multi-family house on the corner of Pierce and St. Charles was where the boy of my age we called Sweet Papa. Although we occasionally played ball together and we would see each other at school, we didn't really hang out together.

Houston, for me then was a place of limited geography. I only went to places I could walk. So *my Houston* was mostly Pierce Avenue bounded by Live Oak on one side and St. Charles on the other, with the walk to the Emancipation Park for play some Saturdays and to church at Jordan Grove on Sundays. Although my world of friends expanded substantially in high school, geographically speaking, the world I moved in was almost completely limited to Black Houston. I only went downtown—walking, with eyes downcast—to reach … my summer job, and once my work hours ended, I came right back to the Third Ward. I really don't even know what downtown Houston looked like in my day.

Once I got to Jack Yates, however, my world began to expand. I renewed friendships with old friends from Douglass Elementary and, because all of the ward's elementary schools fed into Yates, made new friends. That Emerick was two years ahead of me meant I'd at least know and be known to some older students, too. So, my circle of friends expanded to include guys like the Baptiste brothers, Roy and Charles, and I spent a lot of Saturdays at their father's service station, washing cars, gassing up cars, changing the oil on cars, and fixing flat tires all for three dollars a day. But that was the gathering place for a number of guys who also became my friends—Andrew Jefferson, Joseph Pierce, Cecil McBride, and James "Bo" McNeil.

Going to Jack Yates swept me into the world of Black Houston that existed beyond the confines of my neighborhood, particularly through the intense rivalry that existed between the three high schools. On the one hand, it was a rivalry that was typically American—rooted in the schools 'identities as representations of their wards 'civic pride and as football, basketball, track and field, and baseball powerhouses. The annual Thanksgiving Day game between Jack Yates and Phillis Wheatley—the Turkey Day Classic— was a high point of civic life for all three communities, typically drawing crowds of twenty to thirty thousand spectators. Nor was it just a local festival. The schools were so good in football that the contest usually ranked among those Thanksgiving Day high school games across the country that drew national attention as well.

But In those decades when Black Americans had so few avenues to show they, too, believed in the pursuit of excellence and so few avenues to do *typically American things* free of the shadow of racism, the intensity of the Yates-Wheatley Classic (as very likely did its Black counterparts elsewhere) made the day's contest and ceremonies something more: a festival of *freedom.*

The more exciting social life wasn't the only reason I was glad to be at Yates. It was clear to me that the high school curriculum, even at the seventh-grade level, was more serious, and the students in the upper grades seemed to be more serious about the schoolwork, and the teachers were definitely more serious about the substantive aspects of education, as opposed to the nourishing and developmental aspects of elementary school curriculums.

In an era when highly educated Black men and women were almost universally limited in the North as well as the South to teaching in Black colleges and predominantly Black or all-Black high schools, the faculty of many Black high schools throughout the country were stocked with teachers who had completed or were pursuing master's and doctorates (often from prestigious White universities in the North and West, because few Historically Black Colleges then had graduate schools at all), and, at Jack Yates, it was clear they were committed to passing on the knowledge they had acquired. They seemed to see themselves as being on the front line of the fight against racial oppression and they insisted that we students learn as much as we could and perform as best we could. They didn't care that you lived in a three-room shack with an outhouse in the front yard. They didn't care if no other child on your block planned to go to college. They believed their job was to prepare each of us not for the world we lived in then but for the one they hoped would come. In Black Houston, as elsewhere, teachers and administrators at every level were held in very high regard.

Being in high school in the seventh grade reinforced my determination to go to college—and to follow Dad's laconic message—*I may not have been to college, but I know the difference between an "A" and a "C." "Don't bring me any Cs."* I was not going to bring him any "Cs." I was not going to disappoint my parents. Getting top grades was my route to college—my route out of poverty.

All through high school, I could never escape the fact of my poverty. When, in senior year, I was chosen to escort Wilma McDade, who was one of the members of the entourage in the Miss Jack Yates Queen's Court at the Turkey Day Classic, I had to borrow a suit from my friend Bo McNeil. That was Bo's only suit, so he attended the festivities in khakis pants and a sweater. And for my graduation I borrowed Jackie Battles 'suit, even though it was two sizes too large for me.

And yet, in my later years, when I talked with former high school classmates about my poverty and how much I had hated it, they were surprised to learn I felt that way— because they never viewed me as being poor. Perhaps that was because my clothes were always clean and well-pressed, and I suppose the way I carried myself and was involved in school extracurricular activities gave no hint that I was weighed down by feeling poor. It probably also helped that, despite the well-to-do Black families among us, Houston's Black neighborhoods were predominantly poor neighborhoods. That undoubtedly meant that many students at all three high schools came from poor families—and were adept, as I apparently was, at *not behaving* as if they were poor. We all had one thing in common that tended to downplay the differences among us; We lived in a segregated country, in a segregated state, and in a segregated city. Regardless of one's economic status, we were all still Black.

In the decades before the 1960s, the limitations imposed by discrimination and poverty meant that being a good high school athlete was an important route to gaining scholarship funds for college for many Black males. But it was obvious

64

that wasn't going to be a possibility for a boy like me—5'6" tall and of a slight build. Being in a school that was an athletic powerhouse like Yates (and Wheatley, and for that matter, Booker T. Washington; East Texas was dotted with Black high schools that could be similarly described) quickly convinced me that I wasn't muscular enough to hold my own in high school football, or tall enough to get on the court in basketball, or fast enough to star in track, or with the arm strength to compete in baseball to get any sort of athletic scholarship for college. ** So, I decided I would just have to work at being smart.

Now, it's not easy being smart when all you have to work with are the textbooks from your school, and the school library has relatively few books beyond the textbooks. I had no awareness of the city's segregated library for Blacks, the *Carnegie Colored Library*, albeit founded with funds from the Andrew Carnegie endowment. It was years later that I learned of its existence, and even during its years, it had only a small selection of books because city officials 'required funding was meager. **(F. 18)** That situation meant I couldn't *see* the knowledge about the subjects I was taking in high school and other topics that were available in the books a library should have had. It reflected the fact that in Black neighborhoods, despite the best efforts of librarians, libraries represented both the wonders the world of learning and achievement could offer and how the separate but equal regime of Jim Crow worked to deny Blacks a chance to climb the ladder of achievement.

In fact, I grew up in Houston with a very limited vision of the world. I had only seen one Black physician and one Black dentist before going off to college, and I had never seen a Black attorney. And, for me growing up in Houston, a *businessman* was the person who had his own barbershop, and the person who ran a service station, and the man who managed the ward's Black movie theater.

That's how limited my vision of the world beyond the Third Ward was. But I did understand that whatever my future was to be, I first had to liberate myself from poverty, and the way to do that was to get to college. The way to get to college was to demonstrate to my teachers, school administrators, and students that I was hard-working, smart, and a good leader. So, I kept my grades up. I never missed a day of school or a class in school. I followed the advice Jack Yates High's renowned football coach, Andrew "Pat" Patterson, always said to the boys in his physical education class: *in order to be smart, all you needed to do was work a little harder than the other folks in the class.* I remembered his advice, and I applied it. I just worked hard at being a good student.

At Yates, as at other high schools in general, girls were always going to be the majority of the students at the top of the grade rankings. Only a relatively few boys competed for spots at the very top of the class ladder. Andrew Jefferson, a year ahead of me at Yates and an exceptional student, was one of them and I wanted to be like him. While I never told him, I tracked his performance and used it as a measuring stick for mine. That focus helped me not only be chosen for the school's honor society but in my senior year, be elected president of it.

But, even though I didn't go out for sports, I made sure to involve myself in several of Yates 'extracurricular activities, and I earned the respect of students. I had roles in two operettas produced by the music department. I was elected President of the a cappella choir even though some boys in the group had better voices. During the first semester of my senior year, I was elected vice-president of the student council and vice-president of the class and then, at the beginning of our second and last semester at Yates, my classmates elected me president of the graduating class.

As I mentioned above, I was interacting with students whose parents were much better off financially than mine. Some may have been driven to school in their parents' Cadillac, but inside the fence of Jack Yates, I could demonstrate that I could be as good a student as any of them. Yes, my father was a laborer who never owned a home or car, and, yes, we didn't have electricity in our house, or gas to heat it, or a gas stove to cook our food on (my mother cooked on a wood stove), and I read my textbooks by a kerosene lamp and bathed in an old wash tub; and while I never owned a new suit and only had a couple of pairs of pants for school, I took the attitude that it was my wardrobe that was limited, not my mind.

I was always conscious of my poverty, but my friends never treated me as if I were. I never invited them to my home, and to my knowledge, they never wondered why I didn't. I worked hard to be a good student, and my work paid off. I made good grades throughout my high school career, and what I learned is that if you were thought to be smart, not only would other students respect you, but their parents would like you even more. Teachers liked me, students respected me, and their parents liked me. I became *that smart little John Jacob.*

During the eighth grade, I began working after school, but I eased into it, working after school on Friday and then all day Saturday at Carolla's grocery store. The store was in the Third Ward, owned by an Italian-American family whose residence was in the back of the premises. The Corollas had two sons: one who was an adult, living elsewhere in Houston and working for a food company as a route salesman, and the younger son who was close to my age. Mom shopped there because she could buy on credit and pay the bill when Dad got his paycheck.

Mr. Carolla must have noticed me with Mom on one of her trips because the next time she went there, he asked her my age. She told him 13, and he asked her if she wanted me to have a job working there. I think that offer came from their respect for Mom's always paying her bills in full at the proper time and the way she carried herself in general. They saw she was a woman who deserved respect, so they figured she had raised me right. I would work at Corolla's right through to junior year at Jack Yates. My salary never changed: three dollars for eight hours of work.

Soon after I began working there, the Corollas moved their store and themselves outside the Third Ward in a lower-middle-class White neighborhood. This created a problem for my mother because now she had to walk to this new community to buy groceries and could only do so when Mr. Corolla would drive her home. I was soon to learn another lesson about race and racism.

When the youngest Corolla boy lived in the black community, he readily associated with the black kids in the community. But now that it was in a new, white neighborhood, he had a standoffish attitude toward me. I didn't belong in his group of new White friends. I understood then that often, Black people were invisible to White people—even when they were standing next to them. Once, when he and his friends heard music coming from the nearby Black community, one of them said to the others, *I hear music over in nigger town. They must be having a parade. Let's go watch!*. These were young boys my age who had already cultivated the attitude and language of racism.

My second job was at "Sam's Modern Market." This store was located in another lower middle-class white community quite a distance from my home. Beyond stocking shelves, my primary duty at Corolla's, I also worked in the meat section, cutting up meats, grinding meats into hamburgers and making sausages. It wasn't unusual for many White retail stores to have Black workers, but no one ever forgot what the rules of Jim Crow were. Black men and boys were especially well aware that you should never look White males, and especially female customers, directly in their faces. Breaking that rule could be hazardous to your health.

While working at Sam's one day, a black man came in walking with a limp, and he attempted to exit. The store owner tried to restrain him while yelling at me to bring him his gun. I didn't know what he was talking about; all I saw was he was trying to hold onto this black man who was walking with a limp and trying to exit. But, at the same time, the store owner was yelling for me to bring him a gun— which I did not do.

When the man finally got away, got into his car, and left, the owner ran to me, demanding to know why I wouldn't bring him his gun. I told him I didn't know what that was about, and he said the man had been shoplifting and sticking stuff down the pants leg of the one he was dragging with the limp. We spent the better part of the next day riding up and down the street looking for the man he said was stealing from the store because now he had his gun with him. Fortunately, we didn't find him, and I didn't have to witness a Black man being shot.

My third job was at Stone's Service Station. Here, my past experiences at Batiste Service Station came in handy. I worked evenings a couple of summers. This was well before today's system of self-service, so I not only gassed up cars, I changed oil and fixed flats, too. Stone's was owned and operated by the parents of two girls who attended Yates with me, and occasionally, when they stopped by the station, we'd chat. But I always got a feeling their father would have preferred they not associate with the help.

Most Black adults I encountered were much more cordial toward me, including Mrs. Rosa Taylor, a teacher at Jack Yates, whose daughter, Dene', was in my class. I never took a course from Mrs. Taylor, but, she always included me in activities she planned for her daughter. In fact, the first and only time I took what I considered at the time to be a major trip was when Mrs. Taylor was taking Dene 'to Baton Rouge, Louisiana to visit some friends. She insisted that I come along: it was the first and only time I'd ever left the state of Texas until I left Houston for college at Howard University. While Baton Rouge is only about 270 miles, about a four-hour drive from Houston to the 17-year-old John Jacob, whose family didn't have a car and who walked everywhere he went in Houston, it was like setting out on a trip to the moon.

But what I remember most about the trip was that when Dene 'and I went to a party for some teens she knew there, I initially spent a long stretch of time just standing against the wall. Finally, one of the mothers came over to me and asked why I hadn't asked some of the girls to dance. And I asked— much to her surprise—"Are they colored"? I had assumed they were not because they were all light-complected, and I didn't have any intentions of getting lynched. *

Dene 'had always invited me to her parties, and Mrs. Taylor was the only teacher to ever visit my house and meet my parents. There, she seemed unperturbed by our dire economic circumstances and was always respectful and friendly toward my parents. She remained a part of my life throughout my college years.

Taking stock as I reached senior year, I felt I was in a good position, even though I hadn't yet figured out how I would solve the money problem in terms of getting myself to college. I had a good extracurricular record, and I was on track to graduate 9th in a class of a couple hundred students in Jack Yates 'Class of 1953. and I had the best grade point average of any boy in the class. I figured being the male graduate with the highest GPA was the best way to ensure I'd be in line for a college scholarship of some kind.

But, suddenly, as the school year began, Edwin Cooper, who was in the junior-year class, had gone to summer school and taken courses which led to his being advanced into the senior class, and he was a legitimately super bright student. While I had had the highest grade point average of all the boys in my original Class every year since the seventh grade, Cooper's GPA was actually higher than mine. And, I might add, he proved his brightness by becoming a tenured professional at UCLA... I looked him up. Well done, Edwin. However, I had an outstanding track record, and I was elected president of our class, so I knew I was recognized by both my classmates and the faculty and administrators of the school. In fact, on a senior day, the day seniors were to be placed in charge of the school, I was chosen to be the principal for the day.

My scholarship chances improved significantly, I thought when I read in the newspaper the summer before I entered my senior year that a white Houston real estate entrepreneur, Evan Edward Worthing, had passed, but he had left a $500,000 scholarship trust fund for poor, but bright Black high school graduates. (F. 20)

When I saw that article in the newspaper, I said to my confident self: *I've just got to college.* And then I said to myself, *you have two challenges that you must meet over the next twelve months: one, you have to stay alive, and two, you have to practice acting surprised when they call your name to award you the scholarship.*

And at the Jack Yates High School Class of 1953 commencement, when my name was called to receive the E.E. Worthing Scholarship, I gave an Academy Award performance. Six Worthing scholarships were awarded to the Jack Yates classes of 1953; two to the January class, a girl, Issie Shelton, and a bot, Merrill Allen. Four were awarded to the June class: two girls, Jewel McFarlin and Audrey Anderson, and two boys, Harold Hudson and me.

With the Worthing scholarship in hand, school officials said I could go to any school I chose, and I believed them— within the strictures of the Jim Crow South, of course. So that meant not the University of Houston, literally just down the street from where I lived, or Rice University, less than three miles away on the other side of downtown, or the University of Texas, 165 miles up the road in Austin. But that was okay with me, and for the same reason, all-Black Prairie View College, 45 minutes to the northwest, and Houston's newly named Texas Southern University were out for me, too: I wanted to leave Houston and Texas and the South. That summer, to build up my savings for the first year of college, I took on five jobs or money-earning activities.

From six in the morning until two in the afternoon, I washed dishes at Lacy's Café in downtown Houston. I had to get up very early because, given my own personal boycott of the segregated buses, I had to walk from my house to downtown Houston to that job. I would then walk back home to my neighborhood to the neighborhood shoe store, where my job was not only to sell shoes but also to do general cleanup work.

When I'd finish there, I'd walk around the corner to Brown's Barber Shop, where I cleaned up and shined shoes. Then, some evenings during the week, I'd take care of the yard of one of my former teachers. And on weekends, I'd assist the custodian at the Colored YWCA with his cleaning and night-watchman duties. I felt I needed all of these little hustles to generate money for college.

Preparing to go to college was quite an ordeal in other ways, too, for someone who had grown up in poverty and never had anyone in his family go to college and had only limited exposure to any young people who were in college. There were so many things about going to college I felt I just didn't know.

My first challenge was to select a college. With the prospect of a sizable scholarship in hand, I thought I could—*I should*—go far away from Texas. One of the teachers at Yates had mentioned he had been working toward an advanced degree at Northwestern University in the Chicago suburb of Evanston, Illinois. And while I didn't know anything about Northwestern or Evanston, I knew it was out of Houston and I assumed it was a good university. So, I only applied to Northwestern, and I was accepted.

As the summer progressed and the September start date for Northwestern began to loom ever larger, I used some of the money I'd earned to pull my college wardrobe together. I bought a new suit, an overcoat, some Stacy Adams shoes, and a nice hat. Someone gave me an old trunk, and Emerick went to the pawn shop and bought a second-hand suitcase as a gift for me. My father made some hangers for the trunk. I packed it and I packed my suitcase and prepared to head off to Northwestern for the school's opening.

One of the items I had plenty of was pajamas. I had never owned any, and because I knew I'd be sharing a room at college with another boy, I felt I didn't want to be viewed as the poor boy from Texas. Many of the church ladies at Jordan Grove were so proud of me, they asked what I needed, and I said pajamas. Well, I was soon gifted with at least six pairs! My wardrobe may have been weak during the day, but at night, I was ready to be the best-dressed man in the dorm.

In mid-August, when I was set to leave for Evanston within a matter of weeks,. I was mowing Mr. Jerome Busby's lawn one evening when he asked about my college plans. "Jacob, where are you going to college? Very proudly, I said, "Northwestern."

But he gave me a strange look, a concerned look, and when I asked what that look meant, he, who knew that I had won a Worthing Scholarship, said, "Well, you have enough money to get through your first two years. What are you going to do about your second two years?"

At that I panicked because I had thought that when they told me I could go any place I chose, I thought my scholarship would cover all four years. Now, I'd learned from Mr. Busby that that wasn't the case. I knew for certain I couldn't go home and tell my parents I needed two years of money to complete my college education. I didn't know what to do. I made a trip to the Colored YWCA the next day for some teen activities, and the teen counselor, Geneva Bolton, now Geneva Bolton Johnson, must have noticed the painful look on my face... (F. 21) Seeing the distressed look I must have had on my face, she straightaway asked me what was wrong. I told her of Mr. Busby's concern, and she said: "Let me try something."

Geneva Bolton was only about five years older than me, but she was a college graduate who had long committed herself to promoting the social good, and she was a very smart and trained *counselor*. She had joined the YWCA movement fresh out of Albright College in Reading, Pennsylvania, with the goal of becoming a teen counselor. She had been in Houston only a few years but was already revered among the teen set for her willingness to listen and for the terrific job setting up programs at the Y that were interesting to young people, both female and male.

Geneva sent a telegram about me to Howard University. I don't know what she said in the telegram. Obviously, she told them about my grades and extracurricular activities and that I had received a Worthing Scholarship that would pay for all of my undergraduate years there. And I'm sure she said something about my background and my character. And, finally, I'm sure she said something else: that I was one of those Black young people who, in the era of Jim Crow, exemplified why Howard existed—I was trying to the best of my abilities to rise, and I needed their help.

What I do know is that I soon received a telegram from the Admissions Office at Howard University telling me: *Please come.*

I cashed in my railroad ticket to Evanston, Illinois, and got a ticket for a Southern Pacific Railroad train heading to Washington, D.C. I was going to college at Howard University.

Chapter 3 — Into The Wider World: At Howard University and Beyond

It was time. I had packed the suitcase Emerick had bought for me as a gift at a pawn shop—on which I had painted my name in bold white paint, so there wouldn't be any mistake about its owner and left the three-room shack on Pierce Avenue in Houston's Third Ward to head to my future.

In the typically warm, humid early evening, I met up with my other Jack Yates classmates also bound for Howard at Grand Central Station, the city's major railroad terminal: Jewel McFarlin and Harold Hudson, both of whom had also won Worthing Scholarships, were there, as was Carl Ards, Cecil McBride and my close friend Dene' Taylor. It would take our Southern Pacific Railroad train about twelve hours to reach St. Louis, seven hundred miles to the north, and then, after a relatively brief layover and boarding a new train, another twelve to fifteen hours—depending on how many stops there would be along the way—to get to Washington.

But the time we were going to spend traveling was no burden to me. This was my first trip by train. I was *traveling to college*, traveling to adulthood, or at least something close to adulthood. And I was setting off with some of my closest friends, a fact made even more special when we were joined by several Yates' classmates headed to Fisk University, another prestigious Historically Black College. To me, the history we all shared and the very moments we were sharing now made up for the fact that, following the rules of Jim Crow, we were shunted off in the east wing of the sprawling,

Art Deco-style facility. Houston had long been the busiest railroad station in the Deep South, and the Southern Pacific, the region's preeminent railroad company, had built its newest station there in the early 1930s, the heyday of train travel in the U.S. I'm sure we college students to be were unaware as we boarded our train that the clock was ticking more and more ominously for passenger train travel. Fewer and fewer trains came and went from the grand facility as air and automobile travel became more affordable for the affluent-society populace of the 1950s. Six years later, in 1959, the Southern Pacific closed it down, sold the property, and moved its operations to a much smaller station.

Eight hours after leaving Houston, our Fisk counterparts left us at Memphis for their three-hour or so trip to Nashville, and we continued to St. Louis. Then, after a layover of about three hours, we left St. Louis in the early evening, crossing the more than 800 miles to Washington in another 12 hours before arriving at D.C.'s Union Station late Saturday morning. On just my second trip outside the state of Texas, I had traversed nearly half the country. In fact, even before we crossed the Texas-Arkansas border, I had never been so far from home.

Lonnie Edmonds, the husband of Dene's cousin Doris, met the train at Union Station to drive the two of us to Howard's campus. We loaded our bags, glimpsing in the distance amid the hustle and bustle of the station's sweeping Columbus Plaza, the dome of the Capitol. The Howard campus, due north of the historic Shaw district and the vest pocket neighborhood of Le Droit Park, both of which had deep historical ties to the University, was just over two miles from Union Station. The faster, utilitarian route to it would have been to swing out of the station's Columbus Plaza traffic circle, take an immediate right on North Capitol Street, which bisects the city's northwest and northeast quadrants, and drive straight up to Florida Avenue, one of the city's many diagonal thoroughfares (all of which are named for states). There, one would take a left and drive less than a mile to Georgia Avenue. A right turn at that intersection, and you were literally on the doorstep of the Howard campus, announced first by the massive presence of the University-affiliated Freedom's Hospital.

But as I recall, we took the more scenic route, following Massachusetts Avenue, always one of the city's imposing boulevards, a mile or so and then turning north on Sixth Street to follow its path through the historic Shaw District that, with a few twists and turns, delivered us to that same Florida-Georgia Avenue intersection and the beginning of the Howard campus. The Shaw district was filled with the city's noted mixture of three-story row houses, all built adjacent to one another—or, as I soon wrote to my parents: "looking like they were stuck together." At first glance, I thought they were a kind of apartment building because we had nothing like them in Houston.

After we arrived on campus and checked in, I was assigned to Cook Hall, one of the all-male Freshman dormitories at the northern end of Howard's compact campus, and soon found myself carrying my luggage four floors up to my room that would house two students. The eastern side of Cook Hall was just across a campus driveway from the college's small (but just the right size) football stadium, and if you had a fourth-floor room, as I did, you could see just over the stadium bleachers the beautiful waters of McMillan Reservoir. For the first time in my life, I had a bed all to myself and a shower right down the hall. Remember, all my life, I had been bathing in the same wash tub we used to do our daily washing; so, on my very first day at Howard, I had reached a new level of happiness. When I would hear the inevitable complaining about the dorm from other guys, I saw them as a bunch of spoiled brats because this was the best housing I'd ever known in my 18 years on this earth.

My single roommate was Dudley Lowe, from Grenada, an island country in the West Indies. We spent a full year sharing a room, and yet we never got to know each other beyond superficiality. I think my lack of knowledge about world cultures and interacting with the people from abroad was inhibiting, and he seemed to have the same issues. I've often wondered what ever happened to him.

But otherwise my first week at Howard was transformational. That Saturday, we met our "campus pals," the upper-class students who were assigned to a small group of new undergraduates through orientation week. Ours was A. B. Spellman, who the world would come to know as a poet, music critic, cultural activist, and arts administrator. (F.1)A.B. took us that Sunday to the movie theater on the famed U Street commercial district to see the motion picture *Shane*, starring Alan Ladd. It was the first time I'd ever gone to the movies on a Sunday. Dad didn't allow the pursuit of worldly entertainment on Sundays; that day was reserved for church and God.

On Monday, as students and faculty began gathering for the new academic year, I began seeing people I had in Houston who only imagined existed. Before walking around

80

Howard's campus, I had only seen one Black physician in my entire life, and he was the doctor who, rightly or wrongly, I felt had let my twelve-year-old sister Gladys die. Now, at Howard, not only did I receive a physical from a Black physician, I saw scores of Black medical students going to and from medical school classes that were being taught by Black doctors. In Houston, I had never seen a Black attorney, although I had heard at Jack Yates that my Latin teacher's brother was one. But, at Howard, not only did I see Black attorneys but also a host of Black law school students—attorneys in training—and Black law school professors.

That sense of excitement from the role-modeling dynamic this could produce was at a peak in those years of the early 1950s because of the role Howard Law School and some of its alumni, faculty and students were playing in the civil rights movement. Indeed, as the landmark *Brown v Board of Education* schools case was making its way through the federal courts toward the Supreme Court's momentous 1954 ruling, Thurgood Marshall and his corps of attorneys held numerous strategy sessions at the law school itself. (F. 2 Interestingly, the undergraduates I hung around with weren't unduly excited about that. Their feeling was: *Of course. This is why Howard exists.* Also ahead of us and America in those years would be the Montgomery (Ala.) Bus Boycott, the Little Rock (Ark) school desegregation crisis, and other hallmarks on the way to the mass-action eruption of the Civil Rights Movement of the 1960s.

For me, the campus itself, though bordered on three sides by the bustling U Street-Georgia Avenue, a northwest commercial district of small shops and businesses, restaurants, and nightclubs, reinforced the university's assertion that *this* was a place where the pursuit of learning was paramount. It was a perfect, relatively small example of the old New England college-in-a-yard ideal—neo-Georgian buildings (for the most part) set around a quadrangle sliced here and there by concrete walkways and the entire scene dominated by the imposing, cathedral-like Founders Library.

In those years, Howard's campus, including the then-named Freedman's Hospital at its southern end, only spread over twenty or so blocks on the eastern side of Georgia Avenue as it climbed a slight, almost imperceptible hill from the Georgia-Florida avenues intersection. That slight rise, however, was enough to provide from the upper floors of some buildings broad views of the flat topography of parts of the Federal Enclave to the south and, especially on the upper campus, unobstructed views of the blue waters of McMillan Reservoir just across a narrow expressway at the campus's eastern edge.

Howard was what a college campus was supposed to look like in those days. The campus contained not only the undergraduate school but also its graduate schools, the medical school, the dental school, the law school, and the school of social work. Every day one could see the physical representation of *the entire purpose* of the University. And you also saw, as a matter of course, *Black* men and women representing that mission by pursuing their ambitions, too. That sense was reinforced by the fact that in the years before the late 1960s, college students *dressed up* to attend their classes and other school functions. This was the case at historically Black colleges as well as White ones, and the photographs of those years prove the point. Often, male undergraduates wore blazers, dress pants or khakis, and dress shirts and ties—when not fully decked out in suits. Female undergraduates wore demure dresses and sweater sets or something similar. Most Howard students — and indeed students at HBCUs in general — meticulously adhered to this form of dressing for success. But they had an additional reason beyond mere conformity for doing so: *Dressing up* was also a silent protest against the many kinds of racist disparagement Black Americans endured no matter what their station in life.

I immediately found myself in the company of some brilliant Black students from all over the country—not just Jack Yates or Houston smart, but flat-out super smart. One of the smartest guys in my Freshman class was my next-door neighbor in Cook Hall, Louis Clayton Jones, from Louisville, KY. He was brilliant and would go on to major in Philosophy and French and graduate Phi Beta Kappa. He then earned a law degree at Yale and ended up working for an investment company based in France. I bumped into Clayton, as we called him, one morning in one of the terminals at LaGuardia Airport when I was Urban League president, and he gave me a ride to the office in his slick foreign automobile. We became friends at the College; never close, but we always respected one another due to both of us being prominent student leaders. His older brother was Reverend Doctor William A. Jones, Jr., pastor of Bethany Baptist Church in Brooklyn and a leading civil rights and human rights activist.

Clayton's roommate was, of all things, a Jack Yates alumnus. Frank Turner had graduated the year before me in the Class of '52 and had spent his freshman year at Tuskegee

University before transferring to Howard. At Jack Yates he had captured the affections of the girl in my class who'd been chosen the *most beautiful* and who I really liked for her winning personality and her beauty. She wrote to both of us at Howard. It was soon clear, however, that her letters to me were nice and friendly, but those to him were loving and passionate. I knew how she felt about him, and I know he knew how I felt about her because he'd often come to my room to read in front of me the letters she sent him. It took time, but I eventually got over my disappointment because two years later, in my junior year, I met the Howard student who would become my wife.

One day, I walked into the Student Council's office, and there sat a beautiful girl banging away on a typewriter. By then, I had served as a Sophomore Class representative on the undergraduate Student Council, had just been elected President of the Junior Class, Vice Polemarch (Vice President) of my Fraternity, and was involved in a slew of other extracurricular activities. I felt I was — or should be— one of the best-known students on campus.

And so I asked her her name, and she told me. Then, she asked me my name, and I replied, "Now, I can understand my not knowing your name, but I can't possibly understand you not knowing mine."

I think she concluded I was either the most talented person she had ever met or I was the most arrogant and conceited student on Howard's campus. As I discovered, she didn't live on campus but at home with her parents and two younger sisters. And because she lived within walking distance of the campus, she spent most of the time on campus working and involved in campus activities that didn't lead our paths to cross, even though she would later join one of the top sororities on campus, Alpha Kappa Alpha. Prior to meeting her, I dated three other young women: one was a college graduate working in the federal government; the other two were–high school graduates working in various jobs. But once I met Barbara and found myself captivated by her beauty and subtle, winning personality, she was the only woman I would ever date. Our meeting was the beginning of a beautiful relationship. I gave her my fraternity pin in my senior year; a year later, we became engaged, and two years later, we were married, a marriage that has now lasted 65 years.

Howard, for me was about stepping out into the world—with apologies to the late 1980s sitcom, in many respects, *a different world* than I had come from. **(F. 3)** A place where competition as well as friendship was the coin of the realm. I really had to learn how to negotiate college life. Despite my gaining leadership positions in extracurricular activities, I felt I wasn't quick at making new friends; I pretty much hung out with the friends I had from high school. I had to adjust to the big lecture classes, which was how many of the non-science courses were taught—to professors only know you by the name on your blue book at exam time. And, from the beginning, I felt enormous pressure to choose a major, though I had no idea of what I wanted to major in. I just knew I had to get a degree in something "useful."

One driver of that, of course, was my constant companion: the determination to leave my poverty behind. That necessarily included searching for the viable means to accomplish that, given that the early and mid-1950s were well before Corporate America began hanging out welcome signs for Blacks to seek jobs in their middle and upper-level positions and before banks were willing to loan Blacks funds to help start their own businesses or grow the ones they had already opened.

The Black business people I had seen in Houston were individuals who owned the barber or beauty shops, men who managed their own service stations, or managed the Blacks-only movie theater. The "Black professional" category essentially included very few other than teachers and educational administrators in Black schools. Entering Howard, the only thing I knew was that I needed a college degree, but I didn't have a clue in what field. My sophomore class roommate was an economics major, so I signed up for some of those classes. Dene's cousin's husband, Lonnie Edmonds, who had ferried us from Union Station to Howard two years earlier, had earned a master's degree in the subject. He and his wife would call on me to babysit their children from time to time, and through talking with him, I gained a better understanding of it.

The subject I most enjoyed was political science. But it became my minor because I realized in junior year I had already taken twelve hours of classes in Economics. I couldn't afford the cost of taking more courses in political science to meet the requirements for double-major status—and I was also very eager by then to get through college and out into the world of work. I knew that some of the economics faculty at Howard also worked for the federal government (a substantial number of the department's classes were held at night), and they might be of help in landing a job after graduation. So, Economics became my major—by default.

I did go home during the summers after my freshman and sophomore years. I missed my parents and my brothers terribly, even though I wrote home often. I made it to practice, never to ask my parents to send me money because I knew they needed all the money my father earned just to support the house. I received thirty-five dollars every two months from the Worthing Scholarship, and I tried to save as much of that as I could to buy a ticket for the trips home. **(F.4)** Every time I made it home, I discovered that not only were members of my family living the college experience through me, but so were the people in my neighborhood and at Jordan Grove Baptist Church. Even the guys hanging out on the neighborhood's corners would laughingly call out to me as I passed, *Hey, college boy, tell me what's going on in D.C.!*

Those summers, I readily found work. Between my freshman and sophomore years, I resumed my old high school job at Stone's service station, washing cars, working the gas pumps, changing the oil, and fixing flats. The next summer, a fellow Howard student knew someone who fixed me up with a job waiting tables in a high-class barbecue restaurant. That didn't work out so well. In fact, I was so bad I didn't even return after the first week to get my paycheck. I knew from that experience that I had to get a college degree because I was a total failure as a waiter. And, it's because of that I've always had the greatest respect for people who can do that job, and I am a great tipper for waiter service.

Back on campus in the late summer, I quickly found a part-time student job at the Association of American

Geographers housed in the Library of Congress, paying twenty dollars a week. That meant that, along with the Worthing Scholarship stipend and the stipend from the Army ROTC program—which I received during my Junior and Senior years. I was in the best financial shape of my life. It is worth pointing out that during my freshman and sophomore years at Howard, for all able-bodied male students, ROTC was mandatory. For juniors and seniors, it was optional. I was honored to be invited to participate in the program for my last two years.

I went to college in the last full decade when Americans — including Black Americans — considered serving in some branch of the military every able-bodied man's patriotic duty. With memories of World War II still fresh, the inconclusive Korean War, the belligerent posture of *Red China*, and the Soviet Union's October 1957 launch of its tiny satellite, *Sputnik*, all seemed to suggest that *World War III* could be but a few years away. In a light-hearted but symbolically important way, the Army's drafting of Elvis Presley in 1958 for a standard two-year tour of duty and then another four years on Army Reserve status underscored both the military's supposed function as the great equalizer of American society, on the one hand, and, on the other, almost every male's obligation to be trained for battle. Those were among the reasons I joined Howard's ROTC unit.

ROTC, the Reserve Officers' Training Corps, was considered a critical part of that double mission of supplying the military with a deep pool of officers drawn from the male graduates of the nation's four-year colleges and universities as well as its service academies in order to produce a broad, well-educated leadership corps. ROTC was deeply appealing to many Black male collegians, too and viewed as a noteworthy pursuit by male undergraduates. For Blacks, in college and more broadly, not only was service in the military—which Blacks had fought for a century to integrate—a way of showing they were fully equal to the duties of American citizenship. Military service in the 1950s unquestionably offered Black males the most *opportunity* for achievement and respectability. In Black communities, Black men wearing military uniforms, especially those who wore officers garb, drew looks of respect. It was, in many ways, probably the best job many young Black college graduates could hope to secure. So, amid my uncertainty about what a degree in economics could lead to, I did have another post-college career option: the United States military.

The summer after their junior year in ROTC, all cadets are ordered to undergo intensive training at one of the branch's facilities. I was ordered to Fort Meade, Maryland, for six weeks. The training was conducted by members of the 82nd Airborne Division, one of the most elite units in the entire armed services. Among the officers conducting the training was Andrew Chambers, a young Howard alumnus. Andy was also a member of Kappa Alpha Psi, my fraternity, as was his younger brother who was still in school with me. Andy was so impressive as an officer, leader, and airborne soldier that I quickly decided I wanted to earn my airborne wings and be like him. I worked very hard at summer camp, an effort vindicated when the Captain in charge of my training unit said he thought I should, upon graduation be designated a Distinguished Military Graduate.

The DMG designation (awarded by each individual ROTC unit) is for deserving cadets who graduate from college with superior grade point averages, strong performances in the Army Combat Fitness Test, and exceptional leadership ability. I felt ready for it. I had two strong years in Army ROTC at Howard, where both the unit's top commander (always given the title of Professor of Military Science and Tactics) and his deputy head praised my work.

But when I returned to Howard for my senior year, I was stunned to find that the unit had a new commander and a new deputy. Those who had been my advocates, who knew me best, one had been demoted, and the other had been shipped out to another assignment—and I had the feeling I was part of the collateral damage within the unit. I had fallen in love with the idea of making the Army my career. Now, I wasn't so sure. Despite the cloud over my future, I felt satisfied that spring at achieving several important goals: I gained my bachelor's degree in economics, and I received my commission as a Second Lieutenant in the United States Army. It was further proof that Howard had been the right place for me. I had gotten a good education, I had joined a great fraternity, Kappa Alpha Psi, which bonded me with a group of men all over the world who pursued achievement in every field of human endeavor, and, most important, I had met the woman who would become my wife.

Once past Howard's graduation ceremonies, I traveled back to Houston to spend some time with my loved ones I hadn't seen for two years; then returned to Washington to spend some time with Barbara before setting off for my seventeen-week active duty posting at Fort Benning,

Georgia. I think because I was an economics major at Howard, I was offered enrollment in the Quartermaster Corps. But I turned that down, emphatically declaring my choice was the infantry. I thought that if I wanted to make the Army a career, the best opportunity for rising in the ranks was in a combat arms branch. That was the choice my idol, Andy Chambers, had made. So, it was in the infantry that I received my commission.

On the day of departure, with my train ticket for Columbus, Georgia, I dressed in my first-class Army uniform with my highly polished 2nd Lt. bars on its shoulders and my spit-polished shoes on my feet, and I said my goodbyes to Barbara before taking the express train all the way to Atlanta. In Atlanta, while waiting on the platform to board the train to Columbus, a white Army Captain approached me and we struck up a conversation on what I could expect when I arrived at my "duty station" — Army lingo for *destination*. He was forthright and friendly, very generous with his information and advice, and skilled at quickly putting strangers at ease. Then, the conductor called out to passengers that the train was now ready for boarding. The Captain and I began walking down the platform together. As we neared one car, a conductor stopped me and directed me to board the one we had just passed as the Captain continued on. I became concerned, even as I took my seat, for the Captain because I thought he was getting on the wrong train. Puzzled, I asked a Black woman sitting near me if the train was segregated, and she said, "No." So, I tried to get off the train to find the Captain I thought had gone to the wrong train, but the conductor stopped me and assured me that I was in the right car for the completion of my trip.

When I returned to my seat, I again asked the Black woman sitting near me if the train was segregated, and this time, she said, "Oh, do you mean can Black people sit with white people?" I said yes, and she said, "Oh, no, Honey, Black people can't sit with white people."

I learned that day something I didn't realize all the years I was traveling back and forth between Houston and Washington: that interstate travel was by law integrated, but *intrastate travel could be segregated.* In the South, it most assuredly was.

When I arrived in Columbus, Georgia, and gathered my luggage, a young White boy on the platform asked if I needed a taxi. When I said yes, he took me to a taxi driven by a White man and put my luggage in the trunk of the car. There were two Black women sitting in the back seat, so he opened the door to the front seat, gesturing for me to sit there. The driver took the women to their destinations in the city—and then told me I had to get in the back seat. I calmly said, "That's OK. I've been sitting here this long; I'll just stay here."

He replied, "I don't think you understand. We have a law in this state that Black people can't ride in the front seat with White people." Having said that, he refused to move the car and he stopped the car until I got into the back seat. I was livid—but I also knew that moment was not the time for me to begin challenging Jim Crow's fundamental rules. I got out of the front seat and got in the car's back seat. **(F. 5)**

By the time I arrived at Fort Benning and found my assigned Bachelor Officers Quarters, my anger still hadn't cooled when in walked my assigned roommate—my *White* roommate. After the day's experiences with picayune racism, I was ready to take it out on him. But he was cool. He simply said, "Hey man, I'm George Merchner from Lafayette College. What's your name?"

I first thought we had likely been assigned to the same room because, as he would soon tell me, he was an economics major in college and because, without seeing me, my last name led many people to think I was Jewish. However, having George as my roommate didn't appear to be the result of a "racial mistake." Only four of the 200 college grads in the course were African-American. Two were from Hampton Institute (now University); one might expect they'd be placed in a room together. The third was Arnie Sowell, the University of Pittsburgh graduate and star track athlete who had competed for the U.S. in the 1956 Olympics. His roommate was also White. George Merchner turned out to be a nice guy, and I regret not staying in touch with him. Years later, in 1985, when I received an honorary degree from Lafayette College, I spoke of my seventeen weeks with George Merchner as my roommate. Sharing that experience led Meryl Streep, who was the College's Commencement Speaker that year, to subsequently send a $5,000 gift to the National Urban League, with a note saying, "I wanted you to know that I heard your message."

I managed to complete the Basic Officers' course in the top half of the class and was accepted into the airborne class to become a qualified parachutist. I got in only by persuading the examining physician to *add* three pounds to my weight to meet the required 120-pound threshold. I think he had concluded if I was that desperate and stupid, why not? Perhaps I was both, but I confess that being able to pin on my chest those airborne wings made me feel like a real soldier, a real officer, and a real leader of men.

But fate had laid out another direction for me. The severe recession meant the Army's Infantry branch had to rid itself of its excess of junior officers: it wasn't extending any tours. So, I was released from active duty to the active reserve. In those years, the commitment to military service was eight years. So, even when you were released from your active duty commitment, you were obligated to join an active reserve unit. I returned to Washington and joined the "K" Company, 3rd Battalion, 80th Division, based in the suburban community of Riverdale, Maryland.

That short-circuiting of my hopes for a military career meant I had to find a civilian job, and it didn't take long for me to realize that Washington, D.C., in the late 1950s was one of the worst places in the country to be unemployed. Precisely because it was overwhelmingly a "government town," good private-sector jobs were scarce—unlike in later decades when there was a significant influx of private companies, and thus a diversification of the kind of jobs one could pursue. That predicament was especially true for Black college graduates, whose search for any positions above menial or entry-level status outside of Black-owned enterprises was often stymied by racism. Pursuing work in the federal government meant first identifying the position of interest, then finding out when the exam for that position was being given, and then taking the exam and, if you passed, waiting to be called to come to work.

In the meantime, you could find yourself slowly starving to death. There I was, fruitlessly running down job leads and becoming increasingly frustrated. Once, I even drove to

Chicago for an interview only to have that company's representative—having seen the color of my skin—spend almost two hours explaining to me why I didn't *want to work for them*. This was the 1950s, after all. But, I needed work. I needed some income, so I took a minimum-wage job at a General Services Administration warehouse. When they discovered I had a degree in economics, they began temporarily assigning me to their headquarters to cover desks of workers taking leave or vacation; positions at the Government Service (GS) lower and even middle-grade levels —while continuing to pay me a minimum-wage salary.

Finally, in sheer desperation, I drove down to the Senate Office Building one day and asked to meet with someone to help me find a decent job. Since legally I was still a resident of Texas, the Senator I sought help from was Lyndon Baines Johnson. Once I proved I was indeed a Texas resident, I was directed to his office, where an aide took my CV and asked me where I had been looking for work. I gave him a long list. When he had finished looking it over, he asked if I had tried the Post Office.

It was a question I had been dreading because working at the Post Office was something I most emphatically did not want. Not because it was a bad job. My fear stemmed from the fact that I had been in Washington long enough to have seen and heard of any number of Howard University graduates, be they of the College or the professional schools, who took to working at the Post Office because nothing but menial work or permanent entry-level work was available elsewhere—and had never left. They would become trapped by the racism of the job structure in the Washington area, by the fact that the Post Office virtually guaranteed a "forever" job, and by the demands of the family lives they were trying to build. I didn't want to spend my entire career in the Post Office.

But, I couldn't tell this man I wanted a job — just not at the Post Office. So I said I had not tried the Post Office because I knew the sign-up period for the examination for jobs there had closed.

He replied: "Not to the Senator."

He picked up the phone, dialed a number, and spoke to someone on the other end of the line. When he hung up, he said, "The exam is closed. But they are going to open it just for you." Then he said, "I want you to go to this address tomorrow. They will give you the exam. When you complete the exam, I want you to sit there while they grade it, and if you pass, you will go to work."

The next day, I went to the designated place at the appointed time. I took the exam and I passed the exam, and they told me to report for work at the main Post Office in two days. Because the Post Office was launching an expansive automation of the entire organization, I was placed in the very first class training operators for the new parcel post sorting machine. Although I had never wanted to work at the United States Post Office, I kept that job for the next twenty-two months.

Chapter 4 — At Howard and Beyond: Baltimore

My nearly two years with the Post Office gave me a much-needed financial life line. I felt myself especially lucky given the brief but sharp recession that gripped the economy from mid-1957, just as I was graduating to the early summer of 1958. While it wasn't the job I wanted, it was better than being out of work, and it gave me the resources to move out of my fraternity house, which my prior low-income Federal paycheck had made a necessity. Most important of all, it enabled me to marry Barbara and afford the rent of our first apartment. To be fair to the Post Office, I really did have a good job there. Being a parcel post sorting machine operator was an innovative step forward, and my usual working hours of 7 a.m. to 3 p.m. were the most sought-after of the system.

But it wasn't where I wanted to be. So, I was always on the lookout for a better opportunity. When a colleague I knew from our undergraduate days came by to say goodbye, I asked him where he was going. He told me he had taken a job at the Department of Public Welfare in Baltimore, Maryland. That was all I needed to hear. I had been at the Post Office for almost two years, beginning in September 1958 and now it July 1960. Despite having very little knowledge of what welfare or social work involved, I offered to take the next day off and drive him to Baltimore for his first day of work. My real purpose was to see where I could sign up to take the qualifying exam for a job there, too.

Mission accomplished: A short time later, I took the exam and passed. Because the welfare agency was continually in need of staff, within months, I was offered a caseworker's position. I immediately resigned from the Post Office position and reported for work at the Baltimore agency. It was unquestionably a financially risky move. Barbara was pregnant, and not only was I losing my health coverage from the Post Office, I wouldn't be eligible for coverage from the department until the end of my six-month probationary period.

To seemingly make matters much worse, while my annual salary at the Post Office had been $4,800, my starting annual salary at the Welfare Department was $4,040. I seemed to have changed my job and location only to worsen my own financial situation. But, while $4,040 doesn't seem like a huge amount of income by today's standards, in 1959, it was a livable wage for a newly minted college graduate. And, Barbara's salary of $3,600 as an accountant pushed our two-income household status to nearly $8,000—which put us firmly in the ranks of the middle class. So, while I was taking a reduction in salary, I knew we'd be fine financially.

However, I soon found out I hadn't done all the homework I should have, for I discovered that the Welfare Department was to Baltimore what the Post Office had been for DC. In Washington, the Post Office was the place where many Howard graduates had gone and never left. In Baltimore, the Welfare Department was the place where many graduates of Morgan State College (now University), the city's Historically Black college, went to work and rarely left. As I mentioned before, that lack of movement on the part of many black workers across the range of occupations couldn't be ascribed to a lack of initiative of the workers. Instead, given the pervasive discrimination Black Americans faced in the labor market at all levels, there was an overwhelming incentive for blacks to hold on to the jobs with relatively good pay that were available to them.

But I wasn't going to let myself be bound by that reality; I was going to challenge it. I just needed to find a way to make an impact in my new job and improve my prospects.

My week of orientation introduced me to the agency's voluminous manual governing guidebook — what our services were, how we were to determine an individual's or family's eligibility for the program they needed — be it the Aid to Families With Dependent Children, or assistance to elderly or adults who had fallen on hard times, or, through the Children's Division, placing children in Foster care and adoption, either because their parents abused them or were otherwise unable to properly care for them. As a new worker, I was assigned cases of general public assistance and old age assistance because they were less complicated than the AFDC cases that usually went to the more experienced workers. Those typically involved not only dealing with the parent's needs but, even more importantly, with the needs, concerns, and problems of the child or children in the home.

Part of our charge in the public assistance section was to do all we could to help as many of our clients move from dependence on government assistance to independence. Our principal responsibility was to make sure the recipients met the state's eligibility requirements for the program in which they were enrolled, that they received their monthly payment on time, that they received the appropriate help they needed, and that, if employable, they were taking the necessary steps to move themselves out of the status of the welfare recipient. But the reality was that, through the 1950s, the welfare rolls had been slowly growing, and the severe 1957-1958 recession had produced a waiting room at the agency packed every day with people of all colors and ages.

The Division's twenty-person caseworker staff in the public western division, always in need of more workers, was always on the verge of being overwhelmed. It seemed that the thirty clients, or "caseloads" we each were responsible for, were growing more and more difficult to guide toward that goal of "independence."

I quickly came to understand that the critical challenge for welfare caseworkers was how they viewed their role and their relationship to the people who needed government help and government dollars. *Do you see yourself as a policeman whose job is to protect the agency from abuse by those people?* Or do you see your role as a service provider to those people, using all the resources available to you to make them whole? In general, that challenge was one all caseworkers had to grapple with, regardless of their own backgrounds.

But, of course, this was 1960, and in those days before the Civil Rights Movement ushered in a new racial era in America, the divisions of race were often right on the surface of things, including in the Baltimore City welfare department. White workers were given caseloads consisting of Black and White clients; seldom were Black workers assigned White clients. The white workers in public assistance were usually from middle-class backgrounds, fresh out of their white colleges and universities, and, while meaning well, seemed to have had very little actual interaction with Black people and certainly even less with

Black *poor* people. Most caseworkers did the best they could for their clients, Black or White. But I came to feel that, though such things were never said in the office, some of my White colleagues tended to think our clients, especially those who were Black, were poor because they were lazy and/or they were poor managers of money, and that their primary job was protecting the agency itself from abuse by these people.

It struck me that one difference between me and many, if not all, of my White colleagues was that I *had been the people we were serving.* I came from a family where lack of money was always a presence. I knew from experience that most poor people were poor just because they didn't have any money to manage, and, in fact, that many poor people— as my parents had—did an excellent job managing the money they had because they were always in survival mode. I had seen that kind of management not only in my own family but in other poor families, too, on my street and in my neighborhood when I was growing up. That enabled me to see my clients as people confronting problems and my job was to use the resources of the agency to help them rescue themselves from those conditions. And sometimes, it took only the simplest of actions to help someone in distress: someone such as Annie Meekins.

Annie Meekins wasn't one of my general assistance section's clients but of the AFDC group. But I had heard of her. She had a fearsome reputation among the caseworkers because, when her check was late, she did not hesitate to show up at the office and unleashed a loud tirade demanding her check. So, I guess I was not surprised when she stomped into the office one day near our 4:30 closing time and promptly laid down on the floor of the waiting room, declaring she would not budge until she got her check. **(F. 1)**

I didn't know who her caseworker was at that point or why she hadn't gotten her check. But it swept through my mind that there were some older ladies in Houston's Third Ward who, in similar circumstances, would likely do something like that.

So, I went and lay down on the floor next to her. That surprised her. I calmly told her I was concerned about her well-being because the agency was going to close at 4:30, and one of two things would then happen: They would either call the police and have her arrested, or they would leave her there but turn the heat off and let her freeze all night. I told her that if she would get up and go home, I would personally deliver her check to her the next day. She said You promise to bring me my check tomorrow?" I said," Yes, ma'am." With that, she got up and went home.

The next day, I did deliver her check. But I also learned something about her: she was taking care of her two grandchildren, one of whom was out of school and of college-aged. When I got back to the office, I grabbed the manual and started thumbing through it until I found a way to provide some money for that grandchild to go to college. The lesson from that experience told me that there's always a way; you just have to keep looking for it.

Later, I was assigned a white family, a husband and wife couple receiving the department's general assistance benefit for the husband's work-related injury, which rendered him unemployed. Their case file had a note attached to it: this couple was not to be visited at home — "The man is crazy," read the warning. However, because I had taken several seminars led by psychiatrists in my simultaneous pursuit of a master's degree in social work, I wasn't put off by the note. Instead, I was intrigued. *How crazy can he be,* I thought, and decided to visit the home anyway.

The man wasn't there when I knocked on the door of their apartment; his wife let me in. I could see she was very nervous, even as she answered my standard agency assessment questions. She said more than once: "He doesn't like people coming here." And then he was at the door, his key turning the lock. She cried out several times, "He's coming". Her fright at the situation made me wonder what I'd gotten myself into. My explanation of who I was only seemed to provoke him into spouting wild conspiracies about what the welfare department and various other government agencies were doing to people. Given that he was taller and bigger than me, I realized my challenge now was to find a way to get out of there without a physical confrontation. And, then he said, you tell Miss Lazarus, the head of the Welfare Department, and at that, I stood up, saying, I want to take down exactly what you want me to tell her. And, when I leave, I'm going straight to her office with your message. After some minutes of furiously writing down his rantings to convince him I was interested in what he had to say, I managed to get away.

But I still thought I might be able to help this family. So when I got back to the office I reread his file, and I found there something I had missed the first time around; that his disability stemmed from his having worked at Bethlehem Steel for over 20 years. I said to myself, *if he is this disabled, why didn't someone file for his disability benefits?* So I did. A couple of months later, the receptionist for our floor called me to the reception area: he was there and had asked for me. I didn't know what to expect. But when I saw him, he wasn't sitting with the other clients waiting for caseworkers. He was standing against the wall, immaculately dressed: a three-piece suit, dress shirt and tie, highly polished dress shoes, dress hat in hand. *This wasn't the man who had harangued me when I visited his apartment months earlier. This was the man he had been in his prime working years, the man he was once again.* Now, he calmly told me he had gotten his first disability check, thanks to me, and that it was a lump sum payment for all the past months he had been eligible. He didn't need welfare assistance any longer, he said, and he wanted me to know how appreciative he was. So, he had made a special trip to the agency just to say thank you.

But even before the Crazy Man incident, thinking about Annie Meekins and the "Crazy Man" who wasn't crazy led me to approach the division's director and offer to take all eleven of the uncovered caseloads in her group. She thought about it for a moment and then accepted my offer.

One reason I made the offer was that I had been at the agency long enough to see it was always understaffed; I felt people's needs shouldn't be held hostage by the number of agency vacancies. And I could relate to the feeling many of those eligible recipients had when they didn't receive their checks on time. After all, I was unemployed before getting the job at the Post Office, and I knew how I felt every day without income coming in. Finally, there was the poverty of my own childhood and adolescence. I knew poor people didn't enjoy running down to the welfare office. They came because they were desperate, and they didn't need to be humiliated. They *were there* out of the sense of humiliation.

Now, I never set out to become a social worker. If I had my life to live over, I'm not sure I would have knowingly followed a path through the Baltimore City Welfare Department and social work. But then, in that environment in the early 1960s, I realized the welfare department was a tremendous resource for helping people I knew and cared about and that I should take advantage of all that it had to offer.

That's why I volunteered to take all the uncovered caseloads. It wasn't that the agency didn't have the money to provide those resources to people in need. It wasn't even that the agency didn't have the will. It was simply that it didn't have the bodies to deliver on that part of the job. I thought I could solve a problem that needed solving, so I told myself to do the best I could.

I soon learned that a Maryland state program allowed employees of certain government agencies — including the Baltimore City Welfare Department — to work part-time (and be paid a reduced salary) while pursuing a graduate degree in social work. I decided to apply for the program, requesting to enroll in Howard's School of Social Work. Howard required enrollees in the program to attend the classes at Howard three days a week, leaving them two days a week to be at their desks in their agencies.

My colleagues were astonished. One reason was that in the past, those who applied for the state partial-leave program had generally been on the job for at least five or more years and had clearly demonstrated managerial potential, while I had been there only a few months. The second was that I had chosen to apply to Howard, bucking the Welfare Department's preference that its employees in the program attend the University of Pennsylvania School of Social Work. That preference might have been helped by the fact that Penn's School of Social Work required their grad students to be in the classroom just two days a week—which meant caseworkers in the program could be at work the week's other days. But any difficulty my choice might have caused was diminished by the fact that the University of Maryland was opening its new School of Social Work that year and it had the same classroom/non-classroom requirement as Howard. So, my choice of Howard was not going to be a problem — if the director of the agency would sponsor me for the program at all. Initially, that seemed to be the sticking point.

About a month later, my supervisor tapped me on the shoulder and told me Esther Lazarus, the department's director, wanted to see me in her office. It would be our first and only meeting. "Mr. Jacob," she said when I arrived. "I understand you have been going around here saying that this agency is racist."

I was taken aback by her comment but recovered quickly. "No, I never said the agency was racist," I responded. "But there has been grumbling among some black employees about the assignments given compared to our white colleagues, and I was often part of those discussions." A recent article in the local Black newspaper had noted that, even though the department's clientele was substantially Black, all its top officials were White. I said that while I hadn't been interviewed for it, I agreed with its basic observations.

I was too busy then working and being a young husband to be involved in civil rights activities. But that didn't mean

I didn't understand systemic racism's effects on the lives of Black Americans. And this agency wasn't any different from every other institution I knew: from the all-white Houston school board that ruled over a separate-and-unequal school system to the military and the welfare agency I worked for, where Black workers were pushing to reap the rewards of superior performance. "No, I never said the agency was racist," I added, "but what I have said is when you look at the organizational chart of this agency, the higher you go, the whiter it gets."

She then said, "I know you want to go to school, and we're approving it."

Now, I don't know if the director knew I existed before she asked me to come to her office. But the 1960s was a time when the social work leadership sought to recruit more men into the profession, and in my case, I think I happened to come along at the right time. My initiative must have caught her attention.

It was so rare for caseworkers to be summoned to the director's office that when I returned to my desk, a colleague asked if I had been fired. "Nope," I responded, "I'm on my way to school!" And I was, as soon as Howard accepted my application to join its School of Social Work Class of 1963.

The early 1960s were the perfect time for me to learn the principles and techniques of social work because the country was ablaze with activism — and controversy. Kennedy's presidency had uncorked the spirit of activism that had been bubbling just below the surface of the 1950s, and his "New Frontier" spirit in promoting such programs as the Peace Corps and his ratcheting up the American space program gave, in effect, government endorsement to that spirit, That spirit was most dramatically seen — to Kennedy's initial dismay, in fact — in the Civil Rights Movement's entering its most intense stage of street-level activism: the Freedom Rides through the Deep South would begin four months after his inauguration in 1961. **(F. 2)**

I don't want to paint myself as something I wasn't. As a Howard undergraduate in the mid-1950s, I had one goal in mind: to get a degree and get it in four years. I was there on the Worthing Scholarship, among the first ones given out by his trust, and I felt my family, my church, my neighborhood, and my school were watching. I couldn't let myself or them down. Because my scholarship covered four years of study, I wanted to be sure I was out with my degree in four years. While Howard was a center for the creation of leaders in all fields of endeavors, students didn't spend much time celebrating our victories. When the Supreme Court handed up the *Brown* decision, we knew Howard had played a major role in that outcome, but there were no bonfires or rallies. It was viewed as: *That is what we do. These are the kind of leaders we develop at our university. With the preparation we undergo, we produce these kind of results. Now, let's produce some more.*

And keep in mind when I received my undergraduate degree in economics, I also received a commission as a 2nd Lt. in the United States Army. When I received my commission, I swore I would protect this country against all enemies, foreign and domestic. When you raise your right hand and make that pledge, you are committing to three things: You will fight for this country. You will kill for this country, and if need be, You will die for this country. When you are part of the military, your mission is very clear.

The clarity of that mission remained in the early 1960s, even as I—still a commissioned officer in the active Army Reserve—was more attuned than most to the then small-scale American military involvement in a small country, Vietnam, on the other side of the world. In fact, I was seriously considering volunteering to return to full active status. Why? Because I considered myself still a soldier, fully willing and able to join my Army colleagues in support of a military undertaking wherever it be.

Social work doesn't challenge that pledge nor call on social workers to make a similar commitment. But it did do something else for me: by giving me the analytical tools to examine some of the things, people, and places American society would rather not talk about, it sent me on an exploratory mission of who and what the real America was. And my exploration and self-examination was taking place amidst the outbreak of *idealistic activism* of the early 1960s. I couldn't help but notice that one of my social work classmates, Walter Carter, then the Field Secretary for the Congress of Racial Equality (CORE), spent his three days in the classroom and the week's other days on picket lines and/or in jail for demonstrating against injustices. **(F. 3)** There was Saul Alinsky, the political activist busy promoting his techniques for the grassroots organizing of poor people, and George Wiley, whose founding of the National Welfare Rights Organization produced an unprecedented mobilization of welfare recipients. More broadly, several books published in those years had a marked influence on progressive thought and activism: among them, Michael Harrington's *The Other America*, which did so much to expose the extent of poverty in America, Rachel

Carson's *Silent Spring*, warning of the indiscriminate use of synthetic pesticides in agriculture, and Betty Friedan's *The Feminine Mystique,* a landmark of feminist thought.

All this ferment was forcing a broader, more open discussion about poverty and racism, sexism and classism. In turn, that was forcing me to ask: what could I, someone who was about to gain a master's degree in social work, do about it. Of course, the event that put that question in the starkest relief came that summer: the March on Washington for Jobs and Freedom at the Lincoln Memorial on August 28.

Truth be told, my presence at the March was less the product of a noble decision and more a response to someone else's initiative. In the early summer, as the March was being publicized, Harold Bell, a fellow Howard graduate and colleague at the agency who was also studying at Howard's Divinity School, suggested to me that we Black social workers not go to work that day as an act of solidarity with the March. I thought it a good idea—an opportunity for us to stand up and stand out on critical issues confronting our people and communities.

We began talking it up and quickly secured the agreement of more and more Black workers and more than a few of our White colleagues, too. I'm sure the Department's administration knew about our plans, but we didn't get any pushback for it. On the morning of August 28, I said goodbye to Barbara as she left for work. What I hadn't anticipated was that about a dozen of my Black colleagues would soon be knocking at my door, asking if I was ready to lead them to the March. That's how I came to join the huge throng of people of all backgrounds at the Lincoln Memorial and the National Mall. What suffused the experience was not anger, but rather a profound sense of patriotism and resolve, too, that the fight for justice and freedom would continue for as long as it took: Now, as King was to eloquently proclaim, "is the time to make real the promises of democracy."

But I didn't respond to that imperative right away. I graduated with my master's in social work degree in June 1963 and returned to the Baltimore welfare agency to fulfill the two years commitment I owed the state of Maryland. My degree had earned me a promotion to a supervisory position in the Foster Care section of the Children's Division. Our responsibility was working with children whom the agency had taken from their parents and placed in homes of substitute parents we believed could give them the care their birth parents hadn't been able to or had not provided.

Each Foster family was put through a rigorous screening process and then, if approved, provided with funds to care for each child in the home. Their job was to show the child the best that parents can be. But, in and of itself, Foster care was never considered the primary desired outcome for a child; rather, it was the first-level temporary alternative when the child's home had proven too unstable for his or her healthy development. Foster parents' task was to work with the agency's caseworker and the parent to help make it possible for the child to return to live with their birth parent or to prepare the child for a full-fledged adoption by someone else.

I had six caseworkers under my supervision: five were White, and one was Black. That was unique because this was 1963, in Baltimore, Maryland. And what made it more unique was that all of the cases my workers covered were

White families. Each worker carried a caseload of several families located throughout the surrounding counties of Baltimore.

One day, Peggy Haley, the Black American worker in my group, called me to report the Foster parent of one of her families wouldn't meet with her and wanted to know what she should do. I told her to return to the office. I didn't call the Foster parent. I just waited for her to call me. Several days later the Foster mother called, saying that she didn't have a worker, so she was calling me for some assistance. She had never met me, and I realized, again, that I have one of those names that often leads people to assume I am something other than Black. I said to her that she did indeed have a worker, a very good worker. I said, "Peggy Haley told me she had tried to visit you a few days ago and that you had refused to meet with her, so I had her return to the office."

The woman said, "Oh, it's not me; it's my neighbors."

I responded, "Madam, your neighbors are not the Foster parents. You are, and what we try to do is assign our most talented and professional staff member to each family, and that's why Peggy Haley was assigned to you. I would think you would want to be careful not to send the wrong message to your foster child."

She said, "Ok, let's try it again."

I never received another complaint about any worker in my group. And I never changed a worker from an assigned case.

But race continued to be an ever-present fact of work in numerous ways. One day, another of the caseworkers I supervised reported a young girl had told her she'd been sexually assaulted by her Foster father and wanted to know what she should do. For me, it was an easy call. I said, "Let's file charges against that foster father," and we did. But, what happened next reminded me how little, in some ways, the United States of America of the early 1960s had changed from Houston, Texas I grew up from the 1930s to the early 1950s. Because the alleged crime had occurred at the home of the foster family on Maryland's Eastern Shore, we had to go there to file charges against the man. To do so meant we'd have to be driven there by Maryland State Police. But because my colleague was a white woman, we couldn't ride in the same car. So, one trooper drove her in his patrol car, and another drove me in a separate patrol car. This was the law in Maryland not just in 1933 but in 1963.

Nor was the state's, shall we say, sensitivity about the presence of Black people in particular places limited to its rural regions. I didn't spend after-work hours in Baltimore. I didn't even move around the city much during the day, either. I worked there, that was all, and when the day was done, I returned to Washington. And I knew, of course, of Baltimore's reputation as a city where "southern attitudes" on race prevailed. So, when my colleague, so pleased we had so quickly acted against that foster father to protect that child, suggested we have a celebratory lunch at a fine restaurant, I agreed but added only half-jokingly that I wasn't interested in staging a sit-in. She assured me she'd select a restaurant frequented by Morgan State students, so she was sure I wouldn't be the only Black person in the place. We set a lunch date for the end of the week before Thanksgiving.

Despite my colleague's assurances, however, when we arrived at the restaurant that day, it turned out that, despite its proximity to Morgan State, I was indeed the only Black face in the room at lunch time. In fact, some diners seemed to give up eating altogether for staring at me. Finally, an older white man finished his meal, paid his check, and headed for the door. Then, as he reached the door, he suddenly turned and headed to our table. I thought— *OK, here it comes.* But, to my surprise, when he reached our table, he said, "I just want to shake your hand and welcome myself into the human race. Oh, I see all the staring, but don't let that bother you; things are going to be all right." I was stunned but relieved to hear his words, and they provided me with a small degree of optimism about the nation's willingness to confront its racial problems.

That day was Friday, November 22. My colleague and I had left for lunch at 11:30 so that we could get back to the office by 1:30 and get on with our work. When we did get to the office, a little later than we had planned, the staff told us the awful news: President John F. Kennedy had been assassinated. As I sat at my desk trying to understand what had happened, I thought that despite the supportive words I had just heard from the kind White gentleman at the restaurant, Fate was telling us America had reached a new low—or perhaps it was just serving notice that this is where the nation had always been and its people better wake up: Because if "they" were willing to kill a President for expressing progressive ideas, they would stop at nothing to take this country back to the days before the Civil War.

In all my five years working in Baltimore, I had always commuted by car, usually driving five of the D.C.-based staffers in the 1960 Ford Falcon I'd bought while still at the Post Office. Each weekday morning, we'd meet before 7:00

114

a.m. near the entrance to the Baltimore-Washington Parkway for the fifty-mile trip to be at our desks before the office opened an hour later and reverse the drive after work. After graduation from the School of Social Work, armed with an advanced degree, a supervisory position, and a bigger salary, I splurged and bought a brand new Pontiac Catalina. However, like my Ford Falcon, it didn't have air conditioning; in those days, that was a luxury, and you had to pay extra for such additions.

As I was nearing the end of my two-year commitment to the State of Maryland, I began looking for a job closer to home in Washington, my five years of commuting–having long since become drudgery. Soon, I learned that while as a Child Welfare Supervisor with a master's degree, I was earning $5,200 a year in Baltimore, caseworkers for the District's Department of Public Welfare were paid $8,500 to $9,000. So, I concluded that if everything else failed, I would pursue a caseworker's position with Washington's public welfare agency.

But as I was considering that a viable option, I got a call from a D.C. Welfare Department colleague who'd also been a School of Social Work classmate. We had car-pooled together during our social work practice assignments. Knowing that I was job-hunting, she told me her husband had just turned down a job with the Washington Urban League; she thought I might be interested. I followed up with a call to the Washington Urban League and was invited in for an interview. My interviewer was David Rusk, the son of JFK's and, subsequently, LBJ's Secretary of State, Dean Rusk.

David, who had undergraduate and graduate degrees from the University of California at Berkeley, had recently joined the Urban League staff himself. He was friendly, very smart, committed to the cause of Black advancement, and well-respected in the organization. He outlined the duties of the job: as director of education and youth initiatives, I was to be its chief advocate within and outside the organization on elementary- and secondary-school matters, and youth development matters in general, and oversee the further development of its *A Future for Jimmy Program*. That was the constellation of Urban League-sponsored tutoring and counseling centers operating in the D.C. communities, housed in churches throughout the city and served by volunteer retired teachers and government workers. In those centers, volunteers tutored students from the city's public schools in mathematics, science, and English. The goal was to substantially raise students' performance levels.

Listening to David, I quickly realized this was the kind of organization I wanted to work for, and David was the kind of person I wanted to work with. Further discussion led to a specific offer at a salary of $8,500 per year (roughly $85,000 in 2024 dollars). I quickly accepted, and we agreed I'd give my 30 days' notice to my old agency and start the first week of June 1965. The news that I'd taken a new job came as no surprise to my colleagues and superiors in Baltimore. Everyone knew I was looking for a position closer to home. I had never relocated to the Baltimore area (and had never been absent from the job, either). I had asked for and gotten a glowing reference for the Urban League from my Division supervisor, Estella Baughman.

When I arrived at the Baltimore Department of Public Welfare five years earlier, I had no clue about the welfare system and even less about the profession of Social Work. Now, with a variety of experiences over five years, a master's degree in hand, and a heightened interest and skill in human rights and civil rights advocacy, I was leaving with a pretty good knowledge and understanding of the system, its services, and what it's impact was—and could be—on the people it served and the nation. I had concluded that one big problem facing the profession was the label we had placed on ourselves of "social work." The label-was too limiting, I thought. It seemed to describe us as mere followers of an agenda defined and prescribed by others. There was nothing in the title to suggest we ourselves had the training and analytical skills to be leaders in devising solutions to the problems bedeviling individuals, families and the larger society. I thought we social workers would do better to view ourselves as *society's consultants.* It was an important insight, I thought, one that I had rather instinctively made good use of during my five years in Baltimore.

Now, I intended to be more deliberate about its use at the Washington Urban League.

Chapter 5 — Signing On: At The Washington Urban League, 1965-1970

My new job and titles — Director of Education and Youth Incentives and Director of a project named " A Future for Jimmy" — was the work of Sterling Tucker, then the Executive Director of the Washington D.C. Urban League, after he witnessed students from a public high school (the losing side)and a Catholic high school brawling after a football game.

It was Sterling's belief that the public school students started the fight for a reason other than a simple loss: They felt the parochial school students thought their school was better, and thus they were better and better educated — and Sterling believed that the public school students, beneath their bravado, might feel the same way. He concluded that if he could create a program that would raise the performance levels of students in public schools, they'd feel better about themselves and less concerned with the opinions of others. The program free to students, enlisted volunteer tutors, retired school teachers and counselors, and government workers to help students with their subjects in the evenings in churches throughout the city. The program proved popular with students and parents.

On my second day on the job, Sterling, whom I hadn't yet met, knocked on my office door and invited me to lunch. He took me across the street to a small restaurant called "The Place Where Louie Dwells." Once we seated ourselves, his first words to me were, "Now that you're here, you'd better go find the money to pay your salary."

I started to laugh, but he cut me short. "This is no joke," he said, "We may have the money to carry you for three or four months. But if you haven't found the money to pay your salary by then, I'm sorry, but you won't be with us".

I was stunned. I had just given up a good supervisory position with a good salary in Baltimore and passed on a more lucrative position with the D.C. Welfare Department, only to come work for this man who now tells me I must find my own salary? What other surprises were in store for me at the Washington Urban League?

What would I say to Barbara? She hadn't complained when I left the D. C. Post Office for a lower-paying job in Baltimore because I thought it had better potential for our future. She had again supported me the two years I was on reduced salary at the Baltimore welfare agency while working on my Master's. Now, we had a five-year-old daughter and a nice two-bedroom apartment in a fine neighborhood, and I had drawn down my retirement from the State of Maryland to buy her a brand new 1965 Ford Mustang. We were headed in the right direction, or so I thought. Now, here I was being told my good job, good salary, and lofty titles existed only if I could find the funds to finance it.

But even as I sat there listening to Sterling, I decided this was a weight I couldn't lay on Barbara. I couldn't go home and tell my wife I have this big-time job, but unfortunately, they don't have the funds to pay me a salary. So, after lunch, I went straight to David Rusk, who I knew to be thoroughly knowledgeable about where in both the federal and the D. C. governments we might find support. David suggested we apply for a vocational rehabilitation grant based on the claim that young people who drop out of school should be considered just as disabled as those with a physical handicap. With David's assistance, I drafted a proposal that drew $150,000 in pilot grant funds to test the idea. **(F. 1)**

Now, I had the money to pay my salary for a good while. Even more important, if the program validated our theories we would have identified another area of service for the Urban League. With the assistance of David Rusk and utilizing some skills I had developed while assisting one of Howard's Social Work professors on a research project she was involved in after my graduation, we were able to validate our theory. The net outcome of our effort resulted in the D.C.Department of Vocational Rehabilitation including in their eligibility policy students who dropped out of school. And, because of that change, monies could be spent to make them employable. Our success caught Sterling's attention, and he soon assigned me to take on another project for which I'd again need to figure out a way to implement it without funds or staff. This time, he wanted to expand the Washington Urban League's footprint into Northern Virginia. He said, I don't have any money or staff to give you at this time, but the League has a small office in Alexandria, Virginia, housing a jobs placement project, and I would have a desk and a telephone to operate from. Go make it happen, he said. Alexandria, Virginia, was a nice little bedroom community just across the Potomac River, and while it was just a very few miles from D.C., it was still Virginia. Now, I understand such projects were a facet of Sterling's mode of operation: Don't let the lack of money in hand stop you from thinking of good ideas; just get a staff member to try to make the idea a reality. I realized I was now one of Sterling's troubleshooters.

My shared office space in a small office building in Alexandria had just a desk and a telephone, nothing more. Like a good soldier, I arrived at my new assignment early one Monday morning, sat at my desk, looked at my telephone, and asked myself: What now? Then I saw on my desk the local daily newspaper, the *Alexandria Gazette*, and there on the front page was an article about a group of White ministers planning to meet that day in nearby Mount Vernon (the location of George Washington's mansion) to discuss, the article said, critical issues facing northern Virginia. (I could tell they were White ministers from the way the article described, just in passing, their churches and their churches' locations.) To me, it proved once again why community newspapers were so valuable for community organizers: their articles and editorials told you what was happening in neighborhoods and small communities that larger city newspapers could only rarely pay attention to. So, I got in my car and drove the eight miles to Mount Vernon and crashed their meeting.

They were somewhat stunned when I showed up because I wasn't white, wasn't a minister—and, most of all, I hadn't been invited. But they were cordial and asked why I was there. I told them about the *Gazette* article and said I wanted to tell them their intentions would come to nothing unless they were willing to eliminate the housing discrimination Black military personnel faced in the region.

Virginia, just across the Potomac River from the nation's capital, in 1963 was still ruled by Jim Crow. Among many other injustices, that meant that if Black service men and women assigned to the Fort Belvoir Army Base, just twenty miles from Washington, couldn't find housing on the base itself, they wouldn't be able to live in the small whites-only residential communities that surrounded the sprawling facility, either. For them, that racist discrimination meant a long commute of at least 48 miles to and from the nearest other Army base—Fort Meade in Maryland, above the Mason-Dixon Line, equidistant between Washington and Baltimore.

The clergymen understood my point. `The minister leading the group turned to one of his colleagues, Reverend John Wells, and asked if he'd be willing to work with me on this issue. He agreed to do so, and he was excused from the meeting to work with me on this issue. We left the meeting to decide on our next steps.

As it turned out, John Wells not only had a divinity degree—from Howard's School of Divinity, no less — but also a law degree from Emory University and had served as a lawyer in the Air Force Judge Adjutant General Corps. With his background as a JAG officer and my Army background, we were both well suited to the task ahead and working with each other. Once we learned that about each other, I said, "Let's go to Ft. Belvoir and challenge the Commanding General to join us in this endeavor." So, we invited ourselves to the Base and asked for a meeting with the Commanding General, General Robert Seedlock.

It so happened that General Seedlock had played an extraordinary role during World War 2 in the Asian theater. A West Point graduate with a master's degree in civil engineering, Seedlock, then a colonel, was assigned in 1944 to rebuild the eastern half of the Burma Road. The road, which crossed the Himalayas, was the only overland route connecting India and China — a vital supply route in the Allies' effort to drive the Japanese forces off the Asian mainland. We would find him to be a man of great competence and integrity. **(F.2)**

He readily agreed to see us that day. Being military men ourselves, Wells and I knew the way military men thought. I told the General I understood housing on the grounds of Fort Belvoir was integrated and that the discrimination in surrounding communities was not the military's doing. But, I went on; while not his problem directly, I also knew that a Commander is responsible for everything his men do or fail to do. So he must be concerned about the fact that he had personnel assigned to Fort Belvoir who, because all the Base housing is occupied, are forced to commute all the way from Fort Meade every day.

He got right to the point. "*OK,* now what do you want me to do about it?"

I said, "Why don't you invite the property owners and managers of properties surrounding the base for lunch at your Officers' Club and let us assist you in your talking about the issue."

The General didn't need much help from us. He had an excellent staff; it included a young Captain, Harold Sims— who Whitney Young would soon recruit to be his Deputy Executive Director. After Whitney's tragic death in the spring of 1971, Harold Sims would serve as the League's acting executive director until Vernon Jordan was appointed.

The invitations went out, and I think every invitee accepted. The meal was first class, and then it was time for General Seedlock to speak. As he stood before his audience, he displayed the bearing of a Commander in total charge of the subject at hand. He essentially made four important points. First, he wanted his guests—homeowners, landlords, rental agents, politicians—to know that Black soldiers were risking their lives in combat, not just for their Black brothers in arms, but all of their brothers, Black and White. Secondly, he reminded them that these fighting men protected the land on which their properties sat, as they did the lives and the properties and livelihoods of all Americans. And then he said he hoped they understood that each year, Fort Belvoir contributed through its official purchases and those of its personnel and their families more than $200 million dollars to the Northern Virginia economy. Finally, he made it clear that the Fort would not do business with companies or stores that engaged in racial discrimination nor allow its soldiers and staff to rent or buy homes from those who did.

After the meeting, it quickly became known that there were 1,500 units of housing in the communities surrounding Fort Belvoir available to be rented to any and all military personnel stationed at the Fort.

Then Frank Bonomo, an attorney at the Defense Department who knew John Wells, called him to ask how we had managed to get housing opened around the Fort. He invited us to the Pentagon to hear firsthand our approach. During our visit, we emphasized the importance of the confident, can-do commitment General Seedlock had displayed and the value of noting the economic impact military bases have on the communities around them. A few months later, Secretary of Defense Robert McNamara issued a pronouncement stating that any housing surrounding military installations that wouldn't rent or sell to Black military personnel would be placed off limits to all military personnel. It was at that point that a substantial slice of residential housing around military bases across the country began opening. **(F. 2)**

[[[*2 — Footnote —link to articles from the WP on this development]]]

Those successes proved I could bring value to the Washington Urban League. Sterling appreciated what I'd done; he was both results-oriented and compassionate, and in the spring of 1968, he asked me to return to headquarters and become his Deputy Executive Director. And then came the Fourth of April.

I was meeting at St. Stephens' Episcopal Church in the Mount Pleasant neighborhood, conducting a membership report meeting. The Washington Urban League had a very active membership support base, and annually, we conducted a membership campaign. For this affiliate, this initiative was about more than the funds it generated; it was also about the volunteer base it mobilized. It was a significant part of my portfolio to manage such meetings, especially when Serling was out of the area, and on this occasion, he was out of town. But shortly after we began, one of the church's staffers was called to the phone. When he returned, he relayed the shocking news to us; Dr. Martin Luther King, Jr. had been shot.

A stunned silence fell over us. We all knew nothing of importance could be discussed now. I closed the meeting, and those present hurried to their cars to drive home. Because I would be carrying cash receipts to put in the Urban League's safe, we had earlier arranged for a city police officer to drive me to the League's headquarters at Sixth and

G Streets, Northwest, in downtown Washington. I waited for his arrival with a few other staff. He soon arrived, <u>like us, moving as if</u> in a state of shock. How could anyone be so cruel as to kill such a man of peace?

That, I am certain, was the question being asked by millions of people of goodwill all over the world.

What happened next caught the DC community off-guard. The next day, what began as a peaceful march to show the Black community's outrage over Dr. King's murder erupted into devastating looting and rioting, particularly along the 14th Street, Northwest, and H Street, Northeast commercial districts. Stores were looted, and property destroyed. People were angry in Washington and in other Black communities across the country, and that anger was on full display.

Sterling returned home to D.C. and immediately went to work. He quickly decided the best thing the Washington Urban League could do was to set up several rumor control centers in neighborhoods across the city that could serve as clearinghouses of information in the hope of preventing Blacks from reacting irrationally, which would only make the crisis worse.

I was assigned the center at our headquarters. Two nights later, on April 6th, when the rioting was still at its zenith, and one heard the continuous wailing of police car sirens and sometimes the distant sounds of what seemed to be gunshots, I said to one of the volunteers helping us that evening "Call the police precinct and let them know it's us on the second floor of our building." I wanted the police to clearly understand that if they saw movement in our offices, they shouldn't panic and start shooting. It was a simple message.

But somehow, the message must have gotten garbled because soon, we all heard a chilling shout, "We know you're in there; come out with your hands up!"

The message was repeated again and again. At first, I thought they were directed at another building nearby, and I ventured down the flight of stairs to try to see what was going on. Nearing the bottom of the steps, I moved my head just a tad around a corner to see if I could see anything from that position. A voice bellowed, "We saw your head, come out with your hands up!"

It finally dawned on me they were talking to me.

So, I headed to the door, but because the door was locked, I put my hand in my pocket to get the key. The voice bellowed again, "Get your hand out of your pocket!"

I was surprised at how calm I was despite the obvious danger. In fact, I yelled back somewhat defiantly, "I've got to get the key to unlock the door."

A policeman, who I now saw had been crouching behind the hedges, stood up, gun trained on me, "Alright," he said, "unlock it." As soon as I unlocked the door and stepped toward the threshold, I was yanked from the doorway and thrown against the wall with a gun pointed at my head. I suddenly realized they seemed to have been more afraid of me than I was of them, and I knew that made for a very dangerous situation. The staff and volunteers who had apparently started to come down the stairs found themselves being grabbed, yanked outside, and thrown against the wall with guns pointed at their heads, too.

What saved us that night was the lucky fact that, as part of local television news blanket coverage of the riot, Max Robinson, one of the local station's most popular anchors, was riding on assignment with that very police unit—and Max's sister, Jewel Robinson Sheppard, was one of the staff members assisting me. **(F.3)** When Max, moving with the police as they pressed us for identification, saw his sister lined up against the wall, he told the officer in charge, "Those aren't snipers! That's my sister! These are Urban League people!" The Precinct Captain soon arrived and we were all soon released, with no apology. However, as the police trooped back to their vehicles, I did overhear him saying, "Now Sterling Tucker will be all over us for this."

Soon after the uprising had been quelled, Sterling gathered a few staff and Board members to begin to talk out what we could learn from what had just happened. As the discussion developed, several said they believed the violence stemmed from poor people acting out of rage and deprivation. But I challenged that view. I said it wasn't just the poor people who smashed the windows and set the fires, trying to take the city apart. I argued that many of the brick-throwers and looters were young people who had sat in those civic classes and read and heard that America was about fairness, justice, and equality and now felt they had been lied to all their lives — who felt this wasn't a nation where all men were created equal, a nation where anyone could rise if they worked hard and were lawful, These were people — some jobless, but many with jobs — who despaired that no one was listening to them. As the riots in the ghettos had become a disturbing feature of American life in the mid-1960s, King himself had warned that riots were "the language of the unheard" — not as a justification for their actions, but in recognition of why they turned to violence. I ended by saying I thought the lesson for the Urban League was that we needed to bring our processes in line with the impatience of those who had been in the streets.

Sterling immediately responded: "Bring our processes in line with their impatience; that sounds like a new thrust!" Sterling was someone who could quickly evaluate the essential worth of almost any idea, from a few sentences in a book or an op-ed article or a few words spoken off-the-cuff in a long meeting; Whitney had long considered him a keen "thought-provider." He understood that in the 1950s and early 1960s, Blacks in the North, as well as the South, had taken to mass political action — boycotts and other direct-action demonstrations — on an unprecedented scale because of the legal struggle to secure civil rights due to them was taking too long. That was a "new thrust," a new phase of Black Americans' struggle for full citizenship. Now, with the great civil rights acts of the mid-1960s having been achieved, the "language of the unheard" had made it clear it was time for another new thrust to bring both the fruits of American society and its chief promise— *opportunity* — to Blacks at the bottom of the socioeconomic ladder.

Within a day or so, he had crafted the basics of a program for the entire Urban League movement — not surprisingly called *New Thrust* — for Whitney and pledged that he himself would sell it into the movement and raise funds for its implementation. Whitney, always on the lookout for ideas that would tie the Urban League and its public image more closely to the Black poor and disadvantaged, quickly accepted it—on one condition: that Sterling take leave from his post in Washington and direct it as a member of the national staff. That's what Sterling, with the consent of the Washington Urban League board, did.

And, at his recommendation, in late August, the board approved my appointment as Acting Chief Executive of the Washington Urban League affiliate.

One of my first actions as Acting Chief Executive was to put a picket line in front of the Government Printing Office. I had already met with Printing Office Black employees when I was the affiliate's second in command about the discrimination in the hiring and promotion of Black workers there. Among their bitter complaints was that senior Black employees were routinely assigned to train new White hires for various positions—and the latter would ultimately be promoted over them to supervisory positions. Now, I supported their decision that it was time for them to take action. Picketing was not a tactic in the Urban League's toolbox, but in the aftermath of the year's ruinous uprisings, the Printing Office employees' dramatic step proved effective. The publicity the picket line generated soon produced a call to me from the agency's director requesting a meeting. He claimed that the complaints were coming from a few disgruntled employees. I responded the complaints certainly seemed valid to me and that in any case, he could gain a greater clarity of the problems by speaking directly with his employees, which he soon did.

Although Sterling had gone on leave, he was still very close to the League's new offices in the tall office building at Sixteenth and P Streets, Northwest. * Indeed, he had merely moved his office from the headquarters on the 16th floor to the 9th floor in the same building. But Sterling didn't "hover," as some CEOs might have. He knew he didn't need to, and he was too excited about bringing the New Thrust program to fruition. Nonetheless, he did make a point of

130

telling me I shouldn't have thrown up a picket line at the Government Printing Office. And he reminded me that as the CEO of the affiliate, its board was still holding him, though absent, responsible for everything the League did. I didn't challenge him, but I told myself I was exactly following the idea of the New Thrust: keep reaching down the socio-economic ladder to bring our processes in line with the impatience of our constituency. **(F. 4)**

Sterling was gone for about 18 months. He wouldn't return until the late winter of 1970, a development which I had something to do with. Early on, I had noticed — and found annoying — the fact that at the affiliate board's monthly meetings, no matter what I was reporting on, the Board's conversation always centered around when Sterling was coming back. Finally, at one meeting in mid-winter, I calmly said to them, "You know, I don't know when Sterling is coming back, but what I do know is that I don't know if I want to continue to work for this Board. Every month [at our meeting], I talk about what the staff and I are doing, and all you talk about is when is Sterling coming back."

One board member broke the stunned silence: "Wow, why didn't you say something earlier?" The board promptly sent a "demand letter" to Sterling, requesting information on if and or when he was coming back to the Washington Urban League.

Well, I knew that Sterling was planning to come back because I'd been with Sterling long enough to know that he had two primary goals: One was to become President of the National Urban League. The other was to become Mayor of Washington. Both of those goals were dependent on his power base in the city, and the foundation of that power base was his position at the Washington Urban League and his close working relationship with Whitney Young.

So, it was very easy for Sterling to decide immediately to resume his CEO duties. Not only was he respected by the affiliate board and the city's power brokers, but he could still oversee the New Thrust Initiative because, by then, the project had fully been taken up by the affiliates; his oversight largely involved funding and keeping track of their work. As for me, I'd always had no fear of leaving jobs without knowing exactly what I was going to do next, and I figured it was time to take that step again. The second day after Sterling had again taken up his duties, I walked into his office and laid my resignation on his desk. I could see he was shaken because I was "his guy." From the moment we met, he had seen something in me and given me several tough assignments—tests to prove myself, and I had.

"Jake," he said, "you don't have to leave. In a couple of years, this will all be yours." I said kindly, not as a reproach, "Sterling, this isn't some kingdom you get to hand down. I always knew you were going to come back. This is your Urban League. You made it what it is today. So I was never confused about your coming back. This is not about your coming back. This is about my knowing it's time for me to go."

Sterling said, "If it's about money, I will pay you what I'm paying me."

But I turned that down immediately. "Sterling, the League can't afford to pay me what it pays you. And it's not about that. I just know it's time for me to go."

Now, again, I didn't have any place to go; my impulsiveness was what drove me to submit my resignation letter. However, I also knew I had built a significant reputation of my own across the Urban League by then, so there had to be someplace for me to go—a senior position within the League or outside it.

Soon, as word got around that I was leaving the Washington Affiliate, Mel King, head of the Boston Urban League, and, I think, Henry Thomas of the Springfield, Massachusetts Urban League, came to see me. Mel, a trained social worker, was tall and direct. He was the "militant" of the Urban League in those days. In the early 1980s, he would mount an inspiring "rainbow coalition campaign for Mayor of Boston, falling just short of Ray Flynn, who, after two terms in office, would go on to become President Clinton's Secretary of Labor. (F. 5) Henry was the epitome of an Urban League chief executive, too—smart, with a broad range of contacts throughout his city and the region, dedicated to improving his community.

They had a proposition for me. They wanted me to train community organizers for the local affiliates in the League's Eastern region (from Washington to New England, New York State, and eastern and central Pennsylvania down to Maryland and Virginia). They said if I agreed, they'd demand that Sterling fund this new entity by pooling all the New Thrust funds he had set aside for the Eastern affiliates.

Well, I didn't think Sterling would go for giving up control over the millions of dollars that encompassed. But, to my surprise, he agreed. I moved down to the ninth floor, to the very space Sterling had just vacated, and got to work. I quickly put in place a smart group of skilled hands: among them, Barbara Lett Simmons, then at the Washington Technical Institute, who was a sharp management training expert; Anita Bellamy Shelton and Ann Turpeau, who had long experience in community organizing in Washington's predominantly Black neighborhoods. They had gotten substantial funding from the Model Cities program for the redevelopment of D.C.'s Northeast Corridor—the predominantly black neighborhoods that abutted the major thoroughfare of North Capitol Street.

We built a residential community organizing program, enrolling two staffers from each of the Eastern Region's twenty-four affiliates to train them in community mobilization and community organization. The training was organized along the lines of Howard's School of Social Work, where I had taught a class as an adjunct lecturer for several semesters: Case Work, Group Work, or Community Organization. Everyone in the program took the same basic courses and then courses in a particular field based on where they were placed for their fieldwork.

But our training stressed that one always had to be ready to adapt to the circumstances of their own community. For example, when I was teaching my class on applying the techniques of community mobilization and community organization, one of the Urban League staffers from the Binghamton (New York) Urban League kept saying, "That won't work in my community …. That won't work in my community."

After several more, I asked him, How many Black people are there in Binghamton?

And he said, a couple of hundred or so. He was right. Binghamton, 175 miles northwest of New York City, just across the New York-Pennsylvania border, was then a very small community. It later grew significantly when the small college there became part of the State University of New York system. (That a community of that size in the 1970s, with a small Black population, had an Urban League affiliate underscored the diversity of the communities in which Urban League affiliates existed.)

I said, "Then, you're right. That won't work in your community. Let me finish with this, and we're going to delve into the techniques of 'casework for you' because you can work with everybody in your community individually."

The idea of Mel King and Henry Thomas exemplified how adaptable the New Thrust concept was, because it was based on responding to the needs of each individual community — a matter of bringing Urban League processes in line with the impatience of our constituencies.

I was in my ninth-floor New Thrust office one day in the early summer of 1969 when the phone rang. I picked it up and heard a voice ask, "Are you going to be in your office?

I said, "Yes".

The voice said, "Good, I'm coming to see you."

I said, "Who are you?"

The voice said, "I'm Henry H. Hill from San Diego," and hung up.

Chapter 6 — San Diego Urban League

I was amused, mystified, and, frankly, somewhat annoyed by Henry H. Hill's brusque telephone call. But, my annoyance was replaced with interest when he and his wife Catherine showed up at my office a little later that morning, and after a few quick pleasantries, he got down to business.

"I've come to tell you," he said, "why you have to come to San Diego and take over our Urban League." Not waiting for a response from me, he moved right along. This was a man, I understood immediately, used to command. "I don't need to hear you talk," he said." I've heard you talk. Just listen to what I have to say. " He told me all the reasons I must come to San Diego and how supportive he would be of my work. When he finished, they got up and left.

Henry highlighted the affiliate's good beginning with the New Thrust program. John Johnson, who had recently become the CEO of the Westchester County, New York Urban League after spending several years leading the San Diego affiliate and had served as the first Executive Field Secretary of the New Thrust program, had done a good job in launching New Thrust in San Diego prior to his departure. But, Henry said, the work was just beginning; that the affiliate now needed an experienced community organizer to finish the process. He pointed out that since I was training community organizers for the entire 24-affiliate Eastern Region, he knew I was just the person to fill that need. Mrs. Hill, who sat quietly, I later learned as I got to know her, was the secretary to all of Henry's endeavors. She was smart, highly efficient, and highly respected in San Diego. She was, in effect, Henry's alter ego.

But before leaving, he added that when I brought my family to San Diego, he would show me how to buy a house with no money down.

I immediately called John Johnson, "John, I've just had a strange visit from a strange man telling me why I had to come to San Diego and take over that Urban League," I told him. John asked what was his name. "Henry Hill," I said. He asked what he promised, and I told him. John said, "He can and will deliver on everything he promised." Now, I was even more intrigued. But I still didn't see why I should move to San Diego.

That summer, when the League held its sixtieth-anniversary conference in New York City, several Board members from the San Diego affiliate asked to meet with me. I agreed, not because I was interested in going to San Diego, but because there were several other League senior executives who were, and I told them I'd use the group's interest in me to get them to boost the post's salary. During our meeting, I gladly discussed what I thought needed to be done in San Diego. I was enjoying an interesting — and, for me, abstract — discussion about a situation very far away from where I was. At its end, one of the group, Carolyn Murdock, a very active board member and very active member of the broader San Diego community, asked, "Mr. Jacob, what would it cost to get you to come and do those things?"

Now, I knew that John Johnson's annual salary there had been $18,000—my salary at the Washington affiliate then was $38,000—and, since I had no intention of going to San

Diego but had promised to get the salary up for my interested colleagues, I said, "Madam, I won't even hold a discussion for less than $25,000."

She calmly replied, "We'll just have to find the money to pay you what you are asking."

When I left the meeting and walked by those waiting to be interviewed, I whispered, "I got a salary of up to $25,000; good luck."

Several days after the conference ended, the San Diego board called my Washington office and invited me to come visit their office and see the sights of San Diego. I initially accepted, then tried to back out via a quick phone call a few moments later. I didn't think it was fair, I said, for them to spend money on me when I wasn't interested in their offer. But they replied, "It's our money; we'll take the chance."

With a clear conscience, I booked a plane ticket to San Diego.

When my plane landed in San Diego, I was met by the affiliate's board chairman, Dr. Robert Matthews, who drove me to a fine hotel overlooking the Pacific Ocean and installed me in a room with an expansive view of the ocean. When the bellhop opened the sliding glass door, a refreshing breeze blew in, making air conditioning unnecessary. The panoramic view of the ocean and a part of the city was spectacular. I thought about my previous firm rejection of their offer and said to myself, "I may have spoken in haste. I may want to reconsider this."

Meeting with the board the next morning, I backtracked. "I know I said I wouldn't have a discussion for less than $25,000," I told them, "and please understand that I had earned $38,000 last year, so to accept the position for

$25,000, I'd be taking a huge reduction in pay. But, given that I introduced the $25,000 number, here's my offer. I will take the position for $25,000 if you will agree that when I raise more money for the organization, you will pay me more money."

They immediately replied, "You've got a deal. I told them I'd report for duty on the first of November. I headed back to Washington to tell Barbara we were moving to San Diego and to say goodbye to the Community Organizing Training Program I had created and enjoyed leading.

When Barbara and I first got married, and I was only making $4800 a year and she $3600, I promised her that when my salary rose to $12,000 a year, she could stop working to come home and raise our child. She had taken me up on that offer in 1968. Now, I had a good salary: we had bought our first home—a nice brick colonial in a nice *Black* middle-class neighborhood. I emphasize that it was a black neighborhood because it had been a white neighborhood— so recently that in the title attesting to our purchase, it still contained a restrictive clause barring its sale to a Black person. Thanks to the 1948 Supreme Court decision of *Shelley vs. Kremer* that declared racist restrictive covenants unconstitutional, we could buy the home at 4821 Sixteenth Street, N.E. we liked in a neighborhood we liked. It was our first home, and it was within walking distance of Barbara's parents' home.

Barbara and I never discussed salary. We shared a joint bank account, so there was never any question about my money or her money. From the beginning it was always our money. But it's fair to say Barbara was far from excited about my reversal about moving our family to the other side of the country. She had never lived more than a few blocks from her parents and sisters. In fact, the first time she had resided outside of her parent's home was when we had married and moved into our own apartment. Now, I was asking her to move far away from a support system she had always had. And it would disrupt our now ten-year-old daughter's school- and social life. But I felt it was something I had to do, and I trusted that, in the end, it would be good for the three of us. Barbara and Sheryl would stay in Washington so that she could finish the school year among her friends.

As word spread about the move, I began to receive many wishes of congratulation and good luck. One group of friends I would be leaving behind were my fellow members of the Vanguards, an all-male club of young black professionals in the D.C. metropolitan area who annually sponsored several social events. I had been a member for several years and had many good friends on its rolls. Among them was Dino, who, when I told him I was going to be driving cross-country by myself, offered to help me with the drive. Dino was young, single, and I don't think he had ever made the 2,600-mile trek across the nation — facts which prompted his extremely generous offer. I immediately and gladly accepted it.

Having left Washington on Thursday for three days of virtually nonstop driving, we. got to San Diego very early Sunday morning— about 2 am, checked into the same hotel where I had previously stayed, and bedded down for a long, well-earned rest. The next morning, I took Dino to the airport for his flight back to Washington. Then, I set about finding my way to the apartment that Fred Patterson, the deputy John

Johnson had appointed and the staffer I had asked to find me a place to live. He rented for me a nice one bedroom apartment in Clairemont, one of the city's fine, suburban-like neighborhoods, a twenty to thirty-minute drive from the city center.

The apartment complex was recently built, and the apartments were very nice and in a modern Southern California style, taking full advantage of the region's great weather. After I unloaded my car, I went looking for a grocery store, found one a few miles away, and bought some food to stock the kitchen. And then, as one who had grown up in segregated Houston, gone to historically Black Howard University, and lived in predominantly Black Washington for seventeen years, I noticed something peculiar: I had yet to see another Black person. Not in my apartment complex. Not in my drive to the grocery store, or in it, or on the way back to my apartment. Not a single Black person did I see. The question, ridiculous though it was, ran through my mind: are there any Black people in this town? I knew that there were—but where were they?

I had decided to come to San Diego a week before I was scheduled to take up my post to feel out of my new environment. Now, going all day without seeing another Black face, I felt an even stronger imperative to understand San Diego, especially its Black community — the community that was the focus of the organization I was now heading.

Just driving around, it seemed to fully justify the travel brochure boasts of a paradise, significantly different from Los Angeles, its neighbor 120 miles to the north. San Diego was a "Navy town:" then the home port of several aircraft carriers, nearly two dozen jet fighter and helicopter squadrons, and more than 70 different naval operating units. The complex, just southwest of the city across San Diego Bay, was the largest in the entire Navy. It was a facility that, in many ways, seemed as much of a "municipality" as any nearby Southern California community. And the city's population of nearly 700,000 people — White Americans, or "Anglos," Black Americans, and Latino Americans, most of whom were of Mexican descent — was heavily invested in that identity, as they should have been.

The Navy was the area's biggest employer and its dominant economic force, and its presence attracted an increasing number of high-tech firms that serviced both the Navy's needs and the city's growing private sector firms and all sorts of private enterprises, from restaurants to janitorial companies, a thriving city produces.

Although it was the nation's fourteenth largest city in 1970, San Diego was also one of the few major ones to have escaped the kind of devastating racial blow-up that hit so many of its counterparts across the country. One reason why was that the virtual "guarantee" of continuing substantial federal financial support for the Navy base assured a stable economic environment for the area's small and generally well-educated population.

In addition, San Diego's historically small Black population of slightly less than 60,000 people lived in physical and topographical circumstances that differed significantly from "typical" ghettos of the East and Midwest and made it appear a more "racially tolerant " environment. But the appearances were deceiving. In fact, the city's predominant residential single-family style of housing combined with its very terrain of the canyon and elevation differences produced neighborhoods that statistically speaking were integrated, yet, in reality, were significantly segregated.

Those physical differences and comparatively low unemployment rate also concealed a racial dissatisfaction, separately, among Black San Diegans and Latino San Diegans that had grown sharper in recent decades. This would dramatically erupt during my tenure.

I wasn't supposed to report to work until the following Monday. I'd been given that entire week to just acclimate myself to the city and surrounding area. But I got up Monday eager to tour the city's compact downtown and the neighborhood of the Urban League office on Market Street in the heart of the city's historical Black community. That, plus the fact that the affiliate-owned the building and that its New Thrust project was but one example of service effectiveness, meant we were viewed as vital.

After my mini-tour, I headed to the office. Of course, they weren't expecting me. And they didn't know what to do with me. I had some of my new colleagues show me around and told them I'd just camp out in my office for a few days. What I didn't say was that I was looking to get a sense of what a workday looked like there— and I soon found myself bothered by the office's casual culture. I came back to the office on Tuesday, Wednesday and Thursday to confirm I was reading the culture right. On Thursday afternoon, I asked the receptionist to schedule a meeting for me with the full starff Friday morning. I shared with them what I had observed the previous four days and why my style and expectations were different from what seemed to be their practice.

"I've been here a week now observing how you do business, and I need to let you know that's not the way I operate," I said. "I'll admit I'm obsessive-compulsive. That means I come to work on time, and I stay here until I finish my work for the day. I expect my staff to be on the job at the start of the established office hours and at least until the official time for closing unless you have duties elsewhere.

"Now, I realize that way may not work for some of you. That's why I'm calling the assembly today so that you can have the whole weekend to decide if you want to work for me. If you don't, my feelings won't be hurt; I'll understand that you're going to move on. But if you do intend to continue to work here, this is the standard you'll have to meet. And if you decide to leave, no hard feelings."

That Monday, I was in the office early. And everyone showed up on time and ready to work.

Before leaving San Diego, John Johnson, my predecessor and Sterling Tucker's first deputy at the New Thrust project, had put in place a team of community organizers who helped residents establish block clubs throughout the Southeast district. Those block clubs were busy identifying concerns and demanding responses from the city's political leadership. Many of their concerns were seemingly mundane — like seeking a traffic light at a busy intersection, increasing the number of days for garbage collection, and better care of a neighborhood park.

But those issues were far from trivial, for Black Americans as for other Americans. On the contrary, they're fundamental issues of living in the city, and making one's neighborhood better, of exercising the rights of citizenship and having those rights respected. Black Americans pay taxes. They should get from the government what taxes they are supposed to pay for.

The San Diego Urban League was heavily involved in improving the public schools, in community organizing, in economic development, and helping black business people upgrade their businesses so that they stood a better chance of getting business loans. We strengthened our own business development program, pushing the city, state, and federal governments to give more of their business contracts to Black-owned businesses, as we helped Black entrepreneurs become better skilled at seeking business opportunities from the public and private sectors — everything from how to network effectively to proposal writing to best billing practices.

We constantly championed improving educational services to Southeast's children, too. Ambrose Broadus, one of our most effective community organizers, was well-known throughout the city and the school system. With the help of San Diego Gas & Electric, we sponsored a set of classes in particular skills — using employees from their engineering department staff to teach mathematics and from their communications department to teach writing and English.

We did some things that, at first glance, seemed a bit unusual. For example, Planned Parenthood's services were underutilized because San Diego was a heavily Catholic city. So, I took over their operation and turned it into a comprehensive health clinic. We did not do abortions, but we did offer family planning and other medical care services.

I hired Navy doctors to work in the clinic during their off-duty hours — both because they were good doctors and because, in San Diego, the involvement of Navy personnel in something was a seal of integrity. People flocked to our clinic; it was packed every day.

I got a visit from the Commandant of the US Air Force Academy, who said the Academy wanted to increase its enrollment of students of color from the San Diego area, and I'd been recommended as one of the people he should talk to. He actually showed up at my office one day unannounced to seek our assistance in helping to increase the number of cadets of color at the academy. I immediately realized this was a chance to help students improve their grades in math, science, and English and perform better on high school tests and college entrance exams. I proposed a program of courses taught only by volunteer faculty of the San Diego School system. And, we only wanted students who would volunteer to participate and dedicate themselves to the learning process. I wanted to ensure that both teachers and students and, indeed the Air Force Academy were all on the same page and fully committed to the success of the program. I spent several days visiting the Academy in Colorado Springs and learned that cadets could get intensive help in developing good study habits and techniques. So we adapted their program for ours, too.

The program, which San Diego school officials talked up as well, drew an enthusiastic response from the parents and students who well understood the benefits for admission prospects this could provide at any college in the land. The collaboration helped us persuade several businesses in the city to set up student internships and summer jobs. Our initial group of students numbered about 50. By 1975, the year I left San Diego to return to Washington, the program's enrollment had grown to nearly 500 youths. Our success collaborating with the Air Force Academy sparked the Navy's interest in a deeper collaboration—perhaps also because San Diego was a Navy town. With them, I went in a different direction. Knowing that their base offered a full-scale industrial program, and in San Diego, specific skills training by the Navy was practically a guarantee of getting a good job, I proposed they increase by five the number of places in their next class in air conditioning repair and reserve those seats for Southeast residents—giving them, if necessary, the proper tools to join the class. We also successfully sought funding for several projects from the local Model Cities Program, the federal effort created by President Johnson's Great Society legislation that matched our overall goal of spurring the poor and disadvantaged to "maximum feasible participation" — the phrase which became the watchword of the entire anti-poverty program at the federal and local levels.

My involvement in San Diego's civic affairs seemed to be going smoothly until I tried to examine the finances of one of the projects funded through the affiliate. That was the Neighborhood Youth Program, a county-wide project of youth-focused programs and activities ranging from athletics to tutoring in school subjects. Since the San Diego Urban League was the contracted agency for the program and since all of the program's staff were the League's staff, including its director, I asked the director to come to my office to educate me on the complete operations of the program, including its budget.

Leon Williams was not the only director of the program. He was also a San Diego city councilman—the only African American one. That unusual arrangement was a result of tensions between two black militant groups in San Diego — San Diego's Black Panthers Party and the US organization in San Diego — that had ultimately led to a shocking shootout in 1969 in which one of the Panthers was shot to death.

After the murder, the US organization went underground and then re-emerged as the National Involvement Association (NIA), which became the loudest voice in demanding that an African American be appointed to the all-white city council. That appointee was Leon Williams. In the next Council election, he won a term in his own right. But he owed his prominence to NIA, which also claimed that it, not the older, established Southeast community organizations, truly represented the interests of Black San Diegans.

I knew all of this, of course. In that regard, the racial tension in San Diego wasn't significantly different from other cities when so-called militant Black groups challenged the leadership of established Black community organizations, so I wasn't particularly disturbed by it. That tension was part of the ferment of the times in America. For those of us involved in community-based organizations, it was part of the landscape of our work.

On the day we had set to meet, Williams didn't show up for the appointment. Well, I thought, I'll just make another appointment, and this time I'll go to his office for the meeting. So, I called his secretary and made a new appointment. But when that day came, and I got to his office, his secretary told me he had left.

"Was he aware that we were supposed to meet? I asked. She said, "Yes." And I said, "He just left?" and she confirmed that.

My response to her was, "Let him know that he doesn't have to return because he's fired."

That's when all hell broke loose. Williams hired a prominent attorney, a former candidate for Mayor, and sued me and the Urban League. Perhaps they thought I'd be intimidated by that. Instead, I made a telephone call of my own and put the best law firm in town on retainer. I was assigned a young partner with experience as a public defender who would later become chief counsel at the Cummings Engine company. He said to me, "You have to give me something to work with. Can you find something on him I can use?"

I went down to Leon Williams' office — of course, I had barred him from the premises — and began looking through its files. There, I found a document that suggested Williams was renting space from a realtor who had been a big contributor to his city council campaign: the arrangement was certainly something that needed to be investigated. And my attorney agreed. When I took the documents to him, he said, "Oh, we can use this."

The trial lasted just one day. Most of it was spent with Henry Hill testifying in general terms about my competence as head of the affiliate. After it had recessed for the day, my attorney went to Williams' attorney, showed him the files we had, and said, "Let me be clear, If this trial continues, we're going to make this information public." The next day, Leon Williams withdrew the lawsuit.

But my troubles on that front weren't over. The NIA militants went to war against me. They had pushed Williams for the City Council — he was their guy, not only their symbol of influence in the city but also the source of patronage and money from the city government. My firing him had challenged their authority and my forcing him to drop the lawsuit had deepened the insult, and they were determined not to let me get away with it.

They set up a picket line in front of our offices and demanded that the San Diego United Way stop funding us, and I began receiving threatening telephone calls from as far away as New Jersey. Soon, I got a call from Don Morgan, the president of the San Diego United Way. He said he'd gotten calls from some community residents and leaders supporting the NIA's demand. He said he wasn't going to listen to them. Instead, the agency would be " neutral in this fight." — He said the only thing they were going to do was hold up the San Diego Urban League's funded increase.

I quickly responded, "Don, the only thing your 'neutrality' suggests is who you're being neutral *against*."

But he stuck to his position. So I said, " You do what you have to do, and I'll do what I have to do."

I hung up and immediately called Crosby Milne. Crosby was one of my most respected board members and, even more important in this situation, a highly placed senior civilian official at the Navel Air Rework Facility, the complex of industrial plants servicing the planes, ships, and other machinery on the massive North Island base. Explaining the power play the NIA was attempting and

150

Morgan's, I asked Crosby to do me a favor: hold up North Island's substantial annual Combined Federal Campaign contribution to the United Way. He agreed to do so.

Later that day, I got a second call from Don Morgan. He asked if I had stopped their funding from North Island.

"Yes," I said calmly, "I made that phone call." He wanted to know why and I reminded him of what I had said to end our previous phone call. " You did what you had to do," I said, "and I did what I had to do."

Having discovered I wasn't without influence that could affect his agency's operations, Morgan quickly suggested I should meet with the United Way Board to explain my view of the situation. I readily agreed to come to their offices to do so, and we set an appointment for the next day.

When I called my Board members to alert them to the latest developments, Larry Adams, a retired Army colonel, said he was coming with me to the meeting.

The next morning, I arrived at the United Way's headquarters before Larry, so I waited outside for him.

When he arrived he walked over to me and said, "Do you have your piece?" —meaning a gun.

I said, "Not on me, but I have it in my car."

He said, "Well, I'm taking mine in with me." Larry knew as well as I did of the previous year's murderous encounter in San Diego. His words signaled he was taking no chances. So I got my gun from my car, stuck it in my belt beneath my suit jacket in the pit of my back, and we made our way to the United Way board room for the meeting.

The members of the United Way Board were seated around the room's conference table; I took a seat against the wall.

There were two African Americans on the board: Ruby Hubert, who led a well-regarded community agency, Neighborhood House, and Thomas Johnson, a senior executive at one of the city's utility companies. Both were well respected in Southeast San Diego and the city at large. The other Board members included two White military officers, a Naval Captain, and a Marine Colonel, representing the power of the military's presence in southern California. I was most interested in what their reaction to all of this would be.

We were soon "joined" by the slogan-shouting arrival of a dashiki-clad NIA contingent, storming into the room and demanding the United Way stop funding us. All of them had strapped bandoliers full of cartridges across their chests. Their leader, George Stevens, was distinguished by the fact that, in addition to the bandolier across his chest, he was also carrying a bandolier with cartridges in his left hand. He yelled at Ruby, "Don't be a bitch all your life; tell these white folks to get out of here. This is Black folks' business." She looked at him impassively. He moved over to Thomas Johnson, seated a few chairs away, yelling, "Tom, don't be an Uncle Tom all your life; tell these white folks to get out of here; this is Black folks' business." This time, for emphasis, he slammed his hand down on the table. Tom just dropped his head.

The two people I was watching closely were the military officers because I knew they would not be intimidated by the blustering and rough language.

152

As for me, I wasn't about to be intimidated. I'd already drawn a line on the floor and said to myself, if Stevens heads toward me and crosses that line, I'll protect myself and anyone else in the room who needs it.

Now, the irony of this whole episode was the fact that George Stevens' wife worked for the San Diego Urban League. All through my battling the militants, which was to last about four months, I never asked her to say or do anything about this situation, and she never offered to talk about it with me.

Someone in the building must have called the police hotline as soon as the militants entered because two law enforcement officers quickly showed up. Both were African Americans. They introduced themselves to the room as James Hatcher of the San Diego Police Department and Jimmy Wilkins of the San Diego Sheriff's Department. That was for Larry's and my benefit because it was apparent everyone else in the room knew them — including the militants — and knew what was going to happen next. Hatcher and Wilkins immediately ordered the militants to leave, and that order was obeyed despite a surly grumbling. During all of the commotion, I had not said a word.

Once the officers had escorted the militants out and the tension in the room dissipated, so did the United Way's standoffishness. Don Morgan walked over to me and simply said, "John, We don't need to hear from you. We see what you're dealing with. You'll get all the money you're supposed to."

Larry and I left, and I went back to my office. That afternoon, Jimmy Wilkins and James Hatcher came to see me at my office. They said, "Mr. Jacob, we know what you're going through, and we also_know you had a gun in that meeting, and the reason we know it is because it was too large to be fully concealed. It's been a long time since we've seen a .38 that big. So, we're going to do two things for you:" They would ask the County Sheriff to issue me a concealed weapons permit so I could legally carry a gun, and they were going to recommend that I get me a smaller but equally powerful gun to carry. From that point on, for the next two years, every time I stepped outside my house, as the fellas in the hood would say, I was strapped.

As for NIA, they had failed in their attempt to cut off my United Way funding, but they hadn't given up yet, as they tried to use the League's rules to take over the affiliate Board. But they didn't realize I had fully anticipated the maneuver: I knew from experience that just as people could organize for you and with you, people could also organize against you. After the confrontation at the United Way board meeting, it was clear what their next step would have to be, and I was ready to outmaneuver them again.

With our annual meeting, which was open to the public, on the horizon, I suspected that, having botched their top-down tactic, they'd try a bottoms-up approach. That would involve taking advantage of the affiliate's student membership category— we offered high school and college students an annual membership for just one dollar. I figured their plan was to get their youthful supporters to load up on dollar memberships, pack them into our annual meeting, and vote to replace those board members whose tenure was up with their supporters.

I put my counter-strategy to work. I didn't schedule the annual meeting at one of the downtown hotels as had been the normal practice. Instead, I scheduled the meeting at a hotel near the popular Fashion Valley Mall some distance from Southeast, the heart of the Black community. Having it there would require planning for the time. Then, I blanketed Southeast with notices about the meeting and announced it via radio public service announcements. These included the meeting's location and starting time of five o'clock, of course. The notices emphasized our intent to begin the meeting on time.

On the day of the meeting the gavel came down at the appointed time, and, quorum in place, we proceeded swiftly. We conducted all business required by law, elected new Board members and Board officers, and were finished in forty-five minutes. Just as we were packing up, the dissenters arrived. I greeted them warmly, thanked them for coming, and informed them that all official business had already been conducted, and I wished them a good day. I had been successful in coming through the first two rounds of my battle with those who objected to the Urban League's influence unscathed. Round 3 was to be more costly.

Soon after I had fought off the attempt to take over the League, Clarence Pendleton, the director of the city's Model Cities Program, came to my office to tell me San Diego would no longer fund two of our programs and the Youth Program that Leon Williams' led would be transferred to a county agency.

Clarence Pendleton and I had a history. He was the one person in San Diego I had known before coming to the city. We had overlapped at Howard, his alma mater also, and during my college days he was a championship-winning swimming coach there. In fact, he was one of the last people

I saw before I left Washington on the drive to San Diego. "Penny," as friends and acquaintances called him, had married my very good friend and Jack Yates' classmate, Dene' Taylor. They later divorced but shared custody of their two children, a boy and a girl. When I stopped by to say my goodbyes to them, he remarked at the news of my new job, "Why would anyone want to live in that town? They roll up the streets at nine o'clock." Six months later, he called to tell me he was moving to San Diego to run its Model Cities program. And it turned out that while I didn't know his new wife, Barbara did; they had worked together at Howard. So, in San Diego, our families visited each other from time to time, and Penny and I played tennis together and had dinner occasionally to discuss San Diego goings-on. We were well enough acquainted that he called me "Jakey." Those were facets of the relationship that still counted for something despite his political attack against the League's efforts.

But I didn't consider Penny a friend. There was something about him that, to me, seemed untrustworthy. So, when he brought me the bad news, I wasn't really surprised. It was just a matter of who was going to be the messenger. I told Penny that the Urban League would survive the blow, that I would find other funding to provide services to the community, and I predicted that before I left San Diego, he and the Mayor would need my support for something.

All those predictions came true. The San Diego Urban League did continue to prosper with new programs, and both Penny and the Mayor, Pete Wilson — who in the 1980s and 1990s served one as a U.S. Senator and two as Governor of California — did come to me asking for my help. Wilson sought my public support when he was trying to move the airport to another location. Penny's was more personal and more urgent. When the federal government was phasing out the Model Cities program, he found himself, with his new wife and baby on hand, needing a job. It was revealed that the city government found itself able to absorb some of the program's staff but could find nothing for the man who had been its director. He invited me over to his apartment complex, which had tennis courts, for a game or two, but it was his lack of job offers that was really on his mind.

"Jakey, I don't really know what I'm going to do. I don't want to leave San Diego. We have a young baby. We like the city. Maybe I'll just get a job as a skycap at the airport."

I silently dismissed those words straightaway. Even if Penny thought at that moment he meant them, he was never going to become a skycap. I knew that Henry Hill and many of the skycaps felt Penny looked down on them; and, as a result, they had no regard for him. Instead, I said to him, "You know, Penny, I'm sitting here considering the pros and cons of two jobs—the one I have now here in San Diego and the one I was just offered back in Washington to be head of the Washington Urban League."

Unfortunately, I told Penny that if I decided to take the job in Washington, I would recommend him to the board as my replacement. At the time, I thought I was making a pragmatic decision. After all, Penny had been head of a substantial program whose purpose was to aid the development of disadvantaged communities. I wasn't carrying a grudge about the past. He was hurting; I wasn't. And I thought he had the administrative skills that could enhance the growth of the San Diego Urban League. Henry Hill disagreed with me. "That's a mistake," he said when I told him of my intention. "He thinks he's better than everybody else, and, worse, his arrogance is far too obvious. But," he said, "if that's your recommendation, I won't oppose it."

The future proved Henry right and me wrong. I later thought I had been more affected than I realized by the Washington-based associations Penny and I shared. My convincing the board to hire Penny was the worst mistake of my career. He never had any commitment to the Urban League's mission. He only saw it as a "power position" he could exploit for his own benefit. My regret would be compounded in the coming decade when President Reagan, in his scheme to undermine the U.S. Civil Rights Commission, chose Clarence Pendleton as its chairman.

The last time I spoke with Penny was while he was still the highly controversial chairman of the commission (it was not a full-time position) and still President of the San Diego Urban League. I asked him what he planned to do after Ronald Reagan's presidency.

He said, "I'll just get me some corporate boards."

That was enough to tell me he still didn't understand the way the world worked. "Penny," I said, "you don't understand: you don't get corporate boards, corporate boards get you. And corporate boards don't like people with negative baggage, which you have plenty of. So, don't count on corporate boards breaking down your door begging you to join them." Penny would die of a heart attack in late 1987.

On the other hand, things seem to have worked out for George Steven, Leon Williams, and me. George was later elected to the San Diego City Council, Leon to the County Commission, and I became president and CEO of the

National Urban League. Our paths crossed one last time—the day more than a decade later, I was in San Diego, and City Councilman George Stephen picked me up at my hotel and drove me to County Commissioner Leon Williams' office, where he presented me with a lifetime achievement award. I took that to mean that all was well between the three of us.

When I took the job in San Diego, Barbara and I had just bought a house in Washington, so, as I mentioned, I continued to rent the apartment in Clairemont for eight months until Barbara and Sheryl came to San Diego. I now needed to buy a house for my family. So, remembering Henry Hill's pledge to help me whenever I was ready, I found a home at a price I considered reasonable — a nice two-story, three-bedroom house with a garage in a predominantly white middle-class Clairemont neighborhood not far from the apartment I'd been staying in, at 4102 Avati Drive. The seller's price was $40,000 (the equivalent of $400,000 today).

Then I went to see Henry. He gave me his business card and said, "Take this to this guy at the Bank of America, and tell him I sent you, and tell him I said to give you a 90-percent loan on the house."

I did that, and the guy said, "You've got the loan."

I went back to Henry. He said, "Now, I want you to go to the owner of the house and ask if he'd take a second loan for ten percent of the sale price."

The owner agreed—but said he'd only take it for 18 months.

I went back to Henry with that agreement in hand, and he said, "Now, go back to the owner and ask him, if he could sell that second loan tomorrow, how much would he be willing to discount it?"

I did that, and the owner said he'd sell it for $3,000. Henry counted out $4,000 and said: Go buy your second loan; You just made $1,000 on your house.

I bought that house in 1971. I sold that house in 1975 for $50,000. Three years later, in 1978, that house was on the market for $187,000—that's how much property within that community had appreciated in less than a decade. Recently, my daughter found a listing for that same house, 4201 Avati Drive, with some renovations having been made, selling for $1.3 million.

Henry H. Hill was an entrepreneur of the finest type. While he was a college graduate, having attended West Virginia State College, his day job in San Diego was as a skycap at the San Diego airport. He said he took the job because it didn't require spending much time thinking about carrying out those duties.-Instead, he spent time thinking of ways to make money. His main vehicle was his creation, the Timely Investment Club. He and its membership of skycaps and other blue-collar workers and numerous Black physicians, teachers, lawyers, dentists and other professionals, too, discussed investing in real estate and the stock market. They would buy houses and renovate them for sale. And they had purchased a strip mall in Southeast; the same strip mall where the shoot-out between San Diego's Black Panther Party and its US organization had taken place.

One day, I approached Henry and made an offer to buy the property for the San Diego Urban League. He was taken aback. Being chairman of the affiliate's Board, he had a good fix on the money in the League coffers. He asked how we'd make such a purchase.

I told him that I didn't have any money for a down payment, but I did have an offer he might find interesting. I had enough money in several League program contracts to rent office space that would enable us to service the debt by housing those programs in the mall's vacant space. In addition, I'd give the Timely Club a contract to manage the property for the League. Henry said, "I want to congratulate you; you're a fast learner, and you've got a deal." That deal made the San Diego Urban League one of the largest property owners in Southeast San Diego. I bought the property for less than $400,000;' during his tenure as head of the affiliate, Clarence Pendleton sold it for $1.5 million.

I spent 5 years in San Diego, and despite the battles, I really liked the place — its physical beauty, its perfect weather, and, for the most part, my colleagues were terrific. But, it was also a "retirement environment," and as time passed, I was conscious of the fact that I was too young to retire, and I had to guard against behaving in that fashion. By that, I mean San Diego was a town where many Navy personnel retired once they completed their active service. It was a place where many Black physicians gave themselves Wednesday afternoons off to play golf. In fact, Henry Hill, my board chair, suggested I take Wednesday afternoons off and join them. The "living-in-paradise" dynamic made itself evident in other ways, too.

Early on, when I was invited to speak to a white women's group, I naturally talked about the work the San Diego Urban League was doing. I talked about people living on and below the poverty line. I shared with my audience the need for improvement in the education system. And I challenged them to look around and observe the wealth gap between the White community and the Black and Hispanic communities. When I returned to my office, Esther Gillman, the wife of San Diego Chargers head coach Sid Gillman, paid me a visit. Her message to me was, "Young man, you have a problem. What you need to understand is those ladies to whom you were speaking came to San Diego to escape those problems and the last thing they want to hear is that we have those same problems here also."

In other words, Esther Gillman was warning me that my success in San Diego depended on my ability to overcome the fact that I was operating in a somewhat unaccepting, even hostile environment in which some people didn't want to accept they had the same problems as other American cities.

Very soon after joining me in San Diego, Barbara and Sheryl fell in love with the place. Sheryl quickly found new friends, loved her school, and did very well on the standardized tests given in both her elementary and middle school grades. But even so, the cloud of racism that so often shadows Black school pupils appeared when she took the standardized tests in her middle school. In fact, Sheryl did so well that school officials didn't believe the results and asked our permission for her to be tested individually.

They said they would bring in a tester and test her individually. Ordinarily, I would have considered this action as racist, but I, too, wanted to see how well she would do, and this way, I didn't have to pay for it. This time, she did even better. Her middle school was large—enrolling nearly 3,000 pupils, a very small number of whom were Black: in the ninth grade, Sheryl's cohort, fewer than 30 of the 850 students were Black.

Barbara and I put aside our suspicions because we had faith in our daughter. The result: her second set of scores were higher than the first. Then, she was asked to meet with her counselor to discuss the courses she wanted to take in high school. The invitation was sent to Sheryl, but I said to Barbara, "Let's crash this party." So, we arrived at the time of our daughter's scheduled appointment, much to the visible surprise of her counselor.

What quickly became clear to me was that people running the school had assumed all its Black students, most of whom were bussed in from the Southeast San Diego community, had no aspirations, no interest in achievement. I sensed they saw our child, too, as just another of the faceless, undifferentiated group of Black children of whom little should be expected. When the three of us met with her counselor, despite Sheryl's test results and excellent grades and our never having missed a parent-teacher meeting, the woman all but completely ignored us.

She asked us no questions about what we wanted for Sheryl, and she only asked Sheryl where she wanted to go to college and what she wanted to major in. Keep in mind this was a 13-year-old child who was in the process of completing the 9th grade. To both questions, Sheryl simply shrugged her shoulders. And, the counselor's response to those non-verbal responses was: "OK, let's work out your program for high school."

I thought, "I want to see how she develops my daughter's high school program from those non-verbal responses." The counselor then mentioned that state law required that all students graduating from a California public high school must have a marketable skill. Therefore, she said, "We have selected a nice cosmetology class for you. We will have transportation pick you up for your class and return you back to the campus when it's over."

I was convinced and said to myself, "That's the best they can do for a child with my child's potential; that's what this counselor sees in my child with all the data she has on her? I'm willing to bet that would not have been the recommendation she would have proposed had she been white."

But, of course, we kept our cool. I said to the counselor evenly, "Madam, I'm not as liberal with my child's education as you are. Let me tell you what I want my daughter to take: all the science, all the English, all the math, and as many foreign language classes as you can manage to squeeze into her schedule. You see, I believe if you can think critically, compute, analyze, and communicate well both orally and in writing, those are also marketable skills."

The counselor got the message, but she didn't seem to particularly like it. There was just a hint of frustration in her voice when she responded, "Now that we know what your father wants you to take, let's work out your program." I kept quiet, but I thought, "What happens to the students whose parents don't attend these conferences?"

As I rolled into my fifth year in San Diego, things had become less chaotic. Even the group I had been at war with now sought me out to help on some matters. One such call came when the director of a housing program they had a friendly relationship with was indicted for illegal activities through his stewardship of the program. NIA leaders asked me to meet with the district attorney to discuss whether the matter could be resolved without their friend ending up in prison.

I knew the person they were concerned about, and while I didn't have any intimate knowledge about his management of the program, I agreed to seek a meeting and see if I could bring some relief to the situation. I did meet with the San Diego District Attorney, and he was pleasant. But he pointed out he wasn't the one trying the case. He put me in touch with his assistant, who was.

In walks a young attorney who carried himself as if he thought this case would put him on the map. In my pursuit of sympathy for the accused, I suggested that there were no victims resulting from his actions — to witch the young lawyer responded, "Mr. Jacob, I don't agree that this is a victimless crime. I say you are a victim, and your community is a victim." And he capped that off with these words I've never forgotten: "Mr. Jacob, it is the responsibility of the law to protect people even when they don't want to be protected." With that, we ended the meeting because I could not refute the position he had articulated.

Yet, although I had not gotten the District Attorney's Office to drop the charges against their friend, I felt I had gained a new level of trust and respect from them because I had tried. They had come to me because they knew they had little, if any, credibility with the District Attorney's Office themselves, but the San Diego Urban League did. With that appreciation, we both moved on with our work.

Chapter 7 — Back To Chocolate City:
The Washington Urban League, 1975-1978

If one picture is worth a thousand words, one photograph that appeared atop a news story in *The Washington Post* of November 5, 1974, could be as valuable as a century's worth. In it, standing at a podium and obviously reflecting the jubilation of a throng, are three people exulting in a long-sought, hard-fought victory for themselves and for a cause. Home Rule had returned to Washington, D.C. — a city whose majority Black population had led many African Americans in Washington and elsewhere to label it "Chocolate City."

One of the people in the photograph was the duly elected occupant of the city government's top job, Walter E. Washington. The photograph also included his wife, Bennetta Bullock Washington. Arms held high in triumph, the two were flanking the victor for the city's second most prestigious post, the newly elected Chairman of the first popularly elected City Council in Washington's history, the chief executive of the Washington Urban League, Sterling Tucker.

In fact, it was no surprise at all that both Washington and Tucker would emerge as victors of the new "experiment" in democracy in 1974 in the nation's capitol. (**F. 1**) In 1967, when the city was still governed by president appointees subject to the — often interfering — oversight of Congress, President Johnson had appointed Washington as Mayor and a nine-member city council. In 1969, President Nixon appointed Sterling vice-chairman of the latter. (**F. 2**) No one doubted that these two men (and most others holding appointed positions) would sweep to victory when Congress in 1973 finally enacted legislation enabling residents of the District of Columbia to vote for the city offices. **(F. 3)**

From my perch in San Diego I was well aware of the excitement stirring local politics in the District. I'd recently been elected an alumni member of the Howard University Board of Trustees, and, in addition to keeping in touch with Washington goings-on by telephone, I'd regularly fly back to the city on Urban League and Howard business and be able to take the pulse of the city that way, too. Of course, all of Washington knew that Sterling, long a vigorous advocate for Home Rule, intended to be at the top of the city government when that goal was reached.

When Sterling turned in his resignation from the Urban League, I wasn't surprised that, with my five years of experience serving under Sterling (including the eighteen-month stint as Acting Director), the Washington Urban League board formally invited me to apply for the top job. But at that moment, I had no interest in moving. I felt I was doing good work at the San Diego affiliate. I had grown to love living there, as had my wife and daughter. So, I wasn't inclined to work up a formal letter of interest with all the paperwork that was required. I replied that I wouldn't be submitting information for consideration and that I was happy in my current position — and I added that, given my record at the League in general and in Washington in particular, if the Washington board didn't know me by now, they never would. I closed by saying that If they wanted to make me an offer, I would consider it.

The board quickly asked me to come to discuss what I thought they should be looking for in a new President. I agreed to do that when I was next in town for a Howard Trustees meeting.

As promised, on my next trip for a Howard Trustees meeting, I did sit with them. Then, as our talk closed, one of the Board members asked what it would take to get me to come and take on that job. I said, "Make me an offer, and if I like it, I will give you an answer." They soon made me an offer, and I accepted.

My return to Washington was uneventful. There was no parade, no releasing of balloons, no fireworks being shot off in the night and no welcome mat being laid out. But if Washington didn't notice me all the much, I certainly felt I had returned to a changed city — a city in some ways very different from the one I had left five years earlier.

For one thing, one could still feel the reverberations of the Nixon Administration's implosion in the once-hard-to-imagine Watergate scandal. That was a high-crimes saga to which the stunning 1973 indictment and forced resignation of the Administration's blowhard Vice President, Spiro Agnew, for garden-variety financial corruption provided a tawdry confirmation that something was rotten at the highest levels of the national government.

The soul-searching aftermath of those two episodes was exacerbated by the shocking, confused retreat of American military forces from Vietnam, Laos, and Cambodia — a retreat that very clearly left the citizens of those countries who had aided the American side in profound peril. There was no hiding the truth: the American nation had suffered a calamitous defeat but one whose consequences were going to be most severely felt by those the country claimed to be fighting for.

For many Americans, those blows were surpassed by the sharp 1973 OPEC-driven reduction of oil delivered to the U.S. The embargo's immediate effect was to hammer the American economy, producing the much-reported-on spectacle of long lines at gasoline stations, gas rationing, and damaging spikes in prices throughout the economies of the U.S., Japan, and Western European countries. It also produced an immediate spike in unemployment that was to ensnare Black Americans in a devastating, two-decade-long record of mostly double-digit official unemployment rates — which actually didn't capture just how bad the true unemployment situation for Blacks was.

For example, after OPEC triggered the embargo in October 1973, the overall U.S. unemployment rate rose to a high of 8.4 percent in October 1975 before sliding down to 6.3 percent in January 1980. The overall White unemployment rate during those two years rose from below 5 percent to a high of 7.7 percent before dropping to 5.5 percent in January 1980. But the unemployment record of African Americans in the mid-and late 1970s was strikingly worse. In January 1973, ten months before the OPEC action, Blacks' official overall unemployment rate was 9.1 percent—nearly twice that of Whites. By October 1975, it was 14.9 percent, again nearly twice that of Whites. From that month on, it would not dip below 10 percent in any month until 1995. The situation, as one might expect, was even worse when one separated out the rates for Black men and women, and throughout the 1970s, the official monthly rates for Black youths aged 16 to 19 were consistently at or above 35 percent. Black unemployment rates in the 1980s would be far worse.

However, one could well say that for Black Washingtonians and many Whites who actually made the city their home, too, local affairs were even more pressing than the national and international problems. The expansion of Home Rule was occurring when the city, and especially its predominantly Black neighborhoods, were still beset by the damaging effects of two events: the federally-sponsored urban renewal program of the 1950s and early 1960s, on the one hand, and, on the other, the continuing impacts of the deeply destructive 1968 riot that erupted following the assassination of Martin Luther King, Jr. That stunning episode of widespread looting and setting ablaze scores and scores of stores and other buildings produced a physically scarred landscape in several Black city neighborhoods and business districts that lasted for more than a decade. **(F. 4)**

One effect of this terrible combination was to sharply increase poverty among the city's black residents and sharply reduce the supply of adequate housing available to them. The decline in tax revenues from the destroyed and damaged apartment buildings and businesses led to a deterioration in such city services as garbage pick-ups and street cleaning, which made neighborhoods look worse and contributed to the rapid increase in White residents fleeing the city for the suburbs.

At the same time, however, there existed a highly energetic and extraordinarily varied group of activists who had risen to the challenge over the previous three decades of the crises of urban renewal, improving public school education, destroying the systemic support for anti-Black discrimination in the city, resisting plans to slice highways through several city neighborhoods. In 1975 a goodly number of those who had been highly visible activists when I left Washington five years earlier were now either elected political officials, or their aides, or appointees staffing various city departments. For example, Marion Barry, a veteran of the Student Nonviolent Coordinating Committee campaigns in the South, had been an organizing whirlwind in Black neighborhoods in the late 1960s and early 1970s. Now, he was a member of the new City Council.

So, I, who had spent most of the 1950s and 1960s in Washington, now had returned to a different city — one whose Black residents had gained more political and administrative power, but no one could escape knowing that its *Home Rule* was still incomplete.

Nonetheless, the message being sent by some members of the new political leadership was: *we know what the problems are; just give us time, and we'll address them.* That sentiment, of course, is a trap. *Time,* as a force in human affairs, almost always succeeds in imposing its dominant will — delay. I've always believed it's better to not give Time more time but instead to act as swiftly as possible. After Sterling's long tenure leading the affiliate, I felt it incumbent upon me to show its staff inside and the community outside why I was the right person for the job. I began a determined search through the office's program files to see if there was something we could launch quickly to put to use right away. I soon discovered a proposal written several years earlier by Linda Finkelstein, one of Sterling's senior aides and an excellent writer, discussing the plight of Black youth who get swept up in the criminal justice system.

Exemplifying how Home Rule had changed at least some things, Linda had just joined the city agency under whose auspices this proposal fell. I called her and told her I had a proposal about a project I'd like her to consider. Was she surprised when I showed up with the document!

But I chose that proposal not simply because Linda had written it but because it was an idea whose time had come. In its simplest form, it contended that young people were being locked away in juvenile detention facilities — which were notorious for their lack of rehabilitative programs — when they should be placed in programs that would give them the work-related and personal skills they needed to become productive citizens. Our proposal got attention, and several hundred thousand dollars from the city youth services agency to put it into operation.

That was an example of how the new political office-holders and the activists and community organizations could still work toward common goals — and also that the new politicians need not fear that every community activist was just angling for their job. I was especially aware of such sentiments because, as everyone knew, Sterling had long used the position I was now holding as the foundation of his political ambitions. I constantly tried to make it as clear as possible that I hadn't come back to Washington to challenge any of them for their political office. Instead, I wanted the Washington Urban League to be viewed as a vital resource to this newly elected government.

One person who helped me figure out ways to do that was my new staff hire as director of communications, John Watkins. John was on Vernon's staff in New York but was relocating to Washington. Vernon called me and recommended I speak with him. I did; I thought he'd do well in a similar role for me and hired him. He proved his value right away in helping us work through how to convince city officials the League could be a valuable asset in addressing community needs.

Our brainstorming produced the idea of a first-of-its-kind expansive Urban League survey of residents in the lowest-income census tracks, asking them what they considered their greatest needs and what the solutions to those problems should be. We set as our goal to conduct face-to-face interviews with 3,000 households, far beyond the typical survey sample size even for large national surveys.

Some researchers and even some Urban League staff thought we had lost on minds. They pointed out that for its national surveys, Gallup, the nation's most prominent polling firm, surveyed no more than 1,500 households. How could we reach 3,000 households for face-to-face interviews? Where was I going to get the people to do it? And how long would it take to get it done?

My response to the understandably skeptical was that we needed to oversample to be sure the new city government had an abundance of data on what this cohort of the population — whose opinions were rarely sought — was thinking. I felt with the right planning, and enough survey-takers, we could get it done on a given Saturday.

We set to work. We pulled together a team drawn from the League's own staff and its staff researcher to develop the survey instrument. We contacted college sororities, fraternities, and social clubs to ask for their help in being the front-line survey takers, along with volunteers from churches and other community groups. Because our volunteer survey takers were overwhelmingly female, we recruited our own volunteer security force from such men's groups as fraternities, the Elks, and the Masons. Then, for the week prior to the Saturday we had set for the survey, we sent sound trucks through the target neighborhoods, alerting residents that we were coming and that we wanted to know what they wanted to say to D.C.'s new government.

On the actual day of the survey, our 600 survey takers flooded the neighborhoods. It quickly became apparent that many residents had put off going out to do their Saturday chores so they could speak with the survey takers. Our plan called for speaking with the residents of every third household; in numerous instances, those in the dwellings we skipped wanted to know why they, too, weren't being surveyed. After the survey-takers had finished, I had them load the documents in my car, and I bundled them over to the National Urban League's Washington-based research department for its staff to analyze and help us prepare a formal report. We issued that assessment on July 4, 1976, amid the celebrations of the nation's 200th birth. It was titled *SOS 76.*

The release of such a massive survey articulating the views of residents of Washington's most distressed neighborhoods produced a flood of questions from the media to city officials. Their predominant response: *We're going to work with the Urban League in addressing these concerns.*

Our simple but audacious act had many benefits. It re-established the fact that the Urban League still had a role to play in the city's new political era and that its capabilities could be an asset to the new city government; the information gleaned from the study served as a blueprint for action for the affiliate for years to come. But of equal importance, it put more pressure on city officials to include poor residents's views in tackling problems in their neighborhoods; problems they had identified with solutions they felt would work.

Befitting our mission, our services were broad and comprehensive. For example, we partnered with IBM to establish one of the first word-processing training centers at a time when that technology was in its infancy. It provided high-level secretarial skills and good-paying employment opportunities to hundreds of unemployed and underemployed African Americans and other disadvantaged persons. Interestingly enough, I had approached IBM and requested a computer training center, but they pointed out that such a center in a town with so many Universities in the area with degree programs in computer science would place our students at a decided disadvantage. And, they suggested the word processing center idea with all of the government agencies and companies in need of highly trained clerical staff trained in this new technology. They were right because we had employees bidding for our students before they completed the course. We provided meals to senior citizens, services for military veterans, employment training, and placement. We opened schools for students who had dropped out or were pushed out to get re-acquainted with school or vocational studies, and we prepared some for the General Education Diploma exam.

The Washington Urban League had never owned its headquarters building. We still operated out of the tall office building on Sixteenth Street, Northwest a mile or so due north of the White House. But I felt it was long past the time for the affiliate to own its own lodgings, especially if that enabled us to move into a predominantly Black neighborhood. I learned the former Danzansky Funeral Home building located at 14th and Otis Streets NW was coming on the market for sale. And that property was owned by the family of one of our board members, so, I approached that board member and asked if he'd help us to acquire the property. We didn't have funds for a large down payment. However, we could service the loan through monies we had in our budget for rent. He was receptive to our plea, and we bought the property. Our next challenge was to cover the cost of renovating the site to make it usable for our purposes. Another member of our board was a major Washington-area developer; and volunteered his services to manage the renovation and used his contacts to get us the job done at a very reasonable cost.. For the first time in its history, the Washington Urban League had its own home.

25. I was having a good run at the Washington Urban League and one day, I received a telephone call from Vernon inviting me and Barbara to come up to New York and spend the weekend with him and his wife Shirley. Vernon was known to often invite local executives up to his home for a weekend, but this was the first time he had made me such an offer. And, by the way, Vernon was known for his excellent hosting skills. Most local executives couldn't wait to receive such an invitation. But, I'm not most, so I went home and told Barbara about the invitation, and asked if she wanted to go. She said, "Sure, it would be great to spend some time with Shirley since they had only seen each other at National Conferences, and since they had been in the same graduation

176

class at Howard, it should be fun to get reacquainted. So, we flew to New York on Friday and spent the rest of that day just hanging out. Saturday was more of the same. Early Sunday morning, as Vernon puttered around the kitchen preparing breakfast, he told me the consulting firm Booz-Allen had just completed a study on the management structure of the National Urban League and had recommended, among other things, creating the position of Executive Vice President and Chief Operating Officer. That person would run the organization on a day-to-day basis, while Vernon focused on its "national leadership" work. He wanted that person to be me, and he outlined how he planned to restructure the organization to accommodate this new position. When he finished, I said Vernon, you are the Chief Executive; you can structure your organization in any way you choose. I just want to work in that structure. So, I tell you what I'm going to do: "I'm going to eat your breakfast; I'm going to collect my wife, and I'm going back to D.C." Clearly surprised at my pushback, he said, "What's wrong with the structure?" I said, "Vernon, you can't give me all the people you don't like and keep all the people you like and think the position is going have any kind of stature and standing in the organization. But you are the CEO; it is your organization, and you can run it any way you choose. I just want to work on it. So, I tell you what I'm going to do. I'm going to eat your breakfast; I'm going to collect my wife, and I'm going back to D.C." That's the way we left it. Barbara and I had a good breakfast with Vernon and Shirley, and then we packed up and headed to La Guardia for the flight back to D.C.

Shortly after my meeting with Vernon, one evening, my board chairman, Dr. Benjamin Henley, walked into my office and asked me to stay around for a while because the Board wanted to do my appraisal and would like to discuss it with me when they finish. So, I sat in my office while they were in executive session. Recognizing it had been some time since he had asked me to wait around, I took a look at my watch and realized it was almost 8:00 pm and wondered what they could possibly be discussing that was taking so long. Ben finally came to me again; and said, "I don't want you to think it took us that long to do your appraisal. He said the appraisal took about 10 minutes; the rest of the time, we have been trying to figure out how much more money we can afford to pay you." When he said that, my mind immediately went to work. I thought, if it took them three hours this year to determine how much they can afford to pay me, it'll take them three days next year and three weeks the year after that. So, this probably means I've plateaued out of what they can afford to pay me. And I thought further that if the Urban League couldn't afford to pay me a larger salary, it's likely no community-based organization could either. I also realized the very lengthy discussion about how much they could afford to pay me also indicated that the skills I had shown had gone beyond the requirements of the job —- and beyond the salary scale of the non-profit world into the for-profit world. So, I began contemplating how I could move from the non-profit world into the for-profit world. I knew I couldn't do that in D.C. because Washington is a government town. I needed to get to a city where I could be discovered by the for-profit world. So, I was mentally in the job search mode when Vernon called me at 6:00 AM one

178

morning saying: "Alright, John Jacob, we'll do it your way." So, I came to New York to be Vernon's second-in-command, the first Executive Vice President and Chief Operating Officer in the history of the National Urban League.

Chapter 8 – At The Top

During the press conference, Vernon had called at our headquarters Monday to announce my appointment a reporter asked me about differences between Vernon and me. I aimed for comic effect: "You mean besides him being 6'5" and me being 5'6'? Then I got serious. I said that Vernon was a lawyer and an advocate who supported social work activities while I was a social worker who engaged in advocacy activities. I told them my goal: Help guide the Urban League to new heights of effectiveness, help educate the nation about its unfinished responsibilities, and help bring fresh opportunities to black poor people who were the core constituency of the Urban League because "the period of the 80s requires that we engage more in service delivery as best we can."

Those latter words were important because the Reagan Administration's actions during its first year in office had made clear that the pledge he made to the Urban League Conference in August 1980 — "*What I want for America is, I think, pretty much what the overwhelming majority of black Americans want.*" — had quickly proved hollow.

Instead, in office, Reagan continued playing a dirty game of euphemism and innuendo and outright falsehoods to justify draconian social program budget cuts, install appointees — apparatchiks, really — within the Justice Department, Environmental Protection Agency (EPA) the Labor Department, and the Department of Education, among others, who sought to subvert the official duties of their office, and attack efforts such as affirmative action and busing to end school segregation.

I did indeed have a great deal more to say about the crisis the country was facing, but not to the media that day. Instead, I wanted a forum where I could first — as the new President and CEO — explain at least some of them more comprehensively directly to the Urban League community. And I had the perfect venue for that purpose.

In early November, while the selection process for the League's new leader was still underway, the Greenville, South Carolina Urban League had invited me to speak at its annual dinner. Then, I was Executive Vice President of the National Urban League. Now that I was the incoming *President* of the National Urban League, it was incumbent on me to give a" presidential speech" — a speech that set out *my vision* of the Urban League's responsibilities and tasks for the 1980s. I knew I wanted the organization to focus more of our resources on four specific tasks most of all: reducing the high incidence of pregnancy among black teens, mitigating the spread of single female-headed households, marshaling forces within Black communities themselves to reduce crime, and increasing the political empowerment of Black America.

I was ready to re-introduce myself to the National Urban League.

In my speech, I told the Greenville gala's supporters and guests that I was appearing before them under the "happy circumstance" of being Vernon's successor — the President and CEO of the National Urban League: "a job Vernon has aptly called the best job in Black America," before quickly adding, "I am also aware, it is the most difficult job in Black

America: a grueling job rich in frustrations and hardships ...
[but] supremely rich in opportunities to serve the cause of
Black and poor people, and to help build a pluralistic society
the Urban League has been fighting for over 71 years."

I was sure that most of those sitting before me, connected
in one way or another to the Greenville Urban League, were
well aware that mission had become far more fraught with a
new Administration in Washington whose first year had
been filled with one controversy after another. Nonetheless,
I wanted to underscore to them that the Urban League would
continue to be resolute in facing up to the old and new
realities. I ticked off why I believed the Urban League "faces
one of the most difficult periods of its long history."

"One such reality," I said, was "the bitter recognition of
continued black disadvantage" that "comes on top of an old
reality that found blacks disproportionately disadvantaged."
After all, Black Americans had been severely harmed by the
recessions and rising inflation of the 1970s. Now, blacks
were enduring added hardships from a new recession that
was the most severe since the Great Depression itself and
from the Reagan Administration's cruel cuts to federal social
programs pushing the Black poor deeper into poverty.

Of course, I reminded my audience those developments
were affecting millions of whites and other minorities, too;
government statistics indicated that in 1980 alone, more than
4 million people had fallen into poverty. It was the
disproportion that made Blacks' circumstances the more
dramatic.

The official federal statistics pegged Black
unemployment at 17 percent—more than double that of
Whites. But the League's "Hidden Unemployment Index"

contended that the federal calculations understated the real extent of joblessness for all. Our calculations put overall Black unemployment at 25 percent — and that of Black youth at nearly 50 percent nationwide.

Black Americans made up just 12 percent of America's population, I told my listeners, but a third of all Americans who live in poverty. An even greater tragedy was that nearly half of Black children lived in families with incomes at or below the official poverty line. Those striking facts were rooted in the reality that the typical Black family earned less than the government itself estimated was necessary for a minimum adequate standard of living.

"What is new about this terrible reality," I urged those gathered to consider, was "the concentration of poverty among female-headed households. ... the growth in the numbers of people whose poverty extends over a long period of time and threatens to become permanent. .... [and] the concentration of poverty in urban pockets removed from new job opportunities."

And most distressing of all the *new realities* spreading throughout American society, I warned, "is that the poor are cast adrift, casualties in a war of budget cuts, program terminations, and national indifference."

For Black Americans, this callousness was intensified by the "revival of anti-Black attitudes in a nation that only a short time ago seemed dedicated to racial progress. .... [particularly by] respectable people who would never dream of going to a Klan meeting. Well-dressed, affluent people are saying things they would have been embarrassed to say just a few years ago."

I was directly referring to the *New York Times* reporting a month earlier that the board of an exclusive Park Avenue cooperative had rejected the bid of the New York Public Library, one of the nation's preeminent scholarly and cultural institutions, to purchase an apartment as the family home of its new president, the esteemed scholar Vartan Gregorian.

The co-op board held no animus toward the Library, its president explained to a *New York Times* reporter. It was just, he said, that the "way things are going these days, it's very likely that the president of the library could be a member of a minority group. And no matter how we feel about it, we've got to protect our investments. With a member of a minority group living in the building, the value would go right down like that." He emphasized the point, according to the *Times* report, by making a sweeping, downward motion with his right arm. **(F. 1)**

Times columnist Sydney Schanberg, sarcastically noting the coop board president's rationale in a follow-up column, wrote, "The way things are going, I guess he was talking about someone like Andrew Young or Franklin Thomas of the Ford Foundation."

Schanberg then addressed the larger point. "We all know people who behave in a manner consistent with ... [those] remarks. ... They've been keeping 'the wrong people' — sometimes Jews, sometimes Italians, often blacks and Hispanics — out of their neighborhoods and buildings for generations." Schanberg also noted the coop board's attitudes were apparently widespread among its neighbors on Manhattan's Upper East Side: for the Library's "search for a co-op for Dr. Gregorian ... [has] proved so frustrating that they have decided to temporarily put off the idea of purchasing one. Dr. Gregorian will, for the moment, rent an apartment instead." **(F.2)**

I went on to connect those attitudes with the slashing of federal aid to the poor the Reagan Administration had pursued with a vengeance.

That "new reality" helps account for the anger directed at programs for the poor, which are perceived as *black programs.* "More whites than blacks are on welfare. More whites than blacks are on food stamps. More whites than blacks benefit from all the major social service and income transfer programs. But the public perception of those programs as being *black* helps create " a climate in which they can be cut."

To this point in the speech, I had just been sketching some dimensions of the crisis upon us. I wanted to make sure everyone understood that. But it had never been the Urban League's way to just identify the problems without suggesting what could be done to reduce their impact — that is, to note the tasks the different sectors of the society must take up for the good of the whole society.

For the private sector, I said that meant not just donating funds to national and local organizations but also establishing partnerships with them to provide jobs and training for the disadvantaged. True, corporations have more actively responded to these imperatives since the 1960s. But, I told the audience we shouldn't forget that corporations needed the constant pushing or, more politely, urging to respond to the crisis. We bore an even greater responsibility to do more, given that the Reagan tax cuts Congress had enacted that year allowed corporations to deduct up to ten percent of their pretax income for charitable giving. Before, it had been five percent.

I reminded my listeners that "the typical corporate contribution is a fraction of one percent, and most of that money does not go to social welfare activities. ... So I am saying tonight that self-interest and compassion must drive the private sector to a heightened sense of responsibility in these terrible times for poor people."

In that regard, my words to corporate America drew on the historical injunction to White America explicit in the Urban League's first slogan of six decades earlier: *Not Alms, But Opportunity.* What we sought from the private sector was action and funding based not on the notion of *charity* but on *compassionate, self-interested investment.* The goal was not to ensnare the poor and disadvantaged in debilitating dependence but to enable them to gain the education and marketable skills necessary to become viable members of the workforce—to earn wages that allow them to support their families, make purchases that drive consumerism essential to the economy, and pay taxes that fund the government at all levels to function effectively.

Nor did I ignore the tasks Black Americans had to undertake—namely, to put more energy and resources into tackling "the problems within our own communities" even as they tried to beat back "the hammer blows of Reaganomics."

"Reaganomics is a terrible thing," I said. "Black people will never achieve equality without a government that protects our rights and provides the basic income, health, housing, and educational guarantees necessary for survival. We will never achieve equality without a private sector that actively draws us into the economic main stream. But there are problems within our community that we can and ought to do something about."

Indeed, I declared that the imperative was even greater because of the *positive reality of Black Progress.* The increase of Black college graduates, Black managers in American corporations, Black mayors running American cities, and even Black sheriffs wearing badges in Southern cities and towns once worn by men who clubbed civil rights demonstrators are real, I said. "Changes have come—yes, far too slowly. But we must acknowledge that change … gives [Black Americans] a strong base of people used to dealing with mainstream America, skilled people whose talents and accomplishments can be used for the benefit of the total black community."

I suggested three tasks as among those most important to focus on: increasing voter registration and education efforts, reducing the incidence and impact of teenage pregnancies and single female-headed households, and reducing crime in black communities.

Once I officially took office, I formed a task force at headquarters to develop a coherent program League-wide to pursue those goals. At our first meeting — and against the backdrop of our re-calculating the financial hit we were taking from the federal cutbacks to our programs — I said we couldn't surrender to the cutbacks, that we had to figure out how to do more to help our constituents despite the reduced funding. "We're going to have to figure out how to do more with less," I declared.

Mildred Love, our vice president for programs with direct oversight of the national office's sponsored programs, raised her hand. "Jake," she asked, "given our finances, why don't we figure out how to do less with less—but do what we do better, improve the quality of the services that we can offer?"

That trenchant comment guided our thinking from that moment forward. Mildred had reminded us of the importance of at least reconsidering our original goals, but always with the determination to still produce top-quality results. One result was a new *Youth and Community Initiatives Program* model developed with the aid of our affiliates and designed to deal creatively with four crucial problem areas in the black community: teenage pregnancy, female-headed households, crime, and voting and civic involvement. These had always been pillars of our work, but now we sought to inspire and involve those groups and organizations that made up Black communities' civic infrastructure to pool resources in a cohesive approach.

Finally, I pledged to my audience that the Urban League would establish or bolster its own programs across the board. We would hold true to our founding principles: speaking up for the poor and disadvantaged, most of all, providing the services they need to help overcome their disadvantages, and promoting the interracial cooperation essential to achieve the healthy pluralistic environment critical to America's survival.

I carried the message of the Greenville speech forward in summary form to a broader audience that January in the second *To Be Equal* column of my tenure, with a blunt warning for my readers: "The 1980s are a potentially disastrous decade for blacks. With the rug of federal programs and national sympathy pulled out from under us, black organizations and individuals will have to directly confront the internal problems of the community to a greater degree than in the past. ... because we don't have the luxury of waiting for a more favorable national climate, we now have to redouble our own efforts despite our limited resources."

Even as I urged a greater self-reliance in our approaches to problem-solving I also warned that we shouldn't "fool ourselves that voluntary activity can solve our problems or even significantly reduce them. Most black communities' deepest problems are a direct result of past and present racism. Only strong, activist federal and private sector actions can overcome society's heritage of black disadvantage." Nonetheless, I concluded we had no choice but to make the effort. "Many of our problems can be contained or at least made less critical by community efforts, and that is a new responsibility all of us will have to willingly bear in this difficult decade of trial and trouble." **(F. 3)**

I thought I had explained myself well. The audience seemed receptive. But I soon realized I had perhaps confused some at the dinner in setting out the issues I wanted to give priority to when one board member asked me afterward, "Jake, what does teenage pregnancy have to do with civil rights? What does the problem of single female-headed households have to do with civil rights?"

I told him we shouldn't think that just continuing to fight to protect our civil rights would by itself completely solve the problems Black America was facing. I said that when you looked at the data, you saw that pregnancy was the number one reason for black girls dropping out of school. And seventy percent of Black single female-headed households were living below the poverty line. If we weren't willing to address those issues, we were just kidding ourselves about building a stronger black community able to fully take advantage of their "civil rights." If the Urban League was going to be relevant to our community in the 1980s, we had to figure out how to significantly lessen the severity of those issues. That was why the Urban League existed — to suggest how the problems bedeviling Black Americans could be solved or, at the least, lessened. This — *service and advocacy* — was our foundation. Service was how the League secured the money to fund our programs; advocacy was how it gained credibility with its constituency. The two had to go hand in hand.

Some of my colleagues, both outside and within the League, expressed concern that by publicly discussing issues like Black teen pregnancy, I was airing our dirty laundry. To them, I responded, "Are you kidding me? You don't think this data is already widely known? We need to start speaking out about it and proposing solutions on our own terms." That was the very goal the Urban League declared at its founding in 1910—to address the seemingly intractable crises in cities and established Black communities brought on by the great migrations of Black Southerners to the North's urban centers.

At the same time, however, we also needed to make it clear that the problems affecting Black Americans weren't "Black" problems, no matter how often some politicians and scholars labeled them as such. They were problems rooted in the mechanisms of American society that showed themselves most acutely in their impact on Black

Americans—and they required solutions that would benefit not just African-Americans but the whole society, too.

I repeatedly pushed that same message throughout my first months in office, so I'm sure few were surprised when it was also the centerpiece of my keynote address to the League's annual conference in Los Angeles that August.

"Today, hope hangs by a fragile thread, for America has embarked on a new experiment," I told the throng. "It has embraced a supply-side gospel that promised a born-again economy and instead gave us another Depression. … The belief in Reaganomics amounts to a triumph of blind faith over harsh reality. ….. The poor have become casualties of a war of budget cuts, program terminations, and national indifference. [and] are being abandoned by their national government." …..

"Everybody deserves a chance to make it on their own," I said, referencing the slogan for the new advertising campaign we were unveiling at the conference. "A chance to make it on your own means a chance to get the skills with which to compete. Making it on your own means being equipped to take advantage of opportunities. Making it on your own means overcoming the barriers to success— barriers like poverty, barriers like loss of hope, barriers like having two strikes against you before you start."

One part of the solution, I declared, was establishing a Universal Employment and Training Program that would, on the one hand, hire unemployed men and women who already have the skills to repair America's crumbling infrastructure — its roads, bridges, ports and rail systems, sewer lines and water systems — and, on the other, also establish a program to equip more people with those skills. That would make a serious dent in two of the major problems the society faces.

"Our government doesn't mind running up a half trillion dollar deficit over the next three years to support a supply side fantasy," I continued. "It doesn't mind drilling loopholes in the tax code to give away half a trillion over the next four years to a favored few. It doesn't mind spending one and a half trillion dollars over the next four years on an overblown defense program that increases national insecurity. ... Any country that can afford to waste such vast sums can afford to invest in its human capital and its economic future."

I summarized our new Youth and Community Initiatives Program, explaining that it was young people — who were most directly harmed by the crises of teen pregnancy, female-headed households, and crime — whose positive participation in civic life was crucial for Black America's future. Of course, these tasks had always been part of the Urban League's program matrix. But we felt that emphasizing their importance under the banner of a League-wide initiative would, via the work of our local affiliates, underscore how comprehensive the effort mounted by organizations and groups within the Black community needed to be.

Fortunately, thanks to the foresight of my immediate predecessors Whitney and Vernon, I had two powerful tools to propel the message across the land and position the League at the forefront of the progressive response to the so-called Reagan Revolution: the Urban League's *To Be Equal* column and its annual scholarly journal, *The State of Black America*.

The *To Be Equal* column was Whitney's way of capitalizing on two of the major forces animating American society in the early 1960s. One was the American public's intense interest—driven substantially by its fascination with the new, young president, John F. Kennedy, and his wife, Jacqueline—in following current events. The other was the Civil Rights Movement, which had exploded across the South with new "direct action" campaigns of marches, sit-ins, and "Freedom Rides." Those actions had, in turn, stimulated or ratcheted up the intensity of local civil rights campaigns in the North, largely focused on desegregating public schools and eliminating racial discrimination in the unions and civil service jobs.

Whitney understood that in that era of "activism," the League could no longer just depend solely on the occasional news article or editorial in the mainstream media or the other usual sources of coverage: the weekly Black-owned newspapers and the two most significant publications of the John H. Johnson empire, the weekly Jet Magazine, and the monthly Ebony Magazine. It needed a way to continually directly present its views to a much broader swath of Blacks and Whites. At that moment when newspapers were beginning to expand the number of columns offered on their editorial pages — resulting eventually in the creation of the "op-ed page," that is, *the page opposite the editorial page* — to encompass a wider variety of topics and views, Whitney pitched the idea of his writing a stand-alone column to the Copley News Service syndicate. They readily agreed, and in 1964, the column "To Be Equal" under the byline of Whitney M. Young, Jr. made its appearance as part of Copley's broad mix of columns, cartoons, and news features offered to more than 600 small and mid-size newspapers and magazines across the country.

Thus began a five-decade partnership that, along with the column's appearance in most of the nation's Black weekly newspapers, enabled the views of the National Urban League to each week potentially reach millions of Americans in cities, small towns, and rural areas from coast to coast. Undoubtedly, many readers of the Copley syndicate outlets were conservative-leaning Whites. So much the better, because it enabled us to directly reach that segment of Americans with our ideas and opinions. Nor did we "tailor" or soft-pedal our views. The words comprising the columns that appeared in Black-owned newspapers and Copley syndicate newspapers were the same. No other non-profit organization — civil rights or otherwise — ever had such a forum.

In the mid-1970s, Vernon added to the League's "media platform," *The State of Black America (SOBA)*. Published once a year, it was meant to provide scholarly analyses—a more expansive examination, with a focus on including data—of issues affecting Black America not available in the short-form journalism of daily and weekly newspapers and magazines. Its intended audience was not just reporters in the mainstream media and policy wonks in Congress, state and local governments, and think tanks. We also wanted to supply directors and members of local community and civic groups across the country with statistics and insights to bolster their reform efforts. Many of our own affiliates took advantage of the publication to bolster discussions about conditions in their own areas as well.

The volume was always published in early January — pointedly just before the President's State of the Union address — to alert the media and the nation that Black America's views needed a voice in their coverage of the President's message, too. We introduced it at a news conference either at the National Press Club in Washington, or the Urban League headquarters in New York that usually included a panel discussion by several of the essays' authors.

The 322-page January 1982 volume contained essays exploring the economic status of Blacks, the prospects for advancing Black political power, the role of religion among Black Americans, the plight of Black teenagers, the endangered status of K-12 schools, and the effect of media on Americans' perceptions of race. Also, as with each volume, the offerings included a separate detailed section summarizing the conclusions and recommendations of each essay and another substantial section providing a chronology of some of the previous year's developments and events important to Black Americans.

That January 18, my remarks summarizing its findings to the media at the National Press Club were blunt. "For Black America, 1981 was a year of economic depression, savage cuts in survival programs for the poor, and the betrayal of basic civil rights protections. This time around, the social safety net is in shreds," I said. "Cuts in federal social programs did not just trim the fat; they slashed down to the bone. And those cuts were concentrated in programs in which blacks were a third to a half of all beneficiaries. ... The rich got tax cuts, the Pentagon got a blank check, but poor people lost jobs, training opportunities, food assistance, health care, and much else." **(F.4)**

That bill of indictment was part of the message we declared in literally hundreds of the To Be Equal Columns during Reagan's tenure, in dozens of speeches, and in expansive presentations such as my testimony before the Congressional Joint Economic Committee during the four days of hearings it held on the impact of the Reagan domestic program that July. But along with descriptions of the deprivation and despair poor black Americans and other Americans were enduring, I also always suggested what could be done to reverse the downward momentum. Our descriptions of what was wrong in society were always accompanied by specific proposals to improve conditions.

The whirlwind I faced atop the Urban League wasn't just blowing outside my doors. It was inside, too. I was taking office during the most severe recession since the Great Depression itself, and it had quickly produced a noticeable decline in large and small contributions to the League's coffers. But the withdrawal of Federal support was much worse. In 1981, the Reagan Administration cut its funding for programs sponsored directly by the Urban League headquarters from $29 million to $12 million. And it cut total support to all 118 of our affiliates from $100 million to $54 million.

I must say I wasn't that surprised by the magnitude of the hit. The signs had been clear that a Reagan victory in 1980 meant those organizations that worked with the poor were going to suffer. So we felt within our own walls the pain the Administration imposed on those individuals in the society who most needed help. But I was determined to not let the actions and the voice of the National Urban League be stymied by the loss of funds we were enduring.

With Mildred Love's insight in mind, the senior staff and I sat about using the reality of our shrunken resources to determine what we could keep doing and how we could, even with less money, improve the quality of the programs we offered. And I would soon use her insight multiple times in columns and speeches throughout the years, including in a speech in early March at the Biennial United Way Staff Conference.

"If there is any single message that applies to the private sector, the Urban League, and the United Way," I told my audience, "it is that we all must reassess our priorities. I believe the private sector, for example, must concentrate its philanthropic resources on those areas that serve the disadvantaged who are most in need. That may be less visible and bring less immediate prestige than other forms of activity, but it is the way to make the most positive impact on our society. Our advocacy role must shift slightly toward moving the government to get back into the ball game of service. We will not stand by and watch government—at any level—abdicate its responsibilities."

"At the same time," I continued, "we of the Urban League must also do more for more people ....[despite our] fewer resources. While every Urban League affiliate will have to reassess its local conditions, capabilities, and constituent needs to determine its own proper mix of advocacy and services, we at [national headquarters] are placing a strengthened emphasis on services. Services were always an integral part of the Urban League structure, but today they must take precedence. The needs are simply too great, the misery too deep, for us to do otherwise."

For my part, I knew that if we were to keep our doors open to offer those services, I'd better raise a lot of money both for operating funds and an endowment to prepare for what looked like lean years ahead. My first call on the fund-raising trail had been to Franklin Thomas, the president of the Ford Foundation, to ask if I could meet with him. During the 1970s, when McGeorge Bundy, whose glittering achievements included service to Presidents Kennedy and Johnson as their national security advisor, was Ford's president, the foundation had given the League $1.5 million every two years; so, I figured that was as good a place to start building the League's war chest. Thomas, New York City-born and raised and a graduate of Columbia University's college and law school was one of those Black Americans who were then breaking through some of society's highest barriers. In 1979, he succeeded Bundy as the foundation's leader—the first African American to head a major American philanthropy. He and Vernon were fast friends. Frank and I respected each other, but we were not fast friends.

He readily said yes to my request, and a few days later, I was telling him, "Frank, I've come because I want you to tell me what you think about the National Urban League, not what you thought of Vernon, but the National Urban League."

He got right to the point. "John, I'm glad you called. If you hadn't called me, I was going to call you because I do want to talk with you. We have decided that we're no longer going to fund the National Urban League the way we've done in the past few years. We've decided that we will fund proposals that you submit — if we like them — and that will

198

be the basis of our relationship with the National Urban League in the future."

I immediately thought: So, I've lost $1.5 million. I knew it wasn't personal nor a matter of his not respecting the League's work. The economic downturns of the mid-1970s, loose controls on its own program spending, and an overstaffed bureaucracy had cut the foundation's endowment alarmingly from $4.3 billion to $1.7 billion during Bundy's tenure. Changing its relationship with the League was part of the wholesale restructuring he was undertaking that would secure the foundation's future. I knew I had to pivot with him.

"Okay, here's my request: Give me $5 million, and I won't come back to ask you for any money again."

Frank said, "Let me think about that."

After several days of deliberation, he told me, "Tell you what, we won't give you $5 million. We'll give you $4.5 million."

That was enough for me. I said, "Okay, I'll take your $4.5 million and go raise money off of that."

And Frank did one other thing for me. He called the McArthur Foundation and set for me a date to meet with its president. I flew to Chicago and met with him, sharing with him my intent to attack the high incidence of pregnancy among Black teenagers, the plight of Black single female-headed households, crime in the Back community, and the political empowerment of Black citizens.

The MacArthur Foundation gave me $1 million.

Now, I had $5.5 million.

Now, it was time to approach Xerox—the giant chaired by my National Urban League board member, David Kearns. "David," I said to him, "you have to give me $1 million."

Clearly surprised, he said to me, "John, our foundation only gave out $16 million to the whole country last year!" But I countered with, "David, I need you to give me $1 million because I want you to get me an appointment with IBM so that I can ask them for $5 million. When I talk to them, they'll ask me what did you do. So, I need you to give me $1 million."

He said, "Okay, we'll get you a million." And he arranged a meeting with IBM for me

I went to IBM, then at its height as a colossus of American corporations. John Opel was its chief executive officer. He and I had become friends over the years after he appointed me to the company's social responsibility committee. So, when I said to him, "John, I want IBM to give the Urban League $5 million," he started laughing.

"Why, that's the best joke I've heard in years," he said when he finally stopped. He reminded me he was soon to be replaced as CEO—he would become Chairman in another year or two before retiring in 1986. "John, you know it doesn't take long in terms of having influence to go from Who's Who' to Who's He?" He was still joking about the influence he could levy. But his real point was that, given the forthcoming change in his circumstances, it would be improper for him to try to swing that amount of money the Urban League's way. That was for his successor in the CEO's chair to decide.

Then he said, "But let me introduce you to the guy who's replacing me. He sent for John Akers. When Akers joined us, Opel said to me, "Tell John what you asked me." So, having listed the funds I had already collected, I asked Akers for $5 million, and he looked at Opel as if to say, *Where'd you find this guy?* But, as I suspected, he asked, "What did Xerox give you?" and when I responded, "$1 million dollars," John Akers responded, "We'll do our fair share." And IBM gave the Urban League $1 million.

So, now I had $1 million from Xerox, $1 million from IBM, on top of the $4.5 million from Ford. I headed to Coca-Cola to ask them for $1 million. They gave me $1 million. And the Rockefeller Foundation also gave the League $1 million. Thanks to Peter Goldmark, with whom I had served on the LISC (Local Initiative Support Corporation) board, a national housing development program funded by the Ford Foundation. By June, I had raised $8.5 million. But I knew I would need to do more.

One source leading to "more" came via our biannual reception we simply called "The Report Meeting." It was a longstanding tradition of the League to invite all its major funders to an evening reception to hear the League's president discuss our stewardship of the funds and the progress of the programs their funds supported. Corporate suite officers, including those from companies who had given us money, were welcome to attend.

As we were wrapping up the gathering, Hamish Maxwell, the chairman and chief executive of Philip Morris, walked up to me and said, "John, that was impressive. If there's anything that we at Philip Morris can do for you, let me know." After the meeting ended, I couldn't get back to my office fast enough. I drafted a letter to Hamish that I sent directly to Stan Scott, who, as the company's vice president for corporate affairs, was one of several Blacks who held senior positions there and had attended the meeting with Maxwell. Then I telephoned him to say, "Stan, I've addressed this letter to Hamish Maxwell, but I'm sending it to you because I want you to put it in his hands. I don't want anyone else interceding in this. I don't need you to represent me, speak for me, or advocate for me. I just need you to take the letter and put it in Maxwell's hands. That's all I'm asking you to do."

In those years, Philip Morris's institutional interest in art led to their inviting the Whitney Museum of Art, with whom they had a long relationship, to establish an exhibition gallery in the public access lobby of the company's new Park Avenue headquarters across from Grand Central Terminal in midtown Manhattan. I was often invited to their exhibits, so it wasn't unusual I was at the museum's opening in April 1983. I walked in, greeting several acquaintances and friends, and began viewing the beautiful works of art on display.

A moment later, as I was continuing my tour through the exhibit space, one of the company's vice chairmen, a big supporter of the United Negro College Fund, walked over to me and said, quietly but angrily, "You son of a bitch!"

Stunned, I asked, "What?"

"You son of a bitch!" he said again.

"What are you talking about?

"You know what you did! You know what you did! He repeated through clenched teeth as he walked away. I didn't know what the hell he was talking about. Then Margaret Young, Whitney's widow and a member of the Philip Morris board, walked over and quietly said, "You've got your million dollars." **(F. 5)**

I continued building my war chest. The total was up to $9.5 million, but I knew I couldn't afford to rest.

Later that spring, I got a call from Dr. Evelyn Moore, executive director of the National Black Child Development Institute, a prominent New York-based children's agency, who asked if I'd be interested in having lunch with a friend who was a senior official at the United Parcel Service (UPS). I immediately said I'd be happy to and to tell him he didn't need to go through her: he could call me directly. That's how I first met Art McEwen, a senior executive with UPS. UPS was a one-of-a-kind company in that it insisted that its senior officers spend time working in the communities the company served, particularly those at the lower end of the income ladder. Art had been working with Evelyn, and she was thoughtful enough to suggest he talk with us.

When we met for lunch, as soon as the niceties were out of the way and we had ordered, Art handed me a check for $35,000. At his request, we soon met again, and on that occasion, he had a much bigger donation in mind: he said UPS wanted to be the first company to give the Urban League $1 million unsolicited.

We—the National Board and I—felt that a special act of support on their part deserved a special act of gratitude on our part: UPS was invited to Board membership, and Art recommended Calvin Tyler for membership. Cal Tyler, who would ultimately become the company's Senior Vice President for U.S. Operations, proved a valued trustee. He stopped me before a board meeting one morning and asked if he could see me privately for a minute. He told me the UPS

Foundation had just met and, upon his recommendation, had made a major decision. UPS had been paying their contribution in installments of $250,000. But, now, as they approached the time for their last payment, Cal explained, "Our foundation met yesterday, and we've decided that we want to give you another million dollars."

Again, UPS had done this unsolicited. Cal not only made his mark on UPS and the National Urban League, but in retirement he and his wife continued their philanthropy ways through the Calvin and Tina Tyler Foundation, including contributing $20 million to his alma mater, Morgan State University.

The only company that did not positively respond to my funding proposals was Avon Products, Inc., the world's biggest beauty products company—and its new chairman was even on the Urban League board! His predecessor at Avon, David W. Mitchell, had been on the board, too, and he had always been very supportive. He hadn't served long, however, because he came onto the board near the end of his tenure at Avon. His successor, whom we named to the board as a matter of course, wasn't supportive, and he was arrogant, too—the kind of guy who couldn't understand why he got booed by Blacks when he defended doing business in South Africa.

So, when I requested $1 million from Avon and didn't hear back, I wasn't particularly surprised. When the Chairman of the Avons Contribution Committee and I met, he asked me to explain what we were doing to justify Avon's giving us $1 million. I had staff come in to talk about what we were doing and our future plans—the full presentation. And when they finished, he said to me that it sounded like we wanted to do research and planning, and that no one would fund it.

I said, "Wait a minute. When you bring your perfume to the market, and you put it in those bottles, the cost that you charge is not solely for the liquid in the bottle. The cost also includes the cost of all that research that got the liquid in the bottle, right?"

He hurriedly replied, "I don't want you to think I'm opposed to what you're proposing. As chairman of the group, I won't have anything to do with the decision. I'll let them decide."

I matter-of-factly said to him, "Don't piss on my boots and try to tell me it's raining. I know that if you don't support it, they're not going to support it."

He responded, "I'll let you come and make the presentation directly to our management committee." I did that, and I felt and I know I did a very good job, and then I left.

The Avon management committee invited Ernesta Procope, their African American board member, to sit in on the presentation. When I got back to the office, I received a call from Phil Davis, an Avon senior officer. He told me, "Jake, you blew them away. The [chief financial officer] said, "Not only should we give them a million dollars, I know exactly where to take it from."

But, still, I heard nothing from Avon for some time. One day, I bumped into Ernesta Procope, and she asked, "Did you ever get your money?" When I told her we hadn't, she said she'd check on it. In short order, I got a letter from the chairman declining our proposal, and soon after that, he resigned from our board.

That was the only negative response to my fund-raising appeals. Our success proved that the League's long record of contributing to the social welfare of Blacks and the disadvantaged, and its longstanding direct ties to the national and local business communities counted for a great deal. There were many business leaders who, as individuals and as heads of companies, had been meaningfully involved with the League. Those connections also included many of our headquarters and affiliate staff who directly oversaw our programs and had direct contact with their counterparts employed by our corporate and foundation funders. That continuing close contact underscored that the foundations and corporations understood that in a time of outright hostility and heightened indifference to civil rights and social justice progress, they had a heightened duty, as John Akers of IBM had put it, to "do our fair share."

Chapter 9 – It Wasn't Just
About the Benjamins

The need to get the League's financial house in order involved not only serious fundraising but also plugging holes in our internal revenue stream — namely, insisting that all our 118 affiliates pay their annual membership fees. Only three had not, but that group included the Chicago Urban League, long one of the most powerful. In fact, Chicago had not paid its dues for years and years. Such was its importance to the League that both of my immediate predecessors, Whitney and Vernon, had not challenged its delinquency.

But this was a situation I couldn't let continue because, to slightly alter the fashionable saying, it wasn't just about the Benjamins. Even at full strength, the affiliate dues couldn't begin to compensate for the $15-million loss in federal funds we'd sustain from the Reagan Administration during the decade. However the difficulties those losses were causing affiliates did heighten their dissatisfaction about the dues-payment issue. I would later be challenged at one meeting with the CEOs and Board Chairs with the question: *What do I get for my dues?* In other words, the implication was that affiliates were paying a lot of money in dues to headquarters but getting little in return.

What do I get for my dues?

I didn't hesitate. *The right to* belong, I told him. The right to belong to the National Urban League and adopt the label that gave him the ability to raise funds to carry out his activities. It was the Urban League's banner that gave him the credibility and license to help his constituency and community. And it was the Urban League's history that gave his affiliate its recognition and standing in his community.

Nonetheless, I knew it was important for the sense of fairness and unity within the organization to shrink the tension between the affiliates' leaders and national headquarters over the issue. That it had existed was understandable, for although affiliate CEOs reported to the national CEO and the National Board, they had a great deal of leeway in how they managed their affiliates and how they operated in their communities. That was a signal characteristic of the League, an organization dedicated to tailoring the services it provided to local needs and whose affiliates had, in many instances, once been free-standing local community organizations.

The national office did funnel each affiliate a portion of the monies it raised from the private-sector and secured from the federal government. However, each one had to develop the programs for its community and gain the bulk of its operating funds from local businesses, philanthropic organizations, and local and state governments. Those two requirements of the job alone demanded that the men and women who led the affiliates — many of them with graduate degrees in social work and deep experience in community organizing — be independent-minded and resourceful: able, indeed, determined to stand on their own and forcefully advocate for their community's needs. That, in turn, meant they could be expected to resist any perceived infringement from headquarters on what they felt were their prerogatives. Having led two affiliates myself, I knew that feeling well.

The Urban League's affiliate structure was its fundamental strength. To the outside world, it bespoke the organization's united front on issues, even as its affiliates' programs addressed the varied needs of local communities. And yet, I felt that, given the severe difficulties of the 1970s and 1980s and the hostile national administration we were facing, national headquarters and the affiliates needed to act with a greater sense of unity. That had been one purpose of my December 1981 speech to the Greenville League: to suggest a specific set of highly visible national issues all affiliates could focus on in their local communities. Today, such a strategy might be called *solidifying the brand*. Then, amid the attacks from the Reagan Administration and even some liberals that the traditional Black civil rights organizations had ossified and lost a sense of purpose, I wanted to show them all what the Urban League stood for and what it was doing.

I also knew that the dues-payment issue was an internal test of my own authority as President and CEO. Yes, I had been an affiliate CEO myself — and before that, in my seventeen-year career, I had led a program to train community organizers, been a branch office Director, and an acting affiliate Director. That meant in terms of League service I had much in common with what the CEOs were experiencing. That's why more than a few of them clearly felt I would, or should, favor what the CEOs wanted. But unlike any of them or anyone else, I had also been the National Urban League's first Executive Vice President and Chief Operating Officer. My explicit duty in that post was not to favor one bloc or another of the League but to act in the best interests of the whole. That's the imperative I would carry forward to the top job.

So, I anticipated my determination to fully enforce the dues-paying rule would provoke resistance — and that it wasn't dissimilar to what happens in many corporate structures following a change of command. **(F. 1)** That my relationship with at least some of the affiliate CEOs would necessarily become less friendly wasn't going to deter me from pursuing the point I had to make: The League had one set of rules regarding its affiliate structure, and all the affiliates had to abide by them.

That included Chicago, which had become an affiliate in 1919 as that city was being inundated with Black migrants from the South and ever since had been led by a series of powerful chieftains. In fact, I had called on its CEO, James Compton, for help when Vernon had been shot in nearby Fort Wayne, Indiana, not only because of his proximity but because he had superb organizational skills and broad contacts among the area's media. Now, he and I were on opposite sides of an important issue.

Because that issue involved a fundamental violation of the League's bylaws, I had our national Board Chairman, Coy Eklund, Chairman and Chief Executive Officer of Equitable Life Assurance Company, first, write the Chicago affiliate's board chairman and *request* that it pay its dues for the year. We were sure that Jim Compton was immediately given the authority to respond. But there was no response— for months. Then, Coy and I sent a letter to the affiliate under both our signatures asking them to pay their dues— with a warning that non-payment would lead to the Chicago Urban League's disaffiliation.

That sent shock waves through the League. No affiliate had ever even been threatened with that ultimate penalty —

and virtually all the affiliates' CEOs, including those who were paying their dues, vigorously objected. *They were mad at me!* I understood; it was a matter of affiliate CEO solidarity. But when an effort at negotiating our way out of the stalemate failed, I kept my word: I disaffiliated Chicago and the Miami and New Brunswick, New Jersey affiliates, who were also on the delinquent list. I had made my point. The New Brunswick affiliate, which had been struggling to build a role for itself there, collapsed. On the other hand, we and the Chicago and Miami leadership soon agreed on repayment plans for the past dues, and they rejoined the League in good standing.

Chapter 10 – Canaries in the Mine:

Black America and the

Scourge of Unemployment

The imperative I felt to start building a war chest as soon as I took office reflected the grim economic and political realities of the moment for Black America and the larger society, too. The severity of the two-part recession of 1980-1983 **(F. 1),** due in large measure to the tight-money policies of Federal Reserve Board chairman Paul A. Volcker instituted to combat rising inflation, had pushed the overall unemployment rate in December 1981 to 8.6 percent—a full three percentage points higher than it had been just seven months earlier.

Six months later, the overall unemployment rate hit 9.5 percent—in percentage terms, its highest level since the Great Depression. (It would break that record in January 1983, reaching 10.8 percent, a figure that would hold even through the Great Recession of 2008-2009.) More than 10 million Americans were out of work. Those numbers, combined with the public's backlash to the Administration's draconian budget cuts affecting poor people, served to drive Reagan's poll numbers down from the 60s and 50s throughout 1981 into the 40s in 1982 and prompt predictions of significant GOP losses in the November midterm elections.

The predictions proved true. But those political results likely brought no comfort at all to the jobless, and especially to the African-American jobless, for the latter's predicament—always nearly twice as severe as that of Whites in the best of times— was even more dire than the official Bureau of Labor Statistics indicated.

That's because the official government figures were distorted by the fact that the agency never included in its calculations those individuals who had given up looking for work and those who were working part-time or held temporary jobs only because they couldn't find full-time work. No presidential administration—nor Congress, nor politicians in general—wanted the political pressure a true accounting of joblessness would bring. So, the official rates were always significantly lower than the reality.

Indeed, it was apparent by the late 1970s that the reality for Black America was far from the comforting view some scholars put forth that a substantial increase in the number of Blacks achieving middle-class incomes since the 1960s meant there had been an equally substantial decline in discrimination and racism. In fact, while the mid-1970s spike in joblessness for Whites quickly abated (**F.2**), the scourge of unemployment among blacks was escalating with terrifying speed. (**F. 3**) Data gathered by the League's research department, led by the estimable Bob Hill (**F. 4**), produced the first of the National Urban League's *Hidden Unemployment Index.* It pegged the true unemployment situation in the year's first quarter at a total of 19.3 million jobless, a rate of 16.8 percent. That included non-white unemployment at a record level of 4.5 million, which pushed that group rate from 26.2 percent in the last quarter of 1981 to 29.1 percent. The comparable figures for whites were 12.8 percent and 14.9 percent, respectively. Even worse, the figures for non-white teenagers were at astronomical levels:

927,000 non-white teens were jobless — a rate of 65.6 percent — compared to 365,000 White youth. **(F. 5)**

But even the government's official data from 1979 to late 1983 made clear that what were recessions for Whites had trapped Black Americans in a full-blown *Depression* — one that would last for virtually the entire twelve years I was to lead the Urban League.

In June 1979, the official Black unemployment rate had been 8.7 percent. By December 1981, as I was speaking to the Greenville, South Carolina Urban League during the second, more severe recession, the overall official Black unemployment rate had careened to 17.2 percent. The next month, as I formally took office as President and CEO, it was 17.3 percent, on the way to a January 1983 peak for the decade of the 1980s of 21.2 percent. Over the next twenty-two months, it declined in a jagged fashion from just above 19 percent to 15.2 percent.

In June 1979, the official unemployment rate for Black males was also 8.7 percent. By December 1981, it had nearly doubled to 16.1 percent, on the way to a peak of 20.4 percent in January 1983. **(F. 6)** For Black women, the June 1979 official unemployment rate was 11.2 percent. In December 1981 it was 14.2 percent on the way to its peak of 18.2 percent in January 1983. It would continue rising and falling between 18 percent and 12.3 percent for most of the next two years. **(F. 7)** Black workers and would-be workers were to endure that kind of jaggedly moving, double-digit unemployment predicament the entire decade (and for more than half of the 1990s). Not until June 1990 would the official monthly Black unemployment rate be pegged even as low as 10.5 percent. **(F. 8)**

It helped neither Black nor White jobless that Reagan's "voodoo economics" scheme of combining sharp tax cuts for the wealthy with outsized increases in military spending immediately added more instability to the mix. However, two particular developments in American society helped obscure the true extent of economic devastation sweeping over a broad segment of Black Americans. One was, as Bob Hill put it in his tough-minded monograph "The Illusion of Black Progress," the conventional wisdom asserted by conservatives and numerous White centrists and liberals that racial discrimination was a less and less significant cause of the problems Blacks faced. The "behavior" of the Black "underclass" was. (F. 9)

The seriousness of the country's and Black America's economic crisis was exemplified by the swiftness with which job losses raced through what had been a bedrock jobs sector for American men as a whole and particularly for Black men: manufacturing. Black male workers were disproportionately concentrated in factory work because its basic-level jobs required neither a high school diploma nor any appreciable skills that couldn't be learned on the job, just brute strength. From the late 1940s to the 1960s, however, a smaller cohort of Black workers had made significant gains in the skilled-work sectors of manufacturing and other industries, helping to forge an important layer of blue-collar and lower-middle-class stability in many Black communities. Now, all those jobs were at risk. **(F.10)**

"It took years before blacks gained a foothold in prime industrial jobs," I wrote in the fourth To Be Equal column under my byline on 27 January, which announced the publication of the 1982 volume of *The State of Black*

America "and now, instead of solidifying those gains, Black workers are getting layoff notices."

The manufacturing industry had reached its all-time employment peak of just over 21 million in June 1979. Then, as the recession took hold in the next twelve months, "manufacturing firms lost 1.4 million jobs. Only 40 percent of those jobs had been recovered when the recession of 1981-82 began. This recession, much more severe than the first, led manufacturers to eliminate 2.3 million jobs, or 10 percent of the industry's work force." **(F. 11)** In less than four years, the manufacturing industry lost 3.7 million jobs. The twenty-month-long economic recovery that began in late 1983 added 1.5 million jobs to its diminished rolls, but the industry jobs total would never again reach the previous high. **(F. 12)**

Another development that undermined the appeals of the Urban League and others for concerted steps to be taken on the social welfare front was the popularity of Reagan's oft-repeated declaration as candidate and president that "government" was "the problem" because "Washington" was stymieing business profitability and taxing "hard-working" Americans too much.

Buried within that claim was, to many Whites, the appeal of a particular *nostalgia*: the part-real, part-mythical remembrance of and longing for the decade of the 1950s, when, so the myth claimed, America's global political, economic, and military dominance was supreme. The even more important facet of that nostalgic appeal was the posing of the 1950s as a decade of *domestic tranquility* — in contrast to the extraordinary turbulence of the 1960s and 1970s and the greater reach of news media in reporting about

216

it. That misremembered domestic tranquility depended heavily on erasing from view such matters as the polio epidemic, the labor strife, McCarthyism's witch-hunting for suspected communists, the widespread fear among Americans of nuclear war with the Soviet Union, which was intensified by its launch in 1957 of its *Sputnik* satellite, and the momentous developments on the civil rights front: the 1954 *Brown v. Board of Education ruling,* the 1955 Montgomery Bus Boycott and the 1957 Little Rock (Arkansas) school desegregation crisis.

This "Fifties Nostalgia" dynamic wasn't a Reagan creation. It had been welling up in American society since the early 1970s. **(F. 13)** But no political figure used the desire of a large part of White America to believe the myth so effectively. Reagan's career as a Hollywood actor in the 1940s and his ubiquitous presence as a pitchman for General Electric in the 1950s — along with his having been a two-term Governor of California in the 1960s and 1970s (itself the state that more than any other represented the place where the Fifties Nostalgia ideal was perfectly realized) — made him the perfect *salesman* to lead the political Fifties Nostalgia movement. **(F. 14)** In the psychological space of "White" Fifties Nostalgia, social problems virtually didn't exist, and politics in general, and especially the Federal government in Washington, were very far away.

Reagan's proposed solution to the Washington problem was to radically cut taxes, especially for wealthy individuals and businesses, so that wealthy individuals would have more money to spend and save as they chose — including investing in goods-producing businesses — and businesses would have more money to expand their operations. That would result, Reagan declared, in America's economy growing significantly — producing more, not less, tax revenue for the federal government and wiping out the national deficit along the way. This was trickle-down economics theory dressed up with a new 1970s name—*supply-side economics*—and, in turn, quickly came to be called "Reaganomics."

But, in reality, Reaganomics was a Potemkin Village. **(F. 15)** It didn't do what they said it would. Instead of increasing tax revenues and spurring economic growth, Reagan's tax cuts combined with his bloated military budgets to immediately deplete the national treasury and balloon the national deficit. When Reagan took office, the deficit stood at $78.9 billion. By the mid-1980s, it had soared to more than $175 billion before the Administration, pressured by Congress and the financial markets, took concerted steps that cut it to $152.6 billion at the end of Reagan's second term. **(F. 16)** The Gross National Debt also tripled on Reagan's watch, from $995 billion to $2.9 trillion. **(F. 17)**

Reagan's faith in supply-side economics completely ignored two things. One was the likelihood that wealthy individuals would not invest their money in goods-producing companies (thus producing an expanding labor force) but largely in various kinds of financial instruments to gain more money for their own bank accounts. The second was the likelihood that corporations would use the monies they wouldn't have to pay in taxes in two ways: to invest in technological innovations that resulted in their needing *fewer* workers and to increase the dividends they could pay to their shareholders.

Moreover, it rapidly became obvious that one purpose of Reaganomics was to use the tax cuts' hit on federal revenues and the bloated defense spending to justify draconian cuts in government aid programs for the poor and disadvantaged. Even before Reagan adopted the idea in the mid-1970s, many conservatives, as well as liberals, saw the lunacy of supply-side economics. The skewering description George H.W. Bush delivered as he jousted for the Republican nomination during the 1980 presidential primaries — he called it "voodoo economics" — instantly became a classic, widely applied put-down in political debate. The more embarrassing "reveal" of Reaganomics came less than a year into Reagan's first term — in an extraordinary 73-page article in the December 1981 *Atlantic Magazine*. Veteran journalist Bill Greider, a longtime Washington insider, had persuaded one of the President's chief economic advisers, David Stockman, Director of the Office of Management and Budget, to tell the truth about how the Administration's budget was crafted.

Reagan had charged the youthful Stockman, an economics whiz-kid, and former Republican Congressman, with finding a plausible way to balance the budget by 1984 while drastically cutting taxes and spending on social programs, on the one hand, and, on the other, sharply increasing military spending. But Stockman candidly admitted to Greider that trying to implement a "supply-side" budget had caused considerable doubt and confusion among senior Administration officials. The signature line of the piece was: "None of us really understands what's going on with all these numbers." **(F. 18)**

The article immediately caused a sensation, especially because the recessionary downturn was exacerbating Reaganomics' effects. Unemployment was rising sharply, and tax revenues had dropped precipitously. Under pressure from Congress and the public (via Reagan's slipping poll numbers), the administration in early 1982 began grudgingly scaling back the extent of both the tax cuts and the spending cuts in social programs it wanted to make. Those measures were hardly sufficient to ease the damage already done to the economy as a whole and to poor people who needed the government's help the most. The words I used to describe the Administration's urban policy to the Congressional Joint Economic Committee that July fit its efforts to fix the mess Reaganomics had made: "a half dose of a previously impotent prescription." **(F. 19)**

But the hollowness of Reaganomics wasn't "new news" to any observer with common sense. Like Bush, many traditional conservative and liberal analysts had seen through the supply-side fantasy from the beginning. Hobart Rowen, the economic affairs columnist of *The Washington Post,* later described it as a "creation of [conservative] journalists and polemicists that ... had no scientific basis, was riddled with internal contradictions and was rejected as wishful thinking by the vast majority of professional economists. The idea that you could actually increase tax revenues by cutting income tax rates ... no serious economist thought it would happen. Yet this notion was one of the cornerstones of the 1981 tax cuts." **(F. 20)**

I did note that in January, in my fourth *To Be Equal* column, devoted largely to announcing the publication of our *The State of Black America* 1982 edition, that already, "few people believe [the Administration's] current economic policies will work, including the framers of those policies, if the famous Stockman article in the Atlantic Magazine is any guide." And that August in my Keynote Address to the Urban League Conference in Los Angeles — by which time the Administration seemed to have consigned the very phrase "supply-side economics" to political oblivion — I said there was "no way in the world that tight money, tax cuts for the affluent, program cuts for the poor and a renewed arms race [could] lead to prosperity ... [instead] the supply-side gospel that promised a born-again economy ... gave [Black Americans] another Depression."

In short, Reaganomics was making an already bad situation worse. Even though the official figures downplayed the true extent of the crises of poverty and unemployment, that data of double-digit levels of joblessness of Black adult men and women during the 1980s and early 1990s was sufficient to depict a frightening reality: That was that Black America was enduring a vicious dynamic of destabilization because the numerous, tangled forces of the past and *that moment* were making large numbers of Black workers—especially males—*disposable.* **(F. 21)**

For all of the months from September 1974 to November 1994, the Black unemployment rate was greater than 10 percent — and for many of those months, it was greater than 12.5 percent. This meant that after the OPEC-driven oil-shocks recession of the early 1970s, a significant number of poor and low-wage Black workers could expect to be jobless off and on for years to come. Or to fall into the ranks of the long-term jobless or to just stop looking for work altogether as the jobs they were qualified for grew fewer and fewer.

"Pick an industry on the decline," I said in a May 1983 speech to the National Association of Market Developers. "Pick an industry shattered by imports. Pick an industry where jobs are shrinking, and plants are closing. That's where you'll find us. Black workers are concentrated in yesterday's jobs industries, not tomorrow's."

"It is no longer enough to have a strong back and a willing spirit, I continued. "Today's jobs demand skills and knowledge our young people don't get from inferior schools, decaying cities, and insensitive government. Most of today's minority unemployed need to be retrained for growth jobs in growth industries ... this is the time to begin to formulate policies that deal with the implications of the high-tech future we're moving into."

One solution, of course, was to improve the quality of educational and training opportunities for black youth and strengthen and expand retraining programs for adult workers to prepare them for the "high-tech future" — an idea we constantly pushed in various guises in my columns, in the pages of *The State of Black America*, and in speeches throughout my tenure.

For example, in my keynote address to the Urban League Conference that August — my first as President and CEO — we reiterated a proposal we had been making since I took office: for a Universal Employment and Training Program that would guarantee all who were jobless and seeking employment the skills training to find a job. It was, obviously, a response to the need for a large public works effort to rebuild the nation's infrastructure everyone agreed was crumbling.

This was a win-win for American society, I declared: More workers would mean higher productivity. More workers would mean a reduction in social problems. More workers would mean more individuals paying taxes and, thus, more revenue for federal, state, and local governments. All it required was leadership. "The last time we were in a Depression," I told the audience, "our leaders created jobs that produced buildings, bridges, and dams we still use. The last time we were in a Depression our leaders took kids off city streets and gave them jobs building playgrounds and preserving nature."

We put the cost of our proposal at $100 billion annually. "Our Government doesn't mind running up a half trillion dollar deficit to support a supply-side fantasy. It doesn't mind drilling loopholes in the tax code that give away a half trillion dollars over the next four years to the favored few. It doesn't mind spending over $1.5 trillion over the next four years on a bloated defense program." I cited those figures with a positive purpose in mind, I told my audience, declaring, via our new slogan, that any "country that can afford to waste such vast sums ought to be able to see that *Everybody Deserves A Chance To Make It On Their Own.* ... [That] means a chance to get the skills with which to compete. Making it on your own means being equipped to take advantage of opportunities. Making it on your own means overcoming barriers to success — barriers like poverty, barriers like the loss of hope, barriers like having two strikes against you before you start."

Unfortunately, the goal of the Reagan Administration was doing just the opposite — continually claiming such programs were either too costly or had already been tried during the Great Society era and had failed to achieve their goals. I added that all Americans, but especially Whites, needed to understand the purpose of the false implication that Blacks made up the bulk of those helped by these programs.

"There are more white people on welfare than black people," I noted. "There are more white people getting food stamps than black people, and more white people on Medicaid than black people, and more white people living in subsidized housing than black people, and more white people who are in job training programs than black people. The white community has .... never understood that while blacks occupy a disproportionate number of slots in all those programs, they were never most of the people receiving services from those programs. So black organizations like ours, in defending the needs of Black people, have also been defending the needs of poor white people. White people need to understand that if they want to protect their brothers and sisters, ... [they should] start protecting these programs." **(F. 22)**

One of the worst consequences of the unemployment-driven instability within Black America was its drag on small business development in local neighborhoods. Such businesses have always depended on residents to make up nearly all of their customers, and they, in turn, help residents economically by offering many goods, generally at lower prices and often by hiring neighborhood residents as employees.

Of course, what rightly drew the most attention was the profound disruption in Black family stability. Because the scourge of persistently high unemployment throughout these years was greater numerically among Black males than Black females (and all other groups), it had an exponentially more devastating impact on the civic health of small and large Black communities and Black America as a whole.

For one thing, it severely damaged the psychological well-being of many males who, because they either could not find steady work or any work at all, lost that sense of "social legitimacy" having a job establishes and maintains in terms of how individuals — and others — perceive their *place* in a community. That loss was especially burdensome because of the still-pervasive patriarchal nature of American society: It seemed to confirm that Black men were not reliable marriage partners or family providers. In addition, the absence of a steady source of income pushed many toward homelessness, illicit drug trafficking and usage, and other kinds of criminal activity — thus making them prey to the mass incarceration dynamic that swept the nation in the 1970s and 1980s. **(F. 23)** This further diminished any claim these men and young adults had to be considered viable members of their community.

A Bureau of Justice Statistics report, *Prisons and Prisoners*, released in early 1982, described state prison inmates as "predominantly poor young adult males with less than a high school education. Importantly, the report said that among inmates entering prison after 1977, twenty percent had no income in the twelve months before their arrest, and another twenty percent had earned less than $3,000." **(F. 24).** And, overwhelmingly, such males—even those who resisted their circumstances' "financial incentives" to commit crime and honestly eked out subsistence wages—would likely have seen their marriage possibilities virtually disappear. Pragmatically speaking, few women could afford, for their own sakes, to wed men with such uncertain prospects.

That July, in my testimony before the Congressional Joint Economic Committee, I tried to underscore the point that the different sources and impacts of the so-called "street crime" haunting Black neighborhoods demanded a multifaceted approach to reducing it. For example, in our declaring crime as one of our program priorities, we suggested implementing such crime-fighting techniques as helping block associations and community organizations run effective neighborhood watch programs. But we also made clear that justifiable efforts to reduce criminal activity in Black communities must never ignore that the disproportionate incidence of crime was a result of the lack of economic opportunity problem for young Black teens and adults. "Any Federal government policy designed to deal with crime," I said, "must focus on its underlying causes. Serious attempts to reduce crime must certainly focus on programs and policies to reduce high black unemployment and improve the quality of education in inner-city schools."

The mass-incarceration dynamic continued to have devastating consequences for ex-offenders and Black communities as a whole: It "warehoused" them during their prime working years. That produced an additional crushing problem. Because many ex-offenders couldn't find any but low-wage jobs, if that, and nearly all were permanently barred from voting, a felony conviction stripped what were to become millions of Black adults of the two foundations of American citizenship: the right to vote and the right to a decent job. It effectively made them permanent *political exiles* within their own country. This did profound continuing harm to the integrity and power of Black civic activism.

The most visible consequence of the persistently high unemployment rates among African Americans during these decades was the explosive growth in the number of single female-headed households —an increase that was accompanied by a similarly explosive growth in the number of Black families and children living in poverty.

At the time, the negative — and wrong — assumptions and assertions about why this was happening were voluminous, and, beginning with my speech before the Greenville Urban League, I devoted parts or all of at least a dozen speeches and *To Be Equal* columns, and a chunk of my Conference Keynote addresses to untangling the myths and describing the realities.

I returned again to these issues in an 8 September 1982 column, "The Rising Tide of Poverty," writing that there could be no doubt the increase in black poverty was directly tied to the persistence of high black unemployment. "Throughout the late sixties and early seventies [the poverty rate for Blacks] trended downward," I wrote. "By the time the 1974 recession hit, black poverty rates were down to 30 percent. Then there was a slow rise, followed by an accelerated push into poverty over the past three years."

Those were the years when the troubled economy forced spikes in layoffs that, in turn, forged a growing pool of jobless workers even before the recessions of the early

1980s. The official overall unemployment rate for Black Americans rose from 9.5 percent in January 1974 to 15.1 percent in January 1979. Three years later, as I wrote the column in January 1982, the official Black unemployment rate was 17.3 percent. The comparative figures for Whites were 4.6 percent, 5.1 percent, and 7.6 percent. **(F. 25)**

Disaggregated, the increase in joblessness for African-American men and women was breathtaking. The official unemployment rates for men were 6.3 percent in 1974, 9.6 percent in January 1979, and 16.6 percent in January 1982. The comparable figures for Black women were 8.3 percent, 11.4 percent, and 13.7 percent, respectively.

As the overall unemployment rate, and that of Blacks especially, rose sharply during the previous three years, more and more Americans became poor. In 1981, I noted in the column, "2.2 million people became poor ... This year, it's expected that four million more will ..." The poverty rate for Americans was then 14 percent. However, the percentage of Black Americans whose annual income was below the poverty line was 34.2 percent, and it was expected to increase sharply. Black single female-headed households comprised a disproportionate number of Americans below the poverty line, and the percentage of Black children living in poverty was even greater.

Typically, female-headed households bore much of the blame for black poverty because of their low incomes. But, as I wrote in my column, that claim "doesn't make sense." The reason: Black Americans endured discrimination in wages compared to their White counterparts up and down the job ladder. For example, I noted that "Black intact husband-wife families earn less than 80 percent of similar white families. And if being in a female-headed household makes you poor, it should make white female-headed households equally poor. But again, the black family headed by a woman earns only 62 percent of similar white families."

So, for Black single female-headed households, it wasn't their low incomes but the wage discrimination they faced that made them poor. That's not to say that equality in wages with their White counterparts would have solved all the problems of Black families headed by unmarried women. But it likely would have solved some of them. **(F. 26)**

I also noted in the column that, as with the official unemployment rate figures, the discussion about poverty in America was distorted by the fact that some critical information was left out of the official calculations. For starters, the government's poverty line was derived from a crude calculation in a research model made in the mid-1950s to determine the minimal amount of money for food an urban family of four needed to survive. Other calculations were then added to that figure to arrive at a total income that supposedly defined poverty.

That assessment, however, was only meant to be temporary, to provide just enough food for a family of four to survive, literally, just a few tough weeks. It was never meant to stand for what a family needed over a longer period. But that's what happened, producing a safety net for those who were poor that was full of holes. Two-fifths of poor people got no benefits at all, I wrote. "Of those that do, most get only one kind of benefit. So, a family may get Medicaid but not subsidized housing or food stamps. Millions fell through the cracks in the safety net even before [the Reagan] Administration's demolition job on it."

The inaccuracy of the measurements also enabled some opponents of anti-poverty programs to claim some hadn't worked and others were unnecessary. One of the more "tragic" results of this, I said, was that "the so-called 'poverty line' was itself a fiction that obscures the extent of the problem."

I constantly returned to the task of trying to clear away the cobwebs on the issue, as did many others, all to no avail until after the turn of the century. But because that "survival budget" assessment of what constituted a poverty line was so politically useful to presidential administrations and Congress alike, the inaccurate measure that obscured the true extent of poverty outlasted countless attempts to change it. Not until 2010 was that success finally achieved, thanks to the late Rebecca Blank, an economist then working at the Department of Commerce during the Obama Administration.

Blank, from her posts in academia as well as the government, had spent more than a decade trying to persuade Congress to adopt her formulations of how to accurately measure poverty. The breakthrough came when, rather than urging the elimination of the old measure, she urged the adoption of her measure as a "Supplemental Poverty Measure" alongside it. Some scholars on poverty hailed it as "the most important new development in poverty measurement in over 30 years." **(F. 27)**

But that corrective action was still far in the future in my first year in office. Then, I followed Vernon and Professor Robert B. Hill, the League's Research Director *, in a proposal to both work around that flaw and to counter the inflationary spiral's eroding the value of the meager federal subsidies the poor received: a national income maintenance system that would guarantee a minimum income floor beneath every family. It would be based on a refundable income tax credit the government would grant to everyone. Those above a set income line would have the grant taxed away from them on a sliding scale. So, the poor would keep all of the grants, moderate-income people would keep some of it, and the affluent would keep none of it.

This arrangement would lift people who were poor above the poverty line and help families with moderate incomes make ends meet since they could keep part of the Federal grant. It would encourage those with lower incomes to seek work since the grant would only be taxed away on a sliding scale. This was unlike the mechanics of the welfare system in which grants were cut by the amount a worker earned, producing an incentive to not work at all. In addition, we said our proposal would make the tax system fair by ridding it of loopholes and special interest favors, most of which had no rational basis for existing. Finally, we contended it would produce a significant boost to the economy because those with moderate incomes spend to increase their standard of living — which means more money for American businesses and more work for American factories. Depending on the dollar-level set for the basic grant and the tax rate, we put the tab for it at about $25 billion above the present tab for the welfare programs and food stamps. **(F. 28)**

We were hardly the first to argue for an income maintenance system and hardly the last to be unable to overcome the many interests that benefited from an unfair tax system and an unfair system of aiding those in poverty.

Of course, Black America's destabilization dynamic drew much racially-blinkered comment from those who preferred to blame it on a supposed "culture of poverty" that had overtaken Black America, even as numerous Black and White scholars correctly identified the transformation of work and the disappearance of some jobs in America for a particular cohort of workers as the root of the problem.

In fact, the high unemployment of Black males and their resulting decline in the labor force was a harbinger—*a canary-in-the-mine warning*—that the same forces were about to sweep across the lower-wage and blue-collar sectors of White male workers, pushing many of them further and further down the wage ladder, or into the volatile employment/unemployment dynamic, or out of the work force completely.

Those forces made layoffs not the result of an individual's job performance or a momentary downturn in the economy but a matter-of-fact necessity for a significant number of companies to be able to continue to do business. It was to mean that by the early 1990s, as another brief recession gripped the country, more and more workers who were not Black, including some in companies' middle and upper-middle bureaucratic layers, became *disposable*—just as many blue-collar and unskilled Black workers had begun in the 1970s. **(F. 29)**

By the mid-1990s, the phenomenon's visibility had prompted a flurry of news articles, books, and even a popular film, "Falling Down," about an ordinary, law-abiding White man who suddenly breaks down and goes on a violent, rage-filled tear because he feels he had been robbed of his stable place in society by forces beyond his control. Since then, and especially after the election of Trump in 2016, the belief among a significant number of White males that they've been pushed out of society has been seen as one cause of such male-driven social problems among the White working and middle classes as drug use, out-of-wedlock births, and poor performance among boys in elementary and secondary schools, declining college attendance and increasing unemployment. **(F. 30)**

Sound familiar? What's different is the race of the population under stress: With few exceptions, there's been no attempt to blame the problems besieging a sizable cohort of White males on a *culture of poverty among them.* Instead, much of the focus has rightly been on identifying the structural causes of the problems. In other words, there's been a greater willingness to question numerous economic arguments made to justify job layoffs; and many of the analyses have incisively explored the psychological damage to individuals and families periods of unemployment and especially extended unemployment can cause.

To be fair, much of the contemporary discussion also frankly acknowledges that the devastation that struck the Black working class sprang from many of the same large social and economic forces, not a "culture" of Blacks unwilling to meet the requirements of living in a modern society. But during my tenure at the top of the Urban League, that fiercely-held bigoted viewpoint was a standard part of the public discourse on Black poverty, one we had to spend a considerable part of our efforts rebutting.

As terrible as the effects of persistently high unemployment among Black adults were, that specter blighting the future of millions of Black youth seeking work was far worse. Indeed, the early 1990s recession, which pushed the official unemployment rate for Black adults to 14.1 percent in late 1992, continued to wreak havoc on the employment prospects of Black youth. While the rate of unemployment among jobless White youth declined by 10 percent that year, that of Black youth increased by more than 20 percent.

It was a mistake; I had written ten years earlier, in a June 1982 *To Be Equal* column, to dismiss as relatively unimportant the lack of summer jobs or after-school jobs for disadvantaged and minority youth. In addition to putting money in the pockets of those who badly needed it, jobs helped teens and young adults learn how to meet the *requirements of having a job.* It prepared them "to take their place in the economic mainstream. Study after study shows that young people who work while in school or during their summer vacations go on to better jobs and higher pay as adults. Short-changing those kids now means they'll spend years trying to play catch-up, deprived of the work discipline and skills they will need to succeed." **(F. 31)**

The Black youth unemployment crisis also sharply illuminated the breadth of the reach of the "destabilizing effect" of persistently high unemployment among Blacks. At a basic level, it prevented many youths from being able to gain an entry-level job at all while in their teens and early twenties — losing the chance to earn money legitimately and experience the discipline even a basic-level job imposes on an individual. In addition, getting a job as a teenager may give those who aren't particularly interested in school a reason to stay in school and get their diploma because they could see for themselves that a diploma is a ticket to higher pay in the labor market.

Further, given that during the 1980s, a fourth of Black workers were unemployed for some period during a year, it's very likely some significant number of jobless youth were in families where a parent or guardian was also jobless. A 1987 study by the Children's Defense Fund determined that while most young Black males in 1973 earned enough to keep a three-person family out of poverty, by 1987, less than half did. **(F.32)** That terrible family predicament undoubtedly contributed during the 1970s and 1980s to the concentration of joblessness and poverty in particular urban neighborhoods, turning some parts of them into "poverty traps from which people [found] it increasingly difficult to escape." **(F. 33)**

As poignantly, the persistently high youth unemployment rates devastated the marriage and family formation prospects for black young men and women during the 1970s and 1980s. According to the Children's Defense Fund document, young men aged 20 to 24 who earned enough to stay above the poverty line married at rates three to four times higher than those with below-poverty line earnings. Constricted opportunities for young men have cut their marriage rates in half over the past 15 years, significantly contributing to the alarming rise in single female-headed households. **(F. 34)**

One job fair for youth in Los Angeles in early June 1992 vividly illustrated one cost of the Reagan and Bush administration's refusal to properly fund job programs of all kinds for teenagers: their disregarding, in effect, the potential of millions of disadvantaged minorities and poor youth.

Officials from Disneyland had gone to the predominantly Black neighborhood of South-Central seeking applicants in the 17 to 22 age-range for summer jobs at the iconic amusement park. This was a little more than a month after parts of the neighborhood had been virtually destroyed by the violent uprising that occurred in the wake of an all-white jury acquitting four Los Angeles police officers of all charges in the videotaped beating of a Black man, Rodney King.

Disney officials, who had told leaders of local community groups that they were looking to fill 200 summer jobs, wondered what the response would be given that the jobs were available only for the summer, and Disneyland was thirty miles — an hour's commute each way — from South-Central.

But, according to an article in the *New York Times* of June 18, 1992, when Disney officials arrived at a local church to interview applicants, they found "more than 600 young men and women, many in coats and ties or dresses," standing in a line that stretched around the block: college students, hoping to gain some extra funds before heading back to college, and high school students and other youth hoping that a summer job could perhaps lead to permanent employment of one sort or another at the playland. One community leader said that if there'd been time to better publicize the job fair throughout the neighborhood, thousands would have shown up. "People," he said, "just want to work, period." The company's interviewers were "taken aback" at the turnout, the article stated. One Disney interviewer said, "They were wonderful kids, outstanding kids. We didn't know they were there." **(F. 35)**

In going to South-Central, the Walt Disney Company had discovered a critically important reality: that much of the fashionable talk about poor, jobless Black youth in disadvantaged neighborhoods lacking an understanding of how the world works and the ambition to participate in it was not true. So, what the Disney company had done in response was not charity. Rather, they were taking advantage of something crucial to any business: a potential employment pipeline. Disney had simply announced they were coming to look for employees. That was the exploratory *investment* they made in South-Central, and because they did, they discovered "wonderful kids, outstanding kids" they could hire for summer jobs — young people who were determined to make something of themselves and who just needed, as the Urban League's slogan declared: *a chance to make it on their own.*

Chapter 11 – Speaking Truth to Power

There were no words too strong to sound the alarm about Black America's crisis of unemployment or the Reagan Administration's opposition to doing what was necessary to alleviate it. I took advantage of every forum at my disposal to do just that. In the 17 February *To Be Equal* column, "More Budget Blues," on the Fiscal Year 1983 budget Reagan had just submitted to Congress, I warned that his proposals were exacerbating the impact of joblessness among African Americans and the poor. "Unemployment is pushing close to record post-war levels, and some predict it will get a lot worse before it gets better," I wrote. "So what does the administration propose. Another deep slash of $2.7 billion in job training programs. ... Two straight massive budget cuts and the effects of inflation have reduced federal job efforts to a token program at a time of recession and high unemployment. Instead of helping job-seekers find work, the federal-state employment service is slashed to ribbons. And if you want a new definition of meanness, [the proposed budget intends to] round off unemployment compensation checks to the next lower whole dollar — in effect stealing pennies from the jobless."

In April, at the National Conference on Social Welfare in Boston, I addressed how many of the jobless were omitted from the government's official unemployment statistics.

"Almost ten million people are officially counted as unemployed," I said. "Another six million are not counted as unemployed, but they are working part-time while trying to pay full-time bills. Millions more aren't counted as unemployed because they have given up. The jobs aren't there, and [the jobless] no longer look for work that doesn't exist."

"Many of you see the results in your agencies," I went on. "There are few experiences as damaging to self-esteem and to an individual's sense of worth as prolonged unemployment. Study after study demonstrates how even small increases in joblessness result in more crime, alcoholism, drug abuse, child abuse, divorce, bad health, and mental problems. We will be paying for this recession far into the future."

My criticisms of the Reagan Administration policies, with a few exceptions, were plentiful, continual, unstinting—and deserved.

But they weren't personal. If you're the head of the National Urban League, you don't criticize the nation's President merely for publicity's sake. You do it to alert the American public and its decision-makers to critical issues that must be addressed. I was doing my duty, acting as Urban League leaders have always acted: as an advocate for Black Americans as a whole and for the poor and disadvantaged generally, and offering our expertise to the larger society as consultants in identifying how it could achieve the maximum good for all Americans.

We had carried out that duty no matter which Party controlled the White House or the Houses of Congress. There had been no question about its nonpartisanship in the early and middle years of the twentieth century, even as it was clear in the mid- and late 1960s that the friendship between Whitney Young and Lyndon Baines Johnson was rooted in their personalities as well as their ideological commitment to using government to achieve social justice ends. Throughout Jimmy Carter's candidacy and the first months of his presidency, many people undoubtedly thought he and Vernon — both men Georgia-born and -raised who held each other in high regard — would have that kind of public relationship as well. Carter's acceptance of an invitation to speak at the League's annual conference in New York in July 1977 promised, seemingly, to be a friendship fest.

But Vernon made both the League's nonpartisanship and the primacy of its commitment to the poor and disadvantaged strikingly clear when, on the eve of the conference, he alerted the media that he would charge that the new Administration's first six months in office had been a sharp disappointment in "policies, programs, and people."

In those decades, the League's conferences (and those of the N.A.A.C.P.) always drew substantive media attention from the major outlets. But now the prospects of fireworks between the President and one of the Democratic Party's major voting blocs (**F. 1)** markedly swelled the number of journalists in attendance. The 16,000-plus attendees, Urban Leaguers, Urban League-connected individuals, and the public made it our largest crowd ever.

In his keynote address, Vernon did not mince words. "We have no full employment policy. We have no welfare policy. We have no national health policy. We have no urban revitalization policy. We have no aggressive affirmative action policy. We have no national solutions to the grinding problems of poverty and discrimination." He added that because "even an Administration sympathetic to our needs and in harmony with our aspirations needs sustained pressure," the League was meeting in Washington "to recall this Administration to what we feel is its true spirit, the spirit of social reform and racial equality." **(F. 2)**

The frosty relations between the two men, fully on display at the Conference, made national headlines.

President Carter, in his address to the conference the following morning made clear he strenuously objected to Vernon's characterization of his domestic program. He discussed several actions his Administration had taken which he said proved their commitment to live up to their campaign promises, and noted he had appointed more African-Americans to high-level positions in his Administration than any previous president. "We haven't done everything that we'd like to do," the President said firmly, "nor have we done everything that we're going to do. But I have no apologies." And in a humorous aside, he told the audience that his wife, Roslyn, reading Vernon's criticisms, had said, "Jimmy, Vernon doesn't think you're doing as well as I think you're doing.' **(F. 3)**

Carter's speech was well-received by the Urban League throng, an indication that his standing among the Black electorate, which had overwhelmingly supported his election, was still substantial. But, nonetheless, Vernon's criticism did inaugurate a round of fierce criticism of Carter among black politicians and national civic leaders — which itself indicated how much the economic headwinds against Black Americans were worsening in the late 1970s. **(F. 4)**

The friendship between Vernon Jordan and Jimmy and Roslyn Carter long outlasted that dispute because the friendship was personal, while Vernon's criticism of the President was *political*: a matter of Vernon's *service* to and *advocacy* for his constituency. In other words, he was doing his job as President and CEO of the National Urban League.

My following the time-honored standard of Urban League leadership — *nonpartisanship* and *service* and *advocacy* — in sharply criticizing Reagan Administration policies in the six weeks since my appointment had been announced produced the only very brief, one-on-one conversation I ever had with President Reagan. It came amidst the furious reaction to his support of tax-exemptions for discriminatory institutions in the Bob Jones University case and a week or so before the President gave his second State of The Union address.

Just days before I *was to lead* our news conference at the National Press Club in Washington introducing that year's *The State of Black America, m*y words, modeled on the volume's introduction, which I had penned, were not at all complimentary to the Administration. "At no point in recent memory," I wrote, "[has] the distance between the national government and black America been greater than it was in 1981, nor has the relationship between the two been more strained. Throughout black America in 1981, there was a broad feeling of isolation, of a turning back of the clock, of a retreat from civil rights policies and social service programs that were established only after years of struggle and were believed, at least by some, to be inviolate. .... It is difficult," I continued, "to believe that any Administration would deliberately set out to isolate itself from any sector of the American people, and yet this present Administration, both by what it has done and what it has not done, has succeeded to an alarming degree, in doing just that."

On the afternoon of the day we released *The State of Black America*, I received a call from Elizabeth Dole, then a special assistant on the White House staff, inviting me to stop by for a chat with her. **(F. 5)** I had known Elizabeth since her days as head of the American Red Cross. But, I suspected this invitation was no social call. (F. 6) This was a measure of the standing the National Urban League had among the political elite in Washington: Even a hard-right conservative Administration understood — even as they were sharply cutting the federal funds we got for our programs — that they had to be seen to make some sort of gesture of interest in the new guy at the top of the organization.

I hadn't been but a few minutes in Elizabeth's office that day when she said to me," Someone else here wants to see you, and someone will be up to get you in a few minutes." Moments later, Melvin B. Bradley, who had been with Reagan since his days as Governor of California and was one of the few African Americans within the Reagan insider orbit, appeared. Mel carried the title of "Special Assistant to the President. **(F.7)**

I thought Bradley and I were going to have a brief but substantive discussion about a few of the Administration's policies. But as we walked through the White House corridors, I realized we weren't heading to an office he would have occupied, and I suddenly found that we were in the Oval Office. A moment later, the President walked in, dressed in a brown suit and highly polished brown shoes, and Bradley quietly slipped away. As someone who, as a teenager in Houston 40 years earlier, had shined lots of men's shoes and always took care to have my shoes well shined, I was fascinated by one detail: Ronald Reagan had the best shine on his shoes that I had ever seen.

We shook hands, and he immediately set about being gracious and making small talk. He spent a moment lamenting the deaths of the Thunderbird pilots and several other recent tragedies, and then he began moving subtly away from me, clearly signaling that our conversation, such as it was, was at an end.

But I knew I could not let the moment pass. I said to him, "Mr. President, I cannot take my leave from your office without telling you what I think about the Bob Jones situation." **(F. 8)**

He quickly interrupted: "Oh, let me tell you, I've had all of these college presidents," he said, "showing up at the White House, telling me that the I.R.S. is trying to run their schools. I simply told my people we have a problem. The next thing I knew we have this Bob Jones situation."

This, of course, was disingenuous. That very day, he would say something very different at a news conference — very smoothly moving to simultaneously pose the controversy as a matter of the Administration's innocent but clumsy effort to resolve a dispute — while also trying to push it out of the public eye.

But I wasn't going to argue with him. I merely said," Mr. President, if a president expresses something as a problem, there is always a bureaucrat around who is going to try to solve it for him. So, that is your first lesson in presidential policy-making. You have to be careful what you express as a problem."

As I left the White House, a horde of press people descended on me, asking what we had discussed. After I mentioned our brief exchange about the Bob Jones situation, one reporter asked if I trusted the President. I said, "I trust my mother," and turned around and walked away.

After I got back to my office, there were calls from the White House asking me to explain what that statement meant. And I replied, "That's not a complicated statement: I trust my mother, and that's who I trust."

I never met with President Reagan again. But Barbara and I did get invited to the White House in 1985 for the State Dinner held in honor of the visit of the Soviet Premier Mikhail Gorbachev. We were seated at the table with Vice President George H.W. Bush and his wife, Barbara, and they were perfect hosts. And I did begin to have a relationship with the Bushes, but my lack of a connection with Reagan continued.

I pressed on with my critique of Reagan policies in the short form of columns and speeches, and in far more extensive comments when I spoke that July in the hearings held by Congress's Joint Economic Committee on the Administration's urban policy program.

The purpose of the Committee, comprised of 10 members each from the Senate and the House of Representatives, was to hold hearings and produce studies on matters regarding the American economy. That included the report an Administration was to produce every two years on its national urban policy.

The Reagan Administration report was due in February. But, although the Administration had been in office a full year by then, and despite inquiries from the Committee's Democratic chairman, Representative Henry Reuss of Wisconsin, months passed without any sign from Sam

Pierce, the Administration's beleaguered Secretary of Housing and Urban Development, that a report would soon be forthcoming. Finally, Reuss, a 28-year veteran of Congress, short-circuited the Administration's obvious procrastination by arbitrarily setting five days in mid-July as the dates for the hearing—whether or not the Administration had anything to offer. Four days before the hearings were to begin on July 13, Pierce sent over the Administration document.

In addition to several committee members who were to comment on Administration policy, the lineup of speakers included such prominent figures as Coleman Young, Mayor of Detroit and president that year of the National Conference of Mayors; James Rouse, the developer of the planned city of Columbia, Maryland and well-known urban festival marketplaces around the country; Felix Rohatyn, the financier who in the 1970s had helped save New York City from bankruptcy; and Patricia Roberts Harris, the former HUD Secretary under President Carter and Secretary of Health and Human Services.

One thing the hearings confirmed was that my criticisms were fully representative of the mainstream liberal reaction to Reagan's domestic policies from scholars, policy wonks, and Democratic officeholders. Reuss opened the hearings by identifying several significant problems with the report. For one, he said in a tone of jovial sarcasm, referring both to the delay in producing the report and its lack of discussion of the nation's crumbling bridges, roads, and sewer pipelines, "It's six months since the report was due, and one would have hoped that the Federal Government role on infrastructure would not be, as it still is, a matter of high State secrecy."

For another, he noted that while the Administration stated in the report that "the central foundation of the President's urban policy is his economic program,... [that] economic program has brought this country to the highest levels of unemployment and bankruptcies since the Depression. ..." **(F. 9)**

I was the fourth witness before the committee and I quickly stated I fully agreed with Reuss' views. The administration's urban philosophy, I said, "lacks both a unifying vision of America and hope for impoverished city residents left out of the economic main stream. .... No discussion of urban policy can be [taken seriously] unless it addresses the needs and aspirations of the people who live in the cities."

In large measure, I explained, that meant African Americans. By the 1980s, more than 80 percent of Black Americans lived in the nation's metropolitan regions, and more than 50 percent lived in the central city of those regions. Black people were also the poorest Americans, I added, with the typical black family income no more than half that of whites. "We are a tenth of the population, a fourth of the jobless, and a third of the poor. In whatever city you choose, blacks experience serious disadvantage. .... Any urban policy that does not deal constructively with this ugly fact of American urban life is no urban policy at all." **(F. 10)**

In fact, of course, the federal government had played a significant role in the post-World War II decline of the cities. Its massive federal highway construction program and backing in numerous other ways of suburban expansion — which was carried out on the principal of excluding Blacks — helped drain cities off their tax base, weakening their economic foundations. Reagan's so-called New Federalism proposal to transfer responsibility for many social welfare programs to the states was no solution. In the past the Federal government had had to take responsibility for those programs precisely because states couldn't administer them in any fair, rational way. Poverty "is not a local problem. It is national," I said, "[and] national problems require national solutions; ... fairness demands that poor people receive the same treatment wherever they reside." Only the Federal Government could bring that about.

I offered the Committee a solution—a substitute national urban policy: the Urban League's proposal for a Marshall Plan for America. Our idea was to establish a two-part effort—the one part designed to renovate and build America's infrastructure anew in ways that would put to work millions of its citizens, and the second consisting of training and education programs that would enable millions of poor and disadvantaged Americans to acquire the skills they needed to become part of the modern work force.

This was hardly a new idea. The U.S. Marshall Plan for Europe the government carried out from the late 1940s to the early 1950s to help rebuild the war-ravaged countries of Western Europe annually devoted nearly 10 percent of the federal budget (equivalent in 1980s dollars to $100 billion) to help rebuild those countries' shattered infrastructures and agricultural and industrial systems.

The massive rescue effort was driven by self-interest as well as humanitarian concerns: America's own economic well-being depended on Europe becoming a viable outlet for its industrial and agricultural products.

Ten years later, as the civil rights movement was nearing its landmark legislative victories, Whitney Young proposed a domestic Marshall Plan that would do for America's poverty-ridden areas what the U.S. had done for Western Europe — a ten-point program to not only improve the health care and educational opportunities available to poor Blacks and other impoverished Americans but also provide the training in the concrete skills that would make them viable candidates for employment. President Johnson was to incorporate several of those ideas in his Great Society legislation. Indeed, in 1967, a week after the ruinous Detroit uprising had begun, Hubert Humphrey, Johnson's vice-president, had called for a massive effort to aid impoverished areas that he directly likened to the Marshall Plan in a speech to the National Association of Counties convention, held in Detroit. **(F. 11)**

According to a report in the *New York Times*, "Mr. Humphrey emphasized that the same type of aid that had been used to help the underdeveloped countries [should] be used to 'help our own people ... We had a Marshall Plan for the impoverished areas of Europe. Maybe we need an American plan for a new day."

The Vice President added that the massive investment of private capital needed in the world's developing nations, which was insured by the Federal government, was also "needed in America's slums and rural poverty areas. Whatever it will take to get the job done we must be willing to pay the price," said Humphrey, whose commitment to progressive causes had long marked his political career. His remarks were "warmly applauded" by the delegates.

But they had applauded too soon. Within days, Humphrey walked back his words that the government must pay whatever "the price." No doubt he had been reminded of the two great obstacles such a plan would face: opposition in Congress far beyond that faced by the Johnson Administration's Great Society proposals two years earlier and, as a *Times* editorial pointedly noted, the burgeoning cost of the nation's ever more controversial involvement in the Vietnam War.

Without money "in massive amounts," it declared, "the Vice President's brave talk about bringing hope and justice and peace to the ghettos is likely to impress many Negro moderates as further evidence that America accords to the problems of the slums none of the sense of urgency that marks its allocation of additional billions in the Vietnam war." **(F. 12)**

But, of course, we couldn't let past disappointment deter continual effort. "This is the right time to start thinking about another ... Marshall plan for Americans," I told the Committee. 'A Marshall plan for the 1980s would rebuild the cities and get our dying industries producing again for the benefit of all." Most important, it would reach out to the poor and the unskilled with job training opportunities so that they, too, could share in the benefits of a revived economy. Like the original Marshall Plan, doing good for the poor would wind up with America doing well again. We'd have full employment instead of over 10 million jobless. And they would be paying taxes and using fewer resources ... [and our] cities would be strong centers of meaningful activity again, instead of decaying remnants of greatness." **(F. 13)**

I would make the same point within a fortnight in my opening address to the Urban League's annual conference in Los Angeles.

"Just think of a tremendous amount of work to be done in America where millions are idle," I told the conference attendees. "Our national infrastructure is falling apart. Roads and bridges need to be repaired and replaced. Our rail system and ports need to be revitalized. We need to build homes, sewer lines, and water systems. A decade of disinvestment forces us to strengthen the economic infrastructure of America if we want to grow. ... We can put millions to work — paying taxes and buying consumer goods."

This was the message I would reiterate again and again in dozens and dozens of speeches and columns throughout my tenure. At the end of the decade, amid the collapse of the Soviet Union, I, among many others, urged President Bush to reduce the still-bloated defense budget and devote $50 billion of that 'Peace Dividend" to a Marshall Plan effort. In the early 1990s, I would propose that the U.S. victory in the Gulf War should produce billions of dollars for a Marshall Plan-like effort in the U.S. equal to the American-backed reconstruction plans for the Gulf. And still later, I welcomed the Clinton Administration with the same suggestion. None of the League's proposals caught fire. Ideology prevailed over common sense during the Reagan and Bush years.

The Clinton Administration's heart and mind were in the right place: I did note in my January 1994 column, my last year at the helm of the League, that he had sent to Congress an economic stimulus program that had much in common with key features of the Marshall Plan, but that there were two barriers his proposal could not overcome. He was successful in shepherding through Congress a deficit-reduction plan that, in five years' time, would transform the multi-billion deficits into multi-billion surpluses—the first since the 1950s. However, the focus on deficit reduction left Congress with little appetite for new federal spending. In addition, Clinton's having won office by a plurality of votes in the three-way 1992 contest against President Bush and billionaire independent candidate H. Ross Perot meant he had little political capital to spend on controversial proposals. **(F. 14)**

That meant that in Clinton's fiscal year 1995 budget, some programs of special importance to poor people and to the cities—heating-cost subsidies for the poor, funds to modernize public housing, and subsidies for mass transit, among others — were cut significantly. On the other hand, the budget did provide for a big jump in funds for the Head Start educational program aid for the homeless, and for the first time in years, the federal anti-drug program was budgeted to spend more on education and treatment than on drug law enforcement — "recognizing that prevention and cure are more likely roots to cutting drug abuse." And I made one final point. "In some important ways, the budget edges the country towards the necessary investments in the future. But until it embraces a Marshall Plan for America that revives the cities and helps poor people into the mainstream, it represents a missed opportunity."

By the time I appeared before the Joint Economic Committee, Black Americans had plenty of evidence on the "political" front that the Reagan Administration was hostile to their interests and aspirations. Its first year seemed consumed with denouncing the established civil rights leadership as not truly representing the interests of the masses of Black Americans and declaring that the only way "racial equality" could be achieved was a "color-blindness" that ignored the impact of past and present racism.

Its point man for this stance was William Bradford Reynolds, the Justice Department Assistant Attorney General for Civil Rights. Reynolds's legal career had been in corporate work; he had no experience in civil rights law, not even of the *pro bono* kind. But he was to show time and again throughout the coming eight years that he had an Orwellian view of his job: He continually denounced established efforts to further school desegregation and adopted voluntary and mandatory affirmative action decrees to promote equal access to jobs in the public and private sectors; and he orchestrated a concerted, controversial, and ultimately successful effort to undermine the independence of the U.S. Civil Rights Commission. **(F. 15)**

Reagan, in his speech as Candidate Reagan to the Urban League's annual conference in August of 1980, had promised Black Americans that the "perceived barriers between my political beliefs and the aspirations of black Americans … are false. What I want for America is, I think, pretty much what the overwhelming majority of black Americans want." **(F. 16)** But the record of his Administration's first year and the years thereafter bore no relation to that pledge. In his 1980 election victory, he had secured 14 percent of the Black Vote. By December 1981, President Reagan was well on his way to his 1984 mark of just 9 percent of the Black Vote—the lowest percentage for a Republican presidential candidate since the 6 percent won twenty years earlier by Arizona Senator Barry Goldwater —

that June he had been one of only six Republican Senators to oppose the landmark Civil Rights Act of 1964.

Reagan's immediate downward trend in Black support came despite the concerted efforts of GOP operatives and conservative media pundits to promote a new group of political actors: the so-called New Black Conservatives, who publicly espoused the identical principles as the Reaganites of a staunch free-market economic regime and the claim that the effects of past and present racial discrimination could be remedied, not by affirmative action and other positive policies, but simply by not taking race into account at all. They called it "color-blindness." Or "race-neutralism."

Whatever the sloganeering, the notion of race neutralism was, at best, disingenuous — precisely because it claimed that past wrongs had no impact on the present or, even more cynically, that nothing could be done about those effects now. In other words, its proponents used the assertion that practicing color-blindness was *fair* to block mechanisms for redressing past wrongs and expanding opportunities in the present. The so-called Fairmont Conference, convened by Black and White conservatives at San Francisco's Fairmont Hotel and prominently supported by Edwin Meese III, a longtime Reagan friend who was then a White House Special Assistant and later to become Attorney General, was supposed to signal the beginning of the Administration's "Black Alternatives" initiative.

Also among the conservatives present were several Blacks firmly in the liberal camp. They included Percy E. Sutton, a former Manhattan Borough President in New York City who had developed a multimillion-dollar communications empire; economist Bernard E. Anderson of the University of Pennsylvania and a frequent contributor to the Urban League's *The State of Black America*; and two well-known political scientists: Martin L. Kilson, of Harvard, and Charles V. Hamilton, of Columbia University, who had co-authored *Black Power: The Politics of Liberation in America* with famed civil rights activist Kwame Toure (then, Stokely Carmichael).

These men made it clear they believed Republicans had a significant opportunity at hand and that Black Americans could benefit from it.

"The issue regarding politics in the context of the 1980s," Hamilton declared, "is not a matter of party labels ...[nor of] ideological identification .... It is rather what I would call ... the three Ps—process, product, and participation. [W]hen the process is perceived as related to the products the people want, then participation will increase."

Kilson, surveying the wreckage of the Democratic Party a month after the 1980 election, suggested that the conservative ascendancy Reagan's election represented had made the "homogenized black leadership policy" Black Americans had—necessarily—pursued through the early 1970s a hindrance to their full political maturation. He said African Americans now needed to "diversify" their political alliances and allegiances" to achieve the "incredibly pressing need for ... greater policy variation. ... There is too high a cost associated with black policy isolation from conservative initiatives in American political life."

Bernard E. Anderson said that the expanded Black middle class, and especially its cohort of Black business professionals, could be targeted by the Reaganites for concerted appeals just as the GOP in the 1950s, 1960s, and 1970s sliced away at the Democratic political allegiances of the rising White-ethnic working-class and middle classes who were benefiting enormously from the material bounty America's postwar "Affluent Society" had brought to them. **(F. 17)**

As one chronicler of what might have been later wrote, "With this group as the vanguard of a conservative-oriented effort to mobilize Black America, it was just a matter of following Hamilton's advice about the "three P's." Make the process inviting and the product appealing, and the participation—involvement in the conservative movement and voting for Republican candidates—would materialize." **(F. 18)**

While Reagan never met with me again after our very brief chat, or Ben Hooks, head of the NAACP, or others of the traditional civil rights leadership, he did meet with the Council for a Black Economic Agenda, as the group of black conservatives who had access to the Administration called themselves, from time to time. The most revealing occurred on January 15, 1985—the actual birthday of Martin Luther King, Jr. **(F. 19)** and the day before we released that year's volume of *The State of Black America* **(F. 20).** A further calculation in the Administration's choice of that specific day likely stemmed from its trying to obscure the growing spread across the country of demonstrations against the Administration's de facto support of apartheid in South Africa. **(F. 21)**

For their part, these new Black conservatives readily proclaimed their support for the Reagan domestic policies. Robert L. Woodson, the most prominent of this group (and who in the early 1970s had been on the Urban League staff), would later declare the goal of the Council for A Black Economic Agenda, as they called themselves, was "to establish a strategic alliance between the black community and the Reagan administration …. It's unproductive to stand outside and complain." Samuel Pierce, Secretary of Housing and Urban Development, the only high-level Black appointee in the Administration, asserted that "I think a lot of the established black community has taken an attitude that they want to continue dealing in a way that this Administration doesn't want to. We are trying to reduce deficits and get things down into manageable shape, and others just want to have a giant giveaway program and we are not going to do that."

An Administration spokesman dutifully denied the meeting was a deliberate insult to the established black leadership. But that claim was undermined by Reagan himself telling reporters a few days later "that maybe some of those [civil rights] leaders are protecting some rather good positions that they have, and they can protect them better if they keep their constituency aggrieved and believing that they have a legitimate complaint. If they ever become aware of the opportunities that are improving, they might wonder whether they need some of those organizations." **(F. 22)**

However, there were two major clues that, from the beginning, signaled the Administration's disinterest in providing substantive "alternatives" to the traditional liberal cast of Black politics.

For one thing, but for Samuel Pierce, Reagan's Secretary of Housing and Urban Development, few of these Black Conservatives had any record of significant involvement in

257

Black civic life at even the local level. Nor had any appeared to have ever run for political office. These men and women were not like the traditional Black Republicans the civil rights forces always included in their ranks — such as Senator Edward W. Brooke and William T. Coleman, or like Colin Powell and Condoleezza Rice. Some were academics, some occupied vice-presidential-level positions in corporate America, and some appeared to be owners of small businesses or directed small community organizations in various cities.

There were two exceptions to this general description. One was Clarence Pendleton, the newly-appointed Chairman of the U.S. Civil Rights Commission — yes, the same Clarence Pendleton who, in 1975, I had nominated to be my successor as the CEO of the Urban League's San Diego affiliate. The other figure had recently been appointed an assistant secretary in the Department of Education and, a few months later, would be successfully nominated as head of the Equal Employment Opportunity Commission. His name was Clarence Thomas.

Otherwise, in terms of public notice, nearly all the New Black Conservatives would follow the same path through the Reagan-Bush presidencies: Their names would be touted a few times in the mainstream media as possible harbingers of a substantial swing among Blacks to the GOP — and then, politically speaking, they would disappear, leaving no footprint or a substantial trail of advocacy even for conservative causes. It's still astonishing to realize—the more so given the Republicans' vaunted vote-getting success of the two decades from Reagan's election to that of Barack Obama—that in those twenty-eight years, only two Black

Republicans were elected to the House of Representatives, and neither served more than three terms. * Furthermore, according to data gathered by the Joint Center for Political and Economic Studies, during those years, only about fifty of the more than nine thousand Black elected officials in the U.S. were members of the Republican Party. **(F. 23)**

The GOP record stands in stark contrast to the roster of the Carter Administration, which included Patricia Roberts Harris as Secretary of Housing and Urban Development (HUD) and Andrew Young as United Nations Ambassador fort several years, and in the Clinton years included, among many others, Ron Brown as Secretary of Commerce — Vernon Jordan, most famously as Clinton's "First Friend."

But then, the role of the Black Conservatives — under Reagan and his Republican successors down to the present — wasn't to help develop a significant black presence within the Republican Party. The GOP well understood the workings of Charles V. Hamilton's definition of the basics of politics. They had been expertly applying it to the White ethnic working and middle classes for decades. Their "three Ps" relationship with Black Americans and the Republican Party never got off the ground because Black Conservatives' sponsors didn't want substantial, involved Black participation. They were just using the presence of a few Black faces and a few rhetorical expressions of goodwill to try to obscure their hostility to racial equality.

But a *Washington Post* story shortly after the much ballyhooed January 1985 meeting between Reagan and the CEA revealed another layer to the cynical game the Administration was playing. It said that several longtime Black Republican political operatives, including the chairman of the National Black Republican Council, had complained to Vice President Bush that they hadn't been invited to the Reagan Council meeting and that this was just another instance that the White House staff was ignoring their policy suggestions and not funneling any political appointments or government business contracts their way.

"White Republicans, even the boys in the White House, are making millions off the president," a *Post* source said. "They have no problem with connections when you are white, but if blacks try to get into the game, they say it's not fair; it's affirmative action." Another anonymous source bluntly labeled the pledges Reagan made to them when he was campaigning in 1980 as "a sham seduction." **(F. 24)** In other words, while the administration was using their New Black conservatives to justify ignoring black civil rights leaders, it was also playing one group of black conservatives against another.

The Administration's New Black Conservatives Council quickly faded from sight, as I had predicted to the *New York Times*. "I don't think [Reagan's] meeting is tantamount to meeting with blacks who have a constituency and who have provided services over some period of time. He does himself a disservice by ignoring reality." **(F. 25)**

But ignoring the reality of race — and racial discrimination in all its guises — would continue to be the true Republican policy on race throughout the Reagan and Bush presidencies. As I wrote in the introduction to the just-published 1982 edition of *The State of Black America,* we released that month:

At no point in recent memory [has] the distance between the national government and Black America been greater than it was in 1981, nor has the relationship between the two been more strained. Throughout Black America in 1981, there was a broad feeling of isolation, of a turning back of the clock, of a retreat from civil rights policies and social service programs that were established only after years of struggle and were believed, at least by some, to be inviolate..... It is difficult to believe that any Administration would deliberately set out to isolate itself from any sector of the American people, and yet this present Administration, both by what it has done and what it has not done, has succeeded to an alarming degree in doing just that.

Chapter 12 – Do What the Spirit SayS Do:
The Black Political Mobilization of the
1980s and 1990s

Black Americans felt besieged as I took office in January 1982. The recession had thrown millions of Blacks out of work and into unemployment. The Administration's budget cuts had cast many poor Black families deep into poverty. Its blunt disparaging of affirmative action policies meant employers had a license to trim their hiring of Black workers. And its thinly disguised opposition to enforcement of the Voting Rights Act of 1965, which had to be renewed that year (under the Voting Rights Act of 1982) and cloaked efforts to restore tax exemptions for segregated schooling struck at the very foundations of full citizenship Blacks had always fiercely fought for.

Those were just a few of the reasons I repeated the themes of my Greenville Urban League speech in my January 13, 1982, *To Be Equal* column, "New Responsibilities For Blacks."

"The 1980s are a potentially disastrous decade for blacks," I warned. "With the rug of federal programs and national sympathy pulled out from under us, black organizations and individuals will have to directly confront the internal problems of the community to a greater degree than in the past …. One problem that must be tackled is the near-suicidal withdrawal from political activism as measured by the depressingly low voter registration figures in black communities."

"Part of the reason anti-black policies have prevailed," I continued, "is the absence of political risk attached to them. Politicians look at low black voter turnout and swiftly conclude black interests can be ignored. ... It is a general truism that as the black vote decreases, black vulnerability increases. Election-year-get-out-the-vote campaigns ... simply will not effectively deal with this problem. There has to be a permanent citizenship education campaign mounted in black communities by community organizations and concerned individuals. That's a responsibility that cannot be shirked." (F. 1)

All these developments and more underscored for many Black Americans that their entire post-World War II legacy of finally fully gaining their rights as American citizens was under threat.

But, contrary to the predictions following Reagan's 1980 election that the conservative ascendancy had broken Black America's political spirit, it was about to show itself over the next two years in ways that had enormous consequences for the next three decades of American life. No indicator of the Reagan Administration's hostility toward Black America was more infuriating than its reversal, announced eight days after I officially took office, of an eleven-year-old federal policy that barred tax-exemptions for schools, colleges, and other institutions that racially discriminated.

The decision was meant to effectively restore government sanction to more than 100 schools and other organizations whose tax exemptions had been revoked by the IRS in the previous decade. The IRS would also now provide exemptions to many other private segregated schools — so-called 'seg academies' in the South — that had opened since the 1960s to enable white families to escape the mandated desegregation of public schools.

The proposed reversal directly involved Bob Jones University of Greenville, South Carolina, and the Goldsboro Christian Schools of Goldsboro, North Carolina. Strikingly, it was the exact opposite of the position the Justice Department had taken just the previous September in arguing before the Supreme Court that the denial of tax exemptions to the two schools was lawful. Now, in January 1982, the Administration claimed the old policy was unlawful because it was a rule of the Internal Revenue Service, and such policies could only be approved by Congress. (F. 2)

Tellingly, although departmental spokesmen claimed the policy reversal had been recommended to Reagan by Attorney General William French Smith and Treasury Secretary Donald T. Regan, the two Cabinet officials were nowhere to be seen or heard the day it was announced — a sure sign the Administration was concerned about a backlash to the proposal's double purpose: to pander to institutions that discriminate directly and to establish a precedent for granting tuition-tax credits for private elementary and secondary schools, and thereby undermine the viability of public schools.

They were right to worry, for a furious criticism of the action immediately erupted in Washington and across the country. (It was amid this furor that I had my brief, one and only face-to-face meeting with President Reagan.) The Washington-based Lawyers Committee for Civil Rights, which had been formed in the early 1960s to support challenges to Jim Crow laws in the South, announced a lawsuit against the action the next day. A tidal wave of support from other civil rights groups, educational associations, cities, and other private and nonprofit organizations, as well as newspaper editorials quickly took shape that day as well and showed no signs of letting up. (F.3)

My *To Be Equal* column of 20 January was one of many commentaries to point out that the IRS policy had been affirmed during the 1970s by rulings of the Supreme Court and several Federal courts. There was no doubt about its validity.

"Perhaps more than any other of its acts," I wrote, "[the proposed reversal creates] a huge gulf between itself and the white and black majority that despises racial discrimination as an immoral, ugly relic of the past. [It] cannot be excused on any grounds. Even the President's fast backtracking and his endorsement of congressional action to authorize refusal of those exemptions does not take away the bad taste, nor does it change the real issue."

I stated plainly what that real issue was. "Currying favor with the far right has a lot more to do with [the Administration's action] than the technical, procedural question of who gets to rule on tax-exempt status. ... Now any crackpot segregating Academy can raise the flag of open brutal race schism and still line up for its federal tax exemption."

It was another indication, as I and others asserted in those years, that American society had been infected — again — by a *meanness mania* that employed such code words and phrases as the *culture of poverty* and *forced busing* and *reverse discrimination* to mask their opposition to public-

265

and private-sector efforts to help Blacks, other minorities and the poor. (F. 4)

The day before, after nearly a week or so of twisting this way and that, the President tried to have it both ways in a news conference, declaring he had no intent to foster racial discrimination while maintaining that the IRS had no authority on its own to bar such tax exemptions. Reagan said he would send a bill to Congress outlawing tax exemptions for racially discriminatory institutions — a face-saving act since, by that time, it was clear the Supreme Court would once again take up the matter. It was enough, however, to draw a furious rebuke from Bob Jones III, the president of Bob Jones University and grandson of the founder. He called Reagan "a traitor to God's people." (F. 5)

During the January 19 news conference, Reagan wasn't at all defensive. Rather, he was at his easy-going, affable best. While acknowledging being the "originator" of his Administration's stand, he denied his actions pandered to those who practice racial discrimination. "I won't deny that it wasn't handled as well as it could be. Maybe we didn't act as quickly as we could have [proposing legislation to bar tax exemptions for such institutions]. ... But don't judge us by our mistakes ... judge us by how well we recover and solve the situation."

The geniality didn't fool liberal analysts. *Times* columnist Anthony Lewis wrote, "The lawlessness of the whole affair is breathtaking ... But Ronald Reagan gives us his aw-shucks look, and we forgive him. There is just that nagging thought: is it really 'conservative' to play fast and loose with the law?" (F.6)

266

That explanation wouldn't stand scrutiny. The Supreme Court signaled later that spring what its eventual decision would be when, after the Administration stated it wouldn't argue for the old policy, the Court appointed William T. Coleman, the former Secretary of Transportation under President Ford, to argue for continuing the ban. (F. 7)

Coleman, head of the Washington office of a powerhouse law firm, had impeccable legal and civil rights credentials. A University of Pennsylvania graduate, he had become in the late 1940s the first Black member of the prestigious Harvard Law Review and subsequently became part of the group of Black and White attorneys whom Thurgood Marshall led in crafting the winning arguments in the 1954 *Brown vs. Board of Education of Topeka* Supreme Court case. A lifelong traditional Republican, Coleman was emblematic of the close pre-Reagan links along the civil rights front between Blacks Democrats and Blacks Republicans.

In May 1983, the Court voted 8 to 1 in "unusually unequivocal and forceful language" to reject the proposed policy change. "There can be no doubt," Chief Justice Warren Burger wrote, "that racial discrimination in education violates deeply and widely accepted views of elementary justice. It would be wholly incompatible with the concepts underlying tax exemption to grant the benefit of tax-exempt status to racially discriminatory educational entities."

Associate Justice William H. Rehnquist, whose opposition to civil rights laws was well-known and whom Reagan would appoint as Chief Justice in 1986 to replace the retiring Warren Burger, cast the lone dissenting vote.

The President's terse, one-sentence response— "We will obey the law."— spoke volumes, as did the fact that, according to a *New York Times* report, "some lawyers in the [Justice Department's] civil rights division greeted the ruling with backslapping elation." The previous year, when the Administration had sought to change the policy, more than 100 of the division's 175 lawyers had signed a letter of protest. (F. 8)

Those and other developments on the political front were points of light amidst the economic gloom. But I wasn't the only one who noticed that, albeit the eventual victory, the *Bob Jones* gambit also exemplified how difficult the progressive coalition's position had become: under the Reagan Presidency, we were continually battling against the conservative movement's stratagem of forcing the civil rights and progressive groups to spend time and money re-litigating old, hard-fought victories.

That truth was also exemplified by the Administration's persistent and eventually successful effort to undermine the U.S. Civil Rights Commission on Civil Rights, the independent federal advisory body directed to suggest improvements to federal enforcement of civil rights laws. Although it did not itself have enforcement power, the thoroughly researched reports of the Commission, established under the 1957 Civil Rights Act, were of great use to the civil rights forces in pressing federal, state, and local legislators to better combat racial and other forms of discrimination.

That's why the Reagan Administration, from the moment it took office, was determined to destroy its effectiveness. Since its creation, the Commission had typically had a somewhat tense relationship with whoever the occupant of the White House was — because its mandate was to be a gadfly. But Reagan's predecessors generally respected its independence. Perhaps they actually did grudgingly believe it served a proper purpose, and, more pragmatically, they understood there was little to gain by taking on a body fervently supported by the civil rights community, the editorial boards of most heavyweight liberal and centrist newspapers, and a critical mass of Democrats and Republicans in the Congress.

But now, as Reagan attacked, it was suddenly vulnerable. That was partly due to what became the public focus of the battle—not its nonpartisan independence, but the bureaucratic disputes over the scope of its work and how appointments to the six-member commission would be split between the Office of the President and the leadership of the Congress.

That meant that, while the civil rights community and its allies in Congress fought vigorously, the Commission's predicament could not compete for mass attention and support of the kind given to either the Martin Luther King, Jr. Holiday, the Free South Africa Movement, and the Jesse Jackson 1984 presidential campaign—all of which were also at the top of the political agenda in the early and mid-1980s. Indeed, one could say that because the Administration's efforts to defeat legislation creating a Martin Luther King, Jr. national holiday and destroying its material support for South Africa's apartheid regime was going badly, it was even more determined to *win* this battle. By early 1985, the newly restructured commission gave Reagan what he wanted: a majority of reliable Reagan-friendly votes on the eight-member body and a chairman and staff director who acted as if they were adjuncts to the Reagan White House. (F. 9)

What made the Civil Rights Commission battle even more infuriating for me was that Reagan, after having to withdraw two nominees with laughably inadequate credentials, nominated Clarence Pendleton as its new chairman. Yes, the same Clarence Pendleton I had recommended in 1975 as my successor at the San Diego Urban League, and one of the biggest mistakes I ever made in my life. He quickly proved a reliable, voluble spokesman for the Reagan stance on racial discrimination and discrimination against other groups of Americans. His words and actions underscored for me perhaps the biggest mistake I had ever made in my professional career in recommending him as my successor in San Diego. However, over time, complaints about Pendleton's seeming to promote himself as a "chief adviser" to Reagan himself and increasing questions about his management practices and expenditures at the Commission began to erode his usefulness to the Administration, but he remained in office until his death from a heart attack in June 1988.

In that regard, the eventual fate of the Civil Rights Commission—the destruction of its integrity under the Reagan and Bush administrations—epitomized the conservative movement's relentless, systematic efforts to transform federal agencies from guardians to opponents of civil rights laws and regulations.

For me, however, the aftermath of the Bob Jones University controversy confirmed that Reagan wasn't going to suffer any lasting political damage for trying to restore government sanction for racial discrimination or his draconian social welfare policies. Soon after that controversy was settled, the media took to describing him— the description was actually coined in so many words by Colorado Democratic Representative Patricia Schroeder — as the "Teflon President." (New F. 10)

There has always been a rich, complex discussion among scholars and journalists alike about whether the Teflon description fit Reagan in the broad sense and why it did or did not. That broad discussion is beyond this book's scope. But it is my belief that when it came to Reagan's *harmful* policies toward poor and disadvantaged Americans and toward Black Americans and their civil rights, he certainly was a "Teflon President."

As David Shaw, media critic for the *Los Angeles Times,* wrote in a 1992 column, the description arose within a year of his taking office because "criticisms of him and his policies seldom stuck, seldom diminished his enormous personal popularity." One explanation why, Shaw advanced, was that Reagan "surrounded himself with a sophisticated core of media and marketing advisors who knew exactly how to package their product — the President — and they were unprecedentedly successful at manipulating the media and enabling Reagan to go over the heads of the media, directly to the American people." (New F. 11)

Reagan's popularity slide from the 50s to the 40s in the polls from early 1982 to mid-1983 was largely due to the recession-driven high unemployment affecting Whites and only secondarily, as it turned out, to the terrible impact of his draconian cuts in social programs on the poor and the racial controversies he had ginned up. (The quick, overwhelming push-back to Reagan's Bob Jones gambit, which made it clear that policy would be reversed, dissipated anger over it among the larger populace.) Those developments combined to produce the battering the GOP took in the 1982 midterm elections: Democrats won 26 seats in the House and four governorships in the economically hard-hit Midwest. But the polls also showed that it was Reagan's policies, *not him personally*, that voters disliked. When the economic recovery began to take shape in 1983, his poll numbers improved.

Protected by the allure his promise of a *restoration* of the global dominance, economic prosperity, and misremembered domestic peace of the 1950s had for many Whites, and by his own instinctual and actorly skill for projecting affability and confidence, Reagan would sail on to his resounding 1984 re-election. That was another dramatic example of the "Teflon Shield" dynamic that overrode his many mistakes, distortions of fact and circumstance, and outright falsehoods that were evident from the moment he took office.

However, despite Ronald Reagan's Teflon Shield, the beneficial impact on Black Americans of his Bob Jones gambit had become apparent: It had energized them. Along with conservatives' opposition to the civil rights coalition's long-sought Martin Luther King, Jr. national holiday, it had confirmed their suspicions about the "meanness mood" of the moment. But, contrary to the predictions — and hopes of some — that Blacks' political strength had been diminished by the conservative ascendancy, Black America's battling on those two issues had refreshed its activist spirit.

Indeed, in the late winter and spring of 1983, as the Supreme Court was still considering the Bob Jones case, the performance of Black candidates in four cities' mayoral contests underscored African Americans' renewed sense of political vigor: the victories of Chicago Congressman Harold Washington in the primary and general election; of Wilson Goode, in the Philadelphia mayoral Democratic primary; * and Harvey Gantt, as the first Black mayor of Charlotte, North Carolina,** and the surprising showing in defeat of Melvin B. (Mel) King in the Democratic primary contest in Boston. **(F. 12)**

The contest in Chicago had been brewing for some years, more than a decade, in fact, and when it came, it immediately captured the nation's attention. One reason was because the city had long been a rock-solid Democratic stronghold, even before the two-decade tenure of the combative, dictatorial Richard J. Daley. Another was that Chicago's huge Black population, a mainstay of Democratic power, had long chafed at not getting what they felt was their due in government positions and contracts in exchange for their votes.

When Daley died of a heart attack in office in 1976 and was succeeded by a bland regular of the Democratic machine, the determination to revolt intensified. In 1982, a coalition of Black politicians and community leaders promised Washington that they would meet his central, extraordinary demand: mounting a voter registration campaign in the city's predominantly black neighborhoods that would enroll upwards of 100,000 new voters. In fact, the results exceeded all expectations: by the time of the 1983 primary, the city's voting rolls had increased by nearly

200,000, and most of the new voters resided in predominantly Black neighborhoods. In the primary and general elections, held in February and April, an astonishing eighty-five percent of Chicago's Black registered voters went to the polls. (F. 13) They provided Washington's narrow margin of victory in both elections. The bitter, radicalized tone of the contest in Chicago was the opposite of the contests in Philadelphia and Charlotte, and Washington, despite being a veteran of the vaunted Chicago Democratic Machine, would face a relentless, racially driven opposition from a sizable bloc of White council members throughout his two terms as mayor. (F. 14)

An intensive voter registration effort that sharply increased Black voter turnout also characterized the Boston mayoral contest. But, because of the small size of the city's Black population, it was wrapped within an equally intensive cross-racial appeal that drew heavily on the city's liberal tradition. And it was successful — so much so that both Ray Flynn, the White candidate who won the Democratic primary (tantamount to victory in the general election), and the Black candidate he narrowly beat made numerous concerted efforts to tamp down any racial tension in the city over the results. That latter candidate was Mel King — the former head of the Boston Urban League affiliate who, two decades earlier when I was at the Washington Urban League, had recommended that I play a pivotal role in the national headquarters "New Thrust" program.

In my April 20 *To Be Equal* column on the Washington victory, I said the "big lesson … is the latent power of the black vote. … The needs of black voters can no longer either be ignored or taken for granted, and that is the real message the Chicago vote sends the national parties."

As it happened, I was speaking at the annual dinner of the Hudson County (N.J.) Urban League the day after Washington's general-election victory. I told my fellow Urban Leaguers and their guests that my elation was tempered by the ugliness of the opposition to Washington.

In a city where Democratic mayoral candidates had been consecutively winning the office by near-landslide proportions for more than half a century, huge numbers of Whites had deserted the Democrats to vote for the GOP's little-known nominee. Washington won by just four percentage points. "Why," I asked, "did so many white Chicagoans find it impossible to vote for the candidate of the party that had claimed their loyalty for so long? ... Why was it all right for black citizens of Chicago to vote for white candidates year after year but not for white citizens to vote for a black candidate just this once? I answered the core of my own question: "[T]he refusal of so many [whites] to acknowledge black competence, black equality, and the need to share power with black people."

But I also noted the positive implications, too: "The black vote went to Washington out of affirmative pride, the same pride that brought Irish-Americans out to vote for John Kennedy in 1960." And I also counted as a positive "the ability of a black candidate to win a significant minority of white voters, even in a city as racially backward as Chicago. That gives hope that our society contains the seeds of racially mature attitudes." (F. 15)

A new source of hope stemmed from the jolt of energy these mayoral developments gave the campaign for creating a federal holiday to honor Martin Luther King, Jr. By the early 1980s, Democratic Representative John Conyers of Detroit had annually been submitting legislation establishing a Martin Luther King, Jr. Holiday since April 8, 1968 — four days after King had been assassinated. And just as often, Conyers' bill (with its numerous co-sponsors) never made it to the floor of the House for a vote. But in 1979, Stevie Wonder, the great singer and composer, took up the cause — writing another of his many hits, "Happy Birthday" — that lit the spark to what became a mass movement. **(F. 16)**

Wonder's financial backing and highly visible, vigorous championing of a holiday changed the dynamics of the campaign. It was an early indication Black Americans were ready once again to undertake campaigns of mass-action in response to the turn toward conservatism that was clear among White Americans. (F. 17) In that regard, after the increased turnouts of Black voters in the 1982 midterm elections and the 1983 mayoral contests, it was no surprise that "Happy Birthday" was a centerpiece of the ceremonies at the Lincoln Memorial in August 1983 when a throng of more than 300,000 gathered to commemorate the 1963 March on Washington and King's iconic speech. By then, the momentum for the Holiday in Congress was unstoppable. In a symbolic, bipartisan act, the Senate Majority Leader, Republican Howard H. Baker, Jr, of Tennessee, guided the final bill to a 78 to 22-vote passage— more than enough to override a threatened Reagan veto.

More embarrassing for Reagan was the revelation two days before he was to sign the legislation of derogatory remarks he had recently made indicating he agreed with an allegation a Southern segregationist head often made: that he was a communist sympathizer. At a news conference, a reporter had asked Reagan whether he believed King had associated with communists. Reagan quipped, "We'll know in about 35 years," referring to F.B.I. documents that were under seal until 2027 because of a dispute between the agency and the King family. (F. 18)

Sought out by reporters, Coretta Scott King icily replied that it was an "insult. It's hard for me," she said, "to see that someone like ... [Reagan] really believes in equality. What kind of America does he want it to be? He doesn't represent America." The President was compelled to telephone her and apologize—although he himself fudged whether he had done so. Quoting a Reagan spokesman, the *New York Times* account reported that the President had told Mrs. King "he just wanted to make sure he hadn't been misunderstood." But a spokesman for Ms. King bluntly said that the President had told her he made a mistake and 'was wrong.'" Less than a week later, on November 2, the President, sitting at a table in the White House Rose Garden with Coretta Scott King and members of the King Family, Representative John Conyers, and a host of other dignitaries arrayed behind him, signed the legislation establishing the Martin Luther King, Jr. Federal Holiday. (F. 19)

The King Holiday campaign was much more than a "feel-good" event. It was a hard-fought *political* struggle and, importantly, a victory that ordinary Black Americans could feel was *their* doing. In the midst of a conservative ascendancy, when the President of the United States was adding to his long record of denigrating African-Americans' claims to full citizenship, their activism had been the crucial element in the multiracial coalition that insisted the society honor the man who was the greatest twentieth-century representative of Black Americans' struggle against oppression — and also the best representative of that bundle of facts, assertions, hopes, and myths called the *American Dream.*

As I noted in a late August *To Be Equal* column when the House of Representatives passed the bill and sent it to the Senate, "the arguments (such as the holiday's cost to the economy) against a holiday honoring Dr. King are specious. The real issue is not cost but the meaning of national holidays. Special days like July 4 or Memorial Day symbolize the nation's deepest ideals. They aim at uniting all Americans behind those ideals. ... They direct our attention to our past, to sacrifices for our freedoms, and to the principles that bind us together."

I went on to write that "a King Day would buttress the principles that undergird American democracy and ideals. ... That's because the ideals of the American revolution — liberty and equality — were often grossly ignored until the civil rights revolution of the 1960s. Barely twenty years ago, this was a country of officially segregated facilities, officially sanctioned violations of civil rights, and officially institutionalized racism. .... Honoring Dr. King ... would constitute powerful symbolism that would have tremendous meaning not only for black people, whose vital contributions to America have never been acknowledged, but for all minorities and for white Americans who understand we are a pluralistic society whose ethnic and racial diversity is a central factor in our greatness."

Finally, I wrote that a King Holiday was necessary "to focus national attention on the uncompleted ideal of racial equality. It would be an annual reminder that the principles Dr. King symbolized are yet to be fulfilled. ... [and] an important indicator of national resolve to fulfill those principles and make ours a society of equals." (F. 20)

Ironically, Black Americans' activism in the early 1980s against the Reagan Administration's obvious attempts to erase the advances and the lessons of the Civil Rights Movement proved that they, too, had a certain nostalgia for the years before the enactment of the Civil Rights Act of 1964 and the Voting Rights Act of 1965, the high-water mark of that era.

But, though intertwined with the larger society's cultural nostalgia for the late 1940s and 1950s — and excepting the nostalgia attached to one's own family and community — the main element of Black Americans' nostalgia was *political.* It recalled the civil rights struggles of those years—including such hallmarks as Jackie Robinson's breaking the color barrier of Major League Baseball, President Truman's executive order integrating the military, the *Brown* school desegregation decision, the murder of Emmett Till, the Montgomery Bus Boycott; the Little Rock school desegregation crisis; the Freedom Rides of 1961, and many more episodes of their long struggle for equal rights.

Black Political Nostalgia implicitly demanded a sense of selflessness and even of self-sacrifice in service to advancing the Race. Honoring that era's strides toward freedom, the Back Political Nostalgia of the 1980s implicitly rebuked the White Fifties Nostalgia dynamic for what it left out about the injustices of the period — and declared that the same passion and sense of solidarity that motivated Black

Americans then were now needed to resist the conservative ascendancy in all its forms.

This holding on to the sense of mission that had made the Civil Rights Movement so powerful would surface more explicitly in Jesse Jackson's campaign for the 1984 Democratic Party presidential nomination. As historian Manning Marable wrote in a comprehensive review of that effort, Jackson understood "that the idealism and religious enthusiasm which was the foundation of the modern desegregation movement had to become the core of his own candidacy. ... This inference produced unprecedented support from Black America's most powerful institution, the Black Church." (F. 21)

By mid-1983, speculation about the new outlet for the excitement and energy that had flared among Black Americans amid the King Holiday battle and the mayoral results in Chicago, Philadelphia, and Charlotte grew to a fever pitch—because it had settled on promoting a black candidate for the Democratic nomination for president.

That idea had begun percolating with an increasing degree of seriousness among some Black politicians, activists and scholars during the late Carter years. That was due in significant measure to the concerns Vernon Jordan and then other Black leaders had leveled at the Carter administration during the summer of 1977, never having been satisfactorily answered as a series of crises at home and abroad overwhelmed Carter's presidency. The feeling that Blacks were being marooned in a political no-man's land by both the Democratic Party and the GOP was part of the impetus behind the voter registration campaigns launched almost as soon as the 1980 election ended.

The result was what numerous political observers had long expected would come at some point during the 1980s: a Jesse Jackson candidacy. Jackson was hardly without critics among the Black civil rights and political establishment who felt his ambitions outweighed his actual accomplishments. (F. 22) But there was no denying that his rhetorical gifts and ability to inspire people to action were unmatched. If there was going to be a black candidate vying for the Democratic Party nomination, it was going to be Jesse Jackson — an outsider to both the Black and the White political establishments.

In that regard, Jackson was following the trail forged a decade earlier by a Black politician who was even more of an outsider: Shirley Chisholm, the first black woman elected to Congress, who was just in her second term in office and relatively unknown when she launched her campaign for the 1972 Democratic presidential nomination. She didn't expect to win it; she wanted to push the Party to take up more progressive legislation, in general, and become more "open" to African Americans and other Americans of color.

At a time when conservative white Democrats still held great power within the party, and the Congress was an unabashed patriarchy, Chisholm's campaign was immediately derided by many Black and White male politicians and pundits as a foolish misadventure. (F. 23) Even most of her Democratic allies — including most of the Congressional Black Caucus and, at the Democratic National Convention, the 1,000-delegate-strong Women's Caucus — did not endorse her, believing that the eventual nominee, South Dakota Senator George McGovern, would need all the political strength the Party could muster to defeat

President Nixon. (F. 24) Nonetheless, Chisholm's determination, political smarts, and considerable charisma took her all the way to the Democratic Convention's first ballot before she was compelled to withdraw in favor of McGovern. She had entered twelve primaries and gained 430,703 votes and nearly 152 delegates, ten percent of the total. (F. 25)

Twenty-some years later, few expected Jackson to do as well, albeit the increased turnouts of Black voters in the 1982 and 1983 elections. The mechanics of a presidential primary campaign were far more complex than those of local and state contests. And, overwhelmingly, most of the Black political establishment thought the effort would hurt the Democratic presidential chances against Reagan the following year and stymie the political progress Blacks were making. (F. 26) My counterpart at the NAACP, Ben Hooks, penned an op-ed for *The Washington Post* opposing the idea, and Coretta Scott King that October worried it would provoke a "backlash" that would undermine Democratic chances to defeat Reagan. Even Jackson's former Southern Christian Leadership Conference colleague among Martin Luther King, Jr.'s top aides, Andrew Young, then Mayor of Atlanta, rejected the idea in a somewhat roundabout fashion. "Blacks ought to be in any campaign," he told the *New York Times*, "where the candidate is likely to be elected president." (F. 27)

I, too, was opposed to a Black candidacy, and I said so in a May op-ed article in the *New York Times*. "The idea of entering a black candidate in the Democratic presidential primaries is being intensely debated in the black community," I wrote straightaway. "There is much to

commend it, but it is an idea whose time has not yet come."
My opposition wasn't a matter of personal animus against
Jesse. As with Vernon's criticism of Jimmy Carter in 1977
and my continuing criticism of Ronald Reagan, my
opposition was driven by a consideration of what was best
for Black America. (F. 28)

For me, it was a matter of weighing potential benefits
against the negatives. Advocates of the idea, I said, claimed
that a black candidate would inspire many Blacks to register
to vote, focus attention on issues of special concern to
Blacks, influence the Democratic Party's platform, and
"condition America to the legitimacy of black political
aspirations on a national scale."

But I felt the attempt to get Black Americans — its
politicians and highly diverse population of civic and
religious leaders, and individuals from all walks of life—on
a national scale to coalesce behind a single Black candidate
"would fragment, not unify the community" — for example,
by disrupting alliances and relationships Black political
officeholders, operatives and business and community
leaders had built with White politicians and mainstream
Democratic organizations at the local, state and national
levels.

And I worried that the idea's supporters, inspired by the
successes of recent Black campaigns, had not accurately
calculated the difficulties such a candidacy would encounter
in a *national* contest. Jesse had no political organization —
both in terms of bureaucratic infrastructure and a cadre of
seasoned political operatives to run it. Nor did he have
relationships with a network of politicians and wealthy
donors that are crucial to mounting an effective national

campaign. Indeed, albeit the formation of the Congressional Black Caucus in 1972 (in 1983, it had 17 members) and the Chisholm campaign that same year, only one Black American — Edward W. Brooke of Massachusetts — had ever been elected to any statewide office in the country in the twentieth century. **(F. 29)**

"This, of course, is not to suggest," I went on to say, "that a Black person should not run for President — several Black political figures come to mine who are equal or superior to the current crop of candidates. But that's different from unifying the black community behind a single candidate chosen by community leaders to speak for it."

But neither my concerns nor those of numerous others in the broader Black leadership could deter Jackson's own ambition. He formally announced his candidacy on November 3, 1983. By then, there were many who believed — correctly, it turned out — that the Democrats were doomed to defeat in 1984 anyway. The Democratic front-runner, Carter's vice-president, the solidly liberal Walter Mondale, was an earnest but unexciting stump speaker, and the Party's main argument against Reagan — the bad economy of the early 1980s — had evaporated in the face of a strong recovery. Indeed, by late 1983, White America was well on its way to a boom. The unemployment rate for both White men and women had fallen to under 6.4 percent as the election year opened; by November's election day, their respective rates would be under 5.7 percent.

The economic picture for Black Americans, however, presented a sharp contrast. As the year 1983 began, Black Americans were still experiencing Depression-level unemployment — 21.2 percent that January. The rate did fall sharply from there. Yet, that still left the official unemployment rates for both Black men and women above 15 percent at year's end. The country's election-year economic boom would lower them further to 12.5 percent and 13.4 percent, respectively, by the general election. But that meant they were more than twice as high as that of their White counterparts.

It was that continuing economic calamity and the Reagan Administration's continuing political warfare against Black Americans that convinced many it was imperative to capitalize on Jackson's potential to intensify Blacks' political enthusiasm. Despite his campaign's noticeable disorganization and the bitter controversy his uttering an anti-Jewish slur to a Black *Washington Post* reporter provoked, which occupied the mainstream media for the rest of the campaign, Jackson would run in twelve Democratic primaries, gain victories in five of them, * and garner a total of 3.2 million votes, 18.5% of the Party's total primary votes. (F. 30) At the national convention, he won the votes of 12.1 percent of the delegates, compared to Senator Gary Hart's 31.1 percent and Mondale's 56.8 percent. (F. 31)

Jackson's showing was substantially the result of the massive support of individual Black churches and their denominational headquarters across the land. Over 90 percent of Black American clergy had endorsed Jackson within two months of his announcement, and by the spring, three powerful denominations — the National Baptist Convention, U.S.A. with its 6.5 million members, the National Baptist Convention of America, with its 2 million members, and the Pentecostal Church of God in Christ, with its 3.7 million members — were pouring all sorts of resources into Jackson's otherwise underfunded and short-staffed campaign: contributing money, transporting Black voters to the polls, distributing literature, and organizing political motorcades. One religious leader commented that "Jesse's running has made people understand the importance of government. The impact of it will be revolutionary." (F. 32)

That forecast seemed credible despite a Reagan victory that was even more massive than in 1980. Given the overall Democratic Party weakness, no one could say Jackson's presence had damaged the vote-getting performance of the Walter Mondale-Geraldine Ferraro ticket. (F. 33) On the contrary, even though Democrats were to lose the 1988 election as well, the energized Black electorate that had come into being in the early 1980s would prove the "silver-lining" foundation of the Party's future presidential successes in 1992 and 2008. The Black electorate's turnout in November 1984 had increased by a remarkable five percentage points over its 1980 showing: 55.8 percent of Black voters went to the polls, compared to a 50.5 percent turnout in 1980 (and a 48.7 percent turnout in 1976). By contrast, the figure for White voter turnout moved only slightly: from 60.9 percent to 61.4 percent, respectively (60.9 percent of White registered voters had also gone to the polls in 1976). (F. 34)

Equally important though far less visible, the Jackson '84 campaign gave a new cohort of Black political operatives hands-on experience in running a national political campaign — an experience that would swell their ranks and make them far more effective in 1988, when

Jackson again ran in the primaries, and 1992 presidential election cycles. And their success in turning out the Black vote helped Black politicians and operatives gain more influence within the Democratic Party's leadership strata. * (F. 35)

Contrary to the propaganda from conservatives that Blacks had unthinkingly tied themselves to the Democratic Party's apron strings — couched in there ugly racist jargon of a "Democrat plantation" — the initial sharp and vocal differences of opinion within the Black political class about the wisdom of a Black presidential candidacy made it clear that Blacks were playing two-party politics *within* the only Party that made room for them: the Democratic Party. For Blacks, the exalted boast of American exceptionalism that both major parties were open to all comers, reflecting the "melting pot" of American society itself, had never been fully accurate. In fact, it had largely been incorrect. They knew that since the Civil War both Democratic and Republican parties had always been characterized by sharp schisms rooted in race.

The most virulent example was the Dixiecrat southern-segregationist faction of the former. But, as mentioned before, the GOP had always had a bloc of office-holders who, wanting the Party to attract more White Southern voters, kept trying to make it more accommodating to segregationist policies. Their breakthrough came when Arizona Senator Barry Goldwater, who had opposed the 1964 Civil Rights Act (and would oppose the 1965 Voting Rights Act), gained the GOP's 1964 presidential nomination. Against Lyndon Baines Johnson, Goldwater went down to a landslide defeat, capturing only five other states besides his home state. However, those states notably comprised the core of the Old Confederacy: Louisiana, Mississippi, Alabama, Georgia, and South Carolina — the most virulently racist states in the nation. The GOP's new posture on racial issues was cemented in 1968 by Richard Nixon's adoption of the so-called Southern Strategy. * (F.36)

In the 1980s, the Black electorate and political class not only proved the strength of their *institutional* presence within the Democratic Party, but they also showed it now consisted of an "establishment faction" (those politicians and leading Black figures who supported Mondale's candidacy) and a more left-leaning faction (those who unreservedly promoted Jackson's candidacy and generally took positions more to the left on a range of issues). In real terms, the differences between these two groups were largely a matter of tactics, not policy — unlike the real policy differences that existed among Whites in the Party's establishment, progressive and conservative blocs.

Nonetheless, the willingness of the Black Democratic political class to openly split ranks in 1984 over the issue of Jackson's candidacy was itself a measure of Blacks becoming more integrated into the operating structure of the Democratic Party.

This starkly contrasted with what was happening in the GOP. There, under Reagan and Bush (and even afterward), as the Party moved further toward extremist conservatism, a slavish regime of group-think and group-speak became the norm for those who wanted to play politics under its wrongly named "Big Tent." Rock-ribbed traditional Black Republicans, including even Samuel Pierce, were ignored.

(F. 37) And, albeit the rhetoric, the GOP's so-called New Black Conservatives were glaringly absent from Administration and Party positions of influence. (F. 38) In sharp contrast, as the 1980s ended, Ron Brown, who in the late 1970s was head of the National Urban League's Washington Office and had been Jesse Jackson's campaign manager in 1988, was taking office as the new chairman of the Democratic National Committee — a position from which he would help produce the Clinton electoral victory in 1992. (F. 39)

Revealingly, despite the Reagan Administration's control of the government and the Party machinery, no Black Republicans were elected to Congress during the entire two terms of Reagan's tenure. **(F. 40)**

Chapter 13 – Free South Africa! The U.S. Anti-Apartheid Movement

If the exact size of the Reagan victory in 1984 over the Democrats' Mondale-Geraldine Ferraro ticket was somewhat of a surprise, few had doubted the election's overall outcome beforehand. So, for Black Americans, the major question in its wake was what would happen to all that political energy they had generated among themselves over the previous two years: would it dissipate now that they had not achieved their electoral goal?

The answer came swiftly, and it would result in a defeat for the Reagan Administration's 'constructive engagement' policy toward South African apartheid, even more bitter than the loss it had suffered in the King Holiday battle. Administration officials had claimed upon taking office that quiet diplomacy and friendly persuasion rather than public criticism would convince South Africa's Afrikaner regime to jettison at least some aspects of its pervasive denial of citizenship rights to the country's 22 million Black South Africans.

Instead, the regime's measures became even more restrictive. For example, it soon announced it would require residents of the Black townships — its ghettos — that were in or near its (White majority) cities to move to isolated and barren rural "homelands" that would be segregated not only by race but also by the different Black African tribes which comprised the total Black population.

By then, it was clear that the Sullivan Principles, the code of conduct for American companies that did business in

South Africa, were of little use. Under it, nearly two hundred companies had pledged to treat their Black and White employees in their businesses equally in wages and job opportunities. The principles had been devised in 1977 by Reverend Leon Sullivan, the Philadelphia-based minister and civil rights activist, whose 1971 appointment to the board of General Motors had made him the first African-American on a major corporate board. But by the mid-1980s it wasn't clear those pledges were being carried out to any significant degree, and, in any case, the number of Black workers covered by the Sullivan code was disappointingly small. [**New F.1**]

That reality was a major provocation for increasing protests among Black South Africans and, in the U.S., the formation of the Free South Africa Movement. In both places, mass street protests were now added to governmental and corporate lobbying to intensify the pressure against the Afrikaner's brutal system of racial oppression. (Similar public protests were erupting in Western European countries, especially England, France, and Germany.)

There had been a small anti-apartheid movement in the U.S. since the early 1960s. Its demands had been almost completely ignored by a public consumed with other matters, by private companies whose profits from their South African operations and trading relationships outweighed human rights concerns, and by a federal government whose Cold War-driven alliance with the Afrikaner regime **(F. 2)** seemed enduring. In the mid-1980s, however, a confluence of forces would completely upend long-held expectations that apartheid there would last well into the twenty-first century. And in those years — my years at the top of the organization — the Urban League would play an appropriate but — except for one particular moment — far from visible role.

The most important force for change was the increased militancy of the freedom movement inside South Africa. The sudden rebellion by residents of the Soweto township (ghetto) of Johannesburg in 1976, which quickly spread to others, had caught the Afrikaner regime off-guard, and they suppressed it with murderous force. But the willingness to challenge the system had not died out. Crucially, it had spread among the Black workers' unions and the middle class. Their gaining the benefits of increased wages (still deeply inferior compared to Whites') intensified their hatred of apartheid even more. Finally, the independence gained by almost all the majority-Black nations of sub-Saharan Africa underscored the depth of Black South Africans' disadvantage in their own country. **(F. 3)**

Still, few in this country or elsewhere in the West could have predicted how fast change was coming. Indeed, in one sense, apartheid's seeming durability was symbolized by the continued imprisonment of Nelson Mandela, the unquestioned leader of the Black South Africans' freedom movement. Mandela had been convicted of crimes against the state in the early 1960s and, along with several of his colleagues, sentenced to life in prison.

At the time, no one believed Mandela would ever be free again. And yet, the poise with which Mandela and those imprisoned with him met their seeming fate turned the tables on the regime. The government reckoned that locking him away would make him fade from the world's attention and throw the freedom movement there into disarray. Instead,

Mandela became more famous than ever. He embodied the durability of the movement's resistance and the courage of those involved in it.

Although the South African government brutally suppressed the Soweto uprising, the protest marked the beginning of the end of apartheid. Within a decade, its foundations would be shaken from within by a reinvigorated freedom movement and from outside by a mass movement in the United States and Western Europe that forced American and European governments and private companies to threaten to destroy South Africa's economy if it did not end its scheme of racial oppression.

Fourteen years after the Soweto uprising and twenty-seven years after his life sentence, Nelson Mandela was released to begin the discussions with the Afrikaner leadership that would lead to the end of white minority rule, and in 1994, he became president of South Africa.

On November 22, 1984, little more than two weeks after President Reagan's overwhelming landslide re-election, the city of Washington's delegate to Congress, Reverend Walter E. Fauntroy, a former top aide to Martin Luther King, Jr., was arrested for staging a sit-in at the South African Embassy in the city. Arrested with him were Mary Francis Berry, a member of the U.S. Commission on Civil Rights, and Randall Robinson, head of TransAfrica, a lobbying group that sought to influence American policy on Africa and the Caribbean. They were protesting the South African government's apartheid policy in general and particularly its ongoing suppression of protests in Black townships in support of a work stoppage by Black workers.

Taken to court, the three pled not guilty to charges of unlawful entry, refused to post bond, and spent the night in jail. They had entered the Embassy with Eleanor Holmes Norton, the former head of the Federal Equal Employment Opportunity Commission under President Carter, but she had left to alert the media to their action.

At a news conference the next day, Fauntroy described their protest as "an act of moral witness. … in response to the repressive action of the South African Government …[against] the noble, nonviolent protest of black South Africans over the last few months." They also said they were preparing to organize daily demonstrations in front of the Embassy. **(F. 4)**

The media reported on their protest in a modest fashion—brief stories on the television evening newscasts and brief articles buried deep within the newspapers. **(F. 5)** That seemed appropriate. After all, when in October, the Reagan Administration delegation at the United Nations had abstained from voting on a Security Council resolution condemning apartheid (which otherwise drew unanimous support), there was no significant public reaction. **(F. 6)** Nor when Bishop Desmond Tutu, one of the leaders of the South African freedom movement and who had just been awarded the Nobel Peace Prize, had declared the Administration was "aligning itself with the perpetrators of the most vicious system since Nazism." **(F. 7)**

By early December, however, it was apparent that small protests were becoming something much bigger.* **(F. 8)** Organized with almost military precision by TransAfrica, the demonstrations were indeed staged daily throughout December, and they brought substantial numbers of people—and prominent figures, ranging from local politicians and members of Congress to well-known entertainers and writers—to stand before the Embassy and be arrested. **(F. 9)** By the next fall, when a National Anti-Apartheid Protest Day was staged, more than 3,000 demonstrators had been arrested at the South African Embassy in Washington, and tens of thousands had participated in protests of one sort or another across the country. **(F.10)**

The protests at the former followed a set routine. The organizers and demonstrators had determined who among them was to be arrested. Those individuals would step forward when the police demanded the crowd disperse. The police would politely handcuff them with zip ties and take them to the city municipal court, where they would be charged and released on their own recognizance. It also quickly became apparent that none of those arrested would ever face trial: the minor charges would be dismissed.

The size and spread of the protests through the winter and into the spring forced President Reagan and his spokesmen into a series of ever more hollow claims of "constructive engagement's" supposed progress. Those were undercut by the media's now-intensive reporting **(F. 11)** on how apartheid in South Africa actually affected the lives of Black South Africans and by the growing criticism from seasoned foreign policy observers and dozens of Republican and Democratic members of Congress. **(F. 12)** By 1986 55 percent of the public felt that the US should apply more pressure on the South African government, 24 percent approved of the current level of pressure; only 14 percent said less pressure was appropriate. **(F 13)**

I stated the obvious in my first column of the new year: the Reagan Administration's 'constructive engagement' had not worked. "South Africa's leaders have taken it to mean American toleration of blatant violations of human rights. And in the absence of outside pressures, they have solidified their system. ... [It's time] for a drastic change in U.S. policy."

I well understood, I added, the arguments that important American commercial and national security interests in South Africa required not antagonizing the Afrikaner leadership. But, I declared, such claims could no longer be "the excuse" for "cooperating with such an evil system."

Instead, I contended, because "apartheid is doomed to fall sooner or later" — Mandela's release from prison five years later would mark the symbolic end of apartheid — the U.S. government needed to support those American and South African companies working for positive change there.

"That would include," I argued, "voting in the U.N. to condemn outrages, embargoes on militarily sensitive materials, and sanctions on new investments, among other steps. At the same time, the U.S. could generally assist educational, training, union, and self-help groups within South Africa that are working for change and from whom the country's future leaders will come. Ultimately, only South Africa's whites and blacks — together — can find a way out of this tragic situation. America's proper role is to be helpful in that process: to nurture it and to support constructive change." **(F. 14)**

I could have begun that column with the line *I told you so* — because of the warning I had delivered in a 1982 column on the Afrikaner regime's illegal occupation of

South West Africa, the territory which was to become Namibia on its independence in 1990.

Then, I wrote, "our southern Africa policy seems doomed to failure. We've been manipulated by South Africa into delaying a final settlement that brings independence to Namibia and South African withdrawal from illegal occupation of that country. ... So long as we are perceived as South Africa's supporter and friend, the U.S. will be unable to help shape events in the region and will only harvest enmity from the people there. It should be obvious that South Africa's apartheid system will one day disappear, submerged in a tide of revolt. ... Sound national policy suggests an arms-length relationship, not close friendship." **(F. 15)**

Now, in the winter of 1985, that prediction—of course, made by many others over the years—had come true. The Free South Africa Movement also acquired a piercing comparative resonance when a furious months-long controversy erupted on news that Reagan had accepted the invitation of West German Chancellor Helmut Kohl to pay homage to World War II German soldiers by visiting a military cemetery in the town of Bitburg. **(F. 16)**

I referred briefly to the controversy in an April 3d *To Be Equal* column written in response to South Africa police having shot to death a reported forty demonstrators and wounded dozens more during a commemoration of the infamous Sharpeville Massacre of 1960. Reagan had accepted at face value South African officials's assertion that the heavily armed police had no choice but to fire on the unarmed marchers, declaring that there was "an element in

South Africa that does not want a peaceful settlement, who want trouble in the streets."

I likened that "remarkable" claim to declaring "the prisoners in a Russian gulag were to be blamed for wanting freedom." And then I added, "Those remarks, along with his [initial] refusal to visit a former Nazi concentration camp on the 40th anniversary of its liberation by Allied troops, betray an insensitivity to human suffering and to American ideals of freedom and liberty." Administration officials, I added, "... condemn the latest South African outrage, but unless they change the policy of 'constructive engagement' that is seen by [the Afrikaner regime] as a continued license for oppression, such statements will ring hollow." **(F. 17)**

I also wrote that the Administration was misreading the reluctance of American corporate leaders doing business in South Africa — caught between their own humanitarian impulses and the economic imperatives of the companies — to publicly speak out. "In recent months," I said, "I have talked with many corporate executives who are deeply troubled by [the government's] inhumane policies and by the economic inefficiencies caused by apartheid. Many are coming to the conclusion that their continued presence in South Africa may no longer be worth the trouble." **(F. 18)**

I noted, too, that even those business executives who supported staying were exerting their own kind of pressure against apartheid — via the dynamic of rising expectations. Measures such as integrating their work forces, training Black employees for higher-level jobs within their companies, and negotiating with Black trade unions over wages and working standards in and of themselves stood in opposition to the stark rules of apartheid. They were, in effect, reinforcing the freedom movement's assertions that change could be achieved quickly. **(F. 19)**

Of course, I said in an October *To Be Equal* column that American companies "operate in many different political environments, often in countries that abuse human rights and violate the most elementary principles of decency. A requirement that countries in which they do business must be democratic would mean abandoning a large part of their overseas operations."

But South Africa," I went on, "is qualitatively different —and corporate leaders know it. Other countries may abuse minorities or trample on their rights. But only South Africa is a state founded on the suppression of blacks, who outnumber the ruling white minority by four to one." **(F. 20)**

Those columns' words underscored the fact that the possibility of an "evolutionary change" from apartheid in South Africa was "outdated now. It is clear that there is only one real issue — sharing power. …[and] U.S. companies are faced with a stark choice: either abandon operations there or become aggressive advocates of change within South Africa. And if South Africa does not begin to dismantle the apartheid system within months, then it seems that the only course left for U.S. companies is to leave."

During the next two years, the business community's confidence that it was a force for good there eroded sharply — along with the financial incentives for hanging on — as the fierce resistance of the Afrikaner regime to change shredded what was left of the fig-leaf policy of 'constructive engagement.' The death blow to that rationalization — and ultimately to the South African regime's existence — came the following year when Congress passed the

Comprehensive Anti-Apartheid Act of 1986. Both Houses of Congress voted for the law by such wide margins that in late September and early October, each easily overrode Reagan's veto. **(F. 22)**

The Act's provisions lived up to its title, for it struck at the very core of the South African economy. Among other things, it barred new U.S. loans and corporate investments in the country and barred U.S. companies from deducting South African taxes from their income; declared that South African governmental agencies could no longer deposit funds in American banks; prohibited the importing of such South African goods as steel, iron, uranium, coal, textiles, and farm products; and banned South African airlines from flying to the U.S. and U.S. airlines from flying to South Africa.

By the end of 1986, the anti-apartheid momentum had made itself felt across the American political and economic landscape: 21 states, 68 cities, and 10 of the nation's largest counties had adopted divestment policies. More than 100 educational institutions had withdrawn nearly a half-billion dollars from companies profiting from apartheid. Some three hundred fifty American corporations operated in South Africa in 1984; eighty of them, including GM, IBM, Coca-Cola, Eastman Kodak, Honeywell, Exxon, and McGraw-Hill, had pulled out by 1987. The Xerox corporation was among that number, too. **(F. 23)**

In late November 1984, I doubt if even the most fervent anti-apartheid optimist in the United States had envisioned the day six years hence — February 1, 1990 — when Nelson Mandela would walk out of his long imprisonment to the rapturous cheers of millions in South Africa and around the globe. He was released to continue the often fraught negotiations with the Afrikaner political leadership that would result in the actual end of the structure of apartheid. I recalled that day four years later, on 4 May 1994 — two days after he had won the presidency of the new South Africa and shortly before I retired as President and CEO of the National Urban League — as one proving that "miracles do happen [and] challenges [can be] overcome …"

But, as Mandela made clear, he recognized the new democracy faced massive challenges. Perhaps the most daunting, I noted, "comes from tremendous expectations aroused among South Africa's black majority" who had long been burdened by a "grinding poverty" as well as a brutal racism limiting every aspect of their lives. "Now, a people impatient for results face the reality of a long, uphill struggle to stabilize a shattered economy and share the jobs and benefits of a society more equitably." **(F. 24)**

Undoubtedly, all those who participated in the demonstrations against South Africa in Washington and across the US were inspired by the pursuit of liberty the movement in South Africa was waging. But for Black Americans, as I mentioned before, this was an issue in which they were driven by the same dynamic of Black Political Nostalgia that underlay the demonstrations for the King Holiday and also the voter registration campaigns responsible for the successes of many Black candidates for notable political offices throughout the decade. **(F. 25)**

The economic and political setbacks of the 1970s and the threat their predicament would grow worse during a Reagan presidency had led Black Americans to forge a powerful political mobilization. Far from being dispirited by Reagan's two landslide electoral victories, Black Americans and their allies challenged those who would have diminished Martin Luther King, Jr. and the achievements of the Civil Rights Movement—*who would have, in effect, diminished their right to be Americans*—and they were victorious.

However, that didn't mean they won the *war,* which would continue. It did mean that in a decade of profound political and economic challenges, Black Americans remained in a mood of determined resistance. They became the foundation of the King Holiday Battle and U.S. Free South Africa Movement — whose effectiveness was buoyed by its use of the mass-movement tactics of the 1950s-1960s civil rights movement — showed once again that *as a group,* Black Americans' feelings of nostalgia were not primarily a sentimental remembering of the past. Sentimental nostalgia — remembering (or misremembering) and celebrating a past — was for individuals and families and civic celebrations.

Black Political Nostalgia, on the other hand, was remembering that the African American past was defined by acts of resistance to the unjust status quo and *movement* toward freedom and that such actions were always necessary. That first sit-in at the South African Embassy was a clarion call to take the issue of apartheid out of the Reagan Administration's hands and beyond the confines of debates in Congress, academia and think-tanks, corporate board rooms, and the newspaper op-ed pages to make it a *mass-movement* issue, a *participatory-democracy* issue, something within the reach of ordinary people.

In the first weeks of the protests at the South African Embassy in Washington, that point tended to get lost in the glare of the well-known politicians, public intellectuals, and entertainers who came for civil disobedience and possible arrest in front of an audience. So did the fact that by the 1985 mid-winter, the protests there, which had settled into a civil, well-choreographed routine that resulted in all charges against arrested protesters being eventually dismissed, were being staffed overwhelmingly, not by the well-known but by ordinary people — Blacks and Whites and other Americans. The civility of those small acts of civil disobedience belied the fervor of the movement spreading across the country (and in Europe) and gathering momentum in the halls of Congress.

That desire to do more than "dialogue" with our corporate partners and aid anti-apartheid lobbying efforts with local and state governments and Congress had spread throughout the League, too. That led, during our 1985 annual conference in Washington in late July, to what had for all the League's history been unthinkable: staff and members of the National Urban League participating in a demonstration.

From its founding, the League had barred its staff from participating precisely because we didn't want to disturb our relationships with the White political and business elite. This wasn't a matter of organizational cowardice but an understanding of our role in the struggle for Black advancement. There were plenty of groups and individuals in Black America willing to walk the picket line to publicly and vigorously demand all the rights Black Americans deserved. The League supported that.

But there were no groups or individuals who could match year in and year out the League's connections to and trust by the White business community — a cohort of people who could and did provide the jobs and job training that Black men and women needed. The League's primary purpose was to expand opportunities in that field, to expand and deepen the economic foundation vital to Black Americans' success — and the work that required was most often best done quietly. Until that summer, the 1963 March on Washington had marked the first and only time the League had relaxed its ban on staff participating in demonstrations; July 23, 1985, would mark the second.

Throughout the winter and spring, I'd been getting more and more calls from affiliate CEOs asking how the Urban League could more publicly demonstrate its support of the anti-apartheid movement. The police murder in early March of 27 adults and children in the Black township of Uitenhage, * likened by some to the infamous Sharpeville Massacre of 1960, was the most shocking of the Afrikaner regime's crackdown on protest there that intensified anti-apartheid opposition in the U.S. and Europe. Some of the executives asked me why I hadn't gone to Washington to protest and even be arrested at the Embassy. (F. 26)

When I threw the question back to them — Why hadn't they?— they said they had their relationships to their Boards to consider. *Well, so do I,* I said, and I reminded them that in the 1970s, when I was Acting Head of the Washington Urban League, I'd had the affiliate join a picket line in front of the Government Printing Office to support the demands of Black printers there for increased wages and promotion activities.

However, both the CEOs and I realized this was a moment for the League to take decisive public action. That the League's annual conference that July was in Washington gave us the perfect opportunity. I called on Clarence Wood,

304

our vice president for field operations, and we all agreed: *If we're going to do something, let's go big.* And we all understood that whatever we were to do, our annual conference, being held that year in Washington, would be just the time to do it.

In the interim we made no announcements about joining the embassy protest. We did invite the Reverend Allan Boesak, who, along with the Reverend Desmond Tutu, was a leader of the struggle in South Africa, to give a major afternoon address at our conference. We were sure, however, that most observers would consider that a typical Urban League approach to furthering dialogue about the issue.

And neither I nor the local executives had forgotten about our being accountable to our boards of directors. I needed to make sure David Kearns understood why we were taking this step — especially since David was not only my board chairman but also the Chairman and CEO of Xerox Corporation, one of the best-known American companies doing business in South Africa. We had already had several discussions about American companies' involvement there. And I respected his opinion: that he believed Xerox was doing some good for its Black South African employees.

But, first, as I settled into a chair in his office, I had a little fun. I said, "David, you have to come and go to jail with me when I lead a demonstration at the South African Embassy while we're in Washington for the national conference."

Startled and a bit breathless, he quickly replied, "Jake, I can't go to jail!"

And I just as quickly answered, "David, that's a joke. I don't want you to go to jail. I need you outside in a position to get *me* out of jail!"

Then, we got down to business, and his response was one I'll never forget. He said, "Jake, I can support your position as long as you don't call me or my company immoral. I can support you because your constituency is different from my constituency, and I recognize you have to do what is best for the people you represent."

I thought then and now what a bold and mature way of viewing things that was. It pinpointed in a few words exactly what the relationship was between the League and its corporate Board members: the trust between us that meant the differences between our constituencies need not preclude our working together. David's words reaffirmed my confidence that I could feel free to have a frank and honest discussion with him on any subject at any time.

In late July, our Conference got underway at the Washington Hilton Hotel in the Connecticut Avenue commercial district, less than two miles from the South African legation's Embassy Row address on Massachusetts Avenue. There were no signs of any leaks to anyone outside the planning circle, which, of course, by then included Boesak. As he finished his remarks, I came to the podium to announce that he and I would be leading a contingent of Urban Leaguers to stand in protest at the South African Embassy.

The response among the conference attendees was electric, and soon, Boesak and I, marching side by side, were leading a throng, various estimates put from 1,200 to 1,500 well-dressed people through the streets of Washington to the embassy grounds. News accounts said it was the largest demonstration at the Embassy to that time. Once there, I banged on the door of its grand entrance until I and some 44 others were politely arrested and taken to court, where we were soon released.

The *Times* news story the following day gave our participation prominent notice— "Urban League Officials Arrested at Embassy," read the headline—as did a sizable swath of the rest of the media in what had long become routine accounts of the action on Washington's Embassy Row. * Their article noted I said at a news conference after being released that, to my knowledge, the League "had never participated in a demonstration such as the one conducted today." It also reported that I said, "I myself had never before been arrested …[and added] 'I don't plan to make a habit of this.'" **(F. 27)**

Chapter 14 – The Complexity of Black Progress

The mass movements Black Americans staged during the Reagan years produced extraordinary achievements. Increased voter turnouts in national, state, and local elections across the country sustained a badly weakened Democratic Party until it could forge a reinvigorated leadership at the end of the decade. They're leading the clamor for a Martin Luther King, Jr. national holiday kept the ideal of equality shining brightly then and ever since. Their vociferous support for ending apartheid in South Africa contributed mightily to forcing the Reagan Administration to reverse its support for that perverse regime. The decade was full of many far less spectacular and less visible actions and achievements that expanded opportunities for Black Americans to live more fulfilling lives.

But those victories were only part of the story—and, as important as they were, they didn't mean that Black America at the end of the 1980s *came out ahead* on most, or even many, of the social and economic indicators of progress. Indeed, in that regard, the decade of the 1980s maintained the vexing "tradition" of Black Americans' experience since Emancipation: one step forward in some areas was always shadowed by one step — or two — backward in other areas.

I said as much in a series of speeches, *To Be Equal* columns, and introductions to *The State of Black America* editions of the late 1980s and early 1990s in assessing the damage the presidencies of Ronald Reagan and George H.W. Bush had done.

Under Reagan, the combination of lower taxes and sky-high defense spending produced an extraordinary increase in the deficit — totaling $1.5 trillion over the course of the decade **(F.1)** — that provided Reagan and the conservative movement with the financial rationale for the massive cuts in social spending they had long advocated. Those deficits would handcuff President Bush throughout his term in office and force Bill Clinton, for his first two years in office to severely moderate increases in social spending his campaign rhetoric had promised. **(F.2)**

They also profoundly deepened the economic havoc that had been undermining Black America's stability since the early 1970s oil shock had turned the American economy upside down: During the Reagan Presidency, federal programs that benefited the Black poor the most were cut drastically. Between 1981 and 1987, the federal government slashed subsidized housing programs by 79 percent, training and employment programs by 70 percent, the Work Incentive Program by 71 percent, **(F. 3)** compensatory education programs for poor children by 12 percent, and community development block grants and community services block grants by well over a third. **(F. 4)**

Those policy actions, along with the persistently high unemployment Black Americans were enduring, added 4 million more people to the poverty rolls in the 1980s, and the real income of the lowest fifth of the population, adjusted for inflation, declined between 1979 and 1986 by $663 per family. In sharp contrast, during those years, the top fifth of the population gained $12,218 in real income. **(F. 5)**

No matter, I wrote, that the polls consistently showed most people disagreed with him on some specific issues, including the harshness of the social program cutbacks and his stance on South Africa. Reagan's likability — his "Teflon Shield" — and the conservative turn of a large segment of White America enabled him to "largely [achieve] the goals he set when he came to office: lower tax rates, a big defense buildup, federal withdrawal from social programs, and less government." **(F. 6)**

The "tragic" result, I asserted, was "many billions wasted on defense programs that don't work could have been invested in training, education and job programs that help[ed] people to get work. And even a conservative program that downgraded the government's role could have been implemented without encouraging anti-social attitudes. After all, true conservatism means conserving what was good in the past and responsibility toward those who have less."**(F. 7)**

In other words, the so-called Reagan boom, I wrote in *The State of Black America*, 1988, "was a false prosperity era, a period in which gains were concentrated on a relatively small portion of the population while large segments of the citizenry saw a real deterioration in their living standards." Not only had the huge transfer of resources from the poor to the affluent worsened the inequality that has been spreading in American society since the late 1960s, but it had also produced a far more unequal society. The "new respectability given to greed and indifference to the suffering of others" had seriously damaged the national unity. (F. 8)

That "tilt in public rhetoric ... to a celebration of wealth without social responsibility" and callousness toward those less fortunate also showed itself in the Reagan and Bush administrations' racial rhetoric and actions. Part of Reagan's legacy was to have made both coded and explicit appeals to anti-Black racism a significant part of the GOP's electoral rhetoric and policy goals. During his tenure, the calculated use of bigotry advanced from the briefest of references to "state's rights" and fulminations about "welfare queens" to destroy the independence of the U.S. Civil Rights Commission, demeaning statements about leaders of Black organizations and outright opposition to existing affirmative action policies and effective enforcement of civil rights laws. **(F. 9)**

Unfortunately, even as Reagan's exit from the White House was in its last months, that poisonous racial legacy reached a despicable new low in the 1988 campaign to succeed his vice-president, George H.W. Bush. The vehicle for that was a convicted murderer. His last name was Horton. His given name — the name he had always been called by his family, friends, in the charging documents against him, and even the state penitentiary correction officers — was *William*. But Bush's campaign managers changed his first name to fit their purposes. They called him "Willie."

William Horton, of course, was the Black convict who escaped from a Massachusetts prison furlough program in 1986 during the governorship of Michael Dukakis, the Democratic Party nominee, and fled the state. The next year in Maryland, Horton kidnapped a young couple, stabbed the man and raped his fiancee. Dukakis had nothing directly to do with the decision to furlough Horton, and he would ultimately end the furlough program altogether. **(F. 10)**

But Bush and Lee Atwater, Bush's senior political strategist — the same man who eight years earlier had crafted the *racist dog-whistle* strategy of Reagan's campaign and presidency — seized upon Horton's crime and made it a key feature of Bush's campaign. Center-stage in the ads was the soon-to-be infamous, slightly blurred picture of a bearded, menacing-looking Horton. **(F. 11)** It could have been a still photo from the notorious 1915 classic racist movie *Birth of A Nation.* Atwater said, "By the time we're finished, they're going to wonder whether Willie is Dukakis's running mate." **(F.12)**

George H. W. Bush was, in many respects, a decent and fair-minded man. But the consequences of his tarring a legitimate question about the validity of prison furloughs for inmates convicted of serious crimes with a racist smear had consequences that resound to this day.

For one thing, it frightened the Democratic Party into taking a harder line on crime and downplaying the necessity of attacking the social roots of much of the "street crime" committed by poor people. As one analyst put it, that approach — on top of the "war on drugs" that in the 1980s had swept hundreds of thousands of Black and Latino men and women into prisons, most of them for low-level, nonviolent, drug-related offenses — came "at the expense of a generation of African-American men and women who were locked up under tougher sentencing laws championed by President Bill Clinton, among others." **(F. 13)**

For another, such racist rhetoric — from an establishment Republican figure who, in his acceptance speech at the Republican National Convention that August had pledged to promote allegiance to "a kindler, gentler" America — once again dragged overt anti-Black thought, language, and actions to the surface of respectable society. Some expressed hope the following year that the

312

gubernatorial victory of Doug Wilder in Virginia and the mayoral election of David Dinkins in New York City * meant that "'Willie' Horton" was an outlier in American politics and American society. **(F. 14)** But that quickly proved to be wishful thinking.

Indeed, its profound utility became apparent in four explosive race-driven controversies that spanned the new president's first two years in office — and whose reverberations continue in the present: the political rise of white-supremacist David Duke in Louisiana; the infamous Central Park Jogger criminal attack in New York City in 1989; the notorious Stuart Murder Case, which occurred later that same year in Boston; and, finally, the 1990 contest for the U.S. Senate in North Carolina between the unreconstructed segregationist Senator Jesse Helms and Harvey B. Gantt, the first Black mayor of Charlotte, North Carolina.

In February 1989, David Duke, who had been a very minor public figure among the state's racist fringe for years, ran under the GOP's banner to win his only victory in what would come to be three decades of otherwise futilely seeking political office. He served for two years as a Representative in the state legislature, then ran unsuccessfully in 1990 for U.S. Senate, in 1991 for Governor, and against Bush in the 1992 Republican primaries.

Bush and other Republican officials denounced Duke and claimed they bore no responsibility for his popularity with White voters. But, in describing the meaning of Duke's presence in national as well as Louisiana politics in the introduction to the 1992 volume of *The State of Black America*, I said that the link from one to the other could not

313

be denied. Duke's rise "strips away the veil of American racism and exposes it to full view. Had Duke donned his Klan hood and waved *Mein Kampf* at election rallies, he would have been dismissed as a lunatic. But with his newly adopted guise of a populist conservative, he mouthed sentiments and code words made familiar through long usage by national leaders, making his sewer ideology appear respectably mainstream."

I added that the "Duke phenomenon cannot be dismissed as a transient or localized exception to national norms. It is a wakeup call to Americans to re-examine our fundamental beliefs and principles and to reject appeals to the dark, vicious side of our history."

I also dismissed the viewpoint some asserted that Whites' "middle-class anger" over their economic difficulties explained the votes he was getting. "From the black perspective," I stated, that "rings false. [Black Americans] have been subjected to four centuries of slavery, oppression, discrimination, and inequality; our middle class has been subjected to tokenism and glass ceilings. Our resentments encompass not merely vague feelings of no longer being preferred over other races but widespread discrimination and daily pinpricks of racially inspired sleights and slurs. If the privileged white middle class is so burdened that it is driven to support an admirer of Hitler, to what extremes should the disadvantaged black middle class be driven?" **(F. 15)**

Further proof that racist thought and actions remained a fundamental facet of American society came quickly. On 19 April 1989, a young woman, jogging along a lightly traveled road in the northern section of Manhattan's Central Park in

314

the early evening, was attacked, dragged far off the roadway, and brutally sexually assaulted: Beaten severely, she lapsed into a coma that lasted twelve days, and lost her memory of the moments just before the assault against her happened. Her ordeal occurred amid a spree of robberies and muggings that an uncertain number of teenagers were perpetrating primarily at the northern end of the park—the part that bordered Harlem.

Police officials immediately mounted a massive response and that evening arrested six Black and Latino teenagers from Harlem, none older than 16, on suspicion of having committed the crime. One of the six was quickly separated from the case, although he was charged with committing another crime in the park that evening and would serve time in prison for that crime.

The five other teens would ultimately be charged with attempted murder, rape, sexual abuse, assault, robbery and riot. Interrogated by the police — without having an attorney present — that evening and into the next day, the boys confessed to various parts of the crime. **(F. 16)** Unlike the preceding interrogations, each boy's confession was videotaped. Within two weeks, each of them recanted, claiming they had been threatened and denied the right to an attorney during the interrogations.

Because they were no older than 16, their identities were not supposed to be made public. But within a week of their arrests, even before they had been formally indicted, their names began appearing in newspapers in New York City and other cities. On May 1, less than two weeks after the crime occurred, Donald Trump placed full-page advertisements in the city's four major newspapers calling for the reinstatement of the death penalty. "Criminals must be told," it blared, "that their Civil Liberties End When an Attack on Our Safety Begins!" The ad was broadly condemned by city officials and Black community leaders. Despite their subsequent exoneration, Trump has continued to claim the ad was justified. **(F. 17)**

The aftermath, of course, is well known. The teens were tried in two separate trials in the summer and fall of 1990, convicted, and sentenced to long terms in juvenile and adult prison. Their convictions were upheld on appeal, and they served from five to twelve years in prison.

In 2002, the case against the Central Park Five cracked when an inmate, Matias Reyes, incarcerated in the same upstate New York prison as one of the Central Park Five, confessed to prison officials and later to a special task force of the Manhattan District Attorney's Office that he — and he alone — had attacked the Central Park Jogger. **(F. 18)** Reyes said that he had met the other inmate, who was in his late 20s, and wanted to end the injustice against him. Reyes, who had worked in a bodega near the northern end of Central Park in 1989, was serving a sentence of 33 1/2 years to life in prison. He had pleaded guilty to raping four women, one of whom he murdered, and attempting to rob a fifth woman during the summer of 1989. Prosecutors also believed he had raped another woman in the same area of the park two days before the attack on the Central Park Jogger occurred.

Reyes' description of how he carried out the attack and of the crime scene, along with new advances in DNA technology, enabled investigators to prove conclusively that his DNA matched the DNA evidence at the crime scene and led in 2002 to the exoneration of the Five. **(F. 19)** In subsequent lawsuits against New York City and New York State, they won a total of more than $44 million. (F. 20)

I opened my *To Be Equal* column on the Central Park Jogger case, written in late May, a month after the arrest of the teens, by saying that the story was being "played out in terms that shed light on some of the nastier sides of our national life.

"The nastiest, of course," I said, "is the attack itself — a vicious assault on a defenseless person by a gang of kids bent on destruction and pursuing the twisted notions of 'fun.' The first — and lasting — impression was that this was a racial attack. The young woman is white; the teenagers are black and Hispanic. But the same gang," I continued, "is alleged to have attacked African-Americans and Hispanics who crossed their path that fateful night, and we all know that black-on-black crime is among the African-American community's most urgent problems. So while no one can say what went on in those kids' minds, there is no evidence to suggest the assault was racial."

Then, I moved to a broader point. "But that's how the public perceived it," I wrote, "which tells us a lot more about racist stereotypes and assumptions than it tells us about what happened. Those racist stereotypes were reinforced by aspects of the way the media handled the story. Headlines about "wolf packs" sent coded signals to equate young black males with animals. We didn't read about "wolf packs" when white youths in Howard Beach assaulted three black men who wandered into their neighborhood, leading to the death of one of them."

I referred to a *Newsweek Magazine* column written by Meg Greenfield, editorial page editor of *The Washington*

Post, which trenchantly dissected "the way such racial stereotyping creates …a whole class of innocent victims. There are the poor black youths and their families … who do not commit crimes, who are living honest and hard-working lives against tremendous (and unfair) disadvantages. They are the ones who get slandered, disregarded, and terribly damaged by the mindless generalities in which the rest of us insist on discussing episodes such as that in Central Park."

I added that it was "instructive, too, that similar instances of rape and attempted murders directed against African-American women do not get much attention. In one case, a [Black] woman attacked and thrown off a rooftop was saved by catching onto a cable wire—that's [usually] the kind of story the press feeds on. But … it was largely ignored. One has to wonder whether the Central Park story would have got off the back pages if the victim had been black."

In other words, I continued, "Double-standard suggests that racism is alive and well in America's newsrooms and in the public mind. And it also suggests that the lives and dignity of African-American women are devalued in those same newsrooms and minds. Feminists have pointed out that rather than being a black-white tragedy, the Central Park assault typified anti-female violence, and many African-American women agree."

As I almost always did with my columns and speeches, I concluded by suggesting *what needs to be done now:* That we must "re-examine [our] racial attitudes …[and] understand the consequences of dehumanizing young black men as 'animals' and 'wolf packs,' and … [focus] our attention on the outrageous attitudes that make women more vulnerable to bodily violence. Most of all, there is a clear message to every parent in the country… [we must] instill in our kids the values and controls that enable them to reject violence and inflict pain on others. And the message to the nation is to give our young men something positive to look forward to—jobs, careers, and programs to get them into the mainstream." **(F. 21)**

The same broader poisonous forces were at work later that year when the nation was transfixed by a murder case widely accepted as proof of the danger of crimes committed by Blacks in general, and especially by Black males: the murder in Boston of a young, White wife and mother-to-be, Carol DiMaiti. On October 23 of that year, the Boston police emergency hotline received an anguished call from Charles Stuart, a 29-year-old manager of an upscale fur store in the city's most exclusive shopping district, saying that his wife, who was seven months pregnant, and he had been carjacked and shot as they drove through a predominantly Black neighborhood called Mission Hill on their way home from attending childbirth classes at a nearby hospital. He said their lone assailant was a Black man who had shot his wife in the head and him in the stomach. **(F. 22)**

The gruesome immediate aftermath of the crime was captured in graphic footage by the camera crew of a CBS network reality television series meant to show the drama of the emergency medical services profession. They just happened to be riding patrol with one of the ambulances that responded to the scene. Charles Stuart's claim that their predator was a Black man was broadcast to the nation that night along with the film footage.

Stuart's story was false. The truth was that with the collusion of one of his brothers, he had shot his wife in the car and then himself that October night in part to gain the money from her life insurance account and because he did not want children. But that truth would not come to light for another two months.

Meanwhile, during the following weeks and amid an outcry that reverberated across the nation for get-tough anti-crime legislation, including reinstating the death penalty, Black Boston was besieged by police raids of homes and dragnets in which many Black men and boys were randomly stopped and manhandled on its streets. In mid-November, police arrested two men in connection with the crime and formally charged the second for it. On 28 December, Charles Stuart identified that man as the shooter.

Then, due to the suspicions of some of his own siblings and some police detectives, the story Charles Stuart had concocted rapidly unraveled. In the early morning of January 4, 1990, as police were searching to find and arrest him, Stuart jumped to his death from a bridge spanning part of the Boston Harbor. **(F. 23)**

In the *To Be Equal* column the week following Charles Stuart's suicide, I wrote that the stigmatization and physical harassment his lies had forced Black Bostonians to endure illuminated one of the most common "faces of racism—the readiness of white citizens, including the establishment and the media, to accept the stereotype of African-Americans as murderous ... [whites] were all too willing to believe the story because it fit [their] pre-existing stereotype of black men." **(F. 24)** In fact, The Stuart murder case was the first of several high-profile crime stories reported by the media in the 1990s in which the perpetrator, who was White, tried to cover up their guilt by claiming a Black man had been responsible.

The high-visibility evidence of racism's continuing impact in American politics continued in the 1990 North Carolina Senate race when Charlotte Mayor Harvey B. Gantt challenged the fiercely conservative and bigoted Republican incumbent, Senator Jesse Helms. Gantt possessed an extraordinary record of achievement: South Carolina-born, he successfully filed suit to become the first Black applicant admitted to Clemson University, graduated from its college with an honors degree in architecture, and earned a master's degree in city planning from Massachusetts Institute of Technology. Then, he returned to Charlotte and opened his own architectural firm. Immersing himself in local politics, he served for nearly a decade on the city council, then won two terms as the city's Mayor.

Gantt was viewed within and outside the region as representative of the "New South's" citizenry — those ready to leave behind the South's legacy of conservative politics grounded in racist appeals. And, strikingly, Gantt led Helms in the polls with less than two weeks to go before the November election.

That was when Helms — who until then had downplayed any white solidarity appeals — unleashed a series of television ads that overtly, viciously called up the region's old demons of white racism. One, attacking Gantt's pro-choice stance, repeatedly replayed a statement he had made about it while, first, showing his face in color and then in black and white— with the image of his face becoming darker and darker. The second advertisement became the more infamous. It went down in political lore as "the White

Hands ad." It shows the hands of a white person reading and then crumpling a letter as a voice-over calmly says, "You needed that job, and you were the best qualified. But they had to give it to a minority because of a racial quota. Is that really fair?"

Harvey Gantt would lose the election to Helms by a 53-to-47 percent split. Six years later, he again challenged Helms and lost by a margin that was one percent greater.

In a New York Times article in August of that year surveying the candidacies of several Black politicians in that year's contests, including one in which Andy Young suffered a brutal defeat in the Georgia Democratic gubernatorial primary, University of Virginia political scientist Larry Sabato made an incisive observation: That "Young's race points up again just how extraordinary the [Doug] Wilder victory in Virginia was. While it is possible for a black to win now in the South, it is never likely that a black will win."

The controversies provoked by Bush's "Willie" Horton ads, the Stuart murder case, the two senatorial contests between Jesse Helms and Harvey Gantt, and David Duke's successful and unsuccessful political campaigns occurred largely within the context of a startling backdrop: the fact that 1988 was the twentieth anniversary of the landmark report on America's racial crisis by the presidential commission of the late 1960s, The National Advisory Commission on Civil Disorders, popularly known as the Kerner Commission. (F. 25)That anniversary provoked a voluminous number of reports in the media, and books and scholarly studies from foundations and think tanks on where Black Americans and America stood at the end of the 1980s.

Taken as a whole, those assessments tracked many of the findings and warnings that had filled my columns, speeches, and the pages of *The State of Black America*. More to the point, they showed the continued relevance of the Kerner report's best-known passages:

> *Our Nation is moving toward two societies:*
> *one black, one white—separate and unequal. ...*
> *What white Americans have never fully understood—*
> *but what the Negro can never forget—is*
> *that white society is deeply implicated in*
> *the ghetto. White institutions created it, white*
> *institutions maintain it, and white society condones it.*

Of course, it was apparent the Commission was deliberately not being fully accurate. In racial terms, America had *always* been a separate and unequal society. It was the effort to change that American reality that had always proved so difficult. After all, the first of the series of "dreams" Martin Luther King, Jr. had proclaimed in the iconic *I Have A Dream* speech was the one "deeply rooted in the American Dream that one day this nation will rise up and live out the true meaning of its creed: We hold these truths to be self-evident, that all men are created equal.*"* Note that King — of course — posed that dream as a future possibility, not a present reality. Two decades later, at the end of the 1980s, a raft of new reports assessing the country's ongoing racial crisis confirmed that the *one-step-forward/at-least-one-step-back* dynamic that had bedeviled Black Americans' efforts to advance in American society for more than a century was still operative. That truth would continue to shadow my last years as head of the National Urban League.

Chapter 15 – Moving On

I knew how long I intended to be president of the Urban League from the day I walked into my office in January 1982. I told myself *I'll only do this for ten years. Whitney died in his tenth year. Vernon resigned in his tenth year. Ten years sounds about right for me.* When 1990, my eighth year at the helm, rolled around, I talked to some of the Board members and told them I planned to leave at the end of two more years. Two years later, I reminded them this was the year, and I realized they hadn't taken me seriously! They asked me to stay another two years to give the League time to conduct a proper, unhurried search.

Those conversations were kept private, even from the League staff. I had planned to make an announcement during my last words at the 1993 National Conference, but T. Willard Fair, the President of the Greater Miami affiliate, learned of my intent and urged me not to end the Conference on a downer. So, I held off, even keeping the news from Vernon. But, following the end of the Conference, I publicly announced that, after twenty-nine years, I would soon be resigning from the National Urban League.

When Vernon learned of my decision, he called. Barbara and I were on our way to Richmond, Virginia, to hang out with "The Traveling Team" — a half dozen or so couples, including Doug Wilders, the then governor of Virginia, Earl, and Barbara Graves, Darwin and Val-Marie Davis and Wayman Smith, all who were longtime friends. It was the weekend the Wilder's daughter was getting married, and we had all rendezvoused for the occasion.

"You told them you're leaving, but you don't have anything lined up?" Vernon asked incredulously. I said, "Right because I feel after ten years in a leadership position, you're just repeating yourself. " It was the fact that I hadn't lined anything up that bothered him. "You've lost your .... mind," he concluded. It was true I didn't know what I was going to do beyond continuing to serve on my corporate boards — because I wasn't sure I wanted to do anything more than that, at least not right away, and I wasn't worried about it.

It's protocol when you serve on a corporate board, and you're changing your work status to inform that company's Chairman and CEO of your plans. The reason is your job at your own company — or, in my case, nonprofit organization — may well be part of the reason you were brought onto the board. So, the company officials have the right to determine if you, having changed your work status, continue to have value as a company director. I was on six boards of directors, and all of their CEOs had asked me to remain. One of those six boards was that of Anheuser-Busch, America's leading brewery and one of its iconic brands. Through my service on the board, Barbara and I had become close friends with August Busch III, its chairman and CEO, the founder's great-grandson, and his wife, Virginia.

Soon after my brief telephone conversation with Vernon, I was at the regularly scheduled Anheuser-Busch board meeting, and August told me that while he was at a meeting of the American Red Cross board, one of his fellow board members had asked him, "You know your guy is leaving the National Urban League, what is he going to do?" August told me he didn't know whether he was supposed to know I was leaving, so he avoided directly answering. But he said to himself *Jake is too important for me to let some other company get him.* Coming to his point, he told me, "Jake, before you talk to any other company, I want you to come and talk with me."

Frankly, I didn't take that as his wanting me to join the Anheuser-Busch management team. We were close friends; he could have just been generally interested in my future plans. So I didn't follow up—even when he approached me at the following board meeting and said, "I don't want to badger you with this, but I really want to talk with you." I merely said, "I'll give you a call."

More time passed before I realized I had let things slip. I called his secretary to arrange a time for us to talk. Because of our complicated schedules, both of which involved a lot of travel, his secretary was having some difficulty carving out the face time he wanted to have with me until he invited me to a weekend hunting trip with his sons, August IV and Steven near Albany, Georgia, Now, I had been in the military, and I'd had experience with guns after all, I had been a commissioned officer in the Infantry Branch. It's just that I'd never been hunting before and had no interest in breaking that record.

The comedic elements of the trip multiplied once I arrived; it quickly became clear I didn't have the right clothing for hunting in the rough, bramble-filled terrain. Also, I'd only been on a horse once in my life, which meant a wagon would be our way of getting to the hunting site since motorized vehicles weren't allowed where we were going. Further, when he learned that I had never been hunting before, August asked, "Well, have you ever fired a gun"? I responded, "August, I am a former Infantry, Airborne qualified officer of the United States Army. Yes, I have fired a gun". He said, "OK, give him a gun, but only give him one shell." We boarded the wagon and headed out to the hunting site. It was then that August came to his real purpose for the meeting. "So, tell me," he said, referring to my plan to resign from the League, "what do you plan to do?"

I said, "Listen, August, I have six corporate boards— none of which I'm prepared to give up. So, between my corporate boards, what little retirement pension from the Urban League, and what little consulting I might decide to do, I'm going to practice my putting."

He looked at me as if to say: *Seriously?* Then, he said, "Well, let me tell you what I have in mind for you." What he had in mind was my replacing the retiring executive vice-president who had thought up Budweiser's iconic "This Bud's for You!" slogan and had become over a forty-four years career much more than its chief marketing and public relations executive. With a budget that could be categorized as *spend-whatever-you-think-is-necessary*, he had not only supervised all of Anheuser-Busch's sponsorships and branding events, but he devoted special attention to those with national and global impact — securing the appearance of whichever celebrities from the entertainment, athletic and other fields were needed to produce the maximum impact for the company. *Do we need Frank Sinatra for this? Consider it done.* My title would be Executive Vice President of Corporate Marketing and Communications, making me one of just two executive vice presidents in the entire company.

"This is an offer just for you," August III said, "because I want you in the company. If you don't accept it, I'm going to bust up the unit and spread the people in it among several different units. What do you say?"

I said, "Let me think about it." Let's go shoot some birds."

When a bird popped up in my shooting zone, I took aim and I hit it. One shell, one shot, one bird hit. August couldn't believe it. He yelled, "He *hit that bird; nobody gets a bird on their first shot! Nobody does that!*" My response was: "This is hunting? I'm retiring from hunting right now." And I did. But, just to forever mark the occasion, August had that bird stuffed and mounted and formally presented it to me at the next Anheuser-Busch board meeting.

My immediate hesitancy in taking up August's offer had to do with Wayman Smith, the company's Vice President for Corporate Affairs and its top Black executive. Wayman had brought Anheuser-Busch resources to the National Urban League, as well as all the national Black social services organizations throughout the country. To the Black civic community, Wayman was Anheuser-Busch. He was known by every Black politician, both at the local levels and at the national level. He was the man, and he served on the Howard Board of Trustees with me and now serves on the NUL Board of Trustees. I viewed him to be not only a force for Anheuser-Busch, but for the country as well. And, most of all, he was my friend. I didn't want him to think that I'd block him from getting a promotion. So, I wasn't going to accept the job if Wayman thought he was under consideration for it, too.

When I got back to New York the next day, the first thing I did was call him. "Wayman, your boss offered me a job."

"What's the job?" he asked. I told him.

He said, "What was your answer?"

"I told him I'd think about it," and I was about to tell him I wouldn't take it if he thought he had a shot at it, but he cut me off.

"Why? Do you have a problem being rich? No, I said. If you're worried about me, I know he's not going to offer me the job, so it wouldn't bother me if I get up in the morning and have to report to you the next day."

That satisfied that. I'd done the honorable thing a Black man should do in those circumstances for another Black man. I waited a couple of days and then called August and told him I'd take the job. My title would be Executive Vice President and Chief Communications Officer.

My portfolio would consist of all communications, both internal and external. It included a company called Busch Creative Services, which made creative displays for Anheuser-Busch and other companies, usually for their meetings, including their annual meetings; two post-production companies; corporate promotions, which handled meeting planning for the company; **(F. 1)** and a Consumer Awareness and Education unit. Recognizing that we produced and sold a product—beer—that was unpopular in some quarters and one that some groups would like to see banned from the marketplace, the focus of this unit was to continue to be proactive in educating communities about the proper consumption of the product to guard against causing harm.

All these units were well-staffed and led by competent professionals. I made sure that I didn't come in as a know-it-all but rather as someone who was ready and willing to learn and learn quickly. Before arriving at my new job, several corporate friends offered help and advice. One suggested that since I was one of only two Executive Vice Presidents in the company, I should take some of my staff from the National Urban League with me. I rejected that suggestion, as I also initially rejected including the minority outreach units in my portfolio. I wanted to make sure that people inside and outside the company understood I was no longer President of the National Urban League. My job now was to help Anheuser-Busch achieve its goals and objectives, sell its products and services and add to the company's profitability.

Others offered a few other suggestions. One corporate CEO friend even suggested I make sure I had a written contract; he offered me his own attorney for the negotiations. I rejected that offer, too. I believed August had made me the offer in good faith, and I would trust that I would be treated fairly. I never even discussed with him or anyone in the company what my compensation might be. I was to remain a member of the Anheuser-Busch corporate board — a board on which August and I were the only insiders — so I trusted that I would be treated fairly.

Even before taking office, I understood that some people would think I'd be content with the *flash* and *spectacle* possibilities of the job my predecessor had so expertly enjoyed. But I was determined to prove I knew how to be part of an entity whose bottom line was, above all else, making a profit.

My predecessor had always out-sourced all of Anheuser-Busch's communications work to FleishmanHillard, the communications giant headquartered in St. Louis. They had dozens of employees working on our account. One day,

Francine Katz, the bright young woman I had elevated to the vice presidency and who oversaw the Consumer Aware and Education unit, came to me and suggested that we hire into her unit the young man at

FleishmanHillard she had worked with before. I thought it was a great idea, and immediately wondered, *why don't we bring all of our communications services in-house.*

There was no question that Fleishman had done a tremendous job for the company for many years. But in my mind, there was also no question that given what we were paying for the service, we could do as well with the proper staff at a lower cost. So, after I'd been on the job for a couple of years, I walked into August's office and told him I'd like to bring all of the communications work FleishmanHillard had been doing for us in-house.

He told me, "We've been doing it this way for fifty years. What do you mean you want to bring it in-house?" I told him we were spending twelve to twenty million dollars a year on the Fleishman Hilliard account.

"I can get the job done for $5 million," I told him.

He looked at me skeptically, but now I had his interest because we were talking about money. He said, "I'm willing to let you try, but you have to let Fleishman know you're taking the business away from them." So, I got in my car and drove to FleishmanHillard and sat with John Graham, the Chairman & CEO, and informed him that I was bringing all of our business in-house. After he recovered from the shock, he said, "Jake, I have never sold Anheuser-Busch a service they didn't need, but I have sold them services they could have done themselves."

I told John, "I know this creates some problems for you because you have all these people on your payroll working on our account. So, I'm going to do you a favor. With your permission, I'm going to hire a good number of these workers away from you and bring them in-house to augment our communications functions as well."

I had already identified the best people there working on our account. Now, I went after them. I paid them better, gave them more benefits, and had them 24/7 — and upwards of $15 million dropped to our bottom line. When that happened, it became clear I was not simply paying out money from the company. I was also making money *for* the company.

It was only when a few years later that August came to me to tell me that if I didn't take the outreach units, they were going to disband them because none of the other group leaders wanted them. I agreed to take them because I knew they presented a valuable image of the company to consumers, and I felt I could help them correct a misunderstanding of the role in the company.

When I brought them under my direction, I immediately did two things. First, since the Black, Hispanic, and Asian communities had traditionally been treated as sub-groups, I added Whites as a sub-group, too, and assigned a person to service that group. My rationale for doing so was to make a statement that no group was any more or less important to the company's success than the other. And, while in the past, the groups all operated on the premise that their primary job was a kind of goodwill outreach to the respective communities, I explicitly added to their responsibilities the job of selling — of increasing the sales of Anheuser-Busch products in those communities.

At our first meeting, I told them, "Not only am I your best friend, I'm your only friend. Nobody else in this company wants you. And I know why they don't want you because I don't think you really know why you exist."

I told them they had lost sight of what their job was. "You think your job is to create goodwill for the Company by having it sponsor community programs and such. No, that's not it. Your job is to bring the community to the Company so that people in the community will buy our products. If that involves sponsoring community programs, fine. If it involves the Company doing other things, fine. But, don't forget, this is a consumer products company and we exist to sell people our products."

I said I wasn't suggesting cynical exploitation of community events or organizations or individuals but an accurate understanding of their own relationship with the Company. They had to see themselves not as "spenders" of the Company's money but as *producers of profit* for the Company by working in alliance with other producers of profit inside the Company. They had to use the contributions the Company could make to the community in ways that would both help the community and produce more customers for the Company. They were the Company's men and women on the "front line" of the marketplace, and because they were closest to the consumers, they could become the Company's "eyes and ears" in checking consumer responses to the Company's products — and what the Company's competition was up to in their area. Their relationships with the community should provide an incentive for people to want to purchase our products because of the quality of our products and the value of our community service.

I pointed out to the group members that in Anheuser-Busch, staff are classified into two groups they are numerators and denominators. Numerators make money for the company; denominators spend the company's money or give it away. And I added that right now, they were seen only as denominators but that I would show them how to become numerators. That re-focusing meant those groups would now be able to produce measurable data on boosting the sales of Anheuser-Busch products in their respective communities. That's what would earn them the respect of their fellow employees. Later, when I heard August describe these groups as numerators, I knew we had achieved our goal.

I'm sure many people misunderstood, at least initially, my taking a line position at Anheuser-Busch. They may have thought I was there simply as racial "window dressing." Or, because August Busch III and I, and our wives were close friends, the job was just a "show job" with no real responsibilities.

Neither perception was correct. August Busch III was a tough, shrewd businessman. He had forcibly taken the reins of the Company from his father in the early 1970s when Anheuser-Busch was one of America's leading beer companies and pushed it to unprecedented heights. By the early 1990s, when I came aboard, one of every two beers consumers bought in the United States was an Anheuser-Busch product. He did not take his job — expanding the dominance of the family business — lightly. Our close friendship springs from the fact that we were somewhat kindred spirits. But the offer to become one of the Company's most senior officers was a *business matter*. By then, I have been a member of the Anheuser-Busch board for four years. He had seen me and heard me mix with other C-Suite level men and women and discuss his company's business at board meetings, and he undoubtedly knew of my performance as head of the Urban League —whose own board included more than a dozen CEOs and senior officers of Fortune 500 companies.

I was on the Anheuser-Busch board because, institutionally speaking, the National Urban League knew a great deal about the dynamics of minority communities — a segment of the consumer market they were intent on selling more of their products to and because we could both advise them on how to improve their recruiting of minority-group employees. They knew that our advice was based on data and other kinds of research done by the League's own research department and by independent scholars whose work had appeared, among other places, in *The State of Black America*. So, when I moved inside Anheuser-Busch, I wasn't just armed with my advocacy credentials but also those of a creditable consultant on the issues and peoples of urban America. I was armed with a wealth of knowledge and insights about an important segment of the Company's target audience.

In corporate America, there aren't enough hours in the day to justify the compensation to those who occupy high office: what we are paid for is our *judgment*. And, my relationship with August Busch ripened into friendship because he had seen me exercise good judgment about his business and my own. He knew I was willing to disagree with him when I thought he wasn't making the best decision, and he ultimately appreciated it. And he knew that I always knew he had the power to fire me, but I was not intimidated by that fact. He and his wife Virginia liked me and they liked Barbara, and we liked both of them. I think a big part of his acceptance of me and Barbara was because his wife also liked us very much. While on trips we engaged in a good deal of business, but we also enjoyed each other's company. He sought my opinions, and it was clear to me that he listened to what I had to say and respected my input. And I can say that my annual compensation each year reflected his approval of my performance.

Epilogue

I never intended to write a book: while I believe every life is a story, I don't believe every story is a book. But, my wife had been badgering me for years that I should set down my life story, and I stopped ignoring her command when she said, "Just do it for your granddaughter."

Those words reminded me how little I really knew of my own parents' history. Because I grew up at a time and in a home where children were to be seen and not heard, we never talked about what their lives had been like growing up in Marksville, Louisiana, in the early 1900s. And, I thought maybe, just maybe, our granddaughter might one day want to know what life had been for me in my 90 years on this earth.

My career encompassed an extraordinary experience few other Americans have ever had: At the end of the twentieth century, I led a major national civil rights/social service organization that stood in prominent opposition to the hardline conservative policies of two consecutive presidential administrations, then served as a top-line officer and a board member of a Fortune 200 company, one whose main product had been an iconic American consumer brand since the late nineteenth century. I led and helped lead them when both — separately, of course—faced unprecedented challenges to their very existence. I was charged with being a *leader,* and so I had to figure out what, in each of those circumstances, *leadership* meant.

My personal story does say something about the expansiveness of American society in the mid-twentieth century — and about the character of Black Americans' struggle for racial equality that made it possible. That struggle, from my vantage, included two dimensions. On the one side was the willingness of corporate America from the 1960s onward — driven by altruism, yes, as well as the need to expand into new markets — to become more supportive of efforts to foster a more just society and to open its middle- and upper-level ranks to the *new* talent of women and members of minority groups in small but relatively significant numbers. The other dimension was my involvement in the National Urban League, a product of the early twentieth-century Black freedom struggle. It's helping Black Americans and other disadvantaged people gain a foothold in the American mainstream had a most likely unrecognized by-product: a leadership and staff skilled in the arts of racial diplomacy, trained to smoothly navigate the often tense encounters of Blacks and Whites along the Color Line. It was only in the writing of this book that I fully understood I'd been training for those roles all my life.

I've always felt that if there's a task to be done, then *let's get it done right; let's get it done now, and I'm willing to take the lead in doing that.* That's been my nature since I walked through the doors of Houston's Jack Yates High School seven decades ago. When I was growing up poor in a neighborhood of poor people, my mindset was not just why this was our lot; I was constantly thinking about what I needed to do to change my condition. Not what my parents could do, for I understood they were doing the best they could. It was what I could do.

In high school, I saw that some boys in my classes were well-dressed because their parents had the money to buy them clothes that looked good, so I found jobs that enabled me to buy clothes that were presentable. Seeing that some boys were using their athletic skills to gain scholarships for college, and knowing I wasn't built for athletic success, I decided to work at being smart in the classroom: to get a scholarship to college by being academically successful.

I was never one to shirk leadership positions or opportunities. And while I was willing to be a part of the group, I also wanted my voice to be heard.

My determination was further sharpened during my college years at Howard University, where I could see in numerous undergraduate and graduate students and professors how the wide variety of the ambition and intelligence of Black people expressed itself in a setting where they were relatively free of *White hostility*. So I was well prepared for a career — in social work — that I seemingly just happened to fall into through taking a job three years after college at the Baltimore City Department of Public Welfare. There I discovered I possessed an understanding of and compassion for people in poverty because I had grown up in a poor family and in a poor neighborhood. There, too, I discovered I possessed another skill necessary for true leadership: adaptability.

All those traits and skills helped me not turn away from Annie Meekins when she stormed into the welfare agency and laid down on the floor to keep to my initial decision to visit "the crazy man" and his wife at their apartment.

All those skills would also be essential to my forging a successful career at the National Urban League, too. For, on the one hand, the League was founded on the understanding of and compassion for the poor and the disadvantaged. And, on the other, its very structure of a quasi-independent relationship between local affiliates and its national headquarters created an understanding that policies and programs promulgated by the latter often had to be adapted to fit local circumstances. That, in turn, demanded that its senior staff at both levels be flexible in responding to external events and managing the organization itself.

Flexibility, adaptability—and *persistence* were certainly required of me during my years at the top of the League. I was responsible for the League's financial viability and its service to the people who needed us during a period unique in the organization's seventy-year history. From the 1970s to the 1990s, Black Americans suffered a sustained, corrosive dynamic of double-digit unemployment, exacerbated by three recessions, that helped produce an alarming increase in the number of single unwed mothers and left millions of young and adult Black males jobless for long stretches of time, ultimately driving many from the labor force altogether. That scourge was partly the result of the transformation of the American and global economic system as well as the systemic racism layered through American society. But it was also profoundly exacerbated by the rhetoric and backward policies of the Reagan and Bush administrations. This concerted opposition was the "flip side" of the progress Blacks were making moving deeper into the American mainstream.

The League's mission, and my responsibility, was to fight to reverse the conservative momentum with all the considerable tools at our disposal. We did have an unprecedented media platform in our syndicated To Be Equal columns and *The State of Black America,* our scholarly journal, and in the hundreds of speeches I made every year. Via our affiliate boards and staff, we could discuss both the national impact of governmental policy and their impact on specific local communities. And we were consistent and persistent in stating our own positions on issues and proposing our own solutions to problems. The Reagan administration's slashing funds for some social welfare programs unquestionably hurt our capacity to help our constituents. But we took the advice of Mildred Love, our vice president in charge of programs: We did less with less — but we did it better.

Most of all, we would not surrender; we adapted. I never doubted that we would. And we did score victories. We did succeed in helping millions of Americans live better lives, even in a period of hardship. In some hypothetical universe, I certainly wouldn't have picked the Reagan years to be leading the National Urban League. But in the advocacy business, you play the hand you're dealt. It's important that you show up every day and fight. You won't win every battle, but you must serve notice that you won't be intimidated and you won't quit.

Chapter 1 Footnotes

1. *Vernon Can Read, A Memoir* Vernon E. Jordan, Jr., with Annette Gordon-Reed, 2001, P. 281

2. "Federal Jury Returns Verdict of Not Guilty In Jordan Shooting," https://www.nytimes.com/1982/08/18/us/federal-jury-returns-verdict-of-not-guilty-in-jordan-shooting.html?searchResultPosition=18

3. *Vernon Can Read!*, op. cit., p. 297

4. Reverend Gardner C. Taylor was one of the most extraordinary religious leaders of post-World War II America. Louisiana-born, he was a graduate of Oberlin School of Theology, famed pastor of Concord Baptist Church in Christ in Brooklyn, New York for more than forty years, a colleague and close friend of Martin Luther King, Jr., and a staunch foe of racial segregation in the South and the North.

5. *Vernon Can Read!* Op. cit, , p. 300.

6. This is the correct name of the hospital then — cf. "Jordan Is Flown to New York Hospital; Police Still Seek Clues in Shooting," NYT80/06/13. It is now called New York Presbyterian/Weill Cornell Medical Center. But I refer to it by the former name for purposes of historical accuracy. A measure of its national and international renown is that it was the hospital which in 1979 Henry Kissinger had the Shah of Iran secretly flown to when he was dying of cancer. That act played a significant role in the Islamic fundamentalists in Iran storming the American embassy and taking the staff hostages, provoking the infamous Iran Hostage Crisis.

7. From the 1960s to the early 1990s Louis E. Martin, Jr. played an outsized role in developing a sizable Black political class operating in the upper reaches of national black organizations and the Democratic presidential administrations of Presidents Kennedy, Johnson and Carter. A journalist by training and a co-founder of the National Newspaper Publishers Association, Martin had a voluminous Rolodex and a reputation as a consummate insider who knew well and was respected by the players of high-power politics.

8. The hospital complex was on East 68th Street, hard by the Franklin Delano Roosevelt (FDR) Drive and the East River.

9. Dan was to continue to serve the League in that same capacity during my tenure. In his 2008 book, Make It Plain: Standing Up and Speaking Out, Vernon eloquently captured the quality of Dan's contribution to both Vernon and I—and to the Urban League Movement: I have been very fortunate to be the beneficiary of an almost mystical affinity that in the best of circumstances develops between a speech maker and a speech writer. For thirty-five years, from 1971 to 2006, Dan Davis's expensive and precise thinking and facility with words has been invaluable in helping me flesh out my ideas and convey them crisply and elegantly. Our work together has been exemplified by the combination of trust, loyalty, and friendship that is as crucial as intelligence and skill at word-smithing to the process of collaboration between speech writer and speech maker. We have discussed ideas and concepts frankly and without fear of the other taking offense. He has never objected to my being the final authority on the content of a speech, an authority I have fully exercised. But I've never doubted that at the end of my giving every speech we have crafted, he has always been the proudest person in the room for me. And I have continually

realized and been more and more grateful for our professional relationship and our personal friendship.

10. "Jordan Urges Blacks to Use Their Political Strength," New York Times August 8, 1980

11. "Blacks Want Jobs, Urban League Says," *New York Times*, August 4, 1980

12. Footnote: Reagan ran for and on the California governorship in 1966, defeating the liberal Democratic lion, Edmund G. "Pat" Brown.

13. For all the decades since, Reaganites and their fellow-travelers claimed Reagan's remarks had no racist meaning. But those assertions have faded since 2019 when tapes were discovered of a 1971 White House Nixon-Reagan meeting which caught the two men laughingly referring to African delegates to the United Nations in racist terms.

14. "Reagan Urges Blacks To Look Past Labels And To Vote for Him," *New York Times*, August 6, 1980

15. "Jordan Vows Threat of Violence Won't Interfere With His Duties," *New York Times*, September 10, 1980

16. "Vernon Jordan, in His First Speech Since Shooting, Sees Race Hostility," *New York Times*, October 19, 1980

17. "Blacks, reacting to Vote, Seek Way to Keep Gains," *New York Times*, November 8, 1980

18. Vernon's resignation from the League and his joining the Washington-based powerhouse law firm of Akin, Gump, Strauss, Hauer & Feld was announced publicly September 9, 1981

19. *Vernon Can Read!* Op. cit., pp. 305-306

20. "Jordan Expected To Leave Urban League Post," *New York Times*, September 9, 1981; "Roy Wilkins, 50-Year Veteran of Civil Rights Fight, Is Dead," *New York Times,* September 9, 1981

21. "Black Leaders And Needs," Roger Wilkins, New York Times, September 28, 1981

Chapter 2 Footnotes

1. Founded in 1794, it became the trading center and parish seat of Avoyelles Parish, an area dominated by cotton plantations. For twelve years from the 1840s to the 1850s Solomon Northrup, the free Black man from Saratoga Springs, New York, was enslaved in the area. Northrup's memoir of his kidnapping and enslavement, *Twelve Years A Slave*, was one of the most important slave narratives of the 19th Century, and the basis for the 2013 award-winning movie of the same name.

2. John Barry's *Rising Tide: The Great Mississippi Flood of 1927 and How It Changed America*, remains the definitive account of the tragedy.

3. The city was named after Sam Houston, of course, the former Congressman from and Governor of the state of Tennessee, whose lasting fame and place in history stems from his being among the White American settlers who wrenched Texas away from Mexico and attached it to the United States of America. Houston led the forces which in 1836 defeated the Mexican army led by General Santa Anna at the climactic Battle of San Jacinto, avenging the latter's conquest of The Alamo. He would become the first and the third Governor of the Republic of Texas, which lasted for the next nine years until Congress enacted and President James K. Polk signed legislation accepted Texas into the Union in 1845.

4. https://www.history.com/topics/landmarks/spindletop; The Galveston hurricane was the worst natural disaster in American history. The storm killed at least 10,000 people, destroyed more than 2,600 homes and severely damaged

thousands more. The total cost of the damage was estimated at at least $28 million. That it completely wrecked Galveston's port facilities tipped the scales for Houston officials of the necessity of creating their own port facility by significantly deepening the waterway, the Houston Ship Channel, that flows from Houston to the Gulf. https://www.galvestonhistorycenter.org/research/1900-storm

5.   Although they faced considerable discrimination from Anglo Texans, Texans of Hispanic descent had civil rights in Texas: they could vote, and attend the University of Texas and Texas A & M University.

6.   Three books that provide excellent perspectives on Black Houston's nineteenth- and twentieth-century history are: Robert D. Bullard, *Invisible Houston: The Black Experience in Boom and Bust,* (1987; Tyina L. Steptoe, Houston Bound: Culture and Color in a Jim Crow City, (2016); and Howard Bleeth and Cary D. Wintz, eds., *Black Dixie: Afro-Texan History and Culture in Houston,* (1992)

7.   Mexican immigrants and Texicans were concentrated in the Second Ward

8.   The two institutions were virtually Third Ward neighbors; the vast campus of the University of Houston was just a few blocks away from the much smaller grounds of the Houston Junior College for Negroes, whose course offerings were expanded in the 1950s to four-year college level status and, with the addition of a law school, it was renamed Texas Southern University. State officials made these moves in an unsuccessful attempt to prevent the desegregation of the University of Texas. Such were the idiosyncrasies of Jim Crow.

9. The decision, a critical step toward the Court's landmark Brown vs. Board of Education of Topeka case that came four years later, also immediately applied to another case involving graduate education, *McLaurin vs. Oklahoma State Regents*. In that case, George McLaurin had been admitted to the graduate program in education at the University of Oklahoma but had been deliberately isolated from the normal activity a student would undertake. In effect, he was being forced to endure an internal segregation within the program.

10. Sweatt, however, did not succeed at the law school. This was due to a combination of factors: a result of his inadequate preparation at the segregated schools he had attended; his having been out of an educational institutional environment for more than a decade; and the tremendous strain he was under not only from the racial situation but from the strain the years of effort took on his personal life and marriage. He failed his first year and left the school (three of five other Black students admitted with him as part of the suit also dropped out before graduation). But Heman Sweatt would have a productive professional career, nonetheless. As Gary M. Lavigne tells the story in his *Before Brown: Heman Marion Sweatt, Thurgood Marshall and the Long Road to Justice,* in the summer of 1952, Whitney M Young Jr. , who was then preparing to take up his post as Dean of the School of Social Work at Atlanta University, invited Sweet to enroll as a graduate student on a full scholarship. Two years later, Sweatt earned his master's degree with an emphasis in community organizing and began a 23-year career with the Urban League — first in Cleveland and then in Atlanta. There he became assistant regional director responsible for organizing new affiliates in

the Southeast. During his service, the number of affiliates in the region tripled. Hemann Marion Sweatt died in October 1982

11. The Reverend Jack Yates was one of the group of committed, astute leaders who in the nineteenth century laid the foundation of businesses, homes, churches, and a park—Emancipation Park—that enabled the then-small Black Houston community to achieve a measure of security and progress in he twentieth, despite the restrictions o Jim Crow. Born into slavery in Virginia, and having been taught to read by the plantation owner's son, Yates achieved his own freedom, but asked to be re-enslaved in order to remain with his wife, Harriet Willis, whose enslaver as moving to Texas. They were there when the Civil War ended, and Blacks in Texas learned of the Emancipation Proclamation President Lincoln had signed two years earlier. That was the genesis of the successful effort of the Yates (who had moved to Houston) and other community leaders to purchase a ten-acre plot of land in 1872 at the intersection of Dowling and Elgin streets in the Third Ward for use as a place, most of all, to celebrate the day Lincoln had actually signed the document.

12. Phillis Wheatley, seized as a child in Senegal / The Gambia in the 1760s, by American slavers and brought to Boston to serve in the home of a prominent Boston businessman and his wife, became "one of the best-known poets of the pre-19th century America, … '[L]ionized in New England and England," Wheatley's name "was a household word among literate colonists and her achievements a catalyst for the fledgling antislavery movement." (The Poetry Foundation, https://www.poetryfoundation.org//poets/phillis-wheatley)

13. *Houston Bound: Culture and Color in a Jim Crow City,*
    Tyina L. Steptoe, 2016, p. 43

14. *Black Dixie: Afro-Texan History and Culture in Houston,*
    Howard Beeth and CaryD. Wintz, eds. 1992, pp. 134, 144]

15. Until 1940, Emancipation Park was the only recreational
    space in Houston Blacks weren't barred from. Its original
    owners had donated the park to the city, in exchange for
    their pledge to properly maintain it. The pledge was not kept,
    of course —another example of what *separate but equal*
    really meant.

16. Established in 1879 and named after the great orator and
    activist, Frederick Douglass, it was the first school for Black
    Americans in Houston.

17. The school, built in the late 1920s, was named for the
    Reverend Jack Yates, who, along with his wife, was Black
    Houstonians' most prominent leader. He did much to put the
    small, developing community on firm footing. In the 1930s
    and 1940s, Houston had two other high schools for Black
    children. Jack Yates High was for pupils in the Third Ward.
    Booker T. Washington High, the city's first and for many
    years only Black high school, enrolled those who lived in the
    Fourth Ward, and Phillis Wheatley, named for the colonial
    era Black poet, was built at the same time as Yates for
    children in the Fifth Ward. There was an intense, athletics-
    based rivalry among all three schools, but especially between
    Yates and Wheatley, both of whom had more pupils than
    Washington.

18. Between 1886 and 1919 Andrew Carnegie, the industrial
    who was at the turn of the twentieth century the richest man
    in America, donated more than forty million dollars to build
    public libraries in cities, towns and rural communities all

across America. Importantly, use of the libraries was free. Before that, many libraries charged individuals a fee to take out books. In segregated Houston, as throughout the South, the city's libraries were closed to Blacks. Black community leaders petitioned the Carnegie endowment for six years before they it gave funds to build the Carnegie Colored Library—directed by a Black librarian—in the Third Ward. The library opened in 1913 and became a branch of the city library system in 1921. However, Black community leaders would spend decades trying to correct its severe underfunding. The situation was so bad, the black community weekly wrote, "This branch is poorly equipped, and it would be a joke (a very sad one) to compare its opportunities for intellectual and cultural development with the municipal library which Negroz are tax to support, but from which they are excluded." *Black Dixie: Afro-Texan History and Culture in Houston,* Howard Beeth and Cary D. Wintz, eds., Texas A& M University Press, 1992 pp. 187-188.

19. Dad made it clear I could not work on Sundays, because that was the Lord's Day.

20. Evan Edward Worthing was born in Michigan but went to college at Texas A&M University, Class of 1902. His signal achievement of athletic glory in the annals of that institution is that he was captain of the football team his senior year when they did the University of Texas. Worthing went on to make millions in commercial and residential real estate in Houston. He gained the reputation of being fair in his dealings with his Black tenants. He is establishing a scholarship fund for black students was an extraordinary act for a White individual in the South in those years. In the late

1950s the Houston school department built a new high school and named it after him.

21. Geneva Bolton's abilities would soon take her out of Houston—to a master's degree in social work from Case Western Reserve University, and then to a series of ever more challenging positions in the field. That also meant a series of African-American "firsts" in the 1970s and 1980s that matched in importance the racial breakthroughs being made in politics, in higher education, and in the corporate sector. In the late 1970s she would become the first African American and woman senior vice president of the United Way of America, and in the early 1980s she would become the first African American woman to be appointed president and CEO of Family Service America, the largest and oldest social service organization in the country.

Chapter 3 Footnotes

1. Spellman recently added to his long list of contributions to world and American culture in providing the spoken-word contribution to the Jeff Scott concert-length oratorio, *Passion for Bach and Coltrane*, inspired by the *Goldberg Variations of J.S. Bach* and John Colttane's *A Love Supreme.* The collaboration, which included the Imani Winds ensemble, won the Grammy Award for Best Classical Compendium.

2. Charles Hamilton Houston, a brilliant graduate of Amherst College and Harvard Law School, served as Vice-Dean and then Dean of the law school in the early 1930s. He left Howard officially in 1935 to return to his father's law practice in Washington, but continued, via the NAACP and the law school itself to develop the legal theories and a cohort of Black attorneys across the country—including Thurgood Marshall—who would be instrumental in destroying the legal justifications for racial discrimination in America.

3. The reference is to the sitcom "A Different World," the spin-off of "The Cosby Show" series that initially followed the adventures of the Huxtables' daughter, "Denise" at a fictional Historically Black College, but came to focus more on the adventures and experiences of an ensemble of the college's students. In doing so, it took on some topics—sexual assault, the Equal Rights Amendment, and in one episode, AIDS—"The Cosby Show" never discussed.

4. It's worth noting that the value of one dollar in 1953 would in today's terms have a value of between twelve and thirteen dollars. So, $35 then would have a value of around $400

today. The average salaries in 1953, the year I entered college, and 1957, the year I graduated, were $4,011 and $4,494, respectively. A nice two-bedroom house could be had for $8,200 and $10,000. Prices for Ford automobiles were $1,537 and $2,403 in 1953, depending on the model and between $1,879 and $3,408 in 1957, respectively. A gallon of gasoline cost twenty-two cents in 1953 and twenty-four cents in 1957; a loaf of bread cost sixteen cans in 1953 and nineteen cents in 1957.

5.   In 2023, as part of the Pentagon's renaming military bases which had carried the names of Confederate military officers or politicians, the name of Fort Benning was changed to Fort Moore. The new name honors for the first time in American history a military couple: Lt. General Harold G. Moore, Jr., a highly decorated troop commander during the Vietnam War, and his wife, Julia, a leader in improving Army family programs. Her vigorous efforts compelled the military to stop notifying families of deceased service members by telegram and instead do so by military officials' personal visits.

Chapter 4 Footnotes

1. Much of the contact between caseworker and client was carried out via the caseworkers' home visits. But clients could come to the office when emergencies arose.

2. Indeed, in the first months of the new Administration, John and Robert Kennedy tried everything they could to tamp down the activism exploding across the South—in his words, "this Goddamned civil rights mess." JFK well understood that the South's racist laws and customs were wrong. He supported racial equality. But, whipsawed by the competing demands of foreign and domestic politics, and his need to "get along" with a Congress dominated by the Southern segregationist bloc, he wanted the Movement to… *wait.* But the Movement would not wait—a fact one of JFK's emissaries sent to try to convince Freedom Riders to do just that realized with striking clarity in talking to Diane Nash. In May of 1961, Nash, a Fisk University student, was already a veteran of civil rights work. "It was like talking to a brick wall," said John Seigenthaler, the journalist the Kennedys had called upon to be a go-between. "She never listened to a word. She said nothing could stop them now: 'We're going to show those people in Alabama who think they can ignore the President of the United States. … This has to go forward,' she continued. 'Nobody is go to turn us around.'" *President Kennedy: Profile of Power*, Richard Reeves, p. 126]]

3. Walter Carter was a significant figure in the state of Maryland, in CORE, and in the national Civil Rights Movement.

Chapter 5 Footnotes

1. This is he equivalent of nearly $1.5 million in 2024 dollars.

2.
    https://www.washingtonpost.com/archive/local/2004/05/21/g
    en-robert-seedlock-dies/bbeef7de-0957-45f8-9ed7-
    d92de0a93c6a/

3. Max Robinson was the first African-American local
    television anchor in Washington and in 1978 would become
    the first African American anchor for a national television
    network newscast when he served as co-anchor of ABC's
    World News Tonight. He died in 1983.

4. The building was sixteen streets due north of the White
    House on perhaps the most prestigious of Washington's
    numbered streets, well within walking distance of the
    Capitol's universe of Federal agencies, lobbying firms,
    prestigious law firms, the Washington offices of major
    corporations, and many, many nonprofit organizations.

5. https://www.bostonglobe.com/2023/03/28/metro/mel-king-
    whose-1983-mayoral-campaign-ushered-new-era-boston-
    race-relations-dies-94/?p1=BGSearch_Advanced_Results

Chapter 7 Footnotes

1. The coming of Home Rule took place against the backdrop of extraordinary turmoil. In the fall of 1973, as Congress was enacting the legislation establishing Home Rule, the Watergate scandal was shredding the legitimacy of the Nixon Administration — he would resign the following August. The American war effort in Southeast Asia was disintegrating and would produce a humiliating surrender in all but name two years later. And Nixon's bully-boy vice president Spiro Agnew was forced to resign amid charges of financial corruption.

2. Because it was an appointed and officially part-time position, and because the District appointed government was closely watched by Congress, especially its southern Congress members, Tucker was allowed to keep his private-sector job.

3. Congress had granted Washingtonians the right to vote for President in 1962, the first crack in the barrier to local control since Congress had voted to bar male District residents from voting (women did not secure the right to vote in the U.S. until passage of the Nineteenth Amendment in 1919) primarily because many White Congressmen felt too many Black men were taking advantage of their right to vote. In 1968 Washingtonians were granted the right to elect a citywide school board, and in 971 another Congressional act created the elective position of a non-voting Delegate to represent the city in the House of Representatives.

4. Among the books which provide an excellent account of the history of Blacks in Washington, the development of Home Rule, and the 1968 riot and its aftermath are: *Chocolate City:*

A History of Race and Democracy In The Nation's Capital, Chris Myers Asch & George Derek Musgrove, University of North Carolina Press, Chapel Hill, 2017; and *Most of 14th Street Is Gone: The Washington DC Riots of 1968,* J. Samuel Walker, Oxford University Press, 2019

Chapter 8 Footnotes

1. [[* Footnote — — "Public Library Seeks To Buy Apartment For Its Its President," https://www.nytimes.com/1981/11/22/nyregion/public-library-seeks-to-buy-apartment-for-its-president.html?searchResultsPosition=3

2. https://www.nytimes.com/1981/11/24/opinion/new-york-mr-pleasant-regrets.html?searchResultsPosition=1]]

3. "New Responsibilities For Blacks," *To Be Equal*, January 13, 1982

4. "Reagan Actions Called Civil Rights 'Betrayal" *New York Times*, January 19, 1982

5. "Celebrating a New Branch of the Whitney," *New York Times*, April 8, 1983, B-4

Chapter 9 Footnotes

1. I was not surprised that during my twelve years leading the League, the executives of three powerful affiliates — Chicago, Atlanta and Los Angeles, who were either senior or equal to me in length of service — hosted me on League business numerous times but never invited me to speak at their most important event, their annual dinners.

Chapter 10 Footnotes

1. According to the National Bureau of Economic Research, the years 1980 to 1982 actually included two recessions: one in the first six months of 1980; the other, significantly more severe, from July 1981 to November 1982. But at street level, so to speak, there was no "interval" between the periods of economic hardship.

2. "FRED Economic Data , "Unemployment rate - White,https://fred.stlouisfed.org/series/LNS14000003

3. "FRED Economic Data, "Unemployment rate — Black or African American https://fred.stlouisfed.org/series/LNS14000006

4. Robert B. Hill, after earning a bachelor's degree in sociology from City College of New York and a doctorate in the field from Columbia University, began working with the Urban League in the mid-1970s. While teaching at several different universities over the next two decades, he led the League's research unit that was based in the League's political affairs office in Washington.

5. *Hearings Before the Joint Economic Committee Congress of the United States ; Ninety-Seventh Congress; Second Session, Part I: July 13,14,15, 19 and 20, 1982.* https://www.jec.senate.gov/public/index.cfm/1982/12/report-3dfbab75-b79e-40ad-94fc-2e75e9c5372b]]

6. "FRED Economic Data , "Unemployment rate — Black or African American Males https://fred.stlouisfed.org/series/LNS14000031

7. "FRED Economic Data , "Unemployment rate — Black or African American Women
    https://fred.stlouisfed.org/series/LNS14000032

8. "FRED Economic Data, "Unemployment rate — Black or African American
    https://fred.stlouisfed.org/series/LNS14000006 By comparison, overall White unemployment in December 1981 was 7.5 percent and during that period peaked at 9.1 percent in January 1983—its peak, in fact, for the entire fifty-four years from 1955 to September 2009 during the Great Recession. As the early-1980s recession eased that year, White unemployment began a sharp decline through the decade to a low of 4.2 percent in 1989. Thus, the "usual" Black-White unemployment ratio of about 2 to 1 often expanded during the 1980s and 1990s to nearly 3 to 1.

9. Hill's 1978 monograph published by the League, *The Illusion of Black Progress,* marshaled a trove of data to prove that assertions of great progress in reducing racial discrimination and expanding the Black middle class did not match the reality. A shortened version of the report can be found under the title "The Illusion of Black Progress" in *The Black Scholar* of October 1978, pp. 18 to 52.

10. "A Bleak 30 Years For Black Men: Economic Progress Was Slim in Urban America," The Regional Economist, pp. 5-6, Table 2,
    https://files.stlouisfed.org/files/htdocs/publications/regional/10/07/bleak_black_progress.pdf

11. Monthly Labor Review, U.S. Department of Labor, September 1990, pp. 8-9

12. "Between 1980 and 2000, the average share of manufacturing in total employment declined from 22 percent

to 14 percent across 361 metropolitan areas." "The Rise in the Residential Concentration of Joblessness in America's Cities," https://www.stlouisfed.org/publications/bridges/winter-20062007/the-rise-in-the-residential-concentration-of-joblessness-in-americas-cities]]

13. The 1985 hit movie, Back To The Future, which launched a series of movies, as well as sequels to its own storyline, captured many of the elements of the White Fifties Nostalgia dynamic.

14. The term Potemkin village refers to a situation in which a grand story is told or show constructed to conceal a modest or disappointing or entirely negative reality. It was supposedly based on the efforts of the 18th-century Russian statesman Grigory Potemkin to construct entire fake villages in the newly conquered agricultural lands of the Crimea in order to convince Empress Catherine the Great that her colonization plans were a success. But, in a neat irony, that story itself was entirely false.

15. Under George H.W. Bush, the deficit rose as high as $290.3 billion before falling back to $255 billion when he left office. President Clinton cut the deficit to zero by the end of his two terms in office, and left his successor a surplus of $128.2 billion. https://www.politifact.com/factchecks/2019/jul/29/tweets/republican-presidents-democrats-contribute-deficit/

16. https://www,pbs.org/wgbh/commaningheights/shared/minitext/ess_reaganomics.html

17. https://www.theatlantic.com/magazine/archive/1981/12/the-education-of-david-stockman/305760/ Reagan, Stockman

and the rest of the top Administration officers, smartly, did not blow up in public over Stockman's indiscretion. Instead, they played it as a somewhat humorous kerfluffle — and the public largely bought it. However, from that point t onward, few Administration officials ever uttered the phrase "supply-side economics" in public.

18. Testimony before the Congress Joint Economic Committee, p. 143

19. "Add Another Murphy's Law," Hobart Rowen, *The Washington Post,* July 3, 1983

20. These included the transformation of work from being heavily industrial-based to information-based, the complete or partial "off-shoring" of many factories and businesses, and the movement of many factories and businesses from cities to suburbs. These developments, along with direct and hidden racial discrimination and the last-hired-first-fired "rule" of the work place, sharply narrowed Blacks access to jobs at the bottom and lower-middle rungs of the occupation ladder.

21. "John Jacob Speaks, Part II, *Los Angeles Sentinel,* circa January 1982

22. See, for example, Michelle Alexander, *The New Jim Crow: Mass Incarceration in the Age of Colorblindess* (2010) and James Forman, Jr., *Locking Up Our Own: Crime and Punishment in Black America (2017)*

23. "Prisons and Prisoners," Bureau of Justice Statistics, 1982

24. "FRED Economic Data, https://fred.stlouisfed.org/series/LNS14000003 and https://fred.stlouisfed.org/series/LNS14000006

25. *To Be Equal,* "The Rising Tide of Poverty," September 8, 1982

26. Blank had a brilliant career in government service and higher education.She left the Commerce Department in 2013 to become chancellor of the University of Wisconsin-Madison, and in 2022 was about to become president of Northwestern University when she was diagnosed with cancer. She died in March of 2023. "Rebecca Blank, Who Changed How Poverty Is Measured, Dies at 67," *New York Times*, March 11, 2023 https://www.nytimes.com/2023/03/09/us/rebecca-blank-dead.html

27. "A Program To End Poverty," *To Be Equal*, October 12,1983

28. *The Disposable American: Layoffs and Their Consequences,* Louis Uchitelle, Vintage, 2007; *Pinched: How the Great Recession Has Narrowed Our Futures And What We Can Do About It*, Don Peck, Crown, 2011

29. See, for example: *Dying of Whiteness: How the Politics of Racial Resentment Is Killing America's Heartland* , Jonathan Metz; *Deaths of Despair and the Future of Capitalism,* Anne Case and Angus Deaton; and *American Made: What Happens To People When Work Disappears,* Farah Stockman

30. "Help Wanted: Summer Jobs For Youth," *To Be Equal,* June 16, 1982

31. "Black America, 1987: An Overview," *The State of Black America 1987,* p.2

32. "The Rise in the Residential Concentration of Joblessness in America's Cities,"

https://www.stlouisfed.org/publications/bridges/winter-20062007/the-rise-in-the-residential-concentration-of-joblessness-in-americas-cities

33. "Black America, 1987: An Overview," *The State of Black America 1987, p. 2*

34. "Job Opportunities Bring Out Young People (and their Idealism) in Riot Area," *New York Times*, June 18, 1992

Chapter 11 Footnotes:

1. Vernon's words had led other national Black leaders and politicians to voice their dissatisfaction with the President as well ….. will note some of the news articles here

2. "Carter and Jordan," *New York Times*, July 20, 1977

3. "Carter: 'No Apologies' to Blacks, Poor," *Washington Post*, July 7, 1977

4. "Black Leaders Supporting Jordan In His Criticism of Carter's Policies," *The New York Times*, July 7, 1977

5. In 1983 Reagan would nominate Dole to be Secretary of Transportation.

6. Dole was married to Senator Bob Dole, the Kansas Republican, would be the Party's presidential candidate against Bill Clinton in 1996.

7. That morning, January 18th, the worst crash in the history of the elite US Air Force flying squad, the Thunderbirds, had occurred during a training session in the Nevada desert. "4 Pilots Killed As Stunt Planes Crash in Desert," https://www.nytimes.com/1982/01/19/us/4-pilots-killed-as-stunt-planes-crash-in-desert.html?searchResultPosition=4

8. Donald T. Reagan, the Treasury Secretary, and William French Smith, the Attorney General, had announced a few days earlier that they were reversing an Internal Revenue Service policy barring schools and other non-profit institutions that practiced racial discrimination from receiving tax exemptions. It had provoked an immediate and widespread condemnation — and a lawsuit that was clearly

headed for the Supreme Court. See pp. X-Y in Chapter 12.
— to put in the Final Manuscript

9. *The Administration's 1982 National Urban Policy Report,* Hearings before the Joint Economic Committee, Congress of The United States, Ninety-Seventh Congress, Second Session, Part 1, p. 2-3

10. *Ibid.,* pp. 115-118

11. On July 23, 1967 Blacks in Detroit erupted in what was to become the most violent and destructive of the series of uprisings that convulsed American society from the mid-1960s to the early 1970s. President Johnson appointed the eleven-member blue-ribbon group, chaired by Otto Kerner Jr., then Governor of Illinois, on July 28, 1967, the last day of significant violent activity in the city. It would issue its 426-page report seven months later. The report was immediately published in book form by several publishing houses and quickly became a bestseller.

12. "Humphrey Urges New Aid To Poor," *New York Times,* August 3, 1963

13. *The Administration's 1982 National Urban Policy Report,* Hearings before the Joint Economic Committee, Congress of The United States, Ninety-Seventh Congress, Second Session, Part 1, pp. 119-120

14. "The Clinton Report Card," *To Be Equal* column, January 5, 1994

15. In 1985 Reagan would nominate Reynolds to be the Justice Department's Associate Attorney General, its third-ranking officer. The Senate rejected him after a bruising battle waged by civil rights and progressive forces. Reynolds would remain head of the department's civil rights division and the

point man of its anti-civil rights actions until the end of the Reagan presidency. But the Senate's blocking his promotion was a stinging symbolic defeat for the Administration.

16. "Reagan Urges Blacks To Look Past Labels And To Vote for Him," *New York Times*, August 6, 1980

17. *Last Chance: The Political Threat to Black America,* Lee A. Daniels, pp. 104-106

18. Daniels, op. cit. pp. 104-106

19. The King federal holiday wasn't due to take effect until the following year, but it was already being celebrated in many local jurisdictions.

20. "President Meets With 20 Blacks; Intent Disputed," NYT 85/01/16 In the article the *New YorkTimes* described the *The State of Black America* as a "report widely viewed as an accurate barometer of the status of black Americans [and which] has been harshly critical of the administration's policies ... [as] callous toward blacks."

21. "Protests Spreading in U.S. Against South Africa Policy," *New York Times,* December 5, 1984

22. "President Asserts Black Leadership Twists His Record," *New York Times,* January 19, 1985

23. Gary Franks, of Connecticut served from 1991 to 1997, and J.C. Watts, of Oklahoma, served from 1995 to 2003), *Last Chance: The Political Threat to Black America*, Lee A. Daniels, Public Affairs, p. 113, (2008) ; and *Republicans and The Black Vote*, Michael K. Fauntroy, Lynne Rienner Publishing (2006)

24. "GOP Blacks Complain of Limited Access, *Washington Post,* January 28, 1985

25. "President Meets With 20 Blacks; Intent Disputed" *New York Times,* January 16, 1985 and "Toward a New Dialogue," *To Be Equal*, January 23, 1985

Chapter 12 Footnotes

1. "New Responsibilities for Blacks," *To Be Equal*, January 13, 1982

2. The Internal Revenue Service is a division of the Treasury Department

3. They included, among others, the NAACP, the American Jewish Committee, the American Civil Liberties Union, and the National Association of Independent Colleges and Universities, which had 900 members with an aggregate enrollment of Two million students, and the National Association of Independent Schools, which represented 800 elementary and secondary private schools across the country enrolling 330,000 pupils.

4. *Meanness Mania: The Changed Mood*, Gerald R. Gill, Institute for the Study of Educational Policy and Howard University Press, Washington, D.C.,

5. *The 1980 Presidential Election: Ronald Reagan and The Shaping of the American Conservative Movement,* Jeffrey D. Horizon, p. 129

6 "Shucks, It's Only the Law," Anthony Lewis, *New York Times*, January 21, 1982

7. Coleman was the second Black American to be a Cabinet member. The first was Robert Weaver, nominated in 1966 by President Johnson to be the first Secretary of the new Department of Housing and Urban Development.

8. "High Court Bans Tax Exemptions for Schools with Racial Barriers," *New York Times*, May 25, 1983

9. A good summary of how this was done can be found in *Civil Rights and the Reagan Administration*, Norman C. Amaker, The Urban Institute Press, 1988, pp. 167 - 179

10 In a speech on the floor of the House of Representatives, Schroeder said that Reagan had made "a Great breakthrough in political technology—he has been perfecting the Teflon-coated presidency. He sees to it that nothing sticks to him. He is responsible for nothing—civil rights, Central America, the Middle East, the economy, the environment. He is just the master of ceremonies at someone else's dinner." https://the baffler.com/civilifications/the-teflon-con-denison

11. Shaw also wrote later in the column that "After Vietnam, Watergate and various other scandals, the public had become increasingly disenchanted with the news media; forced to choose between aggressive journalists and an avuncular President, they generally sided with the President.", https://latimes.com/archives/la-xpm-1992-10-27-mn-796-story.html

12. Goode would also win the general election that November, becoming the first Black mayor in the history of the city. Twenty years earlier, Gantt has been the first Black student admitted to Clemson University.

13. "A Black Sprint in 1984?, Robert Curvin, *New York Times*, May, 11, 1983; and Katherine Tate, "Black Political Participation in the 1984 and 1988 Presidential Elections," *The American Political Science Review,* December 1991, Volume 85, No. 4, p. 1161

14. Washington won 18 percent of the White vote, in a city where for decades Democratic mayoral candidates had continually won office by landslide proportions. That November, Goode easily won the general election with 55

percent of the total vote, including about 27 percent of the White vote. The two candidates won 99 and 98 percent of the Black vote, respectively. In Charlotte, Gantt won with 52 percent of the total votes, which included 36 percent of the White vote. Washington died of a heart attack on November 25, 1987, Six months into his second term.

15. Speech to the Urban League of Hudson County, Jersey City, New Jersey, April 13, 1983; "Race and Politics," *To Be Equal*, April 20, 1983

16.

https://www.azlyrics.com/lyrics/steviewonder/happybirthday.html

17. The activism in favor of the King Holiday, in turn, injected a much-needed shot of publicity and energy into the fledgling voter registration campaign taking shape around the country in preparation for the 1982 midterm elections and the 1984 presidential campaign. The increased turnout of Black voters in several key campaigns in the former head helped the Democrats retake the Houser of Representatives, a sharp defeat for the Republicans.

18. "U.S. Will Create Holiday to Mark Dr. King's Birth," *New York Times*, October 20, 1983

19. "King Holiday; Balky Minority in the G.O.P.," *New York Times*, October 21, 1983

20 "A Necessary National Holiday," *To Be Equal*, August 31, 1983

21. The Rainbow Coalition: Jesse Jackson and The Politics of Ethnicity," Manning Marable, *CrossCurrents*, pp. 21-42, Spring, 1984

22. *Ibid.*

23. In 1972 they were only 13 Black members of Congress — all Democrats. Chisholm, who had first been elected in 1969, was the only woman. The Congressional Black Caucus had been formed just two years earlier. Only two of its members — Parren Mitchell, of Maryland and Ron Dellums of California — would endorse Chisholm's candidacy.

24. Of course, McGovern lost in a landslide, capturing only the state of Massachusetts and the District of Columbia.

25. *The Good Fight*, Shirley Chisholm, (2022); "Chisholm '72: Unsought & Unbossed," (Documentary), Shola Lynch, director (2012)

26. Marable, CrossCurrents, pp. 21-42, Spring 1984

27. "Black Caucus Weighs Candidacy by Jesse Jackson," *New York Times*, September 26, 1983

28. I donated to the second Jackson campaign during the 1988 Democratic primaries.

29. The Congressional Black Caucus was founded in 1971 by the thirteen Black members of the House of Representatives. By 1983 there were 17 members, all Democrats. That year there was no Black Republican in the Congress, due to Senator Edward W. Brooke, of Massachusetts having been defeated in his quest for a third term. A native of Washington, D.C. graduate of Howard University and Boston University Law School, and World War II veteran, Brooke was elected Attorney General of Massachusetts in 1962 and Senator in 1966. During his two terms in Congress, he was aligned with the GOP's liberal wing — which is why his path-breaking career has virtually never been honored by the GOP since Ronald Reagan took office. Although Brooke worked closely with the Congressional Black Caucus on certain

legislation, he never formally joined it. He was awarded the Presidential Medal of Freedom by President George W. Bush in 2004 and the Congressional Gold Medal in 2009.

30. The five he won were: Louisiana, Virginia, South Carolina, the District of Columbia, and two separate primaries in Mississippi.

31. Marable, p. 31

32. Marable, pp. 26-27

33. In 1980, Reagan had won 44 states and 489 electoral votes, to just six states and the District of Columbia for President Carter.In 1984, Reagan won 49 states and a record 525 electoral votes. Mondale won only his home state of Minnesota and the District of Columbia.

34. "Voting and Registration in the Election of November 1984 (Advance Report)," U.S. Bureau of The Census, Series P-20, No. 397, January 1985. On November 2, 1983, the day before Jackson formally announced his campaign, Louis Harris, the well-known pollster, told Jackson

35. After the 1988 presidential contest, in which George H.W. Bush easily defeated Michael Dukakis, Ronald H. Brown, my former Urban League colleague who had become an influential Washington attorney and lobbyist was unanimously elected chairman of the Democratic National Committee, the first African American to hold such a post in either party. This was a crucial step in the formation of the intra-party planet that would propel Bill Clinton to the White House in 1992. Clinton subsequently appointed Brown Secretary of Commerce. He was on a governmental mission to Yugoslavia when the airplane carrying him and thirty-four

other members of his staff and a contingent of Journalists crashed on April 3, 1996. All aboard were killed.

36. Southern Strategy …….

37. During Reagan's two terms, Sam Pierce remained the only African-American Cabinet member, indeed the only Black person holding a position of prominence in the entire Administration. Under Bush 41 Louis W. Sullivan served a distinguished term as Secretary of Health and Human Services. Throughout the Reagan and Bush presidencies, (and ever since), Republicans—include the Black Conservatives — never mentioned the name of Senator Edward W. Brooke, of Massachusetts, who in 1966 had become the first Black American in the twentieth century to be elected to the Senate and had just left office in 1978. Today, two other prominent Black Republicans of the Bush 41 and 43 presidencies, Colin Powell, the first Black Chairman of the Joint Chiefs of Staff, and Condoleezza Rice, the first Black Secretary of State, have also been blanketed with the same invisibility. The reason: Brooke was a liberal Republican, who worked with Democrats on several important legislative acts. Both Powell and Rice in 2003 publicly expressed support for affirmative action in the University of Michigan case that was decided by the Supreme Court.

38. Clarence Thomas, of course, excepted.

39. Brown was the first Black American to chair the national committee of either Party. The GOP would not name and African-American to the post until 2009 — following Barack Obama's election as President of the United States.

40. The Republican Party from the turn of the twentieth century on has compiled an astonishingly bad record when it comes

to electing Black Americans to Congress (or any other legislative body). Since 1935, only 12 Black Republicans have sat in either chamber of the Congress. The five current Republicans members (elected in 2022) make up the largest number of Black Republicans to sit in the national legislature since the Reconstruction Era. By contrast, since 13 Black Democratic Representatives founded the Congressional Black Caucus in 1971, their number grew to 19 at the beginning of the Reagan presidency, 25 at the start of the Bush presidency, and 27 at the beginning of Clinton's first term. That election also produced the first Black Republican elected to the House of Representatives since 1935. In the thirty years since, only 9 Black Republicans have been elected to Congress—only one of whom served more than two terms. During those years the number of Black Democrats has increased from 27 to 60. The failure of Black Republican candidates to win seats in Congress over the last two decades is equally astonishing when compared with their Asian-American and Hispanic- and Latino-American counterparts. In the 118th Congress, there are 21 members of Asian American or Pacific Islander American descent, 4 of whom are Republican. There are 62 members of Hispanic or Latino descent. Since 2000, the number of Americans of Asian descent in Congress has increased from 5 (3 Democratic and 2 Republican) to 34 (26 Democratic and 8 Republican) The number of Hispanic-Americans in Congress total sixty-two: 42 Democrats and 2 Republicans. Sixty-five African Americans sit in the Congress: sixty are Democratic, five Republican. {{ "Membership of the 118th Congress: A profile," Congressional Research Service, Congressional Research Service, November 13, 2023

Chapter 13 Footnotes

1. Sullivan, of Philadelphia, had compiled an estimable record forging job-training and business-development programs for that city's Black residents. He was a principal founder of Opportunities Industrial Corporation (OIC). By 1987 Rev. Sullivan himself had given up on the Sullivan Principles impact. That year at our annual conference in New York, in a rousing speech, he called for the total withdrawal of all American companies doing business in South Africa within nine months.

2. "Constructive engagement permitted closer ties with the South African government and temporarily shifted public perception of the regional crisis to a global framework that interpreted America's primary interest as containing Soviet and Cuban expansionism." —"The Politics of the Anti-Apartheid Movement in the United States, 1969-1986," Donald R. Culverson, *Political Science Quarterly*, Volume 111, Number 1, pp. 127-149; https://www.jstor.org/stable/2151931

3. South Africa had controlled the area on its northwestern border officially known as South West Africa but called Namibia by Black African peoples since the 1920s. A resistance movement had been waging a low-grade war since 1966 to force it to cede control. In the mid-1970s that ripened into a three-way war that involved the opposing forces in the Angolan Civil War, the opposing rebel forces fighting for control of Namibia, and a secret South African military force which the Afrikaner leadership kept secret from the white citizenry.

4. "Delegate Who Was Jailed Calls Sit-In 'Moral Act," New York Times, November 23, 1984

5. "The Politics of the Anti-Apartheid Movement in the United States, 1969-1986," Donald R. Culverson, *Political Science Quarterly*, Volume 111, Number 1, p. 127 https://www.jstor.org/stable/2151931

6. "U.N. Council Condemns Arrests and Apartheid in South Africa," *New York Times,* October 23, 1984

7. "Tutu Assails U.S. On Pretoria Ties," *New York Times,* October 28, 1984

8. "Protests Spreading in U.S. Against South Africa Policy," *New York Times,* December 5, 1984

9. "Jewish Groups Protest South African Policies," *New York Times*, December 26, 1984

10. Culverson, p. 145; "Many in U.S. Protest on South Africa," *New York Times,* October 12, 1985

11. "The Politics of the Anti-Apartheid Movement in the United States, 1969-1986," Donald R. Culverson, *Political Science Quarterly*, Volume 111, Number 1, p. 144 https://www.jstor.org/stable/2151931

12. "An Analysis Of U.S.-South African Relations In The 1980s: Has Engagement Been Constructive," pp. 103-104, https://scholaship.lw.upenn.edu/jil/vol7/iss1/4]]

13. Culverson, p. 146

14. "Protesting Apartheid," *To Be Equal*, January 2, 1985

15. "The Namibia Tangle," *To Be Equal,* November 17, 1982

16. A concise exploration of the controversy can be found in "Ronald Reagan Administration: The Bitburg Controversy"

Jewish Virtual Library,
https://www.jewishvirtuallibrary.org/the-bitburg-controversy

17. "South Africa Strikes Again," *To Be Equal,* April 3, 1985

18. More than 350 large American companies did business in South Africa, including more than half of the Fortune 100 companies, and another 6,000 had relationships with sales agents and distributors there.The U.S. held 57 percent of allure foreign holdings on the Johannesburg stock exchange. "An Analysis Of U.S.-South African Relations In The 1980s: Has Engagement Been Constructive," pp. 103-104, https://scholaship.lw.upenn.edu/jil/vol7/iss1/4 , p. 100. U.S. investments in South Africa totaled $2.8 billion in 1982, but by 1985 amounted to only $1.3 billion.

19. South Africa Strikes Again," *To Be Equal,* April 3, 1985

20. "Business and South Africa," To Be Equal, October 9, 1985

21. "Business and South Africa," To Be Equal, October 9, 1985

22. The votes were 313-83 in the House and 78-21 in the Senate. By then, Reagan had recalled his *White* ambassador to South Africa and replaced him with Edward J. Perkins, a veteran African-American Foreign Service officer who was serving as the U.S. Ambassador to Liberia. Perkins, who served in Pretoria until 1989, faced deep hostility from South African officials for his insistence on meeting with a wide range of South Africans, visiting the townships and holding integrated receptions and dinners at the American embassy. The government's hostility didn't deter him. He later served as Ambassador to Australia and to the United Nations. He died in 2020 at the age of 92.

23. Culverson, p. 146. The impact of the Congressional act also erased the old argument that if American companies pulled

out of South Africa, foreign companies would rush to take their place. As it happened, many European nations and Japan followed the American lead and soon enacted their own package of strict sanctions, forcing the South African economy into a severe recession.

24. "South Africa's Challenges," *To Be Equal*, May 4, 1994

25. A strong Black voter turnout would also contribute to the election of Doug Wilder's victory as the first elected Black governor of Virginia in 1989 and of David Dinkins as the first Black Mayor of New York City that same year.

26. "60,000 Blacks at South Africa Funeral," New York Times, 14 April 1985

27. "Urban League Officials Are Arrested at Embassy," *New York Times,* July 24, 1985,

Chapter 14 Footnotes

1. "Reaganomics — Political Magic For Republicans," David S. Border, *The Washington Post,* August 11, 1991

2. By 1998 Clinton's astute financial management would by 1998 reduce the deficit he had inherited from President George H.W. Bush to zero and leave a budget surplus to his successor, George W. Bush.

3. The Work Incentive Program (WIN) was part of President Johnson's Great Society programs. Its goal was to help welfare recipients gain the skills that would enable them to get the jobs that would enable them to rise out of poverty. The Reagan Administration, via its New Federalism gambit, placed much of the burden for funding and admin interring it on the states.

4. *Ibid.*

5. "Black America,1987: An Overview, *The State of Black America*, p. 1-2]]

6. "Black America,1987: An Overview, *The State of Black America*, p. 2

7. "The Reagan Era Ends," *To Be Equal*, January 11, 1989

8. " Black America,1988: An Overview, *The State of Black America*, p. 2

9. An excellent summary of how this was done can be found in *Civil Rights and the Reagan Administration,* Norman C. Amaker, The Urban Institute Press, 1988, pp. 167-179

10. At the time furlough programs were a staple of the criminal justice system. The prison systems of all 50 states had them, and many allowed prisoners convicted of murder to be

eligible to participate in them. California did during Reagan's two terms as governor. Twice, when inmates on furlough, separately, committed murders, Reagan defended the program's overall record. — "The Campaign That Reshaped Criminal Justice," https: www.wnycstudios.org/podcasts/takeaway/segments/crime-reshaped-criminal-justice

11. http://articles.baltimoresun.com/1993-08-12/news/1993224224_1_willie-horton-willie-horton-jeffrey-elliot

12. "How a murderer and rapist became the Bush campaigns most valuable player," http://articles.baltimoresun.com/1990-11-11/features/19900315149_1_willie-horton-fournier-michael-dukakis

13. "Bush made Willie Horton an issue in 1988, and the Racial Scars Are Still Fresh," https://nytimes.com/201812/03/us/politics/bush-willie-horton-html

14. Wilder became the first Black American to serve as governor of a state since the Reconstruction era and the first ever to be elected as governor. Dinkins became the first Black American to be elected New York's mayor, beating the Republican candidate Rudy Giuliani. Giuliani would narrowly defeat Dinkins in the 1993 contest.

15. "Black America, 1992: An Overview," *The State of Black America,* p. 4

16. The group was labelled "The Central Park Five." After they were proven innocent of the crime, they called themselves the "Exonerated Five."

17. In October 2016, a month away from the presidential election, John McCain withdrew his endorsement of Trump due to series of insults he made against women and other people. McCain included in that list the "outrageous statements" Trump made "against the innocent men in the Central Park Five case." "John McCain Unendorses Donald Trump," HuffPost, 8 October 2016, https:/www.huffpost.com/entry/john-mccain-unendorses-trump_n_57195fc14b0e655eab4f273

18. Because of the statute of limitations then in effect, Reyes could not be charged with the Central Park Jogger attack.

19. The literature — books, media and scholarly articles, documentaries, and innumerable discussion panels before live audiences and on social media—on the Central Park Five/Exonerated Five case is voluminous. Among the most valuable is the Ken Burns' documentary, *The Central Park Five,* of 2012. In addition, the Ava DuVernay 2019 miniseries, the critically acclaimed*When They See Us, a* dramatic telling of the story from the perspective of the Exonerated Five themselves, is also valuable.

20. In 2023, one of the Exonerated Five, Yusef Salaam, now 48? ran for and won a seat on the New York City Council, representing the Harlem district where he had grown up.

21. "Race and Violence," *To Be Equal*, May 24, 1989

22. The baby, delivered by Caesarean section that night, died seventeen days later.

23. In late December 2023 the Boston Globe published an eight-part series on the case. https://apps.bostonglobe.com/metro/investigations/2023/12/charles-stuart/timeline/ After Charles Stuart's suicide, his

wife's family restored to her in death her family name, DiMaiti. Within weeks of Stuart's death, the DiMaiti family established a foundation in her name to provide college scholarships to students who lived in the Mission Hill area. https://www.latimes.com/archives/la-xpm-1990-02-28-vw-1644-story.html Soon the foundation had raised approximately $750,000. Not until December 19, 2023, when Boston's current Mayor Michelle Wu held a formal ceremony of apology to the families of the two men wrongly arrested for the murder of Carol Stuart and to the city's Black community had any city official ever acknowledged the wrong done. https://apnews.com/article/boston-stuart-murder-black-neighborhood-apology-75e0cfcee05920e205f50adc2724e1cd

24. "The Faces of Racism," *To Be Equal*, 15 January 1990

25. The Commission's chairman was Illinois Governor Otto Kerner.

Chapter 15 Footnotes

1. Corporate Promotions was responsible for staging over 140
   events and meetings per year. My division also included the
   Graphic Communications unit, which handled in-house
   printing and mailing activities, and the unit which managed
   the design and use of the company's two thousand different
   business forms.

i

ii

iii

iv

v

vi

vii

viii

ix

x

xi

xii

xiii

xiv

xv

xvi

xvii

xviii

xix

xx

xxi

387

Made in the USA
Las Vegas, NV
09 May 2025

85c38f4d-938e-4e74-a3e8-4f903af2fff3R01